Kevin Ashman lives in South Wales with his wife and dog and has been writing for eight years.

Mainly concentrating on historical fiction books, especially in the Roman and Medieval eras, he found significant success with the India Summers Mysteries, a series of books about a librarian and her Special Forces partner, who delve deep into history to solve modern-day problems.

Also by K. M. Ashman

The India Summers Mysteries

The Vestal Conspiracy
The Treasures of Suleiman
The Mummies of the Reich
The Tomb Builders

The Roman Chronicles

Roman – The Fall of Britannia
Roman II – The Rise of Caratacus
Roman III – The Wrath of Boudicca

The Medieval Sagas

Medieval – Blood of the Cross
Medieval II – In Shadows of Kings
Medieval III – Sword of Liberty
Medieval IV – Ring of Steel

The Road to Hastings

The Challenges of a King

The
CHALLENGES
of a
KING

K. M. ASHMAN

🔟 CANELO

First published in the United Kingdom in 2021 by

Canelo
Unit 9, 5th Floor
Cargo Works, 1-2 Hatfields
London, SE1 9PG
United Kingdom

A CIP catalogue record for this book is available from the British Library.

Print ISBN 978 1 80032 364 3
Ebook ISBN 978 1 80032 363 6

This book is a work of fiction. Names, characters, businesses, organizations, places
and events are either the product of the author's imagination or are used fictitiously.
Any resemblance to actual persons, living or dead, events or locales is entirely
coincidental.

The Author's note on The Mantle of St Brigid is quoted unabridged from Wikipedia,
and can be viewed in full here: https://en.wikipedia.org/wiki/Brigid_of_Kildare.
The work is released under the Creative Commons Attribution-Share-Alike License
3.0, which can be viewed here: http://creativecommons.org/licenses/by-sa/3.0/

Look for more great books at www.canelo.co

Printed and bound in Great Britain by Clays Ltd, Elcograf S.p.A.

1

For my family…

Character List

Anglo-Saxon

Edward the Confessor	King of England
Ealdgyth of Wessex	Queen consort, Godwin's daughter

Nobles

Godwin	Earl of Wessex
Gytha Thorkelsdóttir	Godwin's wife
Sweyn Godwinson	Earl of Herefordshire
Harold Godwinson	Earl of East Anglia
Tostig Godwinson	Son of Godwin
Gyrth Godwinson	Son of Godwin
Leofwine Godwinson	Son of Godwin
Wulfnorth Godwinson	Son of Godwin
Gunhild	Daughter of Godwin
Edyth Swanneck	Harold's wife

Clergy

Bishop Stigand	Bishop of Elmham and Winchester

| **Spearhafoc** | Benedictine monk |

Norman

William the Bastard	Duke of Normandy
Alan the Red	Lord of Richemont
Robert of Jumièges	Bishop of London

Prologue

Normandy, AD 1038

Garnier of Falaise sat in the centre of the wooden hut at the rear of the tannery, carefully nursing the remains of the previous night's fire. In his hand, he held a fistful of straw, feeding it into the glowing embers as he gently blew them back to life.

His wife, Cateline, and their two young boys lay fast asleep under the heavy sheepskin fleeces covering the sleeping pallet, a luxury he had shared only a few minutes earlier. But with the night only half gone, he had arisen to use the last of the firewood, determined to add whatever warmth he could to the bitterly cold hut.

'What are you doing?' asked Cateline quietly from the bed.

Garnier looked over and saw his wife peering at him in the light of the solitary candle.

'I thought you were asleep,' he said. 'I am trying to rescue what is left of the fire.'

'That's the last of our firewood.'

'It is, but I will take the boys to the forest later and gather more, so we may as well use what we have.'

'I told you,' said Cateline, 'if we block all the holes between the lathes, this place will be far warmer.'

'I know,' sighed Garnier, turning back to the fire, 'and I swear that I will do so as soon as I get a chance. Since the duke died, I have hardly had a moment to do what needs to be done.' He leaned forward and resumed his gentle blowing.

'It's been almost three years,' said his wife, as wisps of smoke started to rise upwards towards the roof. 'We should be grateful we still have employment. Many have been left without a roof over their heads. At least we have an income, and our children do not starve.'

'You are right,' said Garnier, kneeling and feeding the tiny flames with kindling. 'We have much to be grateful for.'

'Leave the fire,' said his wife, 'and come back to bed. The night is only half done.'

Garnier sighed and sat back on his heels, but before he could stand up, someone tapped on the door. Cateline sat bolt upright and stared across the reed-covered floor at her husband.

'Who is it?' she whispered.

'How am I supposed to know?' asked Garnier, getting to his feet. 'It's the middle of the night.'

He walked over and placed his ear against the door, jumping when the knock came again, this time accompanied by a voice.

'Garnier of Falaise! My name is Alan of Brittany. Open this door, in the name of the duke.'

The tanner looked over at his wife, now out of bed with one of the fleeces wrapped around her shoulders.

'Who's Alan of Brittany?' she whispered.

'He was one of the duke's trusted men,' replied Garnier.

'What do you think he wants?'

Before he could respond, the voice came again.

'Garnier of Falaise, open this door immediately or I swear I will have you removed as tanner before this day is out.'

Garnier knew he had no option and unbarred the door. The man pushed past, pulling a young boy behind him. He turned around and shut the door, sliding across the wooden bar before turning to face the tanner.

'My lord,' said Garnier, 'is everything well?'

'It is not,' replied the man. 'I assume you are Garnier of Falaise?'

'I am, my lord, and this is my wife.'

'Good. I have heard you were a respected vassal of Duke Robert of Normandy prior to his death.'

'Indeed I was, my lord, and it was my privilege to serve him. He was a great man.'

'Aye, he was,' said the man, 'and these are dark days. But if we are to continue what he started, we are in dire need of your help.'

'If I can help, I will,' said the tanner, drawing himself up. 'What would you have me do?'

'We need you to hide this boy for a few nights. Lock your doors and do not venture out until I return three days hence. Can you do that?'

'I suppose so,' said Garnier, 'but what about my work?'

'I will tell your seconds that you have fallen gravely ill and cannot attend. Your position will not be at risk.'

'My lord,' said Garnier, 'I have to be able to go out, we need food and fuel for the fire.'

'I will have my men bring you food and firewood after dark tonight. Until then, you will have to make do with what you have.' He glanced towards the modest fire. 'If anyone else asks you to open the door, tell them you have been struck down with illness and fear that death creeps towards you.'

'Aye, my lord, but can I ask why?'

'You may not. Suffice to say, it is a matter of life and death, and if you do as I say without consequence, you will be handsomely rewarded. Do I have your oath?'

'Aye, my lord, you do,' said the tanner.

'Good. Now I must be gone. Do not let me down, Garnier of Falaise, the child's life depends on it.' Without waiting for an answer, he disappeared into the night, closing the door behind him.

Cateline ran across and bolted the door before turning to face her husband and the boy. The child was slight and no more than ten years old, but he was clearly healthy and wore a cloak of rich velvet.

'What was all that about?' she gasped, turning to face her husband. 'What trouble have you got us into now?'

3

'None of my own making,' said Garnier, staring at the frightened boy. 'It seems we have been caught up in the politics of the court.'

'What do you mean?' asked Cateline. 'Do you even know this boy?'

'Aye, I do,' said Garnier, looking over to his wife with a hint of fear in his eyes. 'His name is William the Bastard, and he is the Duke of Normandy.'

Part One

Chapter One

Winchester, June, AD 1043

King Edward sat at a table in one of the antechambers in the rear of Winchester Cathedral. With him were several of his advisors, including Robert, the Abbot of Jumièges Abbey, near Rouen in Normandy.

The previous few weeks had been overwhelming; he had finally been crowned King of England after the death of his half-brother, King Harthacnut, almost a year earlier. Harthacnut had ruled England as regent since the death of Harold in AD 1040, on the agreement that, should he die, Edward would inherit the crown. Now, with all his predecessors finally gone, Edward's time had come. At last, he had been acknowledged as the sole King of England.

For the next few hours, Edward signed off the mountain of decrees and treaties that had accumulated over the past few months, until eventually he sat back and held up his hand, causing all the chatter to stop.

'Gentlemen,' he announced, 'it has been a long day and I know there are many more such days to come, but it is time to put our business to one side. Please, gather your things and leave, we will reconvene at midday tomorrow.'

An air of relief rippled around the gathering. The arrangements for the coronation had taken weeks, and their normal business had piled up in the meantime. Now, at last, they could concentrate on their main roles, but were more than happy to end the day early. As they filed from the chamber, the king spoke out again.

'Father Robert, Bishop Stigand, please remain. There is one more piece of business that I would like to discuss before you go.'

Robert of Jumièges stopped and turned to face the king. He enjoyed a favoured position with Edward, having served him and his family faithfully after they had fled England to escape the Danes over twenty-five years earlier. During that time, Edward lived in exile, until eventually he was summoned to Hursteshever by King Harthacnut and named heir to the crown by the thegns and barons of England. As soon as the succession was confirmed, Edward had summoned Robert from Normandy and installed him as his confidant and advisor.

Bishop Stigand also turned to rejoin the king at the end of the chamber.

'Please, be seated,' said the king. 'It has been a long day and I'm sure your legs suffer for the effort.'

Two servants carried over chairs and all three men sat round a small table bearing wine and sweetmeats. One of the servants made to pour the wine but was waved away by the king.

'You may leave us,' he said. 'We will manage from here.'

'Your grace,' said Robert as soon as they were alone. 'May I take this opportunity of congratulating you on your kingship. It has been a long road, but you got here in the end. May God pave your way with honesty, justice and kindness.'

'Thank you,' said the king. 'It has indeed been a long road. It has been over twenty-five years since I fled England as an exile, and for most of those you have been at my side, not only as a spiritual advisor but as a friend. This achievement is as much yours as mine.'

'Thank you, your grace,' said Robert, 'I am just blessed to serve.'

The king smiled and turned to the other man in the room.

'Bishop Stigand,' he said, 'you have also had a huge part to play in this, and I offer you my gratitude. Without your intervention, especially at the meeting of the Witan in Hursteshever two years ago, my succession might not have been agreed.'

'There were others involved, your grace; I was mainly the go-between.'

'You do yourself an injustice,' said the king. 'My own people have reported that it was you and Godwin of Wessex who worked hard in the shadows to ensure I achieved the votes needed. I will not forget that.'

'Thank you, your grace,' said Stigand. 'May God bless your reign with long life and peaceful intent.'

Again, the king smiled before sitting back with a deep sigh.

'So,' he said, 'we come to the reason I have asked you to remain here. First of all, I am well aware that Robert has only just arrived, so I have to ask – have you both met?'

'Briefly, at the coronation,' said Father Robert, looking over to the bishop. 'But unfortunately there has been little time since. I am, however, aware that his grace is highly thought of and served four of your predecessors as a spiritual advisor.'

'Oh, I think he served as far more than that,' said the king. 'But you are, of course, correct, and I intend he continues to play a large part in palace life.'

'I look forward to working with you,' said Robert, nodding towards the bishop.

'And I, you,' said Bishop Stigand, returning the nod.

'So,' said the king, 'let's get down to business. Despite finally being in possession of the crown, the fact that I have been in Normandy for the best part of twenty-five years is a burden that will be difficult to discard. Already I have heard mutterings about this having been a missed opportunity to crown a man born within these shores. We have to address the embers before they turn into a fire.'

'Who says such things, your grace?' asked Robert. 'I will have them dealt with.'

'The rumours are third-hand,' said the king, 'but truth be told, I can understand why some men see it this way. Besides, the last thing I want to do is start my reign by rounding up my doubters.'

'A sensible approach,' said Stigand. 'For no matter what you do, the scrutiny the role brings means there will always be those who wish you ill. It is the nature of kingship.'

'Indeed,' said Edward. 'So, bearing that in mind, I want to move quickly to build trust and alliances across England. I do have an army at my disposal, but should any ill will arise, especially in the early years, it will be no match for the forces of my earls.'

'I do not believe it will come to that,' said Stigand.

'Perhaps not, but better to deal with it now while we enjoy peace.'

'What would you do, my liege?' asked Robert.

'I think there is merit in binding at least one of the noble houses to the throne,' said the king. 'Create unbreakable ties to ensure no man dare rise against me.'

'And how do you intend to do this?'

'I am open to suggestion,' said the king, 'but I was thinking perhaps through marriage. Is there a suitable bride out there who would bind one of the houses of England to the throne?'

'That sounds like a good idea,' said Robert. 'I will send messengers to Lords Siward and Leofric to see if there are any suitable candidates.'

'Actually,' said Stigand quickly, 'there is no need to send anyone northwards when there is a perfect candidate but a few leagues from here.'

'And who is that?' asked the king.

'The maiden, Gytha, daughter of Godwin of Wessex. She is fair of face and of perfect age for such a union. She is also untouched and as graceful as the purest swan.'

'She sounds intriguing,' said the king. 'Perhaps you could arrange a meeting and, if she is agreeable, open negotiations with her father.'

'No,' interrupted Father Robert, his face lined with concern. 'That won't be possible.'

Both men turned to stare at him.

'Why not?' asked the king.

'You know why not, your grace,' said Robert. 'Earl Godwin is responsible for the death of your brother. How could you create an alliance with someone who has spilt the blood of your own family?'

'Earl Godwin denies all responsibility for Alfred's murder,' interjected Stigand, 'and do not forget it was he who was instrumental in ensuring King Edward received the backing of the Witan. Besides, Godwin is by far the most powerful earl in England and the crown would be unassailable with his support.'

'It goes against everything that is decent,' snapped Robert, his face contorting in anger. He turned back to the king. 'Choose one of the other earls, your grace, for even though I have been here only a short while, it is apparent to me that the Godwin family see themselves as above all other men in England. Some say Godwin even has eyes on the crown for himself.'

'That is ridiculous,' snapped Bishop Stigand. 'He was first to support the king at the Witan. His loyalty is unquestionable.'

'Gentlemen,' interrupted the king, 'you are men of the Church, so please act as such.' He fell silent and looked between them both. 'I understand your concerns, Father Robert,' he said eventually, 'and I promise I will make no rash decisions, but I think Bishop Stigand's suggestion is certainly worth exploring. Let us meet this Gytha and take it from there. Agreed?'

'I am yours to command, your grace,' said Robert. 'But I have to register my concerns.'

'And you have done so,' said the king. 'Now, let us bring this long day to an end. Bishop Stigand, please make the necessary arrangements.'

'As you wish, your grace,' said the bishop.

'Good,' said the king, 'you may leave.'

Both men stood and, after the slightest of bows, left the chamber, one excited at the possibility of one of the Godwin family marrying into royalty, the other seething at what had just happened.

Chapter Two

London, January, AD 1045

Godwin of Wessex rode his horse through the gates of South-wark Manor on the outskirts of London. Behind him came a hundred mounted huscarls, all experienced and trusted men permanently employed as bodyguards and enforcers. Towards the centre of the column a team of two horses pulled a covered cart, the waterproof leather richly decorated with woodland scenes.

As the rest of the riders headed towards the stable blocks, Godwin dismounted and handed the reins of his horse to a servant before heading up the steps into the manor to be met by his marshal. Osmund had been at Southwark for several days, ensuring the manor was adequately protected from anyone foolish enough to try to do the Godwin family ill, and he had been waiting for the arrival of his lord for the past few hours.

'Master Osmund,' said Godwin, removing his riding gaunt-lets. 'A good day to you. I assume the past days have been well spent?'

'Indeed they have, my lord,' said Osmund. 'Your guests are well quartered and there is plenty of room for your huscarls. They will be billeted on the other side of the manor in the new barracks.'

'What about stabling?'

'Enough for now,' said Osmund, 'but with little spare. The place is secure, my lord, and I am confident you and your lady will sleep easy.'

'You have done well,' said Godwin. 'During the celebrations, we will let another command the guard so you may sup at the second table.'

'I am honoured, my lord,' said the marshal with a bow.

Godwin looked around and, seeing the steward nearby, beckoned him over.

'Cuthbert,' he said, 'it has been a while. How go my affairs in London?'

'Everything you asked for in your letters has been carried out diligently,' said the steward. 'Lady Gytha has been particularly active in making sure the arrangements are more than suitable.'

'I'm sure she has,' laughed Godwin. 'When it comes to organising celebrations, my wife is nothing if not enthusiastic.'

'That she is, my lord,' said the steward with a smile.

'So, is my daughter here?'

'She is, my lord; she arrived safely yesterday and is looking forward to seeing you. She said it has been several weeks since you last talked.'

'Indeed it has,' said Godwin. 'I had some unpleasant business to attend to on the Welsh borders, but it is sorted now. Where is she?'

'In her quarters in the west wing, my lord. Shall I send for her?'

'That won't be necessary,' said the earl, slapping his hand on the steward's shoulder. 'I am sure you have enough to do.'

One of Godwin's huscarls walked over and gave him a satchel.

'My lord,' he said, 'don't forget this.'

'As if I would,' said the earl. 'Thank you.'

He entered the building, leaving the steward to coordinate the unpacking of the carts. Once inside, he made his way into the west wing and headed up a wide staircase to the floor given over to his daughter. He knocked on the door and was shown in by one of the servants. Across the room, his daughter sat on the bed alongside his wife, Gytha.

'Father!' squealed Ealdgyth, catching sight of him. She ran across to embrace the earl.

Godwin placed the satchel on the floor just in time as the young woman threw herself into his arms.

'Steady, girl,' he laughed. 'I can hardly breathe such is your strength.'

'But it has been so long,' said Ealdgyth, 'I feared you might not make it in time.'

'What, and miss my own daughter's wedding? That was never going to happen. I would have fought every Welshman and Scotsman single-handedly if I had to.'

'And undoubtedly emerge the victor against everyone foolish enough to stand in your way,' said Ealdgyth. She paused and stared at her father for a few moments. His standing amongst the nobles of England grew ever stronger, and hardly a day went by that she did not hear someone extolling his virtues.

'So,' said Godwin, breaking the moment, 'let me look at you.' He held his daughter at arm's length and looked her up and down. 'Even more beautiful than I remember,' he said eventually. 'King Edward is a very lucky man.'

'I still can't get used to being called Ealdgyth,' said his daughter. 'Why can't I be called by the name afforded me by you and Mother? Gytha is such a beautiful name.'

'A small price to pay to become the Queen of England,' said her mother, walking over from the bed. 'Behind closed doors, you will still be the same daughter we watched grow up into such a beautiful young lady.'

Gytha turned to her husband. 'Come, join us. Cuthbert has furnished us with the most beautiful wine and sweetmeats for our reunion.' She led the way over to a table where two empty goblets stood on a gilded tray.

'We need another,' said Ealdgyth turning to one of the servants.

'Wait,' said Gytha, picking up the satchel. 'That won't be necessary. In fact, please take them away.'

'Mother?' said Ealdgyth, as the servant removed the tray. 'I do not understand.'

'Your father has the answer to that,' said Gytha before giving the satchel back to her husband. 'Here, they should come from you.'

Godwin took the bag and retrieved a beautifully wrapped package from inside.

'This is for you,' he said, handing it over to his daughter.

'What is it?' asked Ealdgyth.

'A small token from your mother and me. Something for you to remember us by in the quiet moments when you miss your family, however brief and infrequent I hope them to be.'

Ealdgyth smiled and sat at the table to open the gift. As the silk wraps fell away, her mouth fell agape at the sight before her – one of the most beautiful goblets she had ever seen. The base was painted in vibrant colours and showed a stag bowing to a crowned young woman. Around the top half of the goblet, intricate designs of gold wove themselves amongst precious stones set carefully into the rim.

She unwrapped the rest of the package to see two similar goblets depicting the same character, though in different scenes. One had an eagle perched on her arm, while the other showed a host of multicoloured fish leaping from a lake while the woman looked on from beneath a great oak.

'These are *astonishing*,' she gasped, looking up. 'Is the woman supposed to be me?'

'It is,' said Godwin. 'A reminder that the kingdom of God is not limited to that of mankind but of all the creatures that walk, swim and fly under the sun.'

'They are truly beautiful,' said Ealdgyth. 'I am sure the king will be taken aback by such beauty.'

'Perhaps,' said Godwin, 'but remember they are for you and you alone.'

'For me?' she asked. 'But I do not understand. If they are for me, why are there three? Surely I would need only one.'

'Because they are to remind you of us and are to be used only when we three are together,' said Gytha, arranging the goblets side by side on the table. 'If you please, my lord,' she said after pouring the wine, 'I would like to be the first to toast our daughter.'

Godwin smiled and picked up one of the goblets.

'To Ealdgyth of Wessex,' said Gytha, 'beloved sister to her siblings and daughter to the proudest parents in Christendom. May you be showered with God's blessings and never forget those who love you the most.'

All three clinked the golden goblets together and sipped at the wine. For the next few minutes, they chatted excitedly about the forthcoming wedding until someone interrupted them with a knock on the door.

'Enter,' called Godwin.

A servant came in and walked over to the earl to whisper in his ear.

'Excellent news,' he said. 'We will be down shortly.'

The servant left, and Godwin turned back to join his wife and daughter. 'There is another gift,' he said, picking up his drink. 'One even more precious than the gold you now hold in your hands.'

'What could possibly be more precious than these?' asked Ealdgyth.

'How about the presence of someone you value more than life itself?'

Ealdgyth stared as the implication sank in. Tears welled in her eyes, and her hand flew to her mouth to stifle a cry of joy.

'*Is she here?*' she whispered, hardly daring to hope.

'She is,' said Godwin, 'and she's waiting in the chapel. Go, we will join you shortly.'

Ealdgyth threw her arms around her parents.

'*I love you both so much*,' she whispered. 'Thank you for everything.'

She turned away and ran from the room, leaving her smiling parents staring after her.

'Do you think she is going to be happy?' asked Gytha eventually.

'I hope so,' said Godwin, 'she deserves it.' He held up his goblet and turned to his wife. 'To the future Queen of England.'

'The Queen of England,' repeated Gytha, lifting her own drink. 'May her reign be blessed with love, happiness, and the sound of little children.'

—

Ealdgyth ran across the courtyard and into the manor's private chapel. The plain stone building was sparsely furnished with only a few benches, but at the far end, a beautiful crucifix adorned the wall. Beneath the cross knelt two women with their backs to the door, both in the grey habits of nuns. Ealdgyth suddenly remembered where she was and, despite her excitement, knelt on one of the many velvet cushions before making the sign of the cross and getting back to her feet. She walked quickly to stand just behind the women but, seeing they were still deep in prayer, waited in silence.

Finally, the two nuns stood up, and after making the sign of the cross, turned to face Ealdgyth. One was advancing in years, her face crisscrossed with the lines of age and wisdom, while the other was one of the most beautiful young women Ealdgyth had ever seen.

'*Gunhild*,' gasped Ealdgyth, 'you look radiant!' She held out her arms, and after glancing at the older nun for permission, Gunhild ran into her sister's embrace.

'Gytha,' said Gunhild, 'it is so good to see you again. My heart feels like it is about to burst!'

'I think mine has already done so,' replied her sister. 'It has been far too long, I am so happy you were allowed to come.'

'How could we not allow her to witness her sister's marriage to the king?' said the older nun with a smile. 'We are tutors, not monsters.'

'This is Sister Margaret,' said Gunhild, releasing her sister. 'She is my teacher and my chaperone. Sister Margaret, this is Gytha Godwinson, my beautiful older sister.'

'It is good to meet you at last, Lady Gytha,' said the nun. 'Gunhild has not stopped talking about you since we left the convent.'

'She always was a chatterbox,' said Ealdgyth, 'but I must inform you both that henceforth I am to be known as Ealdgyth.'

'Why in God's name would you do that?' asked Gunhild.

'Child, do not take the Lord's name in vain,' chastised the older nun.

'My apologies, sister,' said Gunhild, 'I was taken by surprise.'

'I am not sure,' said Ealdgyth, 'I believe it was a request from the king himself. But enough of such trivial matters, we have so much to talk about and so little time until the wedding. Come, I will show you my room and then find out where you are to sleep.'

Chapter Three

Earl Godwin of Wessex sat at the centre of the table alongside his wife, Gytha Thorkelsdóttir. To his right sat his sons Harold, Tostig and Gyrth, with an empty seat for Sweyn, who was late for the gathering. At the other end of the table with Gytha sat their daughters, Ealdgyth and Gunhild, alongside another son, Leofwine, and their youngest child Wulfnorth, a boy of just eight years old. The family was almost complete for the first time in years, with only Ælfgifu missing. Ælfgifu, their youngest daughter, had been sent to Wilton Abbey for her education and had been unable to join Gunhild on the journey to Southwark as she was unwell.

Throughout the hall, Godwin's extended family and huscarls shared another four tables, each seated in a strict pecking order. The earl looked around with quiet satisfaction. Over the past few years, especially since the coronation of Edward, his family had become one of the most powerful families in England, if not *the* most. In addition, his daughter would soon be queen, a position that would give their family even more power.

'Godwin,' said his wife, 'Sweyn is obviously not coming. We should begin.'

'He promised me he would be here,' said the earl. 'We will give him a few more minutes.'

No sooner had he spoken when the lower doors opened and their eldest son strode in, still wearing his riding cloak.

'He's here,' said Gytha, with a smile. 'Thank the Lord.' She stood up and walked around the table, accompanied by Ealdgyth.

'Sweyn,' she said, embracing her son. 'We had almost given up on you.'

'As if I would miss my sister's celebration,' said Sweyn, turning to embrace Ealdgyth. 'Even if I were dead, I would have crossed the country, dragging my coffin behind me.'

'That's awful,' laughed Ealdgyth. 'But coffin or not, we have saved you a seat at Father's right hand, as befits your position of eldest son.'

'And favourite brother,' said Sweyn with mock sincerity. 'Let us not forget that.'

'Of course,' said Ealdgyth. 'Come, I am impatient to get started.'

She took Sweyn's hand and led him to his seat before retaking hers between Gytha and Gunhild. With everyone finally present, Godwin got to his feet and lifted his tankard.

'House of Godwin,' he announced, 'dear family, friends and comrades. God has blessed us this day, and we must give thanks that we are all here again under one roof. As you know, I have arranged this feast to celebrate the forthcoming marriage of my beautiful daughter, Ealdgyth, to Edward, the King of England. But let us not forget that, though she will be queen, I will be a constant reminder to her that once a Godwin, always a Godwin.' To shouts of agreement, he turned to face his daughter. 'Gytha – or should I say, Ealdgyth – may God guide your steps and family guide your heart. We wish you happiness, respect and long life, yet above all this, never forget that I will make a wonderful grandfather to any future king.'

Ealdgyth blushed as the room broke into laughter.

'But enough with the formalities,' shouted the earl, turning back to the room, 'for there will be speeches aplenty in the next few days. So for now, I have only one more thing to say.' He lifted his goblet. 'Take notice that not one person present will be allowed to leave this room until the mead barrels are dry, the wine has all gone and the huscarls fight over the last mug of ale. My friends, let the celebrations begin.'

As the musicians started to play tunes of merriment, a line of young boys filed in from the kitchens carrying pitchers of wine, mead and ale. Behind them came the servants bearing the first of many courses – a light potage of leeks, carrots and turnips, heavily laced with aromatic herbs. First to be served were the top table, and Wulfnorth stared into his bowl with obvious disgust.

'Where is the meat?' he asked, looking up at Ealdgyth. 'I thought we were going to have the king of beasts.'

'The feast has hardly started,' laughed Ealdgyth. 'You must be patient, Wulfnorth. Before this night is done, you will cry with pain, your belly will be so full of pork.'

'Never,' said Wulfnorth. 'I am almost nine years old and can eat as much as Sweyn and Gyrth put together.' He looked along the table to his eldest brother sitting next to Earl Godwin, receiving a wave and a smile in return.

'I am sure you can,' said Ealdgyth, 'but it is always good to try new things. Perhaps you should just try a taste.'

'I think not,' said Wulfnorth, pushing his bowl away. 'Sweyn told me that meat gives a man strength, and I need to wield a sword to fight alongside my brothers.'

'There will be time aplenty for such things,' said Ealdgyth, before lifting her head to smile at the serving girl. 'Could you take his plate away and perhaps replace it with a little meat?'

'Of course, my lady,' said the servant before hurrying away to the kitchen.

At the opposite end of the table, Sweyn waited as his tankard was filled with mead before drinking it down in one draught.

'You should take your time, brother,' said Harold at his side. 'The night is long before us. Drink like that, and the huscarls will be dragging you to your quarters before we are half done.'

'Do not worry about me,' replied Sweyn, offering up his tankard to be refilled. 'I can handle my drink. Besides, I have ridden a long way and have a thirst about me.'

'Where have you been?' asked Harold. 'I understand you were with Father in the Welsh Marches, but he returned a few days ago.'

'I had business to attend to,' said Sweyn.

'What business?'

'Business that is none of your concern,' said Sweyn, turning to face his younger brother.

'I see,' said Harold. 'In that case, I can only assume it had to do with a certain abbess?'

'Ah,' interjected Tostig alongside them. 'The beautiful Abbess of Leominster. Please tell me she is not still a concern in our brother's life?'

'Alas, I cannot,' said Harold, 'for it seems Sweyn may still be smitten.'

'What I do not understand,' said Tostig, leaning towards them across the table, 'is why choose someone married to Christ when you could have the pick of so many women across England? Wales too, for that matter.'

'As I said,' replied Sweyn, 'it is of no concern of yours. Let it be.'

'Methinks we may have aggravated an open wound,' said Tostig, sitting back in his seat.

'As do I,' laughed Harold, before delving into the potage with a silver spoon.

'So,' said Ealdgyth, turning to face Gunhild. 'How is life in Wilton Abbey?'

'Wonderful,' said Gunhild, dabbing at the corner of her mouth with a napkin. 'The sisters are really kind, and I am learning so much. I am truly blessed that God called me to his service.'

'Do you see much of our sister?'

'Sometimes, though she is in a different part of the abbey. But I visited her before we set out and she is recovering well.'

22

'I do hope so,' said Ealdgyth, 'I miss her so much.'

'She is in good hands,' said Sister Margaret. 'And when she is well, I shall arrange a visitation.'

'Thank you,' said Ealdgyth, turning to her mother. 'Mother, who is the monk sitting at the end of the far table? I have never seen him before.'

'His name is Spearhafoc,' said Gytha, 'and he is a goldsmith of the highest order. Your father had him brought to London from Bury St Edmunds. He is the one responsible for making those beautiful goblets.'

'Is he?' asked Ealdgyth, turning to stare again at the young man. 'Is that why he is here?'

'Partly,' said Gytha. 'But we were so impressed with his work your father requested his secondment to the House of Godwin for the foreseeable future. The bishop agreed, and there he is – our very own goldsmith.'

'He looks sad,' said Ealdgyth. 'Why does nobody talk to him?'

'He seems to be a bit of an acquired taste,' said her mother, 'but I am sure he will settle soon enough.'

'Once we have eaten, I will engage him in conversation,' said Ealdgyth. 'Nobody should be lonely at my celebration.'

'That would be a very nice thing to do,' said Gytha. 'Now eat some potage before it gets cold.'

–

For the next few hours, the gathering enjoyed the best fare the earl's hunters and farmers could offer. Each table had a leg of venison as a centrepiece, surrounded by silver platters piled high with sliced pork and tureens of fresh green vegetables. On the top table, the centrepiece was a magnificent boar's head, bedded on a sea of roasted onions with a shiny green apple in its monstrous jaws.

'I want a piece of the snout,' shouted Wulfnorth gleefully. 'It is truly the tenderest part.'

'Oh no,' gasped Ealdgyth with a look of disgust. 'Surely not.'

'*Nonsense*,' roared Tostig, rising from his seat. 'If it is snout the boy wants, then snout the boy will get.'

He walked over to the boar's head and, with an overly ceremonious flourish, produced a carving knife the size of a small sword.

'Forgive me, Sir Pig,' he announced, 'but your snout is hereby sacrificed for the greater good.'

By now, the effects of the alcohol were taking hold, and the guests laughed heartily as Tostig carved off the end and threw it over to his younger brother.

'It is nice to see them all so relaxed,' said Gytha quietly to her husband.

'It is,' said Godwin. 'We get together far too infrequently.'

'We do,' said Gytha, 'and should make more effort. So tell me, my lord, how went it in the Welsh Marches? We have hardly had time to talk since you returned.'

'It was difficult,' sighed Godwin. 'King Gruffydd is nothing if not belligerent and not one to take advice graciously. If he continues along his current path, there will be a reckoning with King Rhydderch of Gwent before this year is out.'

'Why does this concern you so?' asked his wife. 'If the Welsh want to slay the Welsh, then why not step back and enjoy the moment?'

'Because,' said Godwin, 'Sweyn's estates share a border with many of the marches, and should there be war, I fear he will be caught up in the aftermath.'

'I fail to see why he is so bent on becoming Gruffydd's friend,' said Gytha. 'He has enough on his plate as it is managing our concerns this side of the Severn.'

'To be fair,' said Godwin, holding up his goblet for a refill, 'Gruffydd is a powerful man and has the potential to be a powerful ally, but Sweyn needs to remember that both men are Welsh and could join forces against him in an instant if circumstance demands.'

'Talk to him again, Godwin,' said Gytha. 'We have too much to lose by antagonising the Welsh.'

'Aye, I will,' said Godwin. 'But for now, let us forget our troubles and enjoy the celebrations.'

For the next few hours, everyone relaxed, with men and women alike consuming far too much alcohol and food. Once the last of the feast had been cleared away, the servants dragged the tables to the edge of the hall, and the guests danced around the fire to the merry tunes played by the minstrels.

After several dances, Ealdgyth walked over to one of the tables for a well-earned drink. Already there was the young monk, running his hand down the side of an ornately designed silver jug.

'Brother Spearhafoc,' she said with a smile, 'are you enjoying yourself?'

The monk removed his hand and turned to face the young woman. He smiled and bowed his head before responding.

'My lady,' he said, 'indeed I am. It has been a long time since I witnessed such extravagance.'

'Oh,' said Ealdgyth with concern. 'I hope the feasting does not offend you too much.'

'On the contrary,' said Spearhafoc, 'it makes my heart sing to see so much happiness in one room.'

'But do not monks take vows of strict abstinence?'

'Some do and are happy to do so. Luckily, I am not such a monk and have enjoyed the fare enormously, though it has to be said, some of those present have the appetites of wolves and the manners of pigs.'

Ealdgyth stared at the monk with mild surprise. To use insults as a guest at any celebration was unheard of and invited contradiction.

'May I ask to whom you are referring?' she said, her smile a little less broad.

'My lady,' said the monk, seeing her look of concern, 'please forgive my turn of phrase. The words were not meant as insults, only as comparisons to two of God's creatures, both beautiful in their own right. The wolf is brave and fearless with an appetite worthy of any warrior, while a pig will fill its belly to contentment with no thought of niceties. Both attributes are God's gifts, and thus there is no reason for ill judgement to be laid upon them. If my choice of words offended you, then I take them back and apologise unreservedly.'

'Of course not,' said Ealdgyth with a sudden grin. 'The misunderstanding was all mine, and it is I who should be apologising to you. All this must be strange for a man who has spent many years cloistered behind high walls with little view of the outside world.'

'It is certainly an interesting experience,' said Spearhafoc, 'and underlines that which I already know.'

'Which is?'

'That I have much to learn and should, perhaps, keep my thoughts to myself until my meanings are better understood.'

'I am sure you will be fine,' said Ealdgyth. 'Oh, I have received the goblets from my father and have to say they are exquisite. Thank you so much for all your hard work.'

'You are welcome,' said the monk. 'The abbey benefited greatly from the price.'

'I hear you are staying with us for a while?'

'Indeed. Your father has some commissions he wants me to undertake, and I am only too pleased to serve.'

'I am not surprised, your work is superb.'

'Thank you,' said the monk. 'Perhaps, once you have married, I could create something for you and your new husband.'

'Of course,' said Ealdgyth, 'I think that a wonderful idea. But for now, you must excuse me. I think Wulfnorth has drunk too much ale for a child and is about to be sick. I should spirit him away before my mother sees him and banishes him to Ireland.'

'Please, do what you have to do,' said the monk with a laugh. 'And thank you for coming over, it means a lot to me.'

'The pleasure was all mine,' said Ealdgyth, 'and I hope we speak again soon.' She hurried away past the drunken guests to drag Wulfnorth from beneath a table and through the northern door.

Spearhafoc watched her go with interest. Since leaving the abbey a few months earlier, not a single day had gone past without him learning something more about the outside world. It was indeed a strange and fascinating place, and the longer it went on, the more he learned about the greed and stupidity of most men.

Sometimes he missed the peace and solitude of his workshop, but no sooner had the thought crossed his mind than the waves of everyday life would once again flood his senses, drowning him in a flood of unexplored opportunities.

He sipped on his cup of mead and looked around the room. Already there were forbidden thoughts forming in his mind, exciting yet terrifying ideas that had no rightful place in the mind of any man wearing the cloth of Christ.

–

Sweyn stood outside at one of the walls, urinating into a bucket. When he finished, he adjusted his clothing and turned to see a young maid standing in the shadows, waiting patiently to replace the full bucket with an empty one. Sweyn stared at the girl, noticing how pretty she was.

'Hello,' he said, walking over. 'And what is your name?'

'Matilda, my lord,' said the girl, her gaze fixed on the floor at his feet.

'Hello Matilda,' said Sweyn. 'I take it you work for my father?'

'Yes, my lord. Tonight I am to keep the latrine buckets empty.'

'Not a very nice role for someone as pretty as you,' said Sweyn. 'Look at me.'

The girl glanced up but quickly returned her gaze to the floor.

'I said look at me,' snapped Sweyn, grabbing the girl under the chin and forcing her face upwards.

The girl gasped in shock and stared into the earl's eyes.

'Yes, very pretty indeed,' mused Sweyn. 'So pretty in fact, I can think of a much better use of your time than carrying buckets of piss.'

'My lord,' gasped the girl, 'please. I have work to do and will lose my employment.'

'Leave that to me,' said Sweyn. 'I will make sure you are suitably rewarded.' He grabbed the girl's arm and started pulling her towards the stables.

'*Please*,' gasped the girl. 'My lord, I have never been with a man. Please let me go.'

'Even better,' said Sweyn without breaking his stride. 'Let me show you what you are missing.' But before they had reached halfway, a voice called out across the courtyard.

'*Sweyn!*'

Sweyn stopped and turned around, annoyed at the interruption.

'Harold,' he said with a sigh. 'I should have guessed.'

Harold stared at the girl, immediately assessing the situation before turning his attention back to his brother.

'Sweyn,' he said, 'tonight is about Ealdgyth. Let the girl go and come back inside.'

'Nah,' said Sweyn, 'I think I'll do as I want, thank you.' He turned away and continued to drag the girl towards the stables.

'Sweyn,' snapped Harold. 'Do you really want your actions to define Ealdgyth's special night?'

'She won't even know,' said Sweyn, pausing. 'Unless, of course, you tell her.'

Harold stared at the young girl's terrified face before looking again at his brother.

'Let her go, Sweyn,' he said, 'she is no more than a child.'

Sweyn returned the stare but, with a heavy sigh, finally released the girl, allowing her to scurry away into the dark.

'What is your problem, Harold?' he asked. 'Why do you always judge me?'

'I worry about you, Sweyn,' replied Harold, 'that is all. Now come back to the celebrations. It is not often that we all get together as a family.'

'You are right,' replied Sweyn darkly as he walked past his brother towards the hall. 'And that is just the way I like it.'

Chapter Four

Two days later, King Edward sat at a table in one of the rooms turned over to the scribes engaged in recording his rule. Three monks sat at similar tables, all deeply concentrating on recording the events since his coronation at the Cathedral of Winchester almost two years earlier. Standing at the far side of the room, examining a completed manuscript by the light of several candles, stood the Bishop of London, Robert of Jumièges.

'Well,' said the king, staring at Robert's back. 'What do you think?'

'I am impressed,' said the bishop, turning around and walking across the room. 'The details are succinct and interesting. History will show you as both strong and forgiving.'

'Forgiving? That is a strange description to use.'

'I disagree,' said the bishop, 'for the manuscript makes no mention of how Godwin of Wessex, not ten years ago, opposed your brother's rightful claim to the throne in support of Harold Harefoot, nor that he betrayed your brother's trust and burnt out his eyes with a red-hot poker.'

'I know,' said Edward with a sigh. 'But Godwin swears that the deed was done by others with no instruction from himself.'

'His claims are lies before God,' said the bishop, 'why else would he have slain all of Alfred's men in cold blood? That alone proves his guilt in my mind, as it did for King Harthacnut, may the Lord rest his soul. If you want my advice, I would have the manuscripts changed to reflect the truth of such matters so men yet unborn can see the blackness of his soul.'

Edward stared at Robert. Back in Normandy, Robert of Jumièges had been a close friend of the family but had been particularly close to Edward's brother, Alfred Ætheling. So when Alfred had been captured by Godwin and handed over to Harold Harefoot to die in his custody, Robert had been particularly affected. His hatred of Godwin of Wessex had run deep ever since.

'If it were only that easy,' said Edward, indicating a chair for the bishop. 'With his daughter about to become my wife, there are all sorts of complications to consider.'

'Your grace,' said the bishop, sitting down. 'We have known each other a long time, and you know my thoughts on these matters. I understand why you are doing it, but I honestly believe you are making a mistake of the highest order. Godwin is one of the most powerful men in England, and by agreeing to this marriage, you will be strengthening his house even more. Make no mistake, he will use the union to advance his family's fortune at every opportunity.'

'So tell me what to do, Robert,' snapped Edward. 'You seem to have all the answers. What measures do you suggest I take to counter the growing influence of Godwin?'

'The answer is simple,' said the bishop. 'Even as we speak, the entire family and their huscarls are sleeping off an indulgent display of gluttony and drinking not five leagues from where we sit. Give the command, and we can have a thousand men fall upon them as they slumber and end their legacy forever.'

'You suggest I murder, in cold blood, the entire family of one of the most powerful houses in England?' asked the king.

'He had your brother murdered, did he not? This would be justifiable retribution.'

'And what would God make of such a heinous act?'

'The Lord is on your side, your grace, else why would he have led your path here after so many years lost in the wilderness?'

'If I attack Godwin, his thegns would rise up against me. I may have the power, Robert, but he has the men, and they are fiercely loyal. By attacking Wessex, this country would be plunged into civil war, leaving it open to enemies from across Europe.'

'There will be risks, yes, but once the earl and his sons are dead, those who served them will quickly see an opportunity to advance their own ambitions, and I have no doubt many will take the knee before you.'

'I have killed many men in battle, Robert,' said the king, 'but I have never killed a man in cold blood. There will be no slaughter in my name, not tonight, not ever. Instead, there will be a marriage, and there will be reconciliation. I freely admit there is anger in my heart still, but I will not risk England for retribution.'

'So you allow him to get away with the killing of your brother?' said Robert.

'I have no other option,' said the king, 'at least not at the moment. The time may well come when circumstances allow me to avenge my brother's death. Until that day, we will bide our time.'

'There is one more scenario we must consider,' said the bishop, 'one that is even more distasteful.'

'And that is?'

'If you sire a son with your new wife, your grace, that boy will be your heir, which means that one of Godwin's grandsons will one day inherit the throne of England, whether we like it or not.'

'That will be many years in the future,' said Edward. 'Why worry about it now?'

'Your grace, if something unfortunate were to happen to you, the earl has enough support to rule England as regent until the child is old enough to wear the crown. Godwin has already overseen the death of one royal, what is one more?'

Edward stared at the bishop for a few moments as the implications sank in.

'I accept your cautionary words,' he said eventually, 'and they perhaps have some merit.' He paused again as his thoughts cleared in his mind. 'There will be a marriage,' he continued, 'and hopefully an alliance; these things are unavoidable. However, what is avoidable is any grandchild of Godwin becoming king.'

'And how will you achieve that, your grace?' asked the bishop. 'Only God can decree the sex of a child.'

'I know,' said the king, 'and that is why there must be no offspring in the first place. Fret not, Robert, for as God is my witness, this union will produce no heirs of either sex.'

–

Twenty leagues away, Godwin's three eldest sons rode side by side across an open field. The morning had gone well, with any trace of hangovers blown away by the excitement of the hunt. Back in the forest, a team of gamekeepers were busy skinning a deer with the promise it would be in the earl's kitchens by nightfall.

'It was a good kill, brother,' said Sweyn to Tostig. 'The first for a long time if my memory serves me well.'

'I have my fair share of success in the hunt,' said Tostig. 'More than your success in the bedchambers, it seems.'

Harold burst out laughing. 'Come, Tostig,' he said, 'you know that such rumours hurt our brother's feelings. We should change the subject and discuss all things military.'

'Very funny,' responded Sweyn with a cold glance. 'Perhaps if you spent more time on your own affairs, then you would not find so much enjoyment in mine.'

'Surely not,' continued Tostig, determined to antagonise his older brother even further. 'Yours are far more interesting.'

Sweyn reined in his horse and waited as his brothers turned around to face him. Harold was still trying to contain his mirth while Tostig had a look of mischief about him.

'Have we upset you again?' asked Tostig. 'Do you want us to summon the Abbess of Leominster to soothe your hurt feelings?'

'Enough!' shouted Sweyn, the anger evident in his voice. 'Is your life so pathetic that you have no other responsibilities than to goad your betters? I am warning you, Tostig, cease with this infantile behaviour, or I will not be responsible for my actions.'

'He was jesting, Sweyn,' said Harold. 'Lighten your mood.'

'Jesting or not,' said Sweyn, 'words have consequences, and his efforts to solicit humour from the concerns of others lessen us all in the eyes of those who look up to the House of Godwin. Every time his jibes are spoken in public, it reveals business that should stay within the family.'

'There is nobody else here,' said Tostig, looking around. 'Your argument is void.'

'You know what I mean,' said Sweyn. 'For instance, in Ealdgyth's celebrations, after you had both enjoyed ridiculing me, I heard several whispered conversations about me and my affairs. This has to stop, Tostig, or it will end in tears.'

'He has a point, brother,' said Harold, turning to Tostig. 'Perhaps it is time to move on from such things.'

'But he is such an easy target,' laughed Tostig. 'His life is one of luxury and demands the scrutiny of mirth.'

'What part of my life is easy compared to yours?' asked Sweyn. 'Without an earldom, you have nothing to worry about apart from whether the ale barrels are dry.'

'Says the man who can call on the riches of Gloucester-shire, Herefordshire, Oxfordshire, Berkshire and Somerset,' countered Tostig.

'Enough,' said Harold. 'This conversation is descending into farce.'

'Then he should shut his mouth,' said Sweyn, 'for he has no idea of what goes on in my life or the pressures it brings.'

'Such as?' asked Tostig.

'You will see soon enough,' said Sweyn, 'and when you do, you will afford me the respect that I am due.'

Before Harold and Tostig could respond, Sweyn kicked his horse into a gallop towards the main path back to London.

'What did he mean by that?' asked Tostig when Sweyn had gone.

'I do not know,' said Harold, 'but whatever it is, I don't like the sound of it. Come on, let us get back.'

They both urged their horses into a canter and talked of other matters. But all the while, deep down inside, Harold had a terrible sense of foreboding. He knew his elder brother better than anyone; Sweyn was a powerful man but was sometimes capable of rash decisions. Sweyn had looked troubled of late, and with his latest comments, Harold suspected that there might be more going on along the Welsh Marches than Sweyn had let on.

Chapter Five

Sweyn Godwinson sat astride his horse amongst the trees at the edge of a wooded hill. Alongside him were Owen of Hereford, one of his trusted thegns, and Hywel ap Steffan, a scout who usually served King Rhydderch of Gwent.

For the past few days, they had made their way down through Wales from Hereford along with a hundred mounted men – not a massive force, but enough for what they had planned. The route was unknown to Sweyn, but Steffan had led them along the lesser-known tracks to avoid being seen by those loyal to King Rhydderch.

Rhydderch had ousted Gruffydd ap Llewelyn from the Welsh kingdom of Deheubarth the previous year and now ruled all across the south of the country. King Gruffydd, in contrast, ruled the north and most of the west coast but desperately wanted Deheubarth back under his banner, which he saw as an important step in uniting the country. Ongoing strife across the rest of Wales meant Gruffydd was unable to commit his whole army against Rhydderch, but when Hywel the scout had approached Sweyn with an offer to betray his master in return for a purse of silver, the earl had realised it was the perfect opportunity to gain favour with the powerful Welsh king.

Now, just a few weeks later, they found themselves deep in Welsh territory, about to attempt an almost impossible task – the capture or, failing that, the assassination of the king of Gwent.

Down in the valley, a slow river meandered southwards towards the sea. In one of the bends, a hunting party had set up camp, and the banner of Rhydderch flew from the largest tent.

'The scout was telling the truth,' said Sweyn quietly. 'I count only fifty men; we outnumber them two to one.'

'I would have preferred better odds,' said Owen, 'but with surprise on our side, there should be no problem.' He turned around and summoned the scout. 'Hywel, tell us what you know about this place.'

'My lords,' said the scout, pointing south along the river. 'This valley opens up onto the mudflats alongside the river. To the west, their path is blocked by marshland, which means if Rhydderch is forced to flee, he can only go north, as you control the eastern approaches.'

'He will not have a chance to run,' said Sweyn. 'I will see to that.'

'My lord,' said the scout, 'I am not doubting your prowess but be warned – Rhydderch is as slippery as an eel and knows this landscape like the back of his hand. If there are any other escape routes, I will wager that he knows about them.'

Sweyn continued to stare down at the camp. Since being made Earl of Hereford, he had been desperate to garner favour with the powerful King of Gwynedd just across the Welsh border. But with little to offer Gruffydd in return for an alliance, he had seized this opportunity to rid him of his worst enemy. Consequently, without Gruffydd's knowledge, he had brought his small army into Wales to kill Rhydderch; or better still, deliver him alive to Gruffydd's court, an achievement that would cement an alliance between the two men for a lifetime.

'How strong are his forces?' he asked.

'He usually hunts with twenty beaters and servants, along with another forty or so bodyguards, all skilled men-at-arms.'

'Does this sit well with you?' asked Sweyn, turning to face Owen.

'The numbers are tighter than I would have liked,' said Owen, 'but with a swift strike, I am confident we will emerge the victors.'

'My thoughts exactly,' said Sweyn. 'And to give us a greater advantage, we will strike while they are still dreaming of warm beds and warmer women.'

'So be it,' said Owen. 'I suggest we approach on foot under cover of darkness and attack at first light.'

'Agreed,' said Sweyn. 'And if God is with us, Rhydderch and his men will be dead before the sun clears the eastern hills.'

'My lord,' said Hywel, 'I have done as I promised and brought you to the king. But this fight is not mine, and I respectfully request payment for my service.'

Sweyn stared at the scout for a few moments, wondering whether he should trust him further.

'Tell me,' said Sweyn, 'if I pay you now, what is to stop you running to Rhydderch and betraying us to collect even more silver?'

'First of all,' replied the scout, 'I would be signing my own death warrant for betraying him in the first place. But mainly because of this.' He lifted his left hand and removed his riding gauntlet, revealing a wooden hand strapped to his forearm.

'Did Rhydderch do that to you?' asked Sweyn.

'No, it was his father, Rhydderch ap Iestyn, who was responsible.'

'Why, what did you do wrong?'

'Nothing,' said the scout, 'for I was still a boy. But when my family was late with the tithe, they hanged my father as punishment and took my hand as a warning to my older brothers that late payment would not be tolerated. Since that day, I vowed to get my revenge, but when Iestyn died, I turned my attention to his son.'

'And Rhydderch has no idea who you really are?'

'Kings do not see men such as I, except when they need our services. I will not betray you, my lord, and if I did not have two little ones at home to feed, I would join you in an instant. That man needs to die. It is as simple as that.'

Sweyn stared at the scout for a few more seconds before making his decision.

'Pay the man,' he said.

Owen threw over a purse of silver, which was immediately concealed inside the scout's cloak.

'Are you not going to count it?' asked Sweyn.

'I trust you, my lord,' said the scout. 'May I go?'

'You may,' said Sweyn, 'but know this. We know where you live, and if I hear that you have betrayed me in any way or have spoken of this day to anyone, I will make what Iestyn did to you seem like a minor inconvenience. Do you understand what I am saying?'

'Aye, I do,' said Steffan.

'Then be gone,' said Sweyn, watching as the man turned away to ride back towards the marches.

Several hours later, Sweyn and his men lay hidden in the undergrowth to the east of the hunting camp, having crawled the last few hundred paces until they could see the campfires at the edge of the river.

'Get ready,' whispered Sweyn.

'A few moments longer,' said Owen at his side. 'We want no man falling in the darkness.'

Owen looked up at the sky. The light rain that had pestered them for the last few hours had gone, and though a breeze meant many shivered with cold, he knew the discomfort would disappear the moment they attacked. The last of the clouds drifted away, and as the full camp came into sight, he knew that their cautious approach had paid dividends. Not only were the hunting party still asleep in their beds, but the two guards nearest them were wrapped in their cloaks and snoring like pigs.

As Sweyn and Owen watched, one of the dogs stood up and looked towards them. Immediately Owen knew that it would only be seconds before it alerted the camp, and in battle, those seconds could make all the difference.

'Now, my lord,' he said.

Sweyn jumped to his feet, and as the hunting dogs filled the morning air with their frantic barking, he pointed his sword towards the camp, roaring the command his men had been waiting for.

'Men of Hereford, *chaaarge*!'

Throughout the camp, Rhydderch's men were torn from their dreams by the terrifying battle cries of the seasoned warriors. Everyone scrambled to get to their weapons, but it was too late – Sweyn's men launched themselves onto the tents, stabbing their blades indiscriminately through the waxed canvas. Those still inside had no chance, and as they tried desperately to disentangle themselves, their screams rang out pitifully in the pre-dawn gloom.

Despite the surprise attack, some of the more experienced soldiers managed to get out and reach their weapons. At first, they fought back furiously, and even without boots or armour, gave a good account of themselves. The fight spread out with more men than anticipated fighting furiously to protect their king, but the element of surprise was with Sweyn, and his men forced the men of Gwent back towards the river.

'Where's Rhydderch?' shouted Sweyn, looking around. 'Has anyone seen the king?'

'He must still be in his tent,' said Owen.

'Follow me,' said Sweyn, and he and Owen ran over, cutting down a dog near the entrance flap before charging into the tent. Inside, a fire still smouldered in a portable iron hearth, and against the far wall, a terrified young woman sat on a bed, holding up a sheepskin to cover her nakedness.

'Where is he?' demanded Sweyn, striding over to the girl.

'He's not here,' she gasped as Sweyn pushed his blade against her chest. 'He left.'

'What do you mean left? We saw nobody fleeing the camp.'

The girl swallowed hard, desperate not to betray the king but equally desperate not to die.

'This is your last chance,' said Sweyn with a grimace. 'Where is the king?'

'There,' she gasped, pointing towards the rear of the tent. 'He made his escape at the first sound of the attack.'

Owen walked over and found an opening cut into the canvas wall. He ducked outside before returning a few moments later.

'There are tracks outside,' he said, 'heading into the forest. Two men, one barefoot.'

'The tracks are his,' said the girl. 'The second man is his personal bodyguard – it was he that told the king to flee.'

Before anyone could reply, another man burst into the tent and launched himself onto Owen's back. Taken by surprise, Owen fell to the floor, but as his attacker lifted his knife to administer the killing blow, Sweyn swung his sword, cutting through the assailant's neck and sending his head flying through the air to land beside the screaming girl.

Owen staggered to his feet and stared at the decapitated body before looking over to the earl.

'You saved my life,' he said.

'Consider it a favour,' replied Sweyn, lowering his sword and wiping the blood from his face. 'Now, what were you saying about those tracks?'

'They can't have got far,' said Owen, 'we can run him down.'

'*My lord,*' shouted a voice outside, '*come quickly.*'

Sweyn turned and ran out of the tent, just in time to see a naked rider galloping south alongside the river.

'*Rhydderch is escaping,*' he roared. 'Someone get me a horse.'

The men looked around with bewilderment. They had not brought their own horses, and those belonging to the camp were unsaddled.

'It is too late,' said Owen. 'By the time you get horsed, he will be long gone.'

'We were told the mudflats are impassable,' said Sweyn. 'He is trapped.'

Sweyn walked over to the river where his men had cornered the last of their opponents, his face still streaked with blood. In front of him, the ten remaining bodyguards stared at him with fear in their eyes. With nowhere to go, the man in front lowered his sword.

'My lord,' he said, 'we are done. We beg quarter.'

'Where has he gone?' asked Sweyn.

'Who, my lord?'

'You know who I am talking about,' said Sweyn. 'The king has ridden south to the mudflats. What else lies that way?'

'Nothing, my lord, apart from the sea.'

'So he cannot escape?'

The man did not answer, but his eyes grew wide with fear as Sweyn lifted his sword to place it at the man's throat.

'You beg for quarter,' he said, 'yet do not answer my questions, so think carefully. Is he trapped that way?'

'No, he is not,' said another of Rhydderch's men, stepping forward. 'And you will never catch him.'

'And what makes you say that?' asked Sweyn, turning his attention to the second man.

'Because Rhydderch knows these parts as well as any,' said the warrior. 'The flats are a death sentence to most men, but to those with the knowledge, there are paths to be found.'

Sweyn cursed and spun around to walk away. Owen followed him.

'My lord,' he said, 'what do you want to do?'

'I need to think,' said Sweyn. 'We have come a long way for this moment only to be thwarted by circumstance.'

'There is no shame in this outcome,' said Owen. 'Rhydderch is as cunning as a fox and has eluded many men.'

'I am not just any other man,' said Sweyn, 'I am Sweyn Godwinson, Earl of Hereford, and I will not have this stain upon my name.'

Owen fell silent, knowing it was the best way to deal with the arrogance of such men. Sweyn walked over to a tree and leaned his head against the trunk while he thought. Finally, he turned back around and walked over to Owen.

'This day has not turned out as we hoped,' he said, 'but we have still achieved a victory. That in itself is to be celebrated, is it not?'

'I do not agree,' said Owen, 'in fact, I would say it would be better if this fight had not happened.'

'Why?'

'Because, my lord, without Rhydderch's head to offer Gruffydd in appeasement, all he will know is that we crossed the border and killed fifty of his fellow Welshmen and, whether they are men of Gwent or not, the fact remains that we broke the treaty without his knowledge. That in itself may be enough to raise his ire, and the last thing we want is Welsh raids into England.'

'So what do you suggest?'

'I think we should burn the camp and take the prisoners back to Hereford. We can sell them as slaves to the French. That way, nobody will ever know who was responsible for the killing, and the relationship between you and Gruffydd remains intact.'

'As usual, you are the voice of reason,' said Sweyn. 'I agree with your plan but with one change.'

'Which is?'

'Prisoners have a habit of escaping,' said Sweyn, 'and we can leave no witnesses.'

'What do you want me to do, my lord? Are you ordering me to kill the prisoners?'

'Spare them, and one day it could be one of their blades that ends your life. It is best that they die today.'

'And the girl?'

'Leave her to me,' said Sweyn. 'I have unfinished business with her. Kill the witnesses and burn the camp. I will join you shortly.'

He walked away, heading towards the king's tent, as Owen watched with distaste. He had no problem killing men, especially those from Wales, but usually it was in the heat of battle and not in cold blood after they had surrendered.

'My lord,' he said, following the earl. 'These men have begged quarter. Let us cut out their tongues and set them free. That way, they will be no burden and cannot retell what happened here.'

'We cannot take the risk,' said Sweyn. 'You have your orders.' He turned away and ducked through the doorway to the king's tent.

Owen sighed with frustration but headed to the river, where all the prisoners were now bound and on their knees.

'What are we to do with them?' asked one of the men.

'The earl wants no prisoners,' said Owen.

'Are you sure?'

'Aye,' said Owen, drawing his sword. 'Now let us get to it. The quicker it is done, the quicker we can get away from here.'

As Owen and his men closed in on the terrified prisoners, a hundred paces away, another sound filled the air – the cry of a frightened young woman.

–

Several weeks later, in Leominster Abbey, Sweyn Godwinson paced the outer hall, growing impatient at the amount of time he had been forced to wait. One of the nuns stood silently in the corner, watching with concern as the earl grew more and more agitated.

'Where is she?' he demanded again, turning to the nun. 'Surely she should be finished by now?'

'My lord,' said the nun, 'Sister Eadgifu leads the sisters in prayer. I have had the message sent, and I am sure she will be along at any moment.'

'Moments I do not have,' Sweyn said. 'Send another message, and tell her that if she does not come immediately, I will go in there and drag her out myself.'

'There will be no need for that,' said a voice, and both the nun and Sweyn turned to see the abbess standing in the doorway.

'At last,' said Sweyn. 'What took you so long?'

The abbess ignored the earl for a moment and turned to the nun.

'Sister Agnes, thank you for hosting the earl. You may leave and join your sisters in the gardens.'

'Thank you, sister,' said the younger nun before hurriedly leaving the room. The abbess gently closed the door behind her and walked over to stand before her visitor.

'Earl Sweyn,' she said, 'are you well? You look exhausted.'

'I have ridden the night through,' said Sweyn, 'and have not slept a moment.'

'Is there a problem?'

'None to concern the abbey, Sister Eadgifu, but I have news and need to share it with you before I leave.'

'What news is this?'

'Tomorrow,' said Sweyn, 'I am to leave Hereford and join with King Gruffydd and his army in Gwynedd. There I will fight alongside him to oust King Rhydderch from Deheubarth.'

'My lord,' said the nun, 'why are you aiding the Welsh? They have caused these lands nothing but heartache for many years. Surely you should let them settle their own differences.'

'Ordinarily I would,' said Sweyn, 'but I have been seeking an alliance with Gruffydd for a long time, and at last he has given me an opportunity. If I do this, and we are successful, I could secure peace along our borders with Wales for a generation. Is that not an honourable cause?'

'I suppose it is,' said the nun, 'but it is also a great risk. Hardly a season goes by without one Welsh king declaring war on another, but if there is one thing certain to unite them in common cause, it is the opportunity to kill an English nobleman. By doing this, I fear you are placing yourself in extreme danger.'

'I agree,' said Sweyn, 'and that is why I am here.'

'I do not understand,' said the abbess. 'Do you seek the bishop's blessing?'

Sweyn threw back his head and stared at the ceiling, knowing what he was about to say would cross all boundaries with the Church. He lowered his head and stared at the nun again.

'Sister Eadgifu,' he said eventually. 'I am here for the same reason I have come so many times before, to beg you to leave this life and live alongside me as my wife.'

The nun sighed, and her shoulders slumped.

'Oh, Sweyn,' she said gently, 'why do you torture yourself so? We have had this conversation so many times, yet still you refuse to take no for an answer.'

'I cannot help it,' said Sweyn, looking at the beautiful young woman who had pledged her life to God. 'You are like a pestilence in my heart and will surely cause my death if untreated.'

The nun walked over to sit on one of the benches.

'Join me,' she said, 'we should talk.'

Sweyn sat opposite the abbess and gazed into her sky-blue eyes. As an earl, he could have the choice of many women, including those born of nobility, but ever since meeting the abbess a few years earlier, he had been smitten and knew there could never really be anyone else.

'My lord,' said the abbess, 'I am flattered by the attention you shower upon me, I really am, and I would be telling an untruth if I said I did not care for you. But alas, as we have discussed on more than one occasion, my life is here amongst my sisters, and I see no route that will ever see us being together as man and wife. I am sworn to God, my lord, and my heart belongs to him for as long as I live.'

'I know,' interrupted the earl, 'but I have taken advice in such matters and have been told that the Holy Father in Rome can grant you release from your vows. If you care for me as much as you say, why can we not travel to Rome and seek that release?'

The abbess looked shocked at the suggestion but knew she had to tread carefully, fully aware that despite his proclamations of affection, he was known to have a temper, and she could not risk raising it.

'My lord,' she said, 'even if I agreed and the Pope issued such an edict, who is to say that our union would be a happy one? You know I am devoted to my work here in Leominster – the poor and the sick rely on my sisters and me to give them succour and hope. If I gave that up, I fear that I would be eternally resentful and would not be the woman you believe me to be.'

'But there is no need to give that up,' said Sweyn. 'Indeed, if you agree to be my wife, I will ensure you have all the money and power you need to look after those you do now. Imagine what good you could do with my influence behind you. Please, Sister Eadgifu, a just God would never deny you happiness, and I swear that, given a chance, I will make you the happiest woman in the kingdom.'

'Oh, Sweyn,' said Eadgifu, 'I do not know what to say. I am flattered, I really am, but I cannot accept your offer. I am married to Christ and will never leave the Church. Can't you see that? Surely no woman has ever been so blessed by such a determined suitor, but I cannot grant your request. I am sorry, Sweyn, the answer has to be no.'

The earl's face fell, and he stared at the nun for several moments before reaching into his cloak and producing a document.

'In that case,' he said, 'there is one more thing I would ask. Grant me this boon, and I swear I will never darken this threshold again.'

'State your request, my lord,' said the relieved nun, 'and I promise I will do what I can.'

'Sister Eadgifu, this document is a promissory note granting you an immediate allowance for the rest of your life. It is a substantial sum and will be yours to do with as you wish. Few women have access to such riches outside of the royal court, and if I should die in the next few weeks, it also bequeaths all my personal wealth and belongings to you. It has been witnessed by a priest and is a legal document. This represents everything I am, everything I am worth, and I am happy to leave it here at the abbey, but I cannot live or die having never experienced your embrace.'

He paused and looked up at the nun, seeing the apprehension in her eyes. 'So,' he continued, 'in return for all that is held within this document, I implore you, with every breath in my body, with my heart, my life, my soul, please spend one night with me in my bedchamber. Do this, and whether I die or not, you will immediately become one of the richest women in the kingdom.'

Chapter Six

Havering Palace, London, October, AD 1046

Gytha Thorkelsdóttir walked along the corridor towards the queen's chambers. Plush tapestries hung along the walls, and the flagstone floors had been covered with polished wooden boards and luxurious Italian rugs. The air smelled of burning wood and incense, a heady mixture creating a warm and welcoming atmosphere.

Ahead of her walked one of the queen's personal servants, a young woman dressed in an ankle-length, tailored blue gown with open sleeves at the wrist. A wide decorative belt fitted snugly around her waist, and her long hair was braided up over the top of her head. As they approached the end of the corridor, two servants bowed deeply and opened the doors before stepping back out of the way.

Across the room, Ealdgyth was being measured up for a new dress by two seamstresses in front of a large mirror leaning against a wall.

'Your grace,' said the servant, with a deep bow. 'Lady Gytha of Wessex has arrived.'

Ealdgyth turned to her mother with a huge grin on her face.

'Leave us,' she said, without taking her eyes off her mother. 'We will continue this in the morning.' The two seamstresses collected their things and, with a last bow, scurried from the room.

'You too, Mildritha,' said Ealdgyth.

'Do you not want my help to get dressed, your grace?' asked the servant.

'Mildritha,' said Ealdgyth, 'the lady Gytha is my mother. I am sure that between us we can manage. Go and get some rest, you have worked hard today.'

'As you wish, your grace,' said the servant, following the seamstresses from the room and closing the door behind her.

As soon as the door was shut, Ealdgyth let out a squeal of excitement and, forgetting all her queenly deportment, ran across the room to throw herself into her mother's arms.

'Ealdgyth,' laughed Gytha, 'temper your excitement, it has only been a few months since last I saw you.'

'Has it?' gasped Ealdgyth, tightening her embrace. 'For it surely seems like a year or more.' She loosened her grip and stepped back. 'Oh Mother, I have missed you so much.'

'And I, you,' said Gytha. 'I am only sorry I did not come sooner, but Ælfgifu fell ill again, so I stayed at Wilton Abbey for a while to help nurse her back to health.'

'Oh no,' said Ealdgyth. 'Has she recovered?'

'A little,' said Gytha. 'But she is a sickly child, and the physicians are struggling to cure whatever ails her.'

'Then perhaps you should still be with her,' said Ealdgyth. 'A child needs her mother, does she not?'

'Aye, she does, but you, too, are my child, and something tells me my presence is required here just as much as at Wilton. Come, help me with my cloak, and you can tell me everything that has happened since last I came.'

Ealdgyth undid her mother's brooch and placed the cloak on the back of a chair as Gytha walked over to a table to pick up a jug of watered wine.

'Is this fresh?' she asked, sniffing the jug.

'It was brought only moments before you arrived,' said Ealdgyth. 'As soon as I heard you were here, I had it brought from the kitchens, as well as the bread, cheese and honey. I thought you might be hungry after your journey.'

'I will try something shortly,' said Gytha before walking over to examine one of three dresses laid out on the queen's bed. 'These look nice; I suggest the blue one. It matches your eyes.'

Ealdgyth smiled and walked over to join her mother. For the next few minutes, Gytha helped her daughter dress, all thoughts of station and duty happily forgotten. Finally, the queen examined herself in the mirror and, satisfied, turned back to face her mother.

'Beautiful,' said Gytha, 'as usual.'

'Thank you,' said Ealdgyth with a mock curtsy.

'So,' said Gytha, 'the last time I came, you were living in a manor house in the north of the city. When did you transfer here to Havering?'

'Just a few weeks ago,' said Ealdgyth. 'Edward has commissioned a new royal palace at Westminster and wanted to be nearer to liaise with his architects, so we moved here until it is finished.'

'Is this place not grand enough for him?' asked Gytha looking around. 'From what I've seen so far, it is a palace in itself.'

'Indeed,' said Ealdgyth, 'and has been four years in the making, but he has grand ideas and wants to build something the likes of which has never been seen before.'

'Vanity is a sin,' said Gytha, 'as well he knows.'

'I have reminded him so,' said Ealdgyth, 'but he says the people of England demand their king resides in a palace unrivalled in size and beauty.'

'Oh well,' said Gytha. 'I suppose that a king can do whatever he pleases.'

'So,' said Ealdgyth, 'tell me of Ælfgifu and Gunhild. Are they happy?'

'Ælfgifu has had to suspend her studies for now,' said Gytha, 'but when she is well, I am sure she will catch up. As for Gunhild, she looks radiant and embraces every opportunity given to her by the sisters of Wilton.'

'I am so glad,' said Ealdgyth. 'For an age, I thought that she had made the wrong decision.'

'As did I,' said Gytha. 'But believe me when I say, I have never seen her so happy, which, dear daughter, is more than

I can say for you.' She lifted her hand and gently touched the skin beneath Ealdgyth's eyes. 'I can see you have been crying, Ealdgyth. Tell me, what has happened? Why are you so unhappy?'

The young queen looked shocked and got to her feet.

'I am not unhappy,' she said, rather too quickly. 'What makes you think that?'

'Ealdgyth,' sighed her mother, getting to her feet. 'I did not come all this way on a whim. There are people working in the king's court who keep us informed of many things. Lately, we have learned that your life here may not be as happy as you hoped.'

'*You have spies in the king's court?*' asked Ealdgyth, shocked.

'Let us call them friends,' said Gytha, 'the term "spy" evokes an image far more unpleasant.'

'Call them what you will,' said Ealdgyth, 'but I do not feel comfortable about such a thing.'

'My sweet daughter,' said Gytha, 'you may be Queen of England, but you have much to learn about politics. Yes, there are people within the court that are loyal to us, just as there are, no doubt, people at Bosham who are *friends* of the king. It has always been so.'

'And you are happy about this?'

'It can be frustrating, knowing that someone in my household has the ear of the king, but often it can be a benefit.'

'In what way?'

'By controlling the information that eventually reaches the royal court.'

Ealdgyth pondered this a moment before comprehension dawned on her face.

'Do you mean you actually know who they are?' she asked.

'Most of them, but alas, not all.'

Ealdgyth shook her head in disbelief. 'Politics is a strange and dangerous game,' she said. 'I will need to be more careful.'

'You just do what comes naturally,' said her mother, taking her hand and leading her to a chair. 'And leave the politics to others. Come, let me redo your hair.'

Ealdgyth sat in front of the mirror as her mother unravelled her braids. For a few moments, both women fell quiet as Gytha gently brushed the tangles from her daughter's beautiful long hair.

'So,' she said eventually, 'why do you not tell me what is causing those bags beneath your eyes? Is he cruel to you?'

'No,' said Ealdgyth with a sigh, 'nothing like that. In fact, he could not be kinder and treats me like the rarest treasure. Every day we spend time together, and at least twice a week he finds time to dine with me.' She paused and stared at her mother in the mirror.

'And?' said Gytha.

'That is just it,' said Ealdgyth. 'He is kind and gentle, but he does not treat me as a woman, as his *wife*.'

Gytha stopped brushing her daughter's hair and returned the stare.

'Are you talking about the bedchamber?'

'Yes,' said Ealdgyth.

'I do not understand,' said Gytha. 'Does he not attend you regularly?'

'He does not attend me at all,' said the queen. 'Most nights he is elsewhere, and on the few occasions he is here at Havering, he walks me to my room before leaving to sleep in his own bed.'

Gytha was shocked. There had been concerns about the lack of any children after almost two years of marriage, but such things were in the hands of God, and never had she imagined the situation that her daughter now explained.

'Are you saying that he has never touched you, not even once?'

'There have been a few attempts…' said Ealdgyth. 'But the experiences were awkward, painful. Now it seems he has given up – he no longer pays me any attention in that way.'

'There must be something wrong with the man,' said Gytha. 'You are a beautiful young woman. What man in his right mind could resist? Perhaps he has a problem and should seek the help of a physician.'

Ealdgyth spun around in the chair and stared at her mother.

'Do not *dare* say anything like that,' she gasped. 'Not to anyone, not even Father.'

'But this is not natural,' said Gytha. 'The country needs an heir. Your father knows people who may be able to help.'

'No!' snapped Ealdgyth, getting to her feet. 'You can repeat nothing you heard here today, not a single word.'

'I was only trying to help,' said her mother, shocked at the reaction.

'But you will not be helping,' said Ealdgyth. 'Can you not see? If this were to get out, it would make Edward a laughing stock and me an object of pity. Whether you like it or not, we are the King and Queen of England, and we must present a strong and united front to all our subjects. As my mother, I trusted you with this information, but you must swear to me that you will repeat it to no one.'

'But what about children?' asked Gytha quietly. 'There must be a succession?'

'I am sure the king and I can sort this out in our own time,' said Ealdgyth. 'But until then, I have a duty to my husband and to our country. My burden is small in comparison to others', so you must swear to me, Mother, swear to me now, before God, that you will take this secret to the grave.'

'Oh Ealdgyth,' said Gytha, walking over to embrace her daughter. But the queen stepped back, holding up her hand to stop her mother in her tracks, suddenly every inch the queen of the realm.

'No,' she said, 'we cannot continue until you vow our conversation will remain between us and us alone.'

'If that is what you want,' said Gytha, 'then so be it.' She looked around the room and saw a crucifix fixed on the wall beside the bed. She walked over to it, dropped to her knees and folded her hands in prayer.

'I swear,' she said, 'before our Lord and Saviour, Jesus Christ, that I will not repeat the conversation held between my daughter and me in this very room today, to any man, woman or child as long as I live.' She bowed her head in silence for a moment before speaking again. 'Join me,' she said, without looking around, waiting as Ealdgyth walked over to kneel beside her.

'Come,' said Gytha, taking her daughter's hand. 'We will pray for him and for you together. May God bless you both.'

Ealdgyth wiped a tear from her eye, and as silence fell in the room, she and her mother closed their eyes in prayer, not just for the king but for the future safety of England.

–

The following morning both women sat in the dining hall to break their fast. The servants brought in smoked fish and freshly baked bread, supplemented with warm, watered wine.

'Mother,' said Ealdgyth, 'I have arranged for someone to join us for our fare this morning, someone you know.'

'Who is it?' asked Gytha.

'It is a surprise,' said Ealdgyth, 'but I think you will be pleased.'

A few moments later, the door opened, and a young monk ran up the hall to bow before the queen.

'Your grace,' he said, holding his head down, 'I am shamed by my lateness. Please forgive me.'

'Never mind about that,' said the queen with a smile, 'look who is here.'

The monk turned to face Gytha, and his worried look disappeared.

'Lady Gytha,' he said, 'it is so good to see you again.'

'You too, Spearhafoc,' replied Gytha, 'it has been a long time.'

'Too long,' said the monk. 'Over a year, perhaps.'

'And more,' said Gytha. 'Please, sit beside me, there is much to talk about.'

For the next hour or so, all three caught up on all the news from the royal court and the House of Godwin until, eventually, Ealdgyth gave her apologies and left the hall to continue with the previous day's dress-fitting.

Once she had gone, Gytha waited until the servants had cleared the table before turning again to face Spearhafoc. After the wedding of Edward and Ealdgyth, the monk had returned to Bosham with the Godwin family and had worked there for almost a year before the queen asked him to attend court to work for the royal household. Since then, he had spent the past year in the queen's employ producing beautiful jewellery and artwork, a position he found both wonderful and terrifying at the same time. On occasion, the Abbot of Bury St Edmunds enquired about when he would be returning to the abbey, but the quality of his work was so high that both Ealdgyth and Edward were keen for him to stay and be involved in the decoration of the new palace at Westminster.

'So,' said Gytha, 'how are you, Spearhafoc?'

'I am well,' said the monk. 'The work is demanding, but I love the fact that I am allowed to embrace my own creativity.'

'And the king, does he treat you well?'

'To be honest, I rarely see him and deal mainly with your daughter.'

'And it is lucky for us that you do,' said Gytha. 'When I received your letter I was filled with concern and came as soon as I could. You were right, she is definitely unhappy.'

'I was just concerned,' said Spearhafoc. 'Has she told you what ails her?'

'She has,' said Gytha, 'but I am sworn to secrecy. Just be assured that it is not a disease of the body. Other than her worries, she is in perfect health.'

'I am glad,' said Spearhafoc. 'These last few months, I have enjoyed her patronage, and we seem to be getting closer.'

'That is wonderful news,' said Gytha. 'I encourage you to nurture that friendship further.'

She paused for a few moments and looked around the room to make sure there was nobody in earshot before pulling her chair closer to the monk.

'Spearhafoc,' she said, 'I would like to speak to you about something, but you cannot repeat it to anyone else. Are you happy to do such a thing?'

'My lady,' said Spearhafoc, 'not only am I a man of God, but I also consider your family to be friends of the closest order. You have my sworn oath that you can trust me with your innermost secrets, should you wish to do so.'

'I thought as much,' said Gytha, 'and we see you more as a family member than a friend.'

'That makes my heart sing,' said the monk. 'How can I help you?'

'Spearhafoc,' continued Gytha, 'you are settling in really well here in the royal household, and the longer you are here, the closer you will get to Ealdgyth. But more importantly than that, by association, you will get closer to the king, and that brings opportunities that can only help the House of Godwin.'

'In what way?' asked the monk.

'Oh, nothing sinister,' said Gytha. 'But these are troubled times, and with our own daughter now so close to those who perhaps may not wish our family the best of success, we hoped your proximity might occasionally provide us with information that will protect us from harm.'

'My lady,' said Spearhafoc, 'the king can be a difficult man to fathom, but I am sure he would never do anything to harm the queen or her family.'

'Spearhafoc,' said Gytha gently. 'Let us not forget that as soon as he was crowned, he rode to Winchester and confiscated all his mother's lands and wealth for no other reason than she had allegedly bestowed more favour upon his brother than him. What sort of man does such a thing?'

'I know,' said Spearhafoc, 'but in his defence, he reinstated her soon after, along with the Bishop of Elmham who, as her confidant, had lost the bishopric.'

'Indeed, and Bishop Stigand's reinstatement was greatly celebrated – he is fast becoming a trusted ally. But nevertheless, the fact that Edward treated his own mother that way suggests he would have no qualms about turning against the House of Godwin.'

'I yield the argument,' said the monk. 'What would you have me do?'

'Nothing that will put you in any danger,' said Gytha. 'Just keep your eyes and ears open, and should you learn anything that may concern the earl or our family, then let us know at the earliest opportunity.'

The monk stared at Gytha for a few moments before nodding his consent.

'Excellent,' said Gytha. 'There is one more thing that I would like to make you aware of.'

'And that is?'

'Do you know the Abbot of Abingdon?'

'Not personally, though I have met Father Æthelstan once in the course of my duties. He is a very godly man, full of love and compassion.'

'So I understand,' said Gytha. 'But I have also heard his health is poor and he struggles every day in the performance of his duties.'

'I shall pray for him,' said the monk.

'As will I,' said Gytha, 'but even with God's grace, none of us lives forever, and if we are truthful, then I suspect he will not be long for this world.'

'A sad but honest truth,' said Spearhafoc. 'Why is this relevant?'

'Because,' said Gytha, taking the monk's hands in her own. 'When the abbot dies, my husband, the Earl of Wessex, will be the one to nominate his successor. As long as you continue to serve us here at the palace, I see no reason why your name should not be at the top of the list. How does that sound to you?'

Spearhafoc was shocked, and he stared at Gytha with wide eyes.

'Me?' he asked, eventually.

'Why not?' said Gytha, releasing the monk's hands. 'You are loyal, talented, pious, and already have the favour of the king. With my husband's recommendation and the support of the queen, I see no reason why the appointment will not be authorised with little opposition.'

'I am honoured,' said the monk, 'but do not think I am ready for such a responsibility.'

'Perhaps not yet,' said Gytha. 'But now you know our intentions, you can study towards that goal, and when the Abbot of Abingdon finally passes, I think you will be the perfect choice.'

'I do not know what to say,' said the monk, 'my gratitude knows no bounds.'

'As I said before,' replied Gytha, 'you are now one of the family, and the House of Godwin looks after its own.'

Chapter Seven

Hereford, April, AD 1047

Harold Godwinson crawled out from beneath a mountain of sheepskin covers and pulled on his clothes before heading down a corridor into the main living space of his brother's manor. When he had arrived two days earlier, he had found out that Sweyn was somewhere in Wales fighting on behalf of King Gruffydd of Gwynedd, and after learning he was unlikely to return any time soon, he had decided to ride back to Bosham.

Harold entered the hall and immediately felt the difference in temperature, as the servants had kept the fire kindled all night and were now busy feeding it with logs to heat the whole building. He walked over to warm himself by the roaring flames but stopped suddenly when he saw Sweyn, fast asleep on the floor next to the fire.

'Sweyn,' he said loudly, causing his fellow earl to stir. 'You have returned.' He nudged his brother with his foot, causing Sweyn to curse and raise himself up onto one elbow.

'Harold,' he said with a yawn, 'I did not know you were here.'

'I have been here for two days,' said Harold, 'waiting for you. When did you get back?'

'Just before dawn,' said Sweyn, 'soaked to the skin and colder than a scorned woman's embrace.'

Harold turned to one of the servants.

'You, bring hot broth from the kitchens, and plenty of it.'

'Yes, my lord,' said the servant before scurrying away as Sweyn groggily got to his feet.

'I hear you have been in Wales,' said Harold, dragging two chairs closer to the fire. 'I take it that you are still pursuing an alliance with Gruffydd ap Llewelyn?'

'I was,' said Sweyn, extending his hands towards the fire. 'But that man is harder to tie down than a live fish.'

'You have not been successful?'

'I have not,' said Sweyn with a sigh. 'The man is full of promises, but when it comes to formalising anything, there is always one more village to attack, one more campaign to fight. I have spent the last month or so killing Welshmen in his name and have lost a fair few of my own men along the way, yet still he wants more.'

'Father has always said that an alliance with the Welsh was unlikely,' said Harold, 'especially with Gruffydd. He is known to have only self-interest at heart.'

'So it seems,' said Sweyn. 'Anyway, enough is enough, and I withdrew my forces a few days ago.'

'Does Gruffydd know?'

'By now he does, but I care not. I am done and will deal with the consequences.'

One of the servants brought him a sheepskin, and Sweyn threw it over his shoulders before sitting in the second chair and staring into the fire.

'Mother sends her regards,' said Harold, picking up a metal rod to push a log further into the flames. 'As does Ealdgyth. They both worry for you.'

'Why would they be worried?' asked Sweyn. 'I am more than capable of looking after myself.'

'Well, for a start,' said Harold, 'it seems foolish to pursue conflict when there is no need to do so. Your continued fascination with Gruffydd can only end in failure.'

'Trying to secure the borders of my earldom is hardly a foolish desire,' said Sweyn, 'and I suggest that any judgement of my methods should not come from a man who rules in the depths of a peaceful earldom.'

'We have our own challenges in East Anglia,' said Harold, 'not least the threat from the Danes.'

'Then you of all people should know that we can never rest with regard to securing our borders. To do so invites even more hardship, even more death.'

The servant returned with three large bowls of mutton broth, a loaf of freshly baked bread and a deep bowl filled with cheese and butter. Harold saw the third bowl and looked around the hall, noticing a previously unseen man sleeping on a table in the corner.

'Who's he?' he asked as the servant took the extra bowl over to the sleeping man.

'Owen of Hereford,' said Sweyn, 'one of my thegns. He took the place of my bodyguard many months ago after he died in a fight and has been with me ever since.'

The man in the corner grunted and sat up to take the bowl before dragging a chair over to join them at the fire.

'Owen,' said Sweyn, as the man dropped into his chair. 'This is my brother, Harold.'

The soldier nodded towards Harold and grunted an acknowledgement before reaching over to carve a chunk of butter from the slab and drop it into his broth. A slice of cheese followed the butter, and Owen stirred the broth until the surface glistened with fat.

'You are a man of few words,' said Harold as the thegn dipped his bread into the broth.

'Forgive me, my lord,' said Owen, 'I am indeed poor company when tired and cold. Allow me to warm my bones, and I will be as chatty as a newly-wed maiden before you know it.'

'Take your time,' said Harold, watching as the man rammed his grease-soaked bread into his mouth. 'So,' he said, turning to face his brother. 'What happens now? Do you intend to settle for what you have and govern Hereford?'

'I will take stock,' said Sweyn. 'I have not given up on the idea of that alliance. But I will not be the one doing the chasing any longer. It is about time that Welshman realised who he is dealing with and affords me the respect I am due.'

'Will you travel to Bosham anytime soon? Father wants to discuss the events in London.'

'What events?'

'Nothing specific as far as I am aware, but you know what he is like, always looking for a way to increase our influence. And it has been a while since we all broke bread together. Ealdgyth wants us all to join her for a Christmas feast at the palace.'

'I'll see what I can do,' said Sweyn. 'How long are you staying?'

'I could only spare a few days,' said Harold, 'so must be on my way by dawn tomorrow. But perhaps we can hunt before I leave.'

'Aye,' said Sweyn, 'that would be good. I'll send word to prepare the dogs.' He paused to look across at his brother. 'It's good to see you, Harold, it has been too long.'

—

The following morning Sweyn and Owen stood in the courtyard as Harold and his men readied their horses for the long ride back to Bosham.

'So what should I tell them?' asked Harold once he was in the saddle. 'Will you be coming or not?'

'Tell them I will join them at Southwark for Christmas,' said Sweyn.

'I will, but try not to let them down, brother. Ealdgyth in particular worries greatly for your safety and misses you more than most.'

'I will be there,' said Sweyn. 'Now, I suggest you be gone. It looks like it's going to rain, and you need to get as many leagues behind you as you can.'

Harold nodded and turned his horse away to lead his men out of the gates. Once they had gone, Sweyn and Owen headed back into the hall.

'My lord,' said Owen, 'the thegns seek an audience regarding the latest tithe. When shall I say you will receive them?'

'Not yet,' said Sweyn, 'for there is one more piece of business that I need to attend to.'

'And what business would that be?' asked Owen, hearing the dangerous lowering of Sweyn's tone that usually indicated he was deep in serious thought.

'The sort of business that lives in Leominster,' said Sweyn, turning to face Owen. 'And goes by the name of Eadgifu.'

–

Later that night, Owen of Hereford paced the very same floor in Leominster Abbey that Sweyn had graced almost a year earlier. His stomach was in knots, for though he feared no man alive, the task that the earl had placed before him was daunting, and it was only the fact that Sweyn had saved his life in Deheubarth that had finally made him agree.

A door opened and the abbess walked in carrying a candle before her, accompanied by two novices.

'I believe you are called Owen,' said the nun, coming to a stop. 'And you are here on the business of Earl Sweyn?'

'I am,' said Owen, 'and I apologise for the lateness of the hour.'

'My sisters here said you were quite insistent, even to the point of rudeness.'

'My apologies,' said Owen, 'but my master will allow no deviance from my task, and if you knew him as well as I, you would know there is no other option but to obey.'

'Oh, I know the Earl of Hereford only too well,' said the abbess, 'and am painfully aware of his stubbornness. What business does he have that will not wait until morning?'

'Sister Eadgifu,' said Owen, 'perhaps it would be better if we were to have this discussion alone?' He glanced at the two novices.

The abbess nodded and flicked her hand towards the door, indicating the two nuns should leave. Once they had gone, she turned back to the thegn.

'What is all this about, Master Owen?'

'Sister Eadgifu,' said Owen, 'the earl has just returned from Wales, where he fought alongside Gruffydd. We lost many men, and the earl himself was wounded.'

'Oh no,' said the nun, 'is it bad?'

'No, physically he is fine, but inside his mind, he is mortally wounded.'

'What do you mean?'

'Ever since he returned, he has failed in his duty as earl. Tithes are not enforced, meetings with allies are missed, and his estates are run by his staff without oversight. He has even failed in his duty to God and is seldom seen in church, such is his obsession.'

'And what obsession is this?' asked the abbess, already fearing the answer.

'You, Sister Eadgifu,' he said. 'The Earl of Hereford is obsessed by you.'

The nun let out a deep sigh and walked over to sit on the bench.

'I do not know what to say,' she said eventually. 'The earl and I have discussed this infatuation on many occasions, and I have made it clear that there is no way I can ever leave this place to be with him. Why can he not see this?'

'I do not know,' said Owen. 'What I do know is we cannot go on like this, for if the king finds out, there could be serious repercussions.'

'In what way?'

'He could have the earl's titles removed and his lands confiscated.'

'Master Owen,' said the nun, 'I share your worries, I really do, but I cannot be held responsible for his actions. If the result of his continued stubbornness is the loss of some power, then so be it. The responsibility is his and his alone.'

'I accept that,' said Owen, 'and if that was the only possible outcome of this situation, then I would ride away from him tomorrow and leave him to the consequences.'

'What do you mean?'

'Earl Sweyn is a proud and stubborn man,' said Owen. 'He is quick to rage, often without forethought. If the king were to strip him of his titles, I fear Sweyn would rise against the Crown.'

'He would never do that,' said Eadgifu. 'Edward could raise a far greater army and defeat him without drawing breath.'

'He could, but what do you think Earl Godwin would do if his son were attacked? The relationship between his house and King Edward is strained at best.'

'I would hope he would be wise enough to mediate between them both.'

'Perhaps he would, but if all else failed, there is no way he could sit back and watch his son slain by Edward, king or not. Godwin is a popular earl, Sister Eadgifu – men would rally to his banner, and this country could be plunged into civil war.'

'This is ridiculous,' said the nun. 'Something needs to be done.'

'Aye, it does, and that is why I am here. I want you to come with me to Hereford and talk some sense into him.'

The nun's face fell, and she got to her feet.

'I cannot do that,' she said quietly.

'Why not?' asked Owen. 'He will listen to you, I know he will.'

'He will not,' said Eadgifu, 'I have tried repeatedly.'

'He will this time, I am sure of it.'

'How can you be so certain?'

'Because he told me so himself.'

She stared at the thegn for a few moments, shocked at the implications. 'You are here because he sent you?' she asked eventually.

'Aye, he did, but...'

'The answer is no, Master Owen,' replied the abbess. 'I will not go there, for I will not be safe.'

'Of course you will,' said Owen. 'He is an earl, and your safety will be a matter of duty and honour.'

'No,' said the abbess.

'I do not understand,' said Owen. 'What scares you so?'

'Because the last time he was here,' shouted the abbess, turning to face him, 'he tried to buy my chastity with money, and when I flatly refused, he threatened to take me against my will. If it had not been for some of the sisters coming back into the room, I do not know what might have happened. What sort of man does that to any woman, let alone a bride of Christ?'

Owen stared at Eadgifu, shocked at the revelation.

'No,' he said eventually, 'you are mistaken. He can be difficult, but he would never do that to you. He cares too much.'

'Whether he would have carried out the deed or not is not the issue,' said the abbess. 'The fact is that he threatened me, and that cannot be tolerated.'

'I do not know what to say,' said Owen. 'All I know is that the man was close to tears when he gave me this task, and though he can be a devil to ride alongside, I have never seen him so broken.'

Silence fell in the room for a few moments before the abbess spoke again.

'Listen,' she said, 'I can come to Hereford two days hence and talk with him then, but there are conditions.'

'What sort of conditions?' asked Owen. 'He is not a man to be bound by tethers.'

'If you want me to come, I need safeguards,' said Eadgifu, 'one of which is that I will stay for one night only and then be escorted back here the following morning with an armed guard.'

'That can be arranged,' said Owen. 'And the second?'

'I want secure quarters for me and my travelling companions, and during my stay, I will never be left alone with him under any circumstances. I want your personal assurance that you will protect me from any unwelcome attention he may offer.'

'I am sure that will not be necessary,' said Owen.

'Nevertheless, I want your guarantee.'

'Then you have it.'

'Good,' said the abbess with a sigh. 'In that case, come back the day after tomorrow before dawn, and we will make an early start.'

'Thank you, Sister Eadgifu,' said Owen. 'I am sure we can sort this out once and for all.'

'I hope so, Master Owen,' said the abbess, 'for it is a situation that can only end in disaster.'

–

Two days later, Owen and a party of ten armed men rode into the courtyard of Sweyn's manor, escorting a covered cart carrying the abbess and her two assistants. They had been on the road since dawn, and the sun was already high in the sky by the time they arrived. Owen dismounted and, after handing his reins to a groom, walked over to open the tailgate.

'Sister Eadgifu,' he said as a page placed a set of wooden steps on the ground. 'We have arrived. Please let me help you down.'

Moments later, all three nuns stood in the courtyard. The two younger women had been at the abbey since they were children and looked around with interest. Seldom did they see outside the abbey walls, so the visit was nothing short of an adventure.

'So,' said Eadgifu, 'where is he?'

'The earl will be along shortly,' said Owen. 'But first you may want to rest and freshen up from the journey in your quarters. When he returns, I will come for you and take you to the main hall.'

'I am grateful,' said the abbess, turning to the junior nuns. 'Sisters, follow me and avert your eyes from those who stare.

They do not know better and are to be forgiven their ignorance.'

'Yes, sister,' said both nuns, and all three followed Owen across the courtyard to the manor house.

Once inside, Owen escorted them to a comfortable room and waited as the nuns looked around with interest.

'This is yours,' he said to the abbess, 'and this is the only key.' He handed it over and turned to the two junior nuns. 'I have given you the room next door,' he continued. 'There are two cots there, and I am sure you will find it more than adequate.' He handed over another key before turning back to the abbess. 'The servants will be along shortly to light the fires and supply you with hot water to wash away the dust of the road. I have also asked the kitchens to bring some food and wine. You must be hungry after the journey.'

'Thank you,' said the abbess, glancing at the lock on the door. 'This will be most suitable.'

'Is there anything else I can get you?' asked Owen.

'No,' said the nun. 'Just let me know when Sweyn is ready to talk. And do not forget your oath, Master Owen – you will be there throughout the audience.'

'Of course,' said Owen. 'I will see you later.'

With that, he turned away and left the room, hearing the door being locked behind him before he had travelled a dozen paces.

–

Later that evening, all three nuns made their way back from the chapel after evening prayers and headed back to the manor hall. Sweyn had still not made an appearance, and the night was beginning to draw in, yet despite Eadgifu's questioning, nobody seemed to know where the earl was.

The evening meal came and went, and the abbess started to think that he would never appear. Finally, all three nuns rose from the table and, after thanking the steward, walked to their quarters.

'Thank you for allowing us to attend the meal, Sister Eadgifu,' said one of the novices. 'Do you want us to come in?'

'Thank you, but no,' said the abbess, retrieving the key from around her neck. 'I will lock myself in and will see you again at dawn for morning prayers.'

'As you wish,' said the first nun, and they waited until the abbess was safely inside her room before going to their own.

Inside, Sister Eadgifu closed the door and placed the key in the lock, hearing the satisfying clang of a heavy metal hook falling into place within the door frame. Holding the candle before her, she turned around and headed towards the bed, watching the floor carefully lest she trip over the rug, but had only gone a few paces when a shape loomed out of the darkness, and a hand shot out to clamp against her mouth.

The abbess froze in fear, her heart racing as the man's face loomed closer in the flickering candlelight.

'Hello, Sister Eadgifu,' said Sweyn coldly. 'Welcome to Hereford.'

Chapter Eight

Godwin and Harold stood outside the king's audience chamber, having both been summoned by Edward a few days earlier. The message had been curt, with little chance of misunderstanding, and though it did not contain the reason for the summons, both men had a pretty good idea – the actions of Sweyn Godwinson in Hereford.

The doors opened, and two servants stood aside to allow them access. Inside, the king sat on an ornately carved throne on a raised dais. To his left stood the Bishop of London and on his right the Bishop of Elmham.

'Your Majesty,' said Godwin, bowing his head. 'You summoned us?'

'I did,' said Edward, his voice devoid of any friendliness or respect. 'And I have no doubt that you are fully aware why.'

'I have my own thoughts,' said Godwin, looking between the three men. 'But you are the king, so it could be one of many things.'

'Do not attempt sarcasm in the presence of the king,' interjected Bishop Robert. 'This is neither the time nor the place. You are required to respond with honesty and with respect.'

Godwin bit his tongue, desperate not to give the bishop, or indeed the king, any further cause for anger.

'My apologies, your grace,' he said eventually, addressing the king. 'My words were a misguided attempt at levity, nothing more. How may I serve you?'

'We have been informed,' announced Bishop Robert before the king could answer, 'that your eldest son, Sweyn Godwinson, a man granted an earldom that includes Gloucestershire, Herefordshire, Oxfordshire, Berkshire and Somerset, has carried out an act so despicable that even the saints shed tears of shame. It has been reported that just before Christmas, he did abduct and violate the Abbess of Leominster, an act so hideous that it insults the Church, the king and God himself.'

'Your grace,' said Godwin, turning to face the bishop. 'I am aware that Sweyn is missing and that he has taken the abbess with him, but there is no evidence that she was abducted or assaulted. For all we know, she went with him of her own accord.'

'Are you saying that a woman who has devoted her life to prayer and celibacy, a bride of Christ, no less, has suddenly abandoned everything she has ever believed in to become a plaything for your wayward son? Come on, Earl Godwin, even you cannot be that naive.'

'Your grace,' interjected Harold, feeling his father's rising anger. 'First, can I assure you that our family is as concerned about this situation as you, and even as we speak, we have men searching for my brother and the abbess across the western counties. But it has to be said that even before this terrible event, Sweyn and Sister Eadgifu had a very close relationship. That is no secret, even to members of the court. So, despite the unlikelihood of the abbess consenting to such a thing, we have to examine the facts before casting judgement.'

'You are correct up to a point,' said Robert. 'His infatuation with the abbess was common knowledge, but that in itself was inappropriate; you condemn your brother even in the act of defending him.'

'We believed it was no more than friendship,' said Godwin, 'and if I had suspected anything like this was possible, I would have taken action immediately.'

'Alas, such sentiment is too little, too late,' said Robert, 'and consequently the king has summoned you here today to intervene personally, such is the shame it has brought upon this great country.' He turned to face King Edward, who had remained silent throughout the exchange.

'Earl Godwin,' said Edward eventually, 'I accept that any father would defend his son, even unto death, but surely even you can see that this situation is abhorrent.'

'If true, then I agree,' said Godwin, 'but Sweyn is a good man and has served you well. All I ask is that we wait until we find out the truth of the matter before we cast judgement.'

'If we agree,' said the king, 'and even if any union was consensual, what then? The very fact that your son pursued such an arrangement is unacceptable and cannot go unpunished. I am at a loss what to do here and am giving you an opportunity to offer a solution before I bring the weight of the Crown down upon his head.'

'All I ask,' said Godwin, 'is that you grant me time to sort this mess out. I swear that the moment I leave here, I will ride to Hereford myself to find my son, and when I do, I promise to deal with him personally.'

'Your grace,' interrupted Robert, 'surely the time for such leniency has long passed. It has been almost three months since the abbess was abducted, three months in which Earl Godwin could have carried out the actions he now promises. Earl Sweyn deserves no more time, and I suggest you send a party of men after him forthwith with the aim of capturing him and returning him here to face your judgement.'

'No,' interrupted Harold quickly, 'you know what my brother is like. If you do that, he will retaliate. This situation is bad enough, your grace; let us not make it worse by spilling blood.'

'If there is blood to be spilt, it will be Sweyn's,' said Robert, his face hardening.

On the opposite side of the king, Bishop Stigand had been listening in silence. He agreed that what Godwin's son had done was truly awful, but he had a fondness for the family and knew he had to act quickly before the king did something drastic. Finally, he took a deep breath and spoke up.

'Your grace,' he said, 'may I say something?'

'Please do,' said the king.

'Majesty,' he said, 'as we have heard, this travesty occurred almost three months ago. What concerns me is why it has taken so long for the news to reach the palace. Surely the disappearance of an abbess should have set the church bells ringing in alarm from coast to coast.'

'The reason is simple,' said Bishop Robert. 'When she told her fellow nuns in Leominster that she was visiting Hereford, they assumed she was talking about the cathedral, not the manor of Sweyn Godwinson, and had decided to stay for a while to pay tribute at the tomb of St Ethelbert. This was a regular occurrence for the abbess, so when she did not return, it did not raise any concerns. Obviously, those at Hereford Cathedral were not expecting her, so her non-arrival did not raise any worries, and they remained blissfully unaware of her disappearance until a few days ago.'

'I have to ask,' said Bishop Stigand, 'does it not worry you that she did not make her intentions clear to those she left behind?'

'Perhaps it was an oversight.'

'Possibly, though could it be that she knew exactly what she was doing and wanted to delay the alarm for as long as possible?'

'Are you saying she engaged in subterfuge to break her vows willingly and lie to the Church?' gasped Robert.

'All I am saying,' said Stigand, 'is that the facts are clouded at best, and we should be careful not to condemn anyone until the truth has been ascertained.'

'Either way,' interjected the king, 'this cannot be allowed to continue. We need them caught and this whole situation brought to an end, no matter where the blame lies.' He turned his attention back to Godwin. 'Earl Godwin,' he said, 'no matter which way we look at this situation, it is clear that your son has brought shame not only on the House of Godwin but on the Crown, and I cannot allow that to go unpunished. His actions demand that he is arrested immediately and taken into custody until he can appear before the Witan. However, out of respect to your long-standing loyalty to the Crown, I will allow you time to find your son.'

'Thank you, your grace,' said Godwin.

'I have not finished,' said the king. 'Time you will get, leniency you will not. Once you have left this hall, I will be arranging a proclamation to state that your son, Sweyn Godwinson, is to be declared outside of the law, and any man bringing him, or his body, to this court, will be given a purse of silver as a reward. That proclamation will not be issued for a period of three months, giving you plenty of time to find him and deliver my ultimatum.'

'Which is?'

'That he releases the abbess into the custody of the Church and leaves these lands on the first available ship. I care not where he goes, but if he returns without pardon, it will be to face the executioner's blade. That is my decision.'

'Your grace—' said Godwin, taking half a step forward, but his objection was cut short by Bishop Stigand.

'And a fair decision it is,' said the bishop, staring at the earl. 'And we welcome it as both sensible and lenient.'

Godwin stared at Stigand for a moment, realising that if his friend was backing the king's judgement, then it was pointless seeking further clemency.

'Well?' said Bishop Robert. 'What say you, Godwin of Wessex?'

'Three months, you say?' replied the earl, looking at the king.

'And not a minute more,' replied Edward. 'If I have not heard that he was seen sailing from our shores by then, I will mobilise however many men I need to flush him from his hiding place and, if needs be, cut him down like a dog. My decision is final.'

'So be it,' said Godwin before bowing his head in acceptance.

'Good,' said the king. 'This audience is now at an end, Earl Godwin, and I will pray that you can repair your family's name.' He got to his feet and left the room, followed by Robert of Jumièges. When they had gone, Godwin turned to Stigand.

'Do you think he will carry out his threat?' he asked.

'I do,' said Stigand, 'for he has no other choice in the matter. If he had let it go, it would have sent a message to all men that it is acceptable to assault the Church without retribution. In fact, I would say you have been very lucky – if it were not for the fact that the king is married to your daughter Sweyn would already be a hunted man. Find him, and get him on that ship with all haste.'

'We will,' said Godwin, 'thank you, your grace.'

'Just finding him will be thanks enough,' said Stigand. 'Now be gone while you still have light.'

Godwin and Harold left the audience chamber and headed out of the palace towards the stables.

'What now?' asked Harold as they reached their horses.

'I am going back to Bosham to gather our huscarls,' said the earl, 'you go and inform Beorn Estrithson of what has happened here. Ask him to bring fifty men and meet us in Hereford seven days hence. He and Sweyn have always been close, and if your brother won't listen to us, perhaps he will pay heed to his cousin.'

'So be it,' said Harold, mounting his horse, and they headed out into the dirty streets of London.

Chapter Nine

Kent, September, AD 1047

King Edward and his wife stood on a hill overlooking the hunting fields of Kent along with the royal falconers. Down below, teams of beaters flushed birds from the undergrowth and no sooner had they taken flight than one of the handlers sent a hawk skywards to bring them down.

For the past two hours, the royal couple had enjoyed some rare time together and had walked miles with the hunting party. The gamekeepers had bagged over a dozen birds as well as an unexpected deer that had broken cover well within reach of the hunting dogs – a welcome yet unexpected bonus.

The ground fell away before them, and they could see the village of Dover. Beyond them was the sea and, in the distance, the shores of France.

'This will be a good place to rest,' said the king to one of the servants walking behind him. 'Set up the tent here, and we will stay a few hours.'

'Of course, your grace,' said the servant, turning away to make the arrangements.

'So far,' said Edward, gazing out across the sea, 'yet so dangerously close.'

'What do you mean?' asked Ealdgyth.

'Over there,' said Edward, 'lies the home of so many who covet the throne of England. If it weren't for the sea, this realm would constantly be at war with enemies from here to Rome and beyond.'

'But not all are foes,' said Ealdgyth, as two servants lowered the chairs they had carried on their shoulders from the caravan several leagues away. 'We also have allies in Europe.'

'Indeed we do,' said the king, lowering himself into the chair and accepting a tankard of ale from a servant. 'In fact, we received good news only yesterday about my cousin, William of Normandy.'

'Really?' said Ealdgyth, lowering herself into her own chair. 'You did not say.'

'It escaped my mind,' said Edward.

'How is the duke?' asked Ealdgyth.

'He is fine now,' said the king. 'But do you recall last year when I told you that his cousin, Guy of Burgundy, led a revolt against him?'

'I do,' said Ealdgyth. 'You said he was ambushed and was lucky to flee with his life.'

'Indeed he was,' said the king, 'and fled to the court of King Henry of France. Since then, they have been raising an army to attack the rebels, and yesterday I found out that not only did they meet in battle at a place called Val-ès-Dunes near Caen, but that William and the king heavily defeated the rebels despite being vastly outnumbered. According to the despatches, the young duke played an impressive part in the victory and led from the front, as all good leaders should.'

'That is good news,' said Ealdgyth. 'I have met him once and he seems like a good man.'

'He is,' said Edward, 'and even more so as he has had to fight for his position ever since his father died. I have lost count of those who have tried to manipulate or even kill him, but he has had good guardians, and at last, it looks like he is forging his own path.'

'What happened to Guy of Burgundy? Was he killed?'

'Apparently not,' said the king. 'He escaped to his castle in Brionne and has holed up there. William has laid siege and aims to force him out to settle the argument once and for all.'

'He aims to kill him?'

'If necessary, but it may not come to that. Once William's ire has calmed, he may accept an oath of allegiance.'

'I hope so,' said Ealdgyth, 'there is so much killing these days. Why can't we just enjoy a few months' peace for a change?'

'Such is the way of the world,' said the king. 'There is little we can do to change it.'

—

In Hereford, Godwin of Wessex sat at a table in his missing son's manor house, nursing a tankard of warm ale. His face was drawn and his eyes dark from lack of sleep, for since he and his men had arrived weeks earlier, he had insisted on leading the search for Sweyn himself, sometimes being in the saddle for days on end. Despite their efforts, there had still not been a single sighting, and he was rapidly losing hope they would ever be found. He poured more ale from the flask into his tankard, knowing full well that time was rapidly running out. If he could not find his son soon, Edward would release the proclamation and Sweyn would be declared an outlaw.

Behind him, the door to the hall swung open, and Harold and Beorn walked in out of the rain. A boy ran over to take their sodden cloaks as the two men joined the earl at the table.

'Well?' said Godwin, looking up. 'Did you find him?'

'We did not,' said Harold, reaching for two of the empty mugs on the table. 'But we have some information that may be of use.'

'I am sick of hearsay and rumour,' said Godwin. 'Every day we hear that someone knows somebody that may know where he is, and every day that information turns out to be useless. We have knocked on the door to every manor house in the west of England, but Sweyn remains as elusive as a wolf.'

'That's because,' said Harold, dropping into a chair opposite his father, 'we have been searching in the wrong place.'

Godwin stared at the two young men.

'Are you saying he has already fled to France?' he asked.

'No,' said Harold. 'We have heard this very morning that Sweyn is currently staying in a manor not far from here.'

'But you said he is not in England.'

'He is not,' said Beorn. 'He is in Wales, enjoying the hospitality of Gruffydd ap Llewelyn.'

Godwin was shocked. It had always been a faint possibility, but they had never taken it seriously due to the continued aggression of the Welsh towards anyone English.

'Are you sure about this?' he asked.

'As sure as we can be,' said Harold. 'There is a man in the next village who occasionally scouts for him, and he said he served alongside Sweyn when he campaigned with Gruffydd against King Rhydderch. The scout said he led Sweyn to a manor house several leagues inside the Welsh border a few months ago but was sworn to secrecy.'

'And was there a woman with him?'

'He could not say, only that there was a covered cart that he was not allowed to see inside.'

'That must be it,' said Godwin, 'the place he is living. We need to go there straight away.'

'Father,' said Harold, 'think about what you are saying. If we cross the border with an armed patrol, the Welsh will fall upon us like a winter's storm. We need to think of some other way.'

'Like what?' asked Godwin. 'The three months is almost up, and there will soon be a price on his head.'

'I know,' said Harold, 'but to ride into Wales invites even more trouble. Sweyn enjoys Gruffydd's patronage at the moment, so at least he is safe where he is. Perhaps all we need to do is wait until he tires of his situation and comes out of his own accord. In the meantime, we tell the king he is hiding somewhere in Wales, and we are still seeking a way to get to him. At least that way it will give us some more time.'

'But he will have to come out sometime, and when he does, there will be a line of men from here to London waiting to claim the bounty.'

'I do not see what else we can do,' said Harold, 'short of me riding in there alone to see if I can reach him.'

'No,' said Godwin. 'I am already on the verge of losing one son, I will not lose another. This scout you spoke of, can he get a message to him?'

'He can,' said Harold, 'and we have brought him with us. He is in the kitchens getting something to eat.'

'At least that's something,' said the earl. 'Let us get some rest, and tomorrow morning draft a message to Sweyn. Well done both, your efforts will not go unrewarded.'

The three men finished their drinks before heading to their quarters. It had been a hard three months, but at least they now knew where Sweyn was. All they had to do was decide what to do about it.

—

The following morning they met again in the hall, this time joined by the scout Harold had mentioned the previous night.

'Hywel,' said Harold as the scout entered, 'help yourself to some food and take a seat.' He indicated a pot of broth sitting to the side of the fire.

'Thank you, my lord,' said Hywel. 'I have already eaten.'

'You are a Welshman, are you not?' said Godwin, carrying his own bowl over to the table.

'I am, my lord,' said Hywel, 'born and bred in Gwent.'

'So why do you live in Hereford?'

'My father fell out of favour with the king of Gwent many years ago, so we had to flee. We had family in Hereford and have been living here ever since.'

'Yet you have served as a scout for his son recently?'

'I have, my lord,' said the scout, 'but he does not know my background. I have already explained all this to your son, Sweyn Godwinson.'

'So I understand,' said Godwin, 'but he has not shared that information with us. I need to understand the relationship between you and the Welsh.'

'I have no loyalties to anyone in particular,' said Hywel, 'only to my family. But I am an honest man, and whoever pays my purse will be served without question or fault.'

'Did you take my son into Wales a few months ago?'

'I did, my lord. I know the people there and was able to arrange a safe passage to the manor he had been loaned by King Gruffydd of Gwynedd.'

'Tell me,' said Harold, 'does he have any of his huscarls with him?'

'He does, my lord, about twenty trusted men, and his second, Owen of Hereford.'

'No women?'

'Not that I could see, though the cart was covered and I did not see inside.'

'If I needed to go there,' said Harold, with a glance towards his father, 'could you take me?'

'I cannot, my lord. I swore to Earl Sweyn that his location would remain a secret, and I am a man of my word.'

'What if I told you his life was in danger and he needed to be warned?'

'As I said, I gave my word and will stand by my oath. I am, however, happy to take a message to him for a price. I can be there by nightfall if I leave now.'

Harold glanced at his father, receiving a nod of approval in return.

'Then that is what we must do,' said Harold. 'I want you to ride immediately and tell Sweyn he has to return here to meet me. Tell him it is a matter of life or death, and if he does not come, he could be dead within weeks.'

'I will pass the message,' said Hywel, 'but it may help if he was to know more about this threat?'

'Alas, I cannot share it with you,' said Harold. 'Just impress upon him that this is no idle matter. His life is at risk and he has to meet with us, if only for an hour.'

'I will do what I can,' said Hywel. 'The price will be two silver pennies upfront and another two if I return with the earl.'

'If you return with the earl, I will double the purse,' said Godwin. 'Just bring him back.'

Harold handed over the two pennies and watched as the scout left the hall.

'We have done what we can,' Harold said eventually. 'Now we must wait.'

—

Five days later, Harold and his father were near the stables examining the legs of a lame horse. The stable hands had been nursing it back to health after it had suffered a fall during a hunt. Luckily no bones had been broken, and it now seemed the horse would make a full recovery.

'Lift the leg,' said Godwin, bending over to examine one of the rear hooves.

As he did, Harold heard a commotion at the manor gates and turned to see three horsemen riding into the courtyard.

'Father,' he said, tapping Godwin on the shoulder. 'Look.'

Godwin stood up and turned around. At the far side of the courtyard, the three men were dismounting, and though he did not recognise one, the other two were known to him – the scout, Hywel, and his son, Sweyn Godwinson.

'Put the horse to pasture,' he said over his shoulder to the groom before wiping the filth from his hand on a rag hanging on the stable wall.

'At last,' he said to Harold. 'Come, let us get this done.'

The two men walked across the courtyard, meeting the three new arrivals halfway.

'Hello, Sweyn,' said Harold as they neared.

'Harold,' responded the earl with a nod, 'you seem to be coming here more and more often these days.'

'Trust me,' said Harold, 'the situation demands my presence. We were beginning to wonder if you would come.'

'Your man here was very persuasive,' said Sweyn, 'and said something about my life being on the line. Is this true?'

'Perhaps we should discuss this inside,' said Harold. 'There are things best left unheard by those who would wish you ill.'

Sweyn turned to Godwin.

'Hello, Father, you look tired.'

'Age is a burden that grows heavier by the day,' said Godwin, 'not helped by the fact that I have wasted almost three months looking for you.'

'My life is mine to live as I see fit,' said Sweyn, 'there was never any need for you to come here.'

'We will see about that,' said Godwin. 'But Harold is right, these things need to be discussed in private.' He turned to the scout. 'You have my gratitude, Hywel, and your work here is now done. Report to the steward and tell him to pay you what you are owed. It has already been authorised.'

'Thank you, my lord,' said the scout. 'If you ever need anything else, you know where I am.'

As Hywel turned away, Godwin addressed the second man alongside Sweyn. 'I know not your name, sir, but I request that you make yourself scarce for a few hours. You will find food and ale in the kitchens.'

'His name is Owen,' interrupted Sweyn, 'and he stays with me.'

'Sweyn,' said Harold, 'this is family business. Your man can join us later.'

'This is still my manor,' said Sweyn, 'and what I say goes. He stays with me.'

'As you wish,' said Godwin, with a sigh. 'Let us go inside.'

The four men headed into the manor and sat at a table, waiting for the servants to leave. The fire had been stacked up, and various meats and bread left on the table along with four jugs of ale.

'Well, Sweyn,' he said when the servants had gone, 'why don't you tell me why you are here?'

Before anyone could answer, the door burst open, and Beorn walked into the room.

'Sweyn Godwinson,' Beorn announced, his voice laced with relief. 'Thank God you have been found.'

'Beorn,' replied Sweyn with equal enthusiasm, 'I did not know you were here.' He got out of his seat and walked over to greet his cousin warmly. 'How are you, you mangy dog?' he said with a laugh. 'It has been an age since last we met.'

'Indeed it has, and you owe me a barrel of ale for causing me so much worry these past few weeks.'

'Ale I have aplenty,' said Sweyn, 'come, we will share some right now.'

Both men joined the others at the table and refilled the tankards.

'So,' said Sweyn, leaning back into his chair. 'What is all this about?'

For the next hour or so, all four men of the Godwin family, along with Owen of Hereford, sat around the table discussing the king's ultimatum. Initially, Sweyn denied all knowledge of the missing abbess, but when he, at last, realised the seriousness of the situation, he conceded she was indeed living with him back in the manor house in Wales.

'So you admit you abducted her,' said Harold.

'Abducted is too strong a word,' said Sweyn. 'Yes, she needed encouragement, but I knew it was only a matter of time before she realised that she was wrong and we could be happy together.'

'You mean you took her against her will,' said his father.

'She did not know what she wanted,' said Sweyn. 'She was confused, and I knew I had to get her away from all the outside influences that told her she had no right to be happy, no right to be a woman.'

85

'So you went to Wales?'

'Aye, we did.'

'Tell me she was not bound,' said Harold, 'in heaven's name.'

'No, she was not bound,' sighed Sweyn. 'What sort of man do you take me for?'

'I do not know any more,' said Harold. 'What sort of man abducts an abbess?'

'If this is the direction this conversation is taking,' said Sweyn, standing up, 'then I am leaving.'

'Sweyn, stop,' shouted his father, 'and sit down. You are going nowhere until this mess is sorted out.'

'And who is going to stop me, old man?' sneered Sweyn. 'You?'

Godwin stood up and stared at his son.

'If necessary, yes,' he said. 'And if you should draw my blood when I am only trying to save your life, then so be it – let God be your judge. But this needs to be sorted out here and now. So be seated, Sweyn Godwinson, and face us like the man I brought you up to be.'

Sweyn hesitated for a few moments before sitting back down and refilling his tankard.

'Right,' said Godwin, 'tell us exactly what happened before you left Hereford.'

Sweyn sighed and took a drink of his ale before responding.

'I have already told you,' he said, 'I asked her to be my wife, but she tried to deny her own affection for me by claiming she was not allowed by the Church. We talked all through the night, and in the morning, I agreed to take her back to Leominster.'

'But on the way, you diverted into Wales?' asked Godwin.

'We did, but she was not aware of the diversion, and by the time she realised there was something wrong, it was too late.'

'What was her reaction when she found out?'

'Anger,' said Sweyn, staring into his ale, 'frustration, upset. It was as if she had forgotten how much we loved each other and would not listen to reason.'

'But still, you continued?'

'Aye. I knew that all she needed was some time, and we have been at the manor ever since.'

'Sweyn,' said Godwin, 'I have to ask, did you force yourself upon her?'

His son raised his head to stare at his father but did not answer.

'Sweyn,' said Godwin again, 'listen to me, I am only trying to help. If this was just a mistake and she returns to the abbey untouched, then perhaps I can get a pardon. But if she has been violated in any way, especially against her will, then my hands are tied. Either way, I have to know, did you or did you not rape the abbess?'

The room fell silent as everyone stared at Sweyn in anticipation. He refilled his tankard but did not answer.

'Sweyn!' said Godwin. 'Tell us what you did.'

'*What do you want to know?*' roared Sweyn, suddenly knocking his tankard across the table and getting to his feet again. 'Do you want to hear all the sordid details about what we did in the bedchamber? Is that what you want to hear, Father, about how other men service their women because you cannot satisfy your own? Is that why Mother ran to the bed of King Cnut, because you were not man enough to treat her as a true woman?'

The room fell silent, each man shocked at the outburst.

'Oh, do not act so surprised,' said Sweyn, 'you know what I am talking about. It is common knowledge that you are not my father, just look at us all. All my brothers look just like you, but me? I am as different as a black sheep in a flock of white. Do not deny it, Earl Godwin, you are not my real father. My sire is Cnut himself because Mother whored herself to the whim of a king.'

Harold started to get to his feet, a look of rage upon his face, but Godwin reached out and grabbed his arm.

'No,' he said, 'sit. This has been brewing for a long time and needs to be addressed.'

'He just accused my mother of having the morals of a whore,' growled Harold, 'and I demand he retracts it or face the consequences.'

Sweyn reached across for the ale, drinking it straight from the jug.

'Ha,' he said after letting out a belch. 'That's right, hold back your favourite son, Harold the honest, Harold the trustworthy. Perhaps he should wear the nun's habit, such is his goodness.'

'*Sweyn,*' shouted Godwin, 'that is enough. We are trying to help you, but all you are doing is pulling more upset and shame down upon yourself. Just answer the question. Did you or did you not rape the abbess?'

'*Yes,*' roared Sweyn, '*I did.* I am the Earl of Hereford and can do whatever I want to all who live in my earldom, and that includes Leominster. The deed is done and cannot be undone, so go ahead, be my judge and jury. Turn me over to the king if you must, I care not. But know this – I will not go peacefully, and there will be blood spilt before any man ties me to a horse.' He dropped back into his chair and drained the ale jug before throwing it into the fire.

For a few moments, everyone stared in silence, shocked at the admission.

'So,' said Sweyn eventually, 'now you all know. I stand condemned before man and God.'

'What do we do now?' asked Beorn.

'There is not much we can do,' said Godwin. 'When the king finds out, as he will, he will condemn him to death. The only hope we have is to get him to France while the offer of exile still stands.'

'I will not leave Eadgifu,' said Sweyn, still staring into the fire.

'You have to,' said Godwin. 'As soon as Edward issues the proclamation and it becomes known about the price on your head, there will be nowhere you can hide, not even Wales.'

'Then I will take her with me,' said Sweyn.

'*Are you not listening to me?*' shouted Godwin, banging his fist on the table. 'It is over, Sweyn, you are a condemned man and have no other option. You must leave this very day and head for Bristol to find a boat to France. Do this, and at least you get to live. But if you want any chance of a pardon in the future, the abbess must stay here. Even then, if she decides to tell the king of your actions, you may still be declared a *niðingr*. You have to understand, Sweyn, you have done a terrible thing, and if it were any other man, I would drag you to the king's judgement myself. But you are my son, and I will do everything in my power to get you through this. All I ask is that you get out of the country as soon as you can.'

'And what about the abbess?'

'Leave her to me,' said Owen, who had remained silent throughout the meeting. 'I will go back to Wales and talk to her.'

'You must not harm her,' said Sweyn, looking up, 'not a single hair on her head.'

'I will not harm her, my lord,' said Owen. 'I will explain to her the seriousness of the situation and appraise her of the need for her to keep her counsel about what happened. I have got to know her well these past few weeks and think she will keep quiet, especially if she knows she is about to be freed.'

'We can't be sure about that,' said Beorn.

'We cannot,' said Godwin, 'but it is all that we have.' He turned back to his son. 'Well,' he asked, 'what is it to be? Go to France for a few years while I work on the king to get a pardon, or stay and face the executioner's axe?'

'What about my lands?' said Sweyn, looking up. 'My earldom?'

'You will be stripped of both,' said Godwin. 'I hardly think you can appeal against the king's decision. The main thing is you will be alive with the rest of your life to look forward to. I will ensure you have enough money, and who knows, in a few years, you could be back amongst us. Please, my son, you must agree to do this, there is no other option.'

Sweyn looked between all the men in the room, knowing his father was right. The situation had gone on for far too long and had to come to an end.

'So be it,' he said eventually, 'tell me what you want me to do.'

Part Two

Chapter Ten

Godwin of Wessex, Bishop Stigand and several other high-ranking nobles gathered around the fire in the bishop's chambers. The mood was sombre following the death of an abbot, but for some, the bad news was tempered by a hint of opportunity.

'Have you sent for him?' asked Godwin.

'Aye, we have,' said Stigand. 'He will be here shortly.'

The muted conversation continued for a few moments until finally, there was a knock on the door.

'At last,' said Godwin, turning to see Brother Spearhafoc entering the room.

'Your grace,' said Spearhafoc, 'my lords, you sent for me?'

'We did,' said the bishop. 'Brother Spearhafoc, please approach.'

Spearhafoc walked across the room and joined the gathering, unsure about what was going on.

'How can I serve you?' he asked, looking around nervously.

'Brother Spearhafoc,' said Stigand, 'we are in receipt of some very sad news. Yesterday, Father Æthelstan of Abingdon passed into God's embrace. I have been told his passing was peaceful, and his last words were extolling the glory of Christ and the kingdom of God.'

'I am sorry to hear of this,' Spearhafoc said, crossing himself. 'He was truly a kind and pious man. I will pray for him.'

'As will we all,' said the bishop. 'And of course, we will be having a service in his name, but first, we have some important business to discuss. Over the past two years, we have been watching you closely. Your devotion to God is flawless, and your service to the king and queen has been second to none. Indeed, the fact that you are so useful here at the palace becomes a slight problem for what we all agree should happen next.'

'Which is?' asked Spearhafoc, hardly daring to breathe.

The bishop looked around the various clergy and nobles from across Wessex.

'We have discussed this in great detail,' said the bishop, 'and are all in agreement. Your name is to be put forward as the new Abbot of Abingdon.'

Spearhafoc gasped with astonishment. He had discussed the possibility a few years earlier with Lady Gytha of Wessex but never had he imagined that it would actually come to pass.

'I do not know what to say, your grace,' he said. 'I am unworthy of such an honour.'

'Nonsense,' said the bishop. 'We have been watching you for over a year, not just with regards to your dedication to God but also your approach to the poor and destitute. Of course, your continued loyalty to the House of Godwin does you no ill, neither does your close relationship with the queen, but it is your piousness that raises you for consideration above all else. Now we have agreed to support your candidacy, I see no reason it will not be granted by the king.'

'Thank you,' said Spearhafoc, 'thank you all.'

'Direct your thanks to God,' said the bishop, 'we are just outlets through which his guidance is channelled. There is one more thing we should discuss while you are here, and that is about your work at Westminster. You will, of course, have to relocate to Abingdon for your new role, and I fear the king will see that as a drawback, so we need to have the answers before we approach him. Do you think this will be a problem?'

'I do not,' said Spearhafoc. 'Father Æthelstan was also a goldsmith, and I believe he has extensive workshops within the abbey. All my sketches and ideas have been approved, so I can easily work from there and can have everything transferred here as and when they are completed.'

'So, can I take it that you would accept this huge responsibility – if, of course, it is ratified by the king?'

'I would,' said Spearhafoc, 'and I would do everything in my power not just to continue Father Æthelstan's wonderful work, but dedicate it to the glory of God in his name.'

'Excellent,' said Stigand. 'In that case, I will approach the king with the news of our brother's death first thing in the morning, along with my recommendation that you are ordained as his replacement.' He turned around to face the rest of the room. 'Gentlemen, thank you for your attendance and your contribution.'

Everyone filed from the room except Godwin, who hung back until only he, Spearhafoc and the bishop were left. Once the door was closed, he turned to the monk.

'Well,' he said, 'did not my wife tell you that we looked after our own?'

'She did,' said Spearhafoc, 'but I thought I was being offered this position on merit?'

'Oh, you are,' said Godwin, 'there are no strings attached, and I see even greater things for you in the near future. All I am saying is that when you reach the top of a climb, it never hurts to remember those who helped you get there.' Before Spearhafoc could answer, Godwin turned away towards the bishop. 'Your grace,' he said, 'it has been useful as usual. Will we see you soon at Bosham?'

'Sooner than you may think,' said the bishop.

'Good,' said Godwin. 'Until then, stay safe.' He left the room, leaving Stigand and Spearhafoc staring after him. The monk, in particular, was still slightly confused.

'What did he mean, greater things?' he asked eventually.

'There's no need to worry yourself about that for now,' said Stigand. 'All you need to concern yourself with is becoming the best abbot Abingdon has ever seen. Can you do that?'

'I will do everything in my power to be the best I can be,' said Spearhafoc.

'Good,' said the bishop, tapping the monk's shoulder, 'that's all we ask. Now come, we have to prepare you for tomorrow's audience with the king.'

Chapter Eleven

Havering Palace, October, AD 1048

Harold Godwinson and his cousin, Beorn Estrithson, walked along a corridor, having been summoned to an audience by the king.

Over the past year, since Sweyn had finally sailed for France, both men had campaigned on behalf of Edward against Magnus Olafsson, the King of Norway and Denmark, harrying his raiding fleet with their own fighting ships based out of Sandwich. But with the approach of winter, the sea conditions had worsened, and all seaborne campaigns had been suspended until the spring.

Magnus the Good, as he was commonly known, had vowed to conquer England and restore the powerful North Sea Empire, the union between England, Denmark and Norway previously ruled by Cnut the Great some thirteen years earlier, to its former glory. To do that, he had to build an invasion fleet, but the attentions of Edward's own ships, led by Harold and Beorn, had kept the ambitious king at bay, at least for the time being.

'What do you think he wants?' asked Beorn. 'It is unlike him to summon anyone without great cause.'

'We will find out soon enough,' said Harold. 'I just hope he doesn't ask us to weigh anchor again, I could do with staying dry for a few months.'

As they approached the door, a herald announced their arrival.

'Your grace, may I present Harold Godwinson, Earl of East Anglia, and Beorn Estrithson of Northampton.'

King Edward looked down from the throne as he waited for the men to cross the hall. Beside him was Queen Ealdgyth, her face already full of happiness at the thought of seeing her brother.

'Welcome,' said the king. 'Please, take a seat.'

'Thank you, your grace,' said Harold, acknowledging his sister with a quick smile. He sat alongside Beorn in one of the two audience chairs.

'Thank you for coming,' said the king. 'Have you travelled far?'

'We were both at my father's manor in Bosham,' said Harold, 'so the journey has not been arduous.'

'Ah, Bosham,' said the king, 'I have fond memories of its fine harbour. Are my ships stationed there?'

'No, your grace, they are anchored in Sandwich. We are taking advantage of the bad weather to replace the sails, but rest assured they can be launched within hours should the need arise.'

'That is good news,' said the king, 'and brings me nicely on to the reason I have asked you here. If what I have been told is true, there may not be any need for either of you to sail again, at least for the near future.'

'My lord?' asked Harold.

'King Magnus Olafsson died a few days ago,' said the king. 'He fell from one of his ships and drowned before anyone could reach him.'

'*What?*' gasped Harold. 'Is this true?'

'I have sent people to verify the claim,' said the king, 'and to convey our sympathies to his family if it proves to be so.'

'But he is not married,' said Beorn, 'nor does he have any sons.'

'But he does have a daughter, Ragnhild, and it is incumbent upon us to convey our condolences from one royal house to another. However, his death, if true, means there will be a crisis until his successor can be agreed. I strongly suspect his kingdoms will be split between Harald Hardrada in Norway and Sweyn Estridsson in Denmark, but that remains to be seen. In the meantime, let us enjoy the peace his death brings and pray it is long-lasting.'

'Your grace,' said Harold, 'I celebrate the death of no man, but this is truly good news for it will allow many others to live. God surely works in mysterious ways.'

'Indeed he does,' said the king, 'and as soon as I hear back from my envoys, we will announce his death publicly. However, there is another reason I have summoned you here, something that has given me great pause for thought.'

'Your grace,' said Harold, 'if there is anything we can do to help the Crown, please let us know.'

'If you cast your mind back,' continued Edward, 'you will recall that unpleasant business with your brother and the Abbess of Leominster.'

Harold's heart sank; the family was still ashamed of Sweyn's actions, and he had hoped the king wouldn't bring the subject up. He glanced at the queen, but her expression held no sign of sympathy or kindness.

'Yes, your grace,' he said, turning back to face the king, 'but Sweyn is long gone.'

'Indeed,' said Edward, 'and I am reliably informed that the abbess has resumed her role at the abbey, though she refuses to discuss her experience in Wales at all. It must be too painful for her still. Her sisters in Christ watch over her day and night, is that not so?' he asked, turning to face Ealdgyth.

'Indeed it is,' said the queen, 'and the king and I remember her in our prayers.'

Harold stared, trying hard not to react. The shame his brother's actions had brought on the family was a heavy burden, but he did not want it to be a focus of the discussions.

'There is also the issue of Sweyn's earldom to discuss,' continued Edward. 'Despite pressure from Earl Godwin, I cannot ignore the actions of your brother. Therefore, I strip him of all titles and lands forthwith.'

Harold glanced at Beorn; it was no worse than they had expected.

'However,' continued Edward, 'it also cannot be forgotten that it was your efforts that brought this situation to an end, yours and your father's. So, after much consideration, I have decided to distribute Sweyn's lands as follows. One quarter will go to you, Harold Godwinson, and another quarter will go to you, Beorn Estrithson. That way, Sweyn has been punished, but you have been rewarded for your part in the resolution of this matter.'

Harold was shocked. He was not sure what he should have expected, but it certainly was not this.

'Well?' said the king. 'Do you accept my award?'

'Um, yes, your grace,' said Harold, 'I am honoured. You have my gratitude.'

'And mine, your grace,' said Beorn, 'thank you.'

'The gratitude is mine to award,' said the king, 'for if it were not for your involvement, who knows where the situation would have led. Thanks to your actions, the Abbess of Leominster has seen justice done for her ordeal, and Sweyn is banished from my lands on pain of death. It is fitting that you are rewarded so.'

'It was an unpleasant experience for all involved,' said Beorn. 'But may I ask a question?'

'Go ahead,' said the king.

'Your grace, you have awarded myself and Harold half of Sweyn's estates, for which we are very grateful. But I have to ask, how is the remaining half to be distributed?'

'Beorn,' said Ealdgyth, 'it would be better not to question the king's award.'

'Forgive me,' said Beorn, 'but it was out of curiosity only, not judgement.'

'I have decided to award the rest to men who have been loyal to me for many years,' responded the king. 'They will ensure the land is well managed and provide protection from the Welsh.'

'Men of Normandy?'

'Perhaps,' said Edward, 'though I fail to see why that should concern you.'

'Forgive me, your grace,' said Beorn. 'Those lands have been in our family for many years; it is concerning that they are being given now to men who were not even born here.'

Edward stared at the young man for a few moments before responding.

'You are young,' he said eventually, 'so I will ignore your impudence. But remember this – I am the king, and I will award whatever I want to whomever I choose. Be grateful that you have something. Now, let us talk of better things. Will you and your family be staying at Southwark this Christmas?'

'I suspect my brother has other things on his mind,' said Ealdgyth, before Harold could answer. 'Is that not right, Harold?'

'I am not sure what you mean, my queen,' said Harold.

'Oh come, dear brother,' said Ealdgyth, 'my sources tell me a certain young lady has caught your eye, and you already court her with a view to marriage.'

Harold let out a laugh before responding.

'Your grace,' he said, 'is there nothing that fails to come to your attention?'

'In matters of the heart, no,' said Ealdgyth with a smile. 'So pray tell, brother, who is this lucky lady, and when can we expect to meet her?'

Harold sighed, knowing that his secret was now out, and further subterfuge was pointless, especially in the gaze of his much-loved but annoying sister.

'The person in question,' he responded, 'is Edyth Swannesha, daughter of Ealdorman Gerald of Wessex.'

'Edyth the Fair?' said the king, his eyebrows raised. 'You surprise me, Harold Godwinson – your choice is beyond reproach. But I am duty-bound to ask, is this a relationship born of political convenience or a true attraction in God's gaze?'

'We both have feelings for each other, your grace,' said Harold, 'and I promise you, the relationship is devoid of politics. However, with regards to marriage, we have not yet discussed such matters, so would ask my queen not to get too excited.'

'You disappoint me, brother,' said Ealdgyth. 'I hear the lady in question has an impeccable pedigree and is without comparison when it comes to beauty. Do they not call her Edyth Swanneck?'

'Some do,' said Harold, 'and I concur, she is indeed a beautiful woman. But the time is not right to think of marriage; there are far more important matters to consider.'

'Perhaps with the death of Magnus, your mind will now be free to consider such things,' said the king. 'But whatever you decide, you have my blessing.'

'Thank you, your grace,' said Harold. 'May we be of further service?'

'Not to me,' said the king, 'but I have no doubt that the queen has a thousand questions.'

'I certainly do,' said Ealdgyth, 'and request that you stay after the king's withdrawal to share refreshment and discuss everything that is happening in our family.'

'Of course, your grace,' said Harold.

'In that case,' said the king, 'I will leave you alone to catch up. I have a meeting with my architects regarding some of Spearhafoc's designs. Beorn, perhaps you would like to join me?'

'I would be honoured, your grace,' said Beorn standing up.

'Good. Ealdgyth, be gentle with your brother, I need him well rested for the next campaign, whenever that may be.'

'Of course,' said the queen with a bow, waiting until he and Beorn had left the audience chamber before turning to face her brother with a beaming smile on her face.

'So,' she said, 'Edyth Swanneck. I would never have guessed.'

'Ealdgyth,' said Harold, 'can I suggest we get some food and wine from the kitchens before we start? I suspect that I am about to be interrogated, and this is going to be a very long night.'

The following morning Harold and Beorn sat upon their horses in the stable yard, ready to ride back to Bosham. Queen Ealdgyth held the reins of her brother's horse, saying her good-byes.

'Tell Mother and Father I am well,' she said, 'and cannot wait until we meet again.'

'I think they are coming to Southwark for Christmas,' said Harold, 'so we could all meet up then?'

'That sounds wonderful,' said Ealdgyth. 'Perhaps the king and I could host them here at the palace.'

'That would be nice,' said Harold, 'but you know what Father is like with formalities. What if we meet up on St Stephen's day and enjoy a proper Godwin celebration at Southwark?'

'I'll find out what is planned and send a message,' said the queen. She paused for a moment before the smile dimmed on her face. 'Harold,' she continued, 'do you know if Sweyn fares well?'

'I do not,' he replied with a sigh, 'we have lost contact. I do know he is in Denmark, but more than that, I could not say.'

'How could he have been so stupid?' she said.

'He was always a hothead,' said Harold, 'and for a while there, I had no sympathy for him whatsoever, especially when he besmirched Mother's good name.'

'What do you mean?' asked Ealdgyth. 'What did he say?'

Harold looked guiltily at Beorn, realising he had said too much.

'It's nothing, just words spoken in anger.'

'What words?' said Ealdgyth. 'I demand to know, Harold, what did he say?'

Harold looked around to ensure there was nobody else in earshot.

'He accused Mother of sleeping with King Cnut when she was younger,' he said, 'and claimed he is Cnut's bastard son.'

'*But that is ridiculous*,' gasped the queen, 'what on earth possessed him to make such a claim?'

'I know not, but that is what was said. Father was going to thrash it out with him, but events overtook us, and by the time I remembered the accusation, Sweyn had long gone.'

'Surely such a thing would have weighed heavily on Father's mind?'

'You would think so, but he did not bring it up again.'

'Why not?'

'Only he knows. Perhaps it was too hurtful a charge to discuss. Unless...'

'Unless what?'

'Perhaps it is true. Sweyn certainly looks different from the rest of us.'

'No,' said Ealdgyth, 'Mother would never have done such a thing to Father. I refuse to believe it.'

'Well, whatever the truth of the matter is, the accusation is out there now. I just hope it does not get back to Mother. Look after yourself, Ealdgyth.' He leaned down and kissed his sister's hand before turning his horse and heading towards the gates.

'Be safe, Earl Harold, cousin Beorn,' she called behind them.

'And you, my queen,' Harold shouted over his shoulder before trotting his horse alongside Beorn's out of the gate to head towards Bosham.

As the two men rode away, Beorn turned to Harold.

'Well,' he said, 'that was unexpected.'

'It was,' said Harold. 'Sweyn's lands were extensive and will add greatly to my own responsibilities, as they will yours.'

'Do you think it was right for us to accept? I mean, I feel a little uneasy about profiting from the misfortune of your brother.'

'If we did not accept,' said Harold, 'then his lands would have been given to someone else. At least this way, his estates stay within the family, and that can only be a good thing.'

'Well, one thing is certain,' said Beorn, 'knowing him as I do, when he finds out he is not going to be a happy man.'

'I agree,' said Harold, 'but we can only deal with that situation as and when it occurs. Until then, we continue as normal.'

The two men rode out of London, not knowing how prophetic Beorn's words were to become.

Chapter Twelve

Bishop Stigand knelt in silent prayer beneath a statue of Christ, giving thanks after a difficult ride from Elmham, his bishopric in East Anglia. The private chapel, built within the walls of Bosham manor, was small but ornately furnished thanks to its sponsor, Earl Godwin of Wessex, and was the place where all the Godwin family and their visitors held their daily worship.

The past few days had been hard for the bishop; the road had been rough, the wagon uncomfortable, and his advancing years meant a journey that once would have taken half as long had worn him out both mentally and physically. Now he had arrived, he looked forward to getting some rest before continuing his journey to Winchester.

Eventually, he finished his prayer and pulled himself to his feet, using his gilded staff as leverage. The two novice priests who had accompanied him stood up and followed him out of the chapel towards the manor house.

Across the courtyard, four servants were unpacking his carts, for though he was only going to be at Bosham for a few days, his baggage was substantial.

As he walked, Godwin's wife emerged from the manor house and hurried to meet him. She bent one knee in deference and kissed the ring on his finger before standing and giving him a warm smile.

'Your grace,' she said, 'it is good to see you again. Welcome to Bosham.'

'And you, Gytha Thorkelsdóttir,' said the bishop. 'I see God has blessed you with even more beauty since last we met.'

'You flatter me, your grace,' said Gytha. 'Have you had a comfortable journey?'

'I've had better,' said Stigand. 'We even saw some brigands following us for a while, but God in his mercy discouraged them from attacking.'

'That and ten fully armed guards,' said a voice from behind him.

The bishop turned to see the Earl of Wessex striding across the courtyard.

'Earl Godwin,' he said, 'you startled me.'

'My apologies,' said the earl, kissing the bishop's hand. 'I was hoping to be here for your arrival but got held up at the port with some business. But I am here now, and we will do everything in our power to make sure your stay is as safe and as comfortable as it can be.' He turned to his wife. 'Gytha, are the guest quarters ready?'

'They are,' said Gytha, turning to the bishop. 'Your grace, we will eat at sundown, but if you would like some refreshment before then, I can have something brought to your room.'

'I do not hunger,' said the bishop, 'nor do I thirst, but I am a bit weary from the journey, so perhaps you would allow me to rest for a while, and I will join you at the evening meal.'

'Of course,' said Gytha. 'Lady Cynwen will show you the way, and there will be a servant stationed outside your door at all times. If there is anything at all you need during your visit, please just let us know.'

'I will,' said the bishop, 'thank you.' He turned away and followed the maidservant across the courtyard towards the manor.

Godwin waited for a few moments before turning to his wife.

'My apologies,' he said, 'I had to deal with something unpleasant.'

'There is no harm done,' said Gytha, 'he's only just arrived and actually seems in a good mood.'

'He is as stubborn as a mule,' said Godwin, 'and can be a bit abrupt, but he is a good man. What I do not understand is why he is here at all. The journey from Elmham to Winchester is shorter via the direct road.'

'Did his letter not say?'

'It did not, only that he wishes to stop over for a few days on his journey and has something of importance to discuss with me.'

'Well, I suppose we'll find out soon enough,' said Gytha. 'Come, the fires have been lit, and I am beginning to feel the cold.'

–

Later that evening, Gytha and Godwin hosted the bishop and his entourage in the main hall, including all his retainers and his bodyguards. The latter were not used to such opulence and looked around them in wonder at the beautiful tapestries and paintings.

The meal was not lavish but nevertheless was a welcome change to the cold meat and potage that the soldiers were used to. During the meal, the bishop and his hosts exchanged pleasantries, and Gytha was particularly pleased to receive a letter from her daughter, the queen.

Finally, with all courses finished and the soldiers despatched to their quarters with half a barrel of ale between them, the bishop, Earl Godwin and Gytha settled into chairs placed before the fire by the servants. Once they were settled with a bowl of autumn fruits and a jug of the best wine, the servants were dismissed, leaving the three alone in the hall.

'Wine?' said Gytha, picking up the bishop's goblet.

'Just a little,' said Stigand, 'my innards are full to bursting. Thank you for the meal, Lady Gytha, the fare was wonderful.'

'You are welcome,' said Gytha, pouring drinks for her and her husband. Once done, she looked at the two men. 'Would you like me to stay, or is this a discussion for men only?'

'You are welcome to stay,' said Stigand, 'for what I have to say concerns us all.'

Gytha lowered herself into a chair as Godwin threw another log onto the fire.

'So,' said the earl, sitting back in his own chair, 'you are on your way to Winchester?'

'I am,' said Stigand, 'for as you are aware, I have been given the bishopric there. However, as I have been so busy in Elmham, there are outstanding issues in Winchester that need attending. I have neglected any oversight for far too long.'

'I am no expert in such things,' said Godwin, 'but I cannot help but wonder why you keep Elmham under your jurisdiction when you have just been given Winchester. Surely one bishopric is enough for any man?'

'You are not the first to say so,' said Stigand, 'though most men are not bold enough to voice their thoughts. And, of course, you are correct. Usually, one bishop controls one diocese, but there is so much of God's work yet to be done in both places I hesitate to let either go.'

'I am sure you know what you are doing,' said Gytha.

'I try,' said Stigand, sipping his wine.

'Just to make it clear,' said Godwin, 'you are always welcome at Bosham, no matter the circumstances, but I am curious as to the reason why you are here. Winchester enjoys a direct route from London, while the road here is harder on the bones, especially in a cart.'

'It is,' said the bishop, 'but it was important I came as there are things I would like to discuss – in confidence, of course.'

'You are free to talk here,' said Godwin, 'and have my word that whatever it is you have to say will remain within these four walls.'

'I never doubted it,' said Stigand, pausing to look at the earl and his wife. 'I grow increasingly concerned about the amount of influence my counterpart holds over the king in London.'

'You are talking about Bishop Robert of Jumièges, I assume,' said Gytha.

'Indeed,' said Stigand, 'and though such things should not concern me, hardly a day goes by without whispers of disquiet reaching my ears.'

'Such as?'

'Most are trivial,' said the bishop, 'and concern minor appointments within the Church. Usually I would not worry myself with such things, but lately, they give me sleepless nights.'

'Why?' asked Gytha.

'Because most of the appointments are of Normans. I fear the religious oversight the English Church so devotedly nurtures on our people's behalf is in severe danger of being watered down.'

'Wait,' said Godwin, 'are you saying that the king is appointing only Normans into positions of religious importance?'

'Essentially, yes, but I have no doubt that his hand is being guided by the Bishop of London.'

'Robert is influencing the king?'

'Indeed he is, and now he has settled into his new position as the Bishop of London, he is getting more confident by the day, almost to the point that he doesn't even try to hide his reasoning.'

'Which is?'

'Look,' said Stigand, 'I know you have declared on many occasions that the death of Alfred Ætheling was not of your doing, but it seems that he and Robert of Jumièges were particularly close and the bishop has held a grudge against this house ever since. Now he is so close to the seat of power it seems he is doing all that he can to strengthen the French influence in court over those with English blood. What is more, the king seems to turn a blind eye to everything he does, even to the point of encouragement.'

'Can he do that?' asked Gytha, turning to her husband.

'He is the king,' said Godwin, 'he can act as he sees fit.'

'That's not entirely true,' said the bishop, 'for usually, with church appointments, he has to have the agreement of the monks of Canterbury. But alas, he seems to have conveniently forgotten that these past two years.'

'Even so,' said Godwin, 'I fail to see what I can do. Edward is king, after all, and matters of the Church are outside of my influence.'

'Not necessarily,' said Stigand. 'I understand that you have a relative at Christ Church Priory, one who is both pious and patriotic.'

'If you are talking about Æthelric, then yes, I do. But how can he help? He is only a monk.'

'He may be only a monk today,' said the bishop, 'but who knows what post he may hold in a year or so.'

Everyone fell silent as Godwin tried to fathom the implications.

'Look,' said the bishop, seeing the earl's turmoil, 'let me spell it out for you. Æthelric is a good man, and I have no doubt God has great plans for him within the Church. All I am saying is that it would be a good investment of your time and effort to remind him that you are not just his family but also a trusted ally of the Church. Do this, and I feel you may be easing the path for your own sons as they negotiate their way through the troubled politics of our country in the years to come.'

'To have any influence at all, he would need to be at least a bishop,' said Godwin. 'Are you saying he is likely to achieve such heights?'

'All I am saying is that a wager of that nature may not be a bad investment,' said Stigand.

'What I do not understand,' interjected Gytha, 'is that you are already in an even more powerful position. What could he possibly do that you cannot?'

'Alas, my reputation is tarnished,' said Stigand, 'at least in the eyes of the king. I have served too many monarchs to suffer fools gladly, and with Bishop Robert at his side, I will never again enjoy the privilege of offering him advice. No, this needs careful planning, so I suggest you give it some thought.'

'Thank you, your grace,' said Godwin, 'we will.'

'So,' said the bishop, taking a deep breath, 'now that we have concluded our business, may I enquire as to the whereabouts of Harold? I thought he was here at Bosham.'

'He should be back in a week or so,' said Gytha. 'Our sons are turning out to be busy young men.'

'And fine sons they are, too,' said Stigand, raising his hand to stifle a yawn. 'Please excuse me,' he said, 'the journey has taken more out of me than I thought.'

'Of course,' said Gytha, 'perhaps you should retire to your quarters, and we can talk again in the morning?'

'I think I'll do that,' said Stigand, getting to his feet. 'Thank you again for the meal and for the excellent company. Sleep well.'

'You too,' said Godwin, getting to his feet and watching as one of the bishop's servants helped him from the room.

'What did you make of that?' asked Gytha when he had gone.

'I think he is a clever, conniving, politically astute man,' said Godwin. 'But more importantly, he seems to have the interests of England at heart, and I am happy he is on our side.' He turned to his wife. 'Come,' he said, 'accompany me to my quarters. I too, am dog-tired, and it has been a very long day.'

Chapter Thirteen

Abingdon, November, AD 1048

Queen Ealdgyth sat alongside Spearhafoc in the monk's workshop in a building attached to Abingdon Abbey, having travelled from London a few days earlier to finalise some designs on behalf of the king.

'That is beautiful,' said Ealdgyth, looking at the sketch upon Spearhafoc's easel. 'Can you create such a thing?'

'Of course,' said the monk. 'The body will be carved in stone, the same as other statues, but when it is finished, we will apply sheets of fine gold and burnish it to the highest sheen. By the time it has been completed, everyone will think it has been cast from solid gold.'

'Your talent never ceases to amaze me,' said Ealdgyth, 'I am so happy we persuaded you to work for us.'

'Thank you, your grace,' said Spearhafoc. 'The hands may be mine, but they only channel God's talent.'

'Whatever the source,' said the queen, 'I am just happy that we are to be the recipients. However, I have a boon to ask.'

'Just name it, your grace,' said Spearhafoc, 'and if it is within my capability, it will gladly be given.'

'Well,' said the queen, 'in St Augustine's Abbey in Canterbury, there lies the tomb of St Letard. Do you know of it?'

'I do,' said Spearhafoc. 'I was blessed with doing some work in the abbey a few years ago.'

'Excellent,' said Ealdgyth. 'Well, as you know, this past summer, we suffered for lack of rain and the king and I prayed at

St Letard's tomb for relief. Within a week, the heavens opened, and the crops were saved. Now we would like to show our gratitude to the saint by adorning his tomb with a gift of gratitude.'

'And you want me to create this ornament?'

'We do,' said the queen, 'and we were thinking about a small golden statuette formed from some of our personal possessions.'

'It sounds very straightforward,' said Spearhafoc. 'I will give the design some thought and come back to you with the weight of gold required.'

'Thank you,' said Ealdgyth, 'but there is one more thing.' She lifted her hands from her lap and removed a ring from her finger. 'When you melt the gold,' she continued, handing him the ring, 'place this also in the melting pot.'

Spearhafoc looked at the ring and gasped at its beauty. Made from solid gold, the intricate design depicted a long-haired woman on a prancing horse.

'It was a gift from the king,' said Ealdgyth, 'and is said to have been worn by one of his ancestors. It will add special significance to our tribute.'

'Are you sure, your grace?' asked Spearhafoc. 'Never have I seen a thing of such fine craftsmanship.'

'I am sure,' said the queen, 'for even the finest gold pales into insignificance when compared to the darkest raincloud in a drought. Add it to the statuette as a sign of my personal gratitude.'

'What about the king? Will he not be annoyed?'

Ealdgyth stared at the friendly young monk, desperate to share the extent of her unhappiness with Edward. But, putting her station above her personal feelings, subdued the desire as quickly as it arose.

'He will be fine with whatever I decide,' said the queen. 'Besides, what better way to show our devotion to St Letard than to relinquish a valued heirloom?'

'As you wish,' said Spearhafoc, placing the ring safely in a pouch hanging from his neck.

Once the queen had left, he retrieved the ring and went over to a window to examine it more closely in the beam of natural light. The detail was exquisite. Having spent most of his life working amid jewellery of the highest order, he instinctively knew it was far too beautiful to be melted down for something as insignificant as a pretentious symbol of piety. He put it away again, but his thoughts once more turned to ideas unbecoming of a monk.

—

Two weeks later, Bishop Robert of Jumièges made his way down the corridor to Spearhafoc's workshop. Inside, as usual, Spearhafoc's two assistants were busy at their benches, each poring over detailed design work on chalices for the new Palace of Westminster. As the bishop walked in, both men jumped to their feet with surprise.

'Your grace,' said one, 'can we help you?'

'Yes,' said the bishop, 'I am looking for Father Spearhafoc. Is he here?'

'He is not, your grace, for he has gone to the Abbey of St Augustine this very morn.'

'For what reason?'

'To pray at the tomb of St Letard for inspiration in the creation of the tribute.'

'Ah, I see,' said the bishop. 'It matters not; my business is easily dealt with. Has he yet melted down the gold items provided by the queen?'

'He has not, but everything is ready, and it is the first task he will perform upon his return.'

'Excellent,' said the bishop. 'In that case, the queen has another item she would like to add, a brooch belonging to her grandmother. Where are the other pieces?'

The monk walked over to a table and retrieved a wooden bowl filled with various items of gold and silver ready for the melting pot. 'Here,' he said, turning around with the bowl.

The bishop placed the brooch in the bowl, but as the monk started to turn away, he reached out and touched his arm.

'Wait,' he said, 'let me see again.'

The monk held out the bowl, and the bishop moved the various items around with a long finger.

'Where's the ring?' he asked eventually.

'I am sorry, your grace,' said the monk, 'I know not what you are referring to. Father Spearhafoc left this bowl here this morning before he left for Canterbury, and it has not been touched since.'

'There was a ring,' said the bishop, 'one that featured a prancing horse. It was of great personal value to the king, and Queen Ealdgyth gave it to Father Spearhafoc herself.'

'I am sure there is a perfectly good explanation,' said the monk, 'perhaps he has it about his person.'

'Why would he do that?' asked the bishop. 'It is meant for the melting pot.'

'Alas, I do not have the answers you seek,' said the monk. 'Would you like me to send him a message?'

'When will he return?'

'In a few days,' said the monk, 'he was not specific.'

'Then it can wait, but as soon as he is back, ask him to present himself to the queen at Westminster. And do not melt these items until I say so. It seems your master has some questions to answer.'

'Of course, your grace,' said the monk, watching as the bishop left the workshop.

'What do you make of that?' asked the second monk.

'I do not know,' said Brother Geoffrey, 'but it doesn't look good. You stay here, I will be back in a few days.'

'Where are you going?'

'To Canterbury,' said the monk. 'Spearhafoc needs to know about the queen's interest.'

'But the bishop said—'

'I know what he said,' said the monk, 'but I do not trust him in the slightest. His loyalties are with the Normans, and it is well known that Father Spearhafoc is a favourite of the House of Godwin. Bishop Robert's intentions are not always honourable, and if he sees any opportunity to disrupt the relationship between the Godwins and the king, I have no doubt he will jump at the opportunity.'

'So you are going to warn Father Spearhafoc?'

'I am. I have worked alongside him for many years, and though there is no doubt an innocent explanation regarding the ring, I will not see him cornered without preparation.'

'As you wish,' said the monk, 'but if Bishop Robert asks about your whereabouts, I will not tell an untruth.'

'I understand,' said the monk. 'I will see you in a few days.' He left the workshop and made his way out to the stables, hoping that the groom on duty was one of those he considered a friend. Fifteen minutes later, he was riding hard towards Canterbury, his cloak blowing in the wind.

–

Several weeks later, Spearhafoc sat in an antechamber in Havering Palace, waiting to enter the queen's chambers. Since returning from Canterbury, his manner had been melancholy, having been accused by Bishop Robert of stealing the ring, and he now found himself summoned to explain himself to the queen.

Alongside him was Father Wilfric of St Augustine's Abbey, who had come along for moral support and to speak on his behalf. The plan was to just speak the truth and trust in the mercy of the queen.

'I hear you have a very close relationship with the queen,' said Wilfric.

'I do,' said Spearhafoc, 'and am honoured to enjoy her patronage. That is why this situation causes me so much anxiety – it looks like I may have thrown it all away.'

'Let us hope that she realises it was what it was, nothing but a simple oversight made by an honest man.'

Spearhafoc's face looked crestfallen, but deep inside, he hoped that the plan he had put into operation was about to come to fruition.

'The queen will see you now,' announced a servant, opening the door. The two abbots walked inside and approached the fire where the queen was sitting in one of the three chairs.

'Please,' she said, 'be seated.'

Father Wilfric was quite taken aback at the informality, but Spearhafoc was well aware of the queen's relaxed attitude to audiences, having shared so many with her over the years.

'Your grace,' said Wilfric, sitting on the edge of his chair, 'we are honoured to be in your presence.'

'On the contrary,' said the queen, 'it is I who am grateful you have both come to give an explanation in person. The king was prepared to lose the ring to form part of our offering to St Letard but is grieved to know it has simply disappeared. But I am happy to listen to the explanation.' She turned to Spearhafoc. 'Father Spearhafoc, how is your new life at Abingdon, have you settled in?'

'I have,' said Spearhafoc, 'and am looking forward to helping the poor and the destitute as much as I am able in the years ahead. That is, of course, if I am still in this privileged position after today.'

'Let us not worry about that too much,' said the queen, 'at least not yet. Would you like some honeyed water? It is warm and will take the chill from your bones.'

'That would be nice,' said Spearhafoc, waiting as a servant filled three glass goblets. When done, all three sipped on the hot drinks before placing them back on the table between them.

'So,' said Ealdgyth eventually, 'I understand my ring has gone missing, but you do not know how. Is that correct?'

'Not exactly, your grace,' said Spearhafoc. 'But first, I wish to make clear that this tragedy is of my own making. Nobody else is to blame; the fault lies with me and me alone.'

'That is very noble of you to say,' said the queen, 'but those matters will be explored as we go along. Now, tell me what happened.'

For the next few minutes, Spearhafoc explained how he had ridden to St Augustine's Abbey with the ring in his pocket and how, when he was finally shown to his quarters by one of the host monks, he had discovered it was missing.

'When was the last time you saw it?' asked the queen.

'Just after reaching the abbey,' said Spearhafoc. 'I remember moving it to a different pocket within my cloak. I do not remember why, but the second pocket had worn thin and had developed a hole. The ring must have fallen through somewhere between the gates and my cell.'

'So we know it is somewhere within the perimeter of the abbey,' said the queen.

'Indeed, your grace,' said Wilfric, 'but the grounds are extensive, for we grow all our own food there. It could be anywhere.'

'Not really,' said the queen, 'for Father Spearhafoc said he went directly to his cell. Is that the case, Father Spearhafoc?'

'Not quite,' said Spearhafoc, 'for I was indeed shown the vegetable beds on my way. They are nothing but turned ground at this time of the year, but as I am keen to do something similar at Abingdon, I asked my host to show me what they had done.'

'Ah, then that must be where it was lost,' said the queen. 'Do you not agree?'

'Possibly,' said Spearhafoc, 'but there were many brothers turning the soil as we passed. If indeed I dropped it there, it could have been forced beneath the surface by anyone's shoe and now lies underground.'

'Possibly,' said the queen, 'but nevertheless, the fact that it remains within the boundaries of a holy place gives me some comfort. The question is, what are we going to do about it?'

The two abbots looked at each other before Wilfric cleared his throat and turned back towards the queen.

'Your grace,' he said, 'alas, St Augustine's Abbey is a poor establishment, and as much as we would like to help, we simply do not have the resources to replace the value of such an item. In addition, I would plead that we are the innocent victims of this regretful incident and should not be made to suffer. My brother here, Father Spearhafoc, is the one that lost the item, and though he is a wonderful person without an evil bone in his body, the fact remains that it was in his custody, so any financial reparations should come from Abingdon, not Canterbury. That is only fair.'

'Reparations?' said the queen, her eyes furrowing in confusion. 'I was seeking no compensation, Father Wilfric, though your rush to defence begs the question, do you all not see yourself as one church beneath the gaze of God?'

'Of course,' stuttered the abbot, his face reddening as he realised he had misjudged the whole mood of the room. 'I was just explaining the position for the sake of clarity, and I was going to go on to say that if Abingdon Abbey were to struggle to pay any financial penalties, then we would, of course, reach out to do all that we could to help our brothers.'

'Were you really?' said the queen staring at the abbot.

For a few seconds there was an awkward silence before the queen turned back to Spearhafoc.

'So,' she said, 'Father Spearhafoc, tell me, what did you do to try and find the ring?'

'I retraced my steps, your grace,' said Spearhafoc, 'many times over, but when it became clear it was lost, I prayed at the tomb of St Letard himself, begging forgiveness and guidance.'

'And do you believe you have received either of those things?'

'I do not, your grace,' said Spearhafoc, 'and therefore I deserve to be punished by you and God alike. I am not worthy of my trusted position, and I fully accept your judgement. Even exile is too good a fate for someone as wretched as I.'

'I think the judgement you place upon yourself is a little harsh,' said the queen, 'but nevertheless, the king has insisted that such an oversight cannot go unpunished. I can assure you that you will not be denied God's grace, nor will you be sent from these shores, but whether you remain in position as the Abbot of Abingdon is yet to be decided.'

'I understand, your grace,' said Spearhafoc.

'Good. Try not to worry too much, but for now, you should return to Abingdon and continue your work. In due course, after further consultation with the king, I will send notification of our judgement.'

'Thank you, your grace,' said Spearhafoc. 'Is there anything else?'

'No, you may leave.'

The two abbots left the room and walked out to the courtyard. Their horses were being fed and watered and needed rest before they could head back to their respective abbeys, so they made their way to the local monastery to pray and seek sustenance in the refectory.

Several hours later, they were heading back to the stables when a cloaked servant ran up to them, an earnest look upon his face.

'Thank the Lord himself,' he gasped, 'I have been searching for you everywhere. You are to return to the queen's audience room immediately. The Bishop of London is already there, and he needs to talk with you as a matter of urgency.'

The two abbots glanced at each other before following the servant back into Havering Palace. Moments later, they were once again standing before the queen, but this time there were two other people present: Bishop Robert of Jumièges and a brother monk whose face was familiar to Spearhafoc.

'Your grace,' said Wilfric, bowing to the queen, 'I hear you have been looking for us. Please accept our apologies.'

'Forget that,' said the queen, 'you are here now, and that is what is important. I take it that you already know the bishop?'

'We have met,' said Wilfric, nodding towards Bishop Robert. 'Your grace, it is good to see you again.'

Robert did not answer, and both abbots could see his mind was in turmoil.

'And of course,' continued the queen, 'you already know Brother Geoffrey of Abingdon Abbey.'

'I do,' said Spearhafoc, 'and I fail to understand why he is here away from his duties.'

'He is here,' said the queen, 'because he has some astonishing news, information that throws this situation regarding the lost ring into a whole new light. But we await the arrival of Bishop Stigand before we continue, for I believe these moments need to be witnessed at the highest level.'

Within a few minutes, the second bishop entered the room and acknowledged the queen before looking around at everyone gathered. The queen quickly recapped what had happened before turning to the monk from Abingdon.

'Brother Geoffrey,' she said, 'please repeat what you told me only a few minutes ago.'

'Your grace,' he said, his voice shaking with nervousness, 'my name is Brother Geoffrey, and I am a humble monk living at the abbey in Abingdon. One of my roles there is to look after the abbey's gardens, and recently we have been turning the soil ready for the new planting. A few days ago, I travelled to St Augustine's with the aim of procuring some seedlings for our gardens, but while I was there, I witnessed what I can only describe as a miracle.'

'Please explain,' said the queen.

'Your grace,' said the monk, 'I stayed at St Augustine's for a few weeks, working alongside my brothers in the gardens until it was finally time to leave. Before I did, I decided to pray at the tomb of St Letard, but just as I lifted my head at the end of the prayer, I noticed something at the foot of the statue, and I fell to my knees in astonishment.'

'What did you see?' asked the queen, leaning forward in her chair.

The monk lifted up his travel bag from the floor and delved inside to retrieve a pot containing a dying plant, but as everyone gathered around, they crossed themselves in astonishment, for wrapped around the thickest part of the stalk was the missing golden ring.

'It's impossible,' said Bishop Robert, 'there is trickery involved here.'

'I swear upon the name of Christ himself,' said the monk, 'I have not interfered with this plant in any way whatsoever. I asked everyone in the abbey if they were responsible, but none were forthcoming. It is as if the plant was placed there by the saint himself.'

'What about you?' said the bishop, turning towards Spearhafoc. 'You could have gone out and set this up while the other monks slept.'

'That is not possible,' said Father Wilfric, 'for he had already returned to London with me.' He thought rapidly, realising that this was a chance to redeem himself and his abbey in the sight of the queen, and though there was a possibility that there may have been some subterfuge involved, he knew this was an opportunity too good to be missed.

'Your grace,' he continued, turning to the queen, 'you of all people know the power of St Letard. Indeed, Father Spearhafoc was there specifically to arrange your tribute and spent most of his time praying at the saint's tomb. Your influence in all this and the reappearance of your ring must surely mean there can be only one explanation.'

'Which is?' asked the queen nervously.

'Your grace, what we see here today must be an act of God enabled by St Letard himself. So, if I am not mistaken, we are witnesses to a true miracle.'

The room fell silent, and the queen looked towards the two bishops. If what Father Wilfric was saying was true, it would need to be confirmed by at least one of them before being taken to the archbishop.

Robert of Jumièges looked angry. For a while, it had looked like he was going to deliver a significant blow to the reputation of those loyal to Godwin, but now he had been put in a position that meant to do so would cast doubt on the wonder and influence of the Church. He thought furiously, forming his response, but before he could say a word, Bishop Stigand seized the opportunity.

'Your grace,' he said, 'I have said little since coming here, but it was only so I could absorb everything that was being said. As far as being a miracle is concerned, I suggest that I should carry out a detailed investigation, and if all these reports turn out to be true, then and only then – and I think I can speak on behalf of my fellow bishop here – can we safely declare that a miracle has truly occurred.'

He looked over at Bishop Robert, who was struggling to contain his frustration. Control of the conversation had been taken away from him, and he knew he had been outman-oeuvred.

'Well, Bishop Robert,' said the queen, 'are you in agreement?'

'I have to admit that I have a healthy scepticism,' said Robert, 'but I agree with Bishop Stigand. There has to be an investigation, and if proved to be true, then we present our evidence to the archbishop and the king for confirmation.'

'Thank you, everybody,' said the queen, 'and if there is nothing else, I declare this audience over.'

Once she had gone, everyone filed out of the room with Spearhafoc and Bishop Stigand bringing up the rear.

'I have to admit,' said the bishop quietly as they walked, 'I am humbled by what has happened here, and if proven true, then it will be an astonishing confirmation of your piety. However, if proved false, it will bring you crashing down and, by implication, will forever stain the name of the House of Godwin. So I have to ask you, Father Spearhafoc, and I need you to tell me the truth so I can put certain things in place. Will I find anything that may cast doubt on these claims?'

'You will not,' said Spearhafoc.

'Good,' said the bishop.

He walked on ahead to join his fellow bishop, leaving Spearhafoc staring at his back. As he stood, the monk who had produced the ring walked up to stand beside him.

'That went better than expected,' said Brother Geoffrey quietly.

'I was getting worried,' said Spearhafoc. 'You left it to the last moment.'

'I had difficulty finding it,' said Geoffrey, 'you had hidden it almost too well. What I don't know is why you hid it in the first place?'

Spearhafoc turned to face his friend; he trusted him but did not want to share the weaknesses that plagued him on a daily basis.

'Brother Geoffrey,' he said eventually, 'I am truly in your debt, I really am, but please don't ask me to explain, for I am not sure I can.'

Brother Geoffrey stared at Spearhafoc before breaking into a soft smile.

'Worry not, my friend,' he said, 'for I know you are a pious man, and whatever the reason, there was only good intended. Now come, let us get back to the abbey. There is work to be done.'

Chapter Fourteen

Sandwich Harbour, March, AD 1049

Harold Godwinson and Beorn Estrithson stood amongst a group of ship's captains on the walls of Sandwich harbour. All their ships had lain at anchor for several days following bad weather at sea, but Harold was in receipt of a letter from the king and was now briefing his captains as to what was expected of them.

'Gentlemen,' he said, 'as you know, the pirates currently ravaging the eastern coast of England are German in origin, and for the last few weeks, our attempts at catching them have been frustrating to say the least. Every time we sail to intercept them, we are always too late, and they are nowhere to be seen. It's obvious someone has been giving them safe harbour, but until now, we knew not who. However, that situation has now changed, and I have been informed by King Edward himself that King Baldwin of Flanders has entered into an agreement, offering the German pirates the use of any port in his kingdom in return for a share of profits.'

'I knew it,' said one of the captains, 'he always was a serpent.'

'If this is correct,' said another, 'it is highly unlikely we can ever defeat the pirates, for all they have to do is head for harbour at full speed and seek shelter. We cannot attack them there else we incur the wrath of Baldwin.'

'Perhaps we cannot prise them out,' said Harold, 'but if we deny them access, they will have to return whence they came.'

'We do not have enough ships to blockade all those ports,' said the captain, 'there are far too many.'

'We do not have to,' said Harold, 'just Bruges, the busiest and most important port in Flanders.'

'Do that, and you will definitely incur the wrath of Baldwin,' said the captain, 'Bruges is the port via which the king obtains most of the city's imports.'

'I know,' replied Harold, 'and that is why we will target it.'

'We will have no chance against his fleet,' said the captain, 'it is just too big.'

'It doesn't matter,' said Harold, 'for we will not be alone. King Edward has allied with Henry III of Germany, who will add his fleet to the blockade. Hopefully, as soon as Baldwin sees the strength assembled against him, he will quickly capitulate, and those pirates will have nowhere to hide.'

'When do we sail?' asked one of the captains.

'We will cede to your better judgement,' said Beorn, glancing up at the skies, 'but the weather seems to be clearing, so we should weigh anchor as soon as we can.'

'I think we will be in a better situation tomorrow,' said another captain. 'We can recall our crews today and be ready to sail by the morning's high tide.'

'That sounds good,' said Harold, 'let us make that happen.'

The captains walked away back to their ships, but as Harold turned to walk back up to his lodgings in the village, a horseman rode down onto the quay, dismounting and walking over to stand before him.

'My lord,' he said, 'I bring news from Dartmouth. A fleet of eight ships was seen yesterday morning just off the coast. I was told to let you know immediately.'

'Why me?' asked Harold. 'I am busy trying to deal with the Germans. Are there not commanders down there capable of dealing with any threat?'

'That's just it,' said the messenger, 'we do not know if there is any threat.'

'What do you mean?'

'The ships are English, my lord, and fly the flag of the House of Godwin.'

Harold's brow furrowed in confusion.

'I do not understand,' he said. 'We have no ships at sea, at least not that I am aware of.'

'You do not,' said the messenger. 'Prior to coming here, I rode to Bosham, and all your ships are safe at anchor.'

'So who is it that flies our banners?' asked Harold. 'It must be an imposter, unless…'

His eyes widened as he realised the implications, and he turned to call down to his cousin, who stood further along the quay.

'Beorn,' he shouted, 'you had better come quickly.'

The earl ran over to join them and stared at the messenger.

'Is there a problem?' he asked.

'I do not know yet,' said Harold, 'but if what this man is saying proves to be true, then I think my brother has returned, and it looks like he is not happy.'

–

Two days later, Godwin of Wessex stood before the Bishop of London. Robert of Jumièges was pacing back and forth like a caged animal, his face red with rage.

'What do you mean he has returned?' Robert shouted. 'Did the king not make himself clear before he left? Your son is not welcome in England, and we will not tolerate his presence.'

'Your grace,' said Godwin, 'I was as surprised as you, and I swear I had no prior knowledge.'

'Yet he flies your colours as if he is the prodigal son returning in triumph,' said the bishop. 'Is the man stupid, or is he just trying to antagonise the king? If it is the latter, he is doing a good job of it.'

'I'm not sure what is going on, your grace,' said Godwin, 'but if I could just speak to the king, perhaps I can make arrangements to remedy the situation.'

'The king is not available to speak to you,' snapped Robert, 'and what is more, it is as clear as the nose upon your face what is going on, for only a few days ago I discovered that Sweyn has been exiled from Denmark, having disgraced himself there. He is now without a homeland and thinks we have short memories, but let me tell you this – I will not allow him to set one foot on English soil. Do you understand, not a single step!'

'Is that you or the king speaking?' asked Godwin coldly.

'Both,' said Robert. 'So tell your son, if he insists on returning, his head will adorn the gates of London.'

'I understand,' said Godwin, 'and will convey your judgement.'

'It is the king's judgement,' said Robert, 'not mine. Now get out.'

Earl Godwin turned and left the chambers, seething at the manner in which he had been spoken to. Outside Osmund stood waiting with the horses.

'Is it true, my lord?' he asked as the earl came up to him. 'Has Sweyn returned?'

'Aye, he has,' said Godwin, 'but there is no welcome for him in the royal court. We have to find him and warn him to stay away, else he will probably face the king's executioner.'

–

Twenty-five leagues away, Harold Godwinson galloped his horse hard over the open fields towards Hampton, followed by Beorn Estrithson and ten of his huscarls. The previous day they had been told that Sweyn and his ships had docked in Hampton for supplies, and Harold and his men had ridden through the night to reach him before he set sail again. The journey had been hard on man and beast alike, but eventually they rode over the crest of a hill and reined in their horses to stare down at the coastal town below.

'There are over a dozen ships there,' said Beorn at Harold's side, 'but none show colours. Do you think any of them are Sweyn's?'

'There is only one way to find out,' said Harold. 'We need to go down there and ask.'

'Wait,' said Beorn, 'those ships will not be going anywhere soon; there are still several hours before high tide. I suggest we find somewhere to stable the horses and get something to eat before we go looking for him.'

'These are my father's lands,' said Harold, 'and he holds a trading house near the docks to collect the taxes on any trading ships. It is run by a man called Jackson – we can go there.'

Beorn agreed, and within fifteen minutes, they rode through a pair of enormous gates into a busy courtyard piled high with barrels and crates. Several rough-looking men left what they were doing and walked over to stand before the riders, most carrying iron crate-levers, and everyone had long daggers hanging ominously from their belts.

'Hold there, stranger,' said the largest of the men – a huge, bearded brute wearing a bloodstained leather apron over his jerkin. 'What business do you have here?'

'Who is in charge of this place?' asked Beorn, not intimidated in the slightest. 'Point me towards your master.'

'That would be me,' said the man, 'and I suggest you curb your manner while you are within these walls. Either that or lose your teeth.'

'If you are the master,' said Beorn, 'then your name would be Jackson, is that correct?'

'It may be,' said the man, 'but I still do not know your name or your business, so spit it out before I set my boys upon you.'

'If you are truly Jackson,' said Harold at Beorn's side, 'then there should be no need for introductions, for surely you would recognise the man who once drank your ale, kissed your woman and stole your best knife?'

'Nobody has ever done any of those things to Jackson and still walks without a stick,' said one of the other dockers.

'One man has,' said the first man, 'and if I recall, he had not even reached his tenth birthday. Isn't that right, master Harold?'

'It is,' said Harold with a laugh, 'and I still remember having to hide from you for a month to avoid a beating. How are you, old friend?'

'Old is the correct word,' said Jackson, walking over to reach up and take the earl's wrist in friendship. 'Look at you, that cheeky little scoundrel who raised my ire at every opportunity seems to have all grown up.'

'I have,' said Harold, 'and alas, with age comes responsibility. I find myself in need of your help.'

'Just say it, and it shall be yours,' said Jackson. 'Your father is a good lord, and every man here is a loyal servant.'

'We seek food and shelter,' said Harold, 'for the horses and for us. One night, two at most. Can you help us?'

Jackson turned to face his gathering men.

'This man is Harold Godwinson,' he announced, 'and is to be treated as if he is the king himself. What he wants, he gets, and if anyone so much as looks at him the wrong way, they will have me to deal with, understood?'

The tension eased in the courtyard and the dockers returned to their duties, unpacking crates from the many ships in the harbour.

'There is nowhere here for your horses,' said Jackson, 'but there are stables down the road. Take them down there and mention my name; they will be well looked after. Once done, return here, and we will see about finding you some quarters.'

Harold nodded and turned his horse to lead his men back out of the gate.

'I do not think I would like to cross him in an ale-fuelled fight,' said Beorn as they rode. 'It looks like he can handle himself.'

'He is the best fighter I have ever seen,' said Harold. 'My father once had to set six of his best men on him with wooden staves to beat him senseless after he wrecked a tavern and knocked a dozen men down.'

'What happened to him?'

'My father paid for the damage and gave every man hurt in the fight ten silver pennies not to report him to the reeve.'

'The earl must have thought a lot of him.'

'He did and still does. Jackson's loyalty is unbreachable; he would lay down his life for my father if the circumstances demanded.'

They carried on down the road and stabled their horses before heading back up to the compound.

'Up here,' shouted a voice as they walked through the gate. They looked up to see Jackson peering down from a hay platform sticking out from the upper floor. They entered the building and made their way through a maze of crates before climbing a ladder onto the next level. Once again, the floor was covered with cargo, and they wound their way through to the rear where several men were moving sacks of grain to create a cleared space.

'Will this do?' asked Jackson, looking around. 'There is plenty of room and the roof is sound.'

'This is fine for the men,' said one of the huscarls, 'but perhaps you can find better lodgings for the earl?'

'An earl now, is it?' laughed Jackson. 'Not bad employment for a snotty-nosed rascal, even if I say so myself.'

'Curb your tongue,' growled the huscarl, 'lest I cut it from your mouth.'

'Enough,' laughed Harold. 'Jackson has a way with words, and if you do not like them, I suggest you stay well clear, for he does not change his manner for man or beast.'

'But my lord,' said the huscarl, 'he was insulting.'

'He was just telling the truth,' said Harold, 'for as I recall, I was indeed a snotty-nosed rascal. Anyway, there is no need for separate lodgings, we will bed down here with the men. But first, we need to talk.'

Back in Westminster, the king walked around the gardens with the Bishop of London, his mood still sour after the meeting with Godwin.

'I am at a loss what to do,' said Edward. 'I am the King of England, yet find my path dictated by a family who, less than a generation ago, were probably thegns at best. Why can I not rid myself of this burden?'

'I fear that the problem may be deeper than you think,' said the bishop, 'and if you are not careful, it could result in your worst nightmare.'

'Which is?' asked the king.

'That upon your demise, the crown of England could sit upon the head of Godwin himself.'

The king stopped walking and stared at the bishop with surprise.

'What are you talking about?' he said. 'He is not royal born and has no claim to the throne.'

'Ordinarily, I would agree with you,' said the bishop, 'but we must examine the facts more closely. First of all, you have no heir and are unlikely to have one with Ealdgyth if the current state of affairs continues as it is.'

'She will bear no child of mine,' said the king, 'of that I am certain.'

'In that case, we must consider the alternatives. Either you must have a child with another woman out of wedlock, which, of course, would be disapproved of by the Church, or you have to accept that when you die, there will be a gathering of the Witan where your successor will be discussed and agreed upon. If that happens, I would suggest that Godwin of Wessex has enough support to potentially press a claim. He also has many allies within the Church who will be keen to support his case. The throne is indeed at very great risk.'

'So, what are my options?'

'I see only three,' said the bishop. 'The first is to sire a child with Ealdgyth. But even if the union were blessed with a son, it would still mean that Godwin's heir would inherit the throne.'

'That is not going to happen,' said Edward.

'In that case, you could divorce Ealdgyth and replace her with someone more suitable. That way, there would be no problem with the succession, should your new bride have children.'

'Divorce her on what grounds?'

'I have to admit that I have no answers,' said the bishop, 'but I am sure that if you come up with something, we will be able to find people willing to testify as witnesses. For a price, of course.'

'Reverend father,' said the king, 'despite the unpleasant situation I find myself in, I will not forge my legacy with untruths. What is the third option?'

'The last resort is for you to nominate a successor while you are still alive and deal with the Witan as and when the inevitable objections arise.'

'And do you have any suggestions as to who this successor should be?'

'Two spring to mind,' said the bishop. 'The first is Edward Ætheling, son of King Edmund Ironside. His pedigree is impeccable, and as his father once ruled England, he has just as strong a case as any.'

'I admit, his name has come to mind on several occasions,' said the king, 'but the last I heard of him, he was enjoying the patronage of the Prince of Kiev.'

'He is indeed,' said the bishop, 'and Yaroslav the Wise places great favour upon him, so we would have to be careful in revealing our thoughts too early lest Yaroslav sees the proposition as an opportunity to gain influence. To that end, we would first have to be sure that Edward Ætheling was committed to England and not Kiev.'

'And how would we do that?'

'By inviting him here as an honoured guest and spending time with him. Even then, he could ultimately maintain his loyalties to Yaroslav, so we would have to be careful.'

The king walked a few more paces, deep in thought.

'And the second candidate?' Edward asked.

'You will probably find the second option far more agreeable,' said the bishop. 'I suggest that you consider the son of Robert of Normandy.'

Again, the king stopped and stared at the bishop.

'Are you suggesting William the Bastard as the future King of England?'

'Why not?' said Bishop Robert. 'He is strong, ambitious and enjoys the patronage of King Henry of France. I know you have had personal dealings with him before coming to England, and I have been led to believe that you got on very well.'

'Indeed I did,' said the king, 'he is an impressive young man. I have to admit it is an intriguing proposition, not least because his ambition knows no bounds, and I have no doubt that England will eventually become an attractive prize, should we ever lower our guard. An alliance with him and the King of the Francs could secure our safety for generations.'

'Then is it not better that such a thing is discussed now while you are alive instead of it being decided over your grave?'

'I will give it some thought,' said the king. 'But overall, I am tilting towards agreement. This has been a very interesting conversation.'

'It was my pleasure, my lord.'

—

Back in Hampton, Harold Godwinson sat at an upturned barrel along with Beorn and Jackson, sharing a flask of ale with them. The rest of the men had bedded down amongst the stores to try to catch up with some much-needed sleep.

'So,' said Jackson, pouring the ale with a poorly hidden amused smile. 'What brings you back to Hampton, my lord? I am assuming it is about your brother?'

'You know about Sweyn?' asked Harold.

'We may not be privy to courtly politics down here,' said the docker, 'but news travels fast, and when he was exiled, he hired ships from this very harbour.'

'I thought he sailed from Bristol,' said Beorn.

'He may have, but he also hired a dozen ships from here to bolster his arrival in Flanders. Now the word is that he has returned with that fleet and seeks redemption.'

'Is he here now?' asked Beorn. 'Are those his ships in the harbour?'

'Some are,' said Jackson, 'at least six. He, however, sailed straight back out again as soon as he had taken on fresh supplies.'

'Damn,' said Harold, sitting back, 'we missed him.'

'Not necessarily,' said Jackson, 'for he left instructions for his fleet to be resupplied and prepared for sea. It seems he intends on going somewhere pretty soon.'

'Where is he now?' asked Harold.

'There are rumours that he has sailed for Bristol, something about a woman waiting for him, but more than that, I do not know.'

'Surely he has not come back for Eadgifu,' said Beorn, turning to face Harold. 'He invites certain death by doing so.'

'Not even he is that stupid,' said Harold. He turned back to Jackson. 'Do you know when he will return?'

'His crews expect to sail in seven days,' said Jackson, 'so it could be anytime between now and then.'

'If we decide to wait,' said Harold, 'do you have quarters for the men?'

'They are welcome to stay here,' said Jackson, 'though there are two alehouses in the town who will offer a bed and a hot meal in return for a coin.'

'Here is fine,' said Harold, turning to Beorn. 'What do you think?'

'We have come all this way,' said Beorn, 'we may as well stay.'

'So be it,' said Harold, turning back to face Jackson. 'Thank you, my friend, your offer is gratefully accepted.'

Chapter Fifteen

Brionne, Normandy, March, AD 1049

Across the channel, the Duke of Normandy sat before a fire in a house in Brionne. Since his victory at the Battle of Val-ès-Dunes near Caen two years earlier, his forces had besieged his opponent, Guy of Burgundy, in his castle. While it had been a long and costly siege, at last it seemed Guy was prepared to discuss terms of surrender.

At William's side, sharing a large jug of ale, sat Alan Rufus, or Alan the Red as most people knew him, first Lord of Richemont in Rouen. Alan was a valued ally and enjoyed a close and trusted friendship with William, much to the dismay of those who desired influence with the duke.

As they sat discussing the strategy of the following day's meeting with Guy of Burgundy, a servant entered bearing a message on a silver platter.

'My lord,' he said, 'my apologies, but you asked to be informed when you received a reply from Bruges.'

'About time,' said William, walking over to the servant before taking the document and tearing open the seal. He picked up a candle and held it up to the letter. For a few moments he read in silence, his manner calm, but Alan the Red could see the tell-tale signs in the Duke's face – he was about to explode.

'Thank you,' Alan said to the servant quickly, 'you may leave.'

'The messenger is waiting for a reply,' said the servant, 'shall I tell him to wait?'

'Make sure he is fed and has a bed,' said Alan. 'The duke will respond in the morning.'

'No,' snapped William, 'tell him to leave. I will respond when I am good and ready.'

The servant left the room, and Alan Rufus carried over the duke's drink.

'Bad news, my lord?' he asked.

'Aye,' said William, 'you could say that. That damned woman in Bruges not only has the audacity to refuse my proposal but also takes delight in questioning my suitability as a spouse due to my parentage.'

'It is well known she has a feisty and somewhat haughty spirit,' said Alan, 'and despite her undoubted beauty, I have always worried about your fascination with her. You could have any woman you want, yet you choose to pursue a wildcat.'

'A wildcat with a bottomless purse and a list of powerful allies,' said William. 'This is not the end of the matter, Alan, I will not accept no for an answer. But prior to that, she needs to be brought down from her haughty perch.'

'What are you going to do?'

'Show her and her father exactly who they're dealing with.'

'But what about the meeting with Guy?'

'He has held out for two years,' said William, 'another few days won't hurt. Tell the stables to prepare the horses, my friend. Tomorrow morning we are going to Bruges.'

—

Harold and Beorn sat in a crowded tavern near the harbour. Woodsmoke filled the room, and already there had been two fights, both over ownership of the fleeting affections of one of the many whores who stalked the streets looking for the next customer. The room was stuffy and smelled bad, but the ale was plentiful and the food hearty.

'How do you think your father is going to react when he finds out about Sweyn?' asked Beorn, dipping a chunk of bread into a bowl of pork stew.

'He already knows,' said Harold, 'and was summoned to court by the king a few days ago, but I know not the outcome.'

'I think he will be supportive,' said Beorn.

'As do I,' said Harold, 'though why I do not know. All his life Sweyn has been nothing but trouble.'

'He is still the firstborn,' said Beorn, 'that counts for a lot.'

'Aye, it does, and it irks me sometimes that everything my father has built these past twenty years will eventually go to Sweyn to manage.'

'Do you covet that succession?'

'Not in the way that you think,' said Harold. 'Only in as much as I have no doubt Sweyn will ensure it all comes crashing down.'

'A lot can happen between now and then,' said Beorn, 'not least the fact that he will first have to be pardoned by the king. Somehow I cannot see that happening anytime soon.'

They continued to eat until one of their men walked in. After seeing them sitting in the corner, he hurried over.

'My lords,' he said, 'I have news. Two ships are waiting to enter the port, and I have been informed that one of them belongs to Sweyn.'

'About time,' said Harold pushing away his bowl and getting to his feet. 'You know my brother, do you not?'

'I do, my lord.'

'Good. Then wait for him to appear on the dock and bring him to the warehouse.'

'And if he refuses?'

'He will not refuse, for without my support he can never hope to achieve a pardon.'

'As you wish, my lord,' said the huscarl before leaving the tavern to return to the dock.

'Harold,' said Beorn, 'finish your food. There is plenty of time.'

–

Two hours later, Harold was pacing the floor of the warehouse, still waiting for his brother to appear. It had been confirmed that it was indeed Sweyn's ship, but as yet there was no sign of him.

'I've had enough of this,' said the earl, grabbing his cloak. He strode towards the doorway, only to find his passage obstructed by ten men coming in through the courtyard gates.

'Hello brother,' said Sweyn, at the head of the group, 'it is good to see you again.' He held out his arm and, after the slightest of pauses, which did not go unnoticed by Sweyn, Harold grabbed his brother's forearm in friendship.

'Sweyn,' said Harold, 'we have been expecting you.'

'So I have heard,' said Sweyn, 'which is convenient as it is you and Beorn in particular that I have come all this way to see. Shall we go inside?'

Everyone followed Jackson into the warehouse. Inside, a table was laden with food and drink in preparation for the meeting.

'Excellent,' said Sweyn, taking a seat. He turned to his trusted huscarl. 'Owen, please join us. You too, Jackson. The rest of you, take a platter and give us some privacy.'

The rest of his men filled trenchers with meat and bread before leaving with a full pitcher of ale. Harold and Beorn sat down alongside Owen and poured themselves a drink but did not pick at any of the food.

'Eat,' mumbled Sweyn through a mouthful of meat, 'this is almost a feast in itself, and the pork is still hot.'

'We have already eaten,' said Harold, 'so fill your boots, brother – there is plenty more where that came from.'

Sweyn and Owen continued picking from the various platters, filling their bellies with meat and ale.

'So,' said Harold eventually, 'you have just returned from Bristol?'

'I did not go to Bristol,' said Sweyn, looking up. 'You need new spies.'

'I have no spies,' said Harold, 'only rumour and hearsay. Did you find what you were looking for?'

Sweyn stared at his brother while stripping a chicken leg of meat.

'If you are referring to the abbess, dear brother, rest assured that though the thought crossed my mind, I have decided to leave the past behind me. I went to the Isle of Wight to pay a debt and to recruit more men.'

'What sort of men?' asked Beorn. 'Fighting men?'

'Perhaps. Why, is that a problem?'

'It depends on who you intend to fight,' said Beorn. 'Bloodshed is always a last resort.'

'Fret not, cousin,' said Sweyn, 'I do not intend to fight anyone of importance, at least not yet.'

'So, why exactly are you here?' asked Harold. 'Your arrival has caused great consternation across England.'

'There is no secret,' said Sweyn, wiping grease from his mouth with the back of his hand. 'I am done with Denmark and with Flanders, so want to come back.'

'You want to come home?' asked Beorn.

'I do, and I intend to present my case to the king at the earliest opportunity.' He drank a few more mouthfuls of ale before letting out a belch and reaching for a chunk of cheese.

'I fear your appeal will fall on deaf ears,' said Harold. 'The king is still angry about what you did to the abbess, and I see no way he will curb his ire any time soon.'

'You are too pessimistic,' said Sweyn. 'I am the eldest son of Earl Godwin, and that holds a lot of sway in the corridors of power. I will admit I lost my way for a while and am happy to beg forgiveness for what I did, but if he refuses, then he will have the House of Godwin to contend with.'

'*What?*' gasped Harold. 'Are you saying that you expect Father to confront the king and support your claim with the threat of conflict?'

'Why not?' said Sweyn. 'He is always preaching that we are stronger as a family when we stand united, so this is an opportunity for him to prove he is a man of his word. If all of us present a combined and united front, then the king would not dare refuse. The country could be plunged into a civil war.'

'You are mad,' said Harold. 'There is no way that Father would agree to that, especially after what you accused Mother of the last time we met.'

'Ah, yes,' said Sweyn, 'I wondered when you would bring that up.'

'How could I not?' said Harold. 'You besmirched the name of your own mother.'

'I do not judge her,' said Sweyn, 'for we do not know the circumstances. However, I did not say anything that is not already the subject of courtly gossip across England. Indeed, if I am wrong, then that is all the more reason for Father to support my case. I am the eldest son and need to be living here in England.'

'I do not know what to say,' said Harold. 'I am shocked by the audacity of your ambition.'

'Shocked or not,' said Sweyn, 'that is why I am here, but I need your support to make it happen.'

'What sort of support?'

Sweyn put down his tankard and turned to stare at his cousin.

'Beorn,' he said, 'if my lands had been given outside of the family, it would have been difficult to get them back. However, as they are being looked after by you and Harold, I know that all I have to do is ask, and they will be returned to me without argument.' He lowered his tone, and his stare pierced Beorn like a blade. 'Is that not the case?'

Beorn hesitated, not knowing how to respond.

'Sweyn,' interjected Harold, 'you cannot just march in here without warning and demand such a thing of either of us – it is not as easy as that.'

'Why not?' asked Sweyn, his manner a lot less jovial. 'They are my lands and should be returned to me.'

'They belong to the king,' said Beorn, 'and even if we agreed, then the final decision would be his to grant or deny as he saw fit.'

'I know,' said Sweyn, 'but if you were to tell him you are happy to return them to me, then I am sure he would see sense and reinstate everything I once had.'

'This is madness,' said Harold, 'the king would never agree to it.'

'It is a bold move, I agree,' said Sweyn, 'but if we all unite as a family and share a position, then I cannot see how Edward can refuse. The House of Godwin and our allies are at least as strong as anything the king could muster. Do not forget he is a Norman at heart, and the needs of our people are of secondary importance to him.'

'He is as English as you or me,' said Harold, 'and you know it.'

'Do not tell me that the twenty-five years he spent in Normandy had no effect on him,' said Sweyn. 'The man is as French as his pet bishop, Robert of Jumièges.'

'I don't know, Sweyn,' said Harold, 'I feel it is too big a step. I am happy to stand beside you and support your plea for clemency, but I will not be part of any threat to the Crown just because you wish to come home.'

'Let us not make any hasty decisions,' said Sweyn. 'I am in port for the next few days, so we can all sleep on it before I sail to Bosham and put my plan to Father.' He looked around the warehouse. 'Are you staying here?'

'We are,' said Harold, 'and there is room for you if you so require.'

'No, I will stay above the tavern until I sail, either that or in my cabin on the ship.' He stood up and stared at the two men.

'Two days,' he said, 'and then I sail to Bosham, with or without your support.'

Harold and the rest of the men stood and watched as Sweyn walked out of the warehouse to join his men.

'What did you make of that?' asked Beorn quietly.

'In short,' said Harold, 'I think the man is deluded.'

Chapter Sixteen

The Port of Hampton, March, AD 1049

Two days later, Harold Godwinson and Beorn Estrithson walked towards Sweyn's ship in the harbour. The last of the supplies Sweyn needed had already been loaded, and the few men-at-arms waiting to go aboard made their way up the gangplanks.

To one side, they could see Sweyn settling his account with the harbourmaster. As they approached, he concluded his business and turned to greet them.

'Ah, there you are,' he said, 'I had just about given up on you.'

'You are fooling nobody, Sweyn,' said Harold. 'You know that without our support, your plan is doomed to certain failure.'

'Not necessarily,' said Sweyn. 'The main player is the Earl of Wessex, and I think I can get our father to agree to an alliance.'

'Funny,' said Harold, 'all of a sudden, when you want something, he becomes your father, when only a day or so ago you claimed to be sired by Cnut himself. Which is it, Sweyn, for you cannot claim both?'

'I will do exactly as I like,' said Sweyn. 'Now, I imagine you are here to tell me your decision, so why don't you spit it out?'

'My position has not changed,' said Harold. 'I will stand at your side to request forgiveness before the king, but I will play no part in any threats to the Crown itself. Should you utter such things in the king's presence, I will immediately stand alongside him against you.'

'You would turn against your own brother?'

'If it meant stopping a civil war, then yes. No single man is worth a country, Sweyn, not even you.'

Sweyn turned to face his cousin.

'What about you, Beorn? You are more of a brother to me than any sired by Godwin. Do you also intend to stand against me?'

'Sweyn,' said Beorn, obviously struggling with his conscience, 'what you did was a terrible thing, and I think the king was generous with his punishment. Even the fact that you stand before us now, alive and well, is hardly believable, but I am unsure that he will be willing to extend his mercy to a pardon. If I believed there was any chance whatsoever, then I would stand beside you, but I just cannot see it, and as Harold said, the chance of bloodshed is just too high.'

'So you, too, are rejecting me?'

'I didn't say that,' said Beorn, 'I just—'

'Just what?' interrupted Sweyn. 'Either you are with me, or you are against me. It is as simple as that.'

Harold stared at Beorn with surprise. Only a few hours ago, they had both agreed to reject Sweyn's plan, but now it seemed his cousin was wavering.

'Well?' said Sweyn. 'What is it to be, Beorn?'

'I... I do not know,' said Beorn at last. 'I need to know more before I commit either way.'

'I'll tell you what,' said Sweyn, 'I have an idea. I have just found out I need to sail down to Dartmouth before going to Bosham. Why don't you join me aboard my ship so we can talk properly? That way, you will hear everything I have to say, and by the time we reach Bosham, you will have decided one way or another.'

'You want me to come with you on your ship?'

'Why not? You have to go back to Bosham anyway, so the method of travel is irrelevant.' He turned to his brother. 'You too, Harold, why don't you spend a few days with me so we can discuss this like men?'

'I have to stop off elsewhere,' said Harold, 'so cannot accept. However, Beorn is his own man, and if he wants to go with you, I will ensure his horses and men get to Bosham before you arrive.'

'Well,' said Sweyn, turning to Beorn, 'what do you think? Are you coming with me or not?'

'Aye,' said Beorn eventually, 'I think I will. Is there room for some of my men to accompany me?'

'Of course,' said Sweyn, 'but make haste, we have to sail within the hour.' He walked away to speak to the ship's captain as Beorn turned to Harold.

'Are you sure about this?' said Harold. 'He is not thinking straight, and I worry for your safety.'

'I do not think that is an issue,' said Beorn, 'we have been friends for too long. I will sail with him and use the time to try and talk some sense into him.'

'Good luck with that,' said Harold. 'He may be my brother, but I fear sense is the last thing he wants to hear.' He grabbed Beorn's forearm. 'Be careful, cousin,' he said, 'and God willing, I will see you in Bosham in a few days.'

'Do not worry, Harold,' said Beorn, 'I will be fine, and this will soon all be over.'

'I hope so,' said Harold, 'but somehow I doubt it; I doubt it very much.'

–

Three days later, across the Channel, William of Normandy rode along the road to Bruges, having been in the saddle for the best part of five days. Alongside him was Alan the Red and behind him a column of a hundred experienced lancers, insurance against the many dangers to be found in the surrounding area. William's mood was sour, and as the journey had progressed, the thoughts about what he would say or do when he confronted Matilda of Flanders continued to darken. There was no doubt that she would have made a perfect match for him, being in possession of both beauty and wealth, but the fact that she had dismissed him outright for no other reason than being beneath her station had left him irate and determined to balance the shame she had placed upon him. Now they were getting close to the city, and he knew that he had to calm his mood lest he do something foolhardy. He turned to Alan the Red at his side.

'We will rest on the crest of the next hill,' he said, 'and wait for our scouts to report back.'

'As you wish, my lord,' said Alan, before passing the information back to the column.

–

An hour later, all the men not on guard sat on fallen logs or their folded cloaks as protection against the damp ground. Each ate whatever food they still had left in their food bags and swilled it down with watered wine or water from one of the many streams they had passed along the way.

William and Alan stood at the edge of the forest, looking down at the vast valley before them. At its centre was Bruges itself, a relatively large town that sat on the banks of an estuary. Recently the upper reaches of the tidal river had become silted up, causing many problems to the town's reliance on seaborne trade, but work was now afoot to alleviate the problem and return the town to its once-thriving best.

'Our scouts are back,' said Alan, looking down at a group of four men riding up the path.

As the men approached, the rider at the front reined in his horse and dismounted before running up to the duke.

'My lord,' he said, 'I have interesting news.'

'Did you locate her father's house?' asked William.

'Aye, we did, but even better than that, we found out his daughter intends to attend church this very morn, and the church in question lies outside the town walls.'

'How did you find that out?' asked Alan.

'We kidnapped one of her servants on her way to the market,' said the scout, 'and after a bit of persuasion, she was only too happy to talk.'

'Where is the servant now?' asked Alan.

'Fret not, my lord, she is still alive and well and is currently walking back to the town. We reckon it will be nightfall before she gets back to raise the alarm.'

'Do you know the location of this church?'

'We do, my lord, and we can be there in less than an hour if you so wish.'

'How many guards accompany her?'

'A maximum of twenty,' said the scout, 'no more.'

William turned to Alan the Red.

'Tell the men to mount up,' said William, 'my task just got a whole lot easier.'

—

Ten minutes later, the whole column rode out of the forest and descended into the valley, heading eastwards to circumnavigate the town. Eventually, the scout reined in his horse and called the column to a halt.

'The church is over that hill,' he said to the duke, 'and the lady's party will be approaching from the north. Here we are hidden from sight, but once we crest the ridge, we will be in full view. What do you want us to do, my lord?'

William thought for a moment, wondering whether to ride with the full force of his column at his back or to approach alone with a view to a private conversation. Finally, he decided that a show of force was necessary, especially as Matilda would be accompanied by a force of bodyguards. He turned to Alan the Red.

'Tell the men to be ready to fight if necessary, but only if they receive my specific command. Is that clear?'

'It is, my lord,' said Alan. 'What are you going to do?'

'Your guess is as good as mine,' said William. 'Come, let us get this done.' With a dig of his heels, William urged his horse forward, followed by a hundred fearless and battle-hardened men.

—

Baldwin V of Flanders and his wife, Adela of France, rode their horses alongside a river leading to their favourite church. The morning was warm, and though the grass was still damp from the overnight rain, the sky was clear and the sun shining. Just behind them rode their eighteen-year-old daughter, Matilda of Flanders, and their youngest son, Robert, a boy of just fifteen years of age. Accompanying the family was a guard of twenty trusted men, for though there was no fear of attack from any of Flanders' enemies, there was always a chance of brigands seeking easy victims.

Matilda, in particular, looked radiant in the morning sunshine. Her white dress was spotless and her golden hair hung in long golden braids down to her waist. Although she was shorter than most women, she was fully aware of her own beauty and position in life. Her status as the daughter of Baldwin meant that she was highly desirable to many potential allies, and she knew that she would soon have to choose a suitor.

As the family chatted amongst themselves, the captain of the guard suddenly reined in his horse and held up his hand. The column came to a halt, and everyone looked up in surprise.

'What is the problem, captain...' started Baldwin, but before he could continue, the captain turned to issue an order to the following column.

'To arms,' he shouted. 'Protect our lord.'

Instantly all the soldiers behind Baldwin raced forward to form a protective wall, causing fear and confusion amongst the family.

'What's happening,' shouted Robert, 'are we under attack?'

'Stay with your mother,' snapped Baldwin, spurring his horse to join the captain. Up ahead, they could see a column of riders coming down the hill towards them.

'Who are they?' asked Baldwin.

'They carry no colours,' said the captain, 'so we should take no chances.'

'They outnumber us five to one,' said Baldwin, 'let us hope they are friendly.' As the column approached, the count squinted his eyes, trying to recognise the man in front. 'I know him,' he said, 'it's William the Bastard, Duke of Normandy.'

The captain swore under his breath, fully aware that William was known for his aggressive ways and lack of patience.

'Be on your mettle, men,' he said over his shoulder, 'we may have a fight on our hands.' He turned to the count at his side. 'My lord, if their intent is ill, then be prepared to ride as hard as you can back to the town. There is no way we can defeat them, but we should be able to delay them long enough for you and your family to escape.'

'I don't think it will come to that,' said Baldwin. 'Besides, if William is coming to attack Bruges, you can guarantee there is an army ten thousand strong on the other side of that hill.'

Both men fell silent as the column rode up to meet them, splitting in two to encircle the whole group. William reined in his horse before the count and waited as his men took their positions.

'Duke William,' said Baldwin eventually, 'your arrival is unannounced. If you had sent a message, perhaps I could have arranged a more, shall we say, friendly reception.'

'There is no need to be alarmed, Count Baldwin,' said William, 'we are not here with any aggressive intention.'

'Your men suggest otherwise,' said Baldwin, looking around at the riders with their swords unsheathed.

William followed his gaze before nodding towards Alan the Red.

'Sheath swords,' called Alan, and immediately the tension eased. Baldwin's men followed suit, but everyone maintained their stance, ready to spring into action if so required.

'So,' said Baldwin, 'to what do we owe this unexpected pleasure?'

'Lord Baldwin,' said William, acknowledging the man's position with the slightest of nods, 'I wish to speak with your daughter, nothing more.'

Baldwin's brow furrowed in confusion.

'Matilda?' he said. 'What business do you have with her?'

'The business of an insulting letter I received from her a few days ago.'

Baldwin stared at William. He knew nothing about any letter, and inside he was furious that she had done such a thing without his knowledge.

'This is the first I have heard of it,' said Baldwin, 'but I'm sure that if it was indeed insulting, then it was written poorly and without forethought.'

'If that is the case,' said William, 'then I would hear her apology from her own lips.'

Baldwin hesitated, not wanting to put his daughter in such a position, but he knew he had no other choice. He turned around in his saddle and called out.

'Matilda, come forward.'

The young woman kicked her heels and urged her horse forward.

'The duke here tells me you have been in correspondence,' he said. 'Is this true?'

'It is,' she said, staring at William, 'but it was nothing of importance.'

'May I ask, what was the subject?' asked her father.

'Count Baldwin,' interrupted William, 'may I suggest that the contents of the letter are private and are better kept between your daughter and me.'

'On the contrary,' said Baldwin, 'as her father and guardian, I should be kept aware of such things.'

'Nevertheless, I would rather speak to Matilda alone.'

'That is not going to happen,' said the count.

'Father,' said Matilda, reaching out and touching the count's arm. 'I agree with Duke William and wish to talk with him alone.'

'Are you sure?'

'I am in no danger,' she said. 'Let me settle this.'

Baldwin nodded, and as William turned his horse to ride away to a nearby knoll, Matilda kicked her horse to follow him. A few moments later, both dismounted and walked away from the horses.

'So,' said Matilda, looking up at the handsome duke, 'I take it you are not impressed with my letter.'

'I am not,' said William. 'You dismissed me out of hand without as much as agreeing to an introduction.'

'I recall no request for such a thing,' she said, 'only one for marriage that was probably written on your behalf by someone else. What sort of woman do you think I would be if I were to respond to such an anonymous letter?'

'One who respects authority and station,' said William. 'An alliance between our two houses would be beneficial to all, but especially to your father.'

'You have a grand opinion of yourself, Duke William,' she said, 'and though you may be fair to the eye, I need more than an exaggerated sense of importance from any man who wishes to take me to his bed.'

'I am the Duke of Normandy,' said William, 'and command respect from anyone who crosses my path. The challenges of my position are vast, yet I have put them aside and travelled many days to face someone who has rebuffed my advances. At the very least, you will grant me the decency of hearing what I have to say.'

'I fear you are wasting your time,' said Matilda, 'for my mind is set, and we are ruining a beautiful day in meaningless conversation.'

'Then tell me what would change your mind,' said William, 'for as you can see, I am not one for prolonged courtship.'

'The fact that you came all the way here certainly helps,' said Matilda, 'but letters and words mean nought without actions. When I marry, it will be to a real man, not one who whines like a beaten child at the first sign of rejection.'

She turned away to return to her father, but William felt a rage erupt like a fire inside him, and grabbing her braids, he threw her to the ground before kneeling beside her with his hand around her throat.

Down near the river, Matilda's mother cried out with fear and men on both sides drew their swords, but before anyone could act, Baldwin called out.

'*Hold*,' he roared. 'Sheath your swords.'

'Baldwin,' shouted his wife, 'do something.'

'Be quiet, woman,' shouted Baldwin, 'this will play out as it will.'

Adela reached out and grabbed the reins of her son's horse, pulling him closer to stop him from doing anything stupid.

'You just stay calm, my friend,' said Alan the Red to the captain of the Flemish guards, 'she is not in any danger.'

'I just hope you are correct,' replied the captain, 'for your sake.'

—

Back on the hill, Matilda looked up at William with no hint of fear.

'*You listen to me*,' hissed the duke. 'I may not be a competent strategist when it comes to matters of the heart, but whether you like it or not, I am the Duke of Normandy, and my name is destined to be written into the history books. I thought that you were the person to share that destiny with me, but it seems

I may be mistaken. Stay here, and you will end up as the wife of a petty lord, destined to be forgotten within generations, but choose me, and I swear we will forge paths yet undreamed of. What is it to be, Matilda – a future of insignificance, or the wife of a man who is going to change the world?'

For a few seconds, they both stared at each other as their anger subsided.

'Let me up,' she said eventually. Realising he had gone too far, William released his grip on her throat and got to his feet.

'No other man alive would have dared do that to me and hope to live,' said Matilda, scrambling to her feet. 'You are lucky that your men outnumber ours.'

'Perhaps that in itself tells you the sort of man I am,' said William. 'But I play no games here, Matilda of Flanders, I have come for an answer. I will give you one more chance – will you be my bride, or will you not?'

–

Back amongst the group by the river, everyone stared at the two people on the knoll, not knowing what they were saying to each other. Inside, Baldwin was seething, but at least he could see that his daughter was not hurt despite the rough treatment she had received at the hands of William. Finally, the young woman turned away from the duke and started leading her horse back down the slope.

Alan the Red looked towards William and, receiving a signal in return, turned to his men.

'Stand down and withdraw,' he shouted, 'our work here is done.'

William's men turned their horses and headed back the way they had come. Once they had gone, Adela rode up to join her husband.

'Never have I been so afraid,' she said quietly, 'or so insulted. We cannot let him get away with this.'

'As soon as we get back,' said Baldwin, 'I will muster the cavalry and ride after him. His head will be atop a pike before the sun sets tomorrow.'

'Good,' said Adela, 'for I will be the first in line to spit upon it.' With a kick of her heels, she rode forward to meet her approaching daughter, closely followed by her husband.

'Matilda,' she said, taking the reins of her daughter's horse, 'did he hurt you?'

'I was surprised, more than hurt,' said Matilda, 'for no man has ever treated me so.'

'Nor should they,' said Baldwin, 'but fret not, he will soon be back, though this time in a cage of iron dragged behind two bulls.'

'And how do you intend to do that?' asked Matilda.

'I will muster the city cavalry,' said Baldwin. 'Duke or not, I will not have him treat my family so.'

'I wouldn't bother mustering the horsemen,' said Matilda, 'for he will be back soon enough of his own free will.'

'What do you mean?' asked her mother.

'Because,' said Matilda, 'William the Bastard intends to ask Father for my hand in marriage.'

'*What?*' gasped her mother. 'You cannot be serious.'

'Oh, I am deadly serious,' said Matilda, 'he will be back within days.'

'And what are your thoughts on this?'

'I am agreeable,' said Matilda, 'for I have nursed the idea for many weeks, and my letter was no more than a ruse that worked perfectly. I already knew about his reputation, but such things are often exaggerated, so I decided to find out the truth of the matter.'

'So you sent an insulting letter?' asked Baldwin.

'I did,' said Matilda, 'and the outcome was better than I had expected. Not only is he handsome of face, but he is also more of a man than any I have ever met. He is the one, Mother – I am going to marry the Duke of Normandy.'

Chapter Seventeen

The Port of Dartmouth, March, AD 1049

Sweyn's ship lay at anchor in the deepest part of the river. None of the men had been given shore leave as they had only left Hampton two days earlier and there were still many tasks to do on board. Sweyn himself had been ashore to meet a man able to supply him with more men-at-arms but had now returned while he awaited his contact to come back to him.

For the past two days there had been little time to talk with Beorn, but now they were waiting, Sweyn decided to take the opportunity to broach the subject they both knew needed to be discussed.

'Beorn,' he called from a doorway, 'I have brought cheese and wine from ashore. Perhaps you will join me to do both some justice.'

Beorn turned around from his position at the stern and looked at his cousin. Both had been very close since childhood, more brothers than cousins, but lately, Sweyn's actions had given him great cause for concern, and he knew he was quickly approaching the point where he could no longer give the son of Godwin his unconditional support.

'Of course,' he replied, 'give me a moment.'

Sweyn retreated into his tiny cabin and sat at the table, pouring wine into two wooden tankards in anticipation. Moments later, Beorn joined him and threw his cloak onto the bed before sitting on the only other chair in the room.

'It looks good,' Beorn said, seeing the cheese.

'I've some venison too,' said Sweyn, lifting a cloth from a platter. 'It's cold but was cooked only this morning. Please, help yourself.'

'Quite a feast,' said Beorn, reaching over for one of the two knives on the plate. He cut a chunk of cheese from the wheel and a thick slice of venison, adding them both to the wooden bowl before him.

'Oh,' said Sweyn, 'I forgot.' He reached to one side and retrieved a loaf of bread, pushing it between the plates to fill the small table. Beorn tore off a chunk and added it to his bowl.

'So,' Beorn said eventually, placing a slice of cheese on a piece of bread, 'did your shore visit go well?'

'It did,' said Sweyn, 'but the cargo I requested will not be here before dawn, so we face another night at anchor.'

'I take it that, by cargo, you mean fighting men?' asked Beorn.

'I do,' said Sweyn. 'Forgive me, cousin, I am used to hiding the true meaning of my words, and old habits die hard. I have requested twenty more men-at-arms, experienced soldiers with loyalty only to those who pay the purse.'

'Mercenaries?' said Beorn.

'You could call them that,' said Sweyn, 'but they are no different to huscarls in that respect.'

'Why would you want so many men?' asked Beorn. 'You do not even know yet whether the king will hear your petition.'

'Just being cautious,' said Sweyn. 'I have notified others who are loyal to me, and they are on their way to London as we speak. By the time I face Edward, I will have a strong force at my command, albeit hidden outside the city.'

'Sweyn,' said Beorn, 'you are heading down a dangerous path. You cannot threaten the king with just a few hundred men – he has the resources of an entire country at his back.'

'As I said to you in Hampton,' Sweyn responded, 'I do not need a full-strength army to sway the king's mind, just the support of my family. The House of Godwin is respected across the land, and if we called our thegns and vassals to muster, they would more than match any force Edward could raise.'

He topped up both mugs with wine as his cousin stared at him, his face lined with concern.

'What?' said Sweyn, seeing his reaction. 'Do you disagree?'

'With regards to numbers, no,' said Beorn, 'but your strategy and ambition fill me with dread.'

'Why?' asked Sweyn. 'With your support, and that of Harold, my father would have no other option but to support me, else he risks tearing apart the precious family he continually preaches about.'

'You heard what Harold said,' replied Beorn, 'he will not support you.'

'He will come round,' said Sweyn, 'especially when you pave the way and we arrive in Bosham as brothers-in-arms.'

'I have not made that commitment yet,' said Beorn, 'as you well know.'

'Yes, but you will, right? I mean, why else would you have agreed to sail with me if not to consider the option?'

'Consideration is one thing,' said Beorn, 'agreement is something else completely.'

'Listen to me,' said Sweyn, 'everyone knows that our so-called king considers himself more Norman than English. The fact that he sits on the throne is a travesty in itself. This may be an opportunity to right that wrong.'

'*What?*' gasped Beorn. '*You intend to challenge the king for the throne of England?*'

'No,' snapped Sweyn, growing frustrated, 'you are not listening to me. All I want is my titles and lands to be reinstated, and to do that, I need the support of all the family. But if the king refuses to see sense, there may be other options...'

'I don't know, Sweyn,' said Beorn, 'it sounds as if all this is getting out of hand.'

'I thought you of all people would understand,' said Sweyn, his voice lowering. 'I have done many favours for you in the past, why will you not support me now? All I ask is that you pledge your backing and assure the king that you are happy to return everything you gained from my banishment back into my hands. Once you have committed, everyone else will follow.'

Beorn set his wine on the table and pushed it away from him.

'I cannot do it, Sweyn,' he said. 'Supporting you is one thing, but to threaten the Crown itself is something else altogether.'

Both men stared at each other without speaking. Eventually, a smile appeared on Sweyn's face and he spoke again.

'Worry not,' he said. 'Perhaps I have been unclear.' He stood up and headed for the door. 'There is something I want you to see.'

Both men headed out onto the deck and descended a ladder into the hold. Hammocks hung from the structural timbers in any space available; the air stank of salt, sweat and urine.

'Over here,' Sweyn said, walking towards an open door in one of the bulkheads. 'Take a look inside,' he said, 'perhaps this will change your mind.'

Beorn stared at Sweyn but eventually sidled past his cousin to peer inside the small room. It was nothing more than a tiny storage space; it was very dark inside, a barred grille in the door affording the only light.

'It's empty,' he said, leaning further in to check the corners.

'Not any more,' snarled Sweyn before pushing his cousin headlong into the opposite wall. Beorn fell to the floor, and by the time he got back to his feet, the door had already been slammed shut and locked.

'Sweyn!' he shouted. 'What do you think you are doing? Open this door.'

'Not until you have had time to reconsider your position,' said Sweyn, standing with his back against the cell's outer wall. 'A few nights' peace and quiet should help you come to your senses.'

'Don't be an idiot, Sweyn,' shouted Beorn, grabbing the iron grille. 'This is helping nobody.'

'Least of all you, cousin,' said Sweyn. 'Think about what we discussed, and when you have had a change of heart, we will talk again, perhaps.' He walked away from the cell but found his way barred by his huscarl, Owen of Hereford.

'What are you doing, my lord?'

'He needs time to think,' said Sweyn. 'Make sure that door remains locked and give him only water until I say so. Hunger may sharpen his thinking.' He pushed past Owen and up the ladder to the deck. Owen followed him into his cabin and closed the door behind them.

'My lord,' he said, 'you are making a grave mistake. When you release him, and the king finds out you kidnapped an earl, not even your father will be able to help.'

'On the contrary,' said Sweyn, staring out of his cabin's window, 'he is just confused and does not know his own mind. A few days' contemplation and he will realise that I am right.'

'Did the abbess finally realise you were right?' asked Owen.

Sweyn spun around and stared at the huscarl.

'Be careful, Owen,' he said, his voice low and menacing, 'there is a fine line between advice and enmity. You would not want me to confuse the two.'

'All I am saying,' said Owen in a placatory tone, 'is that often you are quick to act without thought of consequence. The abbess is one example, and look where that got you. We now have a similar situation with Deorn Estrithson, and no matter what he says from this point on, you will never be sure whether he speaks the truth or only says what he thinks you want to hear in order to secure his release. When we get to Bosham, he could tell Godwin everything.'

Sweyn stared at the huscarl, realising he was right, but there was no way he could back down now.

'I have listened to your advice,' he said eventually, 'and will give it some thought. But whatever happens, make sure he is not released from that cell. Now be gone, I will call you when I need you.'

'As you wish, my lord,' said Owen, leaving Sweyn Godwinson to finish the flask of wine alone.

–

Two days later, Beorn Estrithson lay curled beneath a blanket in his pitch-dark cell, hungry and cold. Despite his pleas, nobody had come to release him, and he had only received water to drink. For the past few hours, he had been aware that the ship was at sea, but he had no idea where they were going. Frustrated, he sat up and leaned against the wall, pulling the blanket tighter around his shoulders. For the next hour or so, the ship continued to sway until eventually, to his surprise, he heard the anchor being dropped. He got to his feet and peered out of the grille. A few minutes later, four men appeared and stood before the door.

'Step back,' said one, 'against the wall.'

Beorn did as requested, and as the door opened, the four men rushed in to overpower him. Once on the floor, they tied his hands behind his back and pulled him to his feet.

'What is all this about?' asked Beorn. 'Where are you taking me?'

'Shut your mouth,' said one, 'or you will share the fate of the other three.'

'What do you mean?' asked Beorn as he was dragged from the cell. 'What have you done with my men?'

Nobody answered, and they dragged him up onto the deck. Night was falling fast but, despite the gloom, Beorn could see they were not out at sea but further up the river. He turned to one of the guards, but before he could say anything, they grabbed hold of him and threw him over the side.

Beorn plunged into the freezing water, kicking wildly, but just as he thought he was about to drown, a hand reached down and pulled him, gasping, to the surface.

'Pull him out,' said a voice, as more hands reached down to drag him into a rowing boat.

'He's in,' said a voice as Beorn landed in the bottom with a thump. 'Set off.'

The boat started moving, but Beorn lay still, hardly willing to breathe such was his fear. A few minutes later, the boat hit the bank, and one of the men kicked him in the ribs.

'Get up,' he said, 'or I'll throw you in again.'

Beorn stumbled to his feet, shivering violently in the cold evening air.

'Where are you taking me?' he mumbled.

'You'll find out soon enough,' said the voice, 'now move.'

Beorn climbed up the bank as best he could and followed the men inland through the trees. After walking for a few hundred paces, he found himself standing in a clearing before Sweyn Godwinson and Owen of Hereford.

'Leave us,' said Sweyn.

After throwing him to the ground, the rest of the men returned to the boat.

'What is all this?' said Beorn, scrambling to his knees. 'Cut me free, Sweyn, or I swear I will see you hanged from the highest tree in England.'

'That disappoints me so much,' said Sweyn with a sigh. 'You see, I brought you here in the hope you would have changed your mind.'

'Not even you are that stupid, Sweyn,' said Beorn. 'After the way you have treated me, how could you ever have imagined that I would agree to your demands?'

'To be honest,' said Sweyn, 'it was a stretched hope, but I thought that might have persuaded you.' He nodded towards an area of ground a little way off. Beorn peered into the darkness, eventually making out what Sweyn was referring to – a mound of loose earth on the far side of a freshly dug grave. For a few moments, he just stared in silence as the realisation sank in, before finally turning back to face his cousin.

'No,' he said, shaking his head, 'you would not do that, Sweyn, not to me. I am family.'

'And that is exactly what I have been saying these past few days,' said Sweyn, 'but still you kept on rejecting my argument.'

'You have made your point,' said Beorn, 'now cut me free.'

'Alas, I cannot,' said Sweyn, walking round behind him. 'You see, as my good friend here said a few days ago, no matter what you promise now, I can never be confident that you will not reveal to the king what has happened to you since leaving Hampton.'

'Sweyn,' said Beorn, his voice shaking, 'don't do this. I swear I will keep my mouth shut. Cut me loose, and we will never talk of these things again. I'll give you my lands, my earldom, anything you want, just let me live.'

'It's too late, Beorn,' said Sweyn, drawing a knife from his belt, 'you had your chance.' He grabbed Beorn's hair and, yanking his head back, plunged the blade deep into his cousin's throat.

—

A week later, Sweyn and Owen walked into the courtyard at Bosham Manor, having arrived from Dartmouth a few hours earlier.

'Sweyn,' said Godwin, walking over to greet his son, 'it is good to see you again.'

'It is good to be here,' said Sweyn, 'though my arrival has put you in a difficult position.'

'Let us not worry about that for the moment,' said Godwin, 'I'm just happy you are safe and well. Mother can't wait to see you.'

'Ah,' said Sweyn, 'about Mother. I have to say I am ashamed about my outburst before I left for Flanders. I was angry and knew not what I was saying.'

'It is in the past and warrants no discussion,' said Godwin. 'You are here now, and that is all that matters.' He looked over Sweyn's shoulder. 'Where is Beorn? I was told he sailed with you.'

'Indeed he did,' said Sweyn, 'and we spent some quality time together while aboard my ship. It was good to catch up, and we came to a mutually beneficial agreement, so much so that there was no longer any need for him to stay aboard. He left the ship in Dartmouth.'

'To what end?' asked Godwin.

'I'm not sure,' said Sweyn. 'He said only that he had business to attend to and left with his men the day before we weighed anchor.'

'It matters not,' said Godwin with a shrug, 'I'm sure we will see him soon enough.'

'Is Harold here?' asked Sweyn.

'He was, but left for East Anglia yesterday. Come, there is a mountain of food and a lake of ale waiting for your attention. Welcome home, son, and whatever it is you have come to do, you can be sure of my support.'

'I hope so, Father,' said Sweyn, slapping Godwin on the shoulder. 'It is good to be back.'

Chapter Eighteen

Bosham, May, AD 1049

Godwin of Wessex stood on a hill above the harbour, staring down at the comings and goings of the many ships that plied their trade out of Bosham. Behind him, down in the lee of the hill and sheltered from the worst of the winter storms, lay Bosham Manor, the place that made him feel safe and warm whenever the trials and tribulations of his station became a difficult burden to bear. Now was such a time, for although matters of state were relatively calm, he had just received some terrible news, and his conscience was tearing him apart as to what to do.

Further along the hill stood two men holding the reins of their horses, but it was not the two men that the earl was waiting for – it was his eldest son, Sweyn.

Sweyn had been staying at Bosham since arriving two months earlier, spending most of his time sailing up and down the coast trading on behalf of Godwin. Technically he was still exiled, but as he was spending most of his time at sea, Godwin reckoned it was a minor transgression, and he fully intended to talk to the king about his son's return at the earliest opportunity. But with his nephew still missing, it was something that would have to wait. Now, at long last, he was in possession of news that he could keep to himself no longer.

'Father,' called Sweyn, climbing the hill, 'you sent for me.'

'Aye, I did,' said Godwin as his son neared. 'I expected you yesterday.'

'I missed the tide in Bristol,' said Sweyn, 'but made good time once we finally made sail.'

'Did you collect the debt from the Bishop of Gloucester?' asked Godwin.

'I did,' said Sweyn, holding up a satchel, 'though it was like trying to get a hungry cat to give up a mouse.'

'He is well known for his reluctance to pay,' said Godwin, taking the purse and peering inside.

'It's all there,' said Sweyn, 'every coin.'

'I'm sure it is,' said Godwin, 'you have done well.' He paused for a moment, not sure how to continue. 'Sweyn—' he said eventually, but before he could continue, his son interrupted.

'Father, have you thought more on taking my petition to Edward?'

'I have not,' said Godwin. 'I have had other things on my mind.'

Sweyn cursed and looked out to sea. 'I am growing frustrated, Father,' he said. 'These past few months, I have done everything you requested of me, from trading pigs to catching criminals. All this I have done without complaint, based on the promise that you would argue my case, but again you stall. Are you going to do this, or should I make my own presentation?'

'You will do no such thing,' said Godwin, an edge to his voice, 'for there are things we must discuss. Mainly, the disappearance of Beorn.'

'Oh, not again,' sighed Sweyn. 'I have already told you a hundred times – he left my ship in Dartmouth saying he had business to attend to elsewhere. That is all I know, and no matter how often you ask me the same questions, you will get the same answers. I do not know where he is.'

Godwin stared at his son before slowly turning to look at the two men waiting a few hundred paces distant.

'Do you know those men?' he asked eventually.

'One looks familiar,' replied Sweyn, 'but the other, no. I have never seen him before.'

'The one on the right is a priest,' said Godwin. 'You probably don't know him, but the other served on one of your ships. His name is Isaac, and he enlisted in Flanders before you returned to England.'

'That's where I must have seen him,' said Sweyn. 'What's all this about?'

'Isaac enlisted with his brother, Jacob,' said Godwin, 'but alas, Jacob died a few days ago, stricken down by the fever.'

'I am sorry to hear that,' said Sweyn, 'I will ensure his family gets some money.'

'They do not want money, Sweyn,' said Godwin, 'for I have already gifted a purse. What they *do* want, however, is absolution from the Church.'

'You have lost me,' sighed Sweyn, growing frustrated. 'Tell me what this is about, Father, for I have more important things to do.'

'Before Jacob died,' said Godwin, 'Isaac sent for the priest to hear his brother's confession. When the priest arrived, Isaac heard his brother say that a few months ago, while he was serving on your ship in Dartmouth, he was tasked with rowing a boat to the shore, a boat carrying a bound man who had been cast overboard from the ship. Once there, he was told to wait, but when he finally returned to the vessel, it was with a different passenger. This passenger was also soaked, though not with river water – he was covered with blood.'

Sweyn stared at his father, his heart racing. His own men were sworn to secrecy and knew the consequences of treachery, but in his rush to recruit extra men-at-arms, it had become necessary to use mercenaries, men whose character he did not know.

'What are you insinuating, Father?' said Sweyn. 'Are you saying someone was murdered?'

'Possibly,' said Godwin. 'Jacob certainly thought so. As does his brother, for Jacob's dying words to his priest were to beg forgiveness for his part in whatever happened that night.'

'I do not know what you are talking about,' said Sweyn. 'You say the man had the fever, so he could have been hallucinating for all we know. What has this to do with me?'

'Well, his confession did not end there,' said Godwin, 'for he named the blood-sodden man.' He paused, meeting his son's stare. 'He named you, Sweyn. He swore that whoever was killed, it was your hand that wielded the knife.'

Sweyn stared at Godwin, knowing he had to keep his wits about him. If his father believed the mercenary, then there was no way he would support his petition to the king.

'Father,' he said, 'I do not know what is going on here, but it seems to me that someone is trying to frame me for a murder I know nothing about. What is more worrying is that you seem to be giving these accusations credence. Surely you would believe your own son's word over that of a dead mercenary?'

'I would,' said Godwin, 'but nevertheless, I had to investigate the accusation and sent Harold down to Dartmouth with the dead man's brother to find the victim. It took two days, but eventually, they found the grave on the banks of the river. Inside was the corpse of a man with his throat cut.' He stared at Sweyn, his eyes cold. 'It was your cousin, Sweyn,' he said, 'the body was that of Beorn Estrithson, murdered in cold blood.'

'Look,' said Sweyn eventually, 'even if it is Beorn—'

'*It is*,' interrupted Godwin, 'for I have seen the body myself. Harold brought him back yesterday. Beorn currently lies at peace within our chapel and is being prepared for a proper Christian burial as soon as it can be arranged.'

'Even so,' said Sweyn, 'it could not have been me, for I stayed on the ship the full time we were in Dartmouth. If this deed did take place, then it was by the hand of someone else. All you have are the second-hand words of a dead man and a brother who is probably just seeking a purse. Do you really expect anyone to believe such men over the word of an earl?'

'You are no longer an earl,' said Godwin, 'let us not forget that. But I agree, there is probably no way of ever knowing for sure who wielded the blade. Yet something does not make sense, Sweyn. When did you last see your cousin?'

'I have already told you,' said Sweyn, 'we finished a meal together before saying our goodbyes. Once done, he and his men left the ship and rode towards Dartmouth town.'

'On their horses?'

'Yes, on their horses,' said Sweyn, 'why do you ask such a stupid question?'

Godwin turned to look towards the two men again.

'See anything you recognise?' he asked.

'They are not known to me,' said Sweyn. 'Where are you going with this?'

'What about the horses,' asked Godwin, 'do you recognise any of them? What about the bay? Is it familiar to you?'

'It is not. Why, should it be?'

'Perhaps not, but it is to me, for it was a gift from me to Beorn. It was one of my favourites, and I would recognise it anywhere.'

'So what?' said Sweyn. 'After Beorn was killed, who knows where it ended up?'

'It didn't *end up* anywhere,' said Godwin, 'and that is the problem. That horse was in the stables down in the docks. It has been there, along with several others, since you returned from Dartmouth. You said that Beorn rode away that night, but if he did, it was on a different horse, and I can assure you that was one thing he would never have done.'

'You don't know that,' said Sweyn, 'there could have been a hundred reasons why he took a different horse.'

Godwin turned his gaze out to sea, his heart aching at his son's desperate attempts to cover up his involvement.

'I do not know where I went wrong with you, Sweyn,' he said eventually. 'What happened that was so bad that, despite your life of privilege, you see fit to continually bring trouble to our house?'

'Are you saying you do not believe me?' asked Sweyn.

'*Stop!*' shouted Godwin, turning back to his son. 'I have heard enough. Every word that comes from your mouth is a lie, and I grow tired of it. Heaven knows I have given you the benefit of the doubt on many occasions, but this time you have gone too far.'

Sweyn returned the stare, knowing that it was pointless continuing the lie.

'So what if I did kill him?' he snarled, taking a step closer to his father. 'The man stole my lands and threatened to stand against me. In my eyes, that makes him my enemy. No, *our* enemy. Now there is one less to worry about when we call our men to arms.'

'Beorn was your friend, Sweyn, your cousin. How could you do it?'

'Friends stand together,' said Sweyn, 'no matter the circumstances, and when I stand before the king, you can rest assured that I will have many friends within an hour's ride of London to aid us.'

'There is not going to be an audience with the king,' said Godwin, 'nor will you have an army at your side.'

'You are going to abandon me?' gasped Sweyn. 'I should have known.'

'I am not abandoning you, Sweyn, I am trying to help you.'

'How?'

'By letting you sail as a free man back to Flanders instead of arresting you for murder.'

Sweyn shook his head. Inside, he was furious.

'No,' he said eventually, 'that title and the estates are mine by right, and I will get them back, by force if necessary.'

'You do not have the means for such a thing,' said Godwin. 'Neither I, nor any of your brothers, will support you in this matter. You are alone.'

'I still have my paid men-at-arms,' said Sweyn, 'and once I stand up to Edward, it is only a matter of time before men flock to my banner. This is England, Father, not Normandy.'

'You do not have any men, Sweyn,' said Godwin. 'Look down to the harbour. Of the eight ships you came with, only two remain; the others have returned to Flanders.'

Sweyn stared at the few ships still left at anchor. His father was right – the majority of his fleet was missing.

'You paid them off,' he growled. 'You betrayed your own family in support of the false king.'

'Yes, I paid them off,' said Godwin, 'though in truth, they did not need much convincing. The crews were already uneasy after what you did at Dartmouth and were on the verge of leaving you anyway. My intervention made their decision easier.'

'*What sort of man are you?*' shouted Sweyn.

'*One that loves you,*' shouted Godwin, '*and has no wish to see you beheaded.* You have to step back from this, Sweyn. The chances of a pardon were slim enough as it was, but now you are implicated in the murder of an earl, the probability is zero.'

'Neither the king nor anybody else can ever prove it had anything to do with me,' said Sweyn.

'Whether you did or not, the fact is that he was last seen with you, and we have a man who will swear that his brother named you as the perpetrator. You have to face facts, Sweyn, the rumours are already out there, and it is only a matter of time before they reach the ears of the king. There is nothing you can do other than leave here while you still can.'

'You want me to leave Bosham?' asked Sweyn.

'Not just Bosham, but England,' said Godwin. 'Go back to Flanders and wait until all this dies down.'

'I'm not going back,' said Sweyn. 'I came here to reclaim my estates, and that is what I am going to do.'

'*With what?*' shouted Godwin. 'You have no men, no money and no lands. If you stay here, you will be charged with murder and hanged by the king. Do what is sensible and go back to Flanders. When tempers have cooled, I will send for you. You are still a young man, Sweyn, time is on your side.'

Once again, Sweyn fell silent. His father was right – without men and money, his ambitions were dead in the water.

'I can't stay over there,' he said, his temper easing. 'I am exiled from Denmark and unwelcome in Flanders.'

'We have friends there,' said Godwin. 'I will furnish you with a letter of introduction, and you can stay with them. It won't be for long, I swear. But you can't stay here, Sweyn, not while Beorn's murder goes unsolved.'

'So be it,' said Sweyn. 'I'll sail at first light tomorrow.'

'No,' said Godwin, 'you will go on tonight's high tide. There is no time, Sweyn – you have to get out of England now.'

–

The following morning Godwin knelt at the fire, stacking logs into the flames. Despite the weather getting better, the night had been particularly cold, and he needed some extra warmth, not least to pull him from his sombre mood.

'Has he gone?' asked a voice. Godwin looked over his shoulder to see Harold standing in the doorway.

'Aye, he has,' said Godwin, getting to his feet. 'He sailed last night.' He turned to face Harold. 'I thought you would have been there to see him go. Where were you last night?'

'I stayed in a tavern in the village,' said Harold, walking over to stand at the fire. 'If I had come here, you would have two murdering sons to worry about.'

'I know you are upset, Harold,' said Godwin, 'as am I, but never forget that he is your brother.'

'Is he?' asked Harold. 'Because he seemed to denounce you at every opportunity. How could you be so loyal to someone who claims to have been fathered by another.'

'Sweyn is your brother,' said Godwin, 'despite what he says. Your mother has sworn to me that she never lay with Cnut, or any other man for that matter, and that is good enough for me.'

'I believe her,' said Harold, 'yet he seems so convinced otherwise it tricks his mind into ideas of grandeur. If he truly believes such a thing, then it is only a small step to believing he has a claim to the throne himself, and that way lies only bloodshed.'

'Aye,' said Godwin. 'But now he has gone, it is time to move on. How long are you staying?'

'My mind has been filled with thoughts of Sweyn for far too long,' said Harold, 'and my own estates suffer because of it. I am riding back this very day and have just come to say goodbye.'

'I understand,' said Godwin. He paused for a moment, judging how his next words might be received. 'These are difficult times, Harold, but do not judge your brother too harshly. He is a troubled young man and needs our support, now more than ever.'

'He is not a troubled young man, Father,' said Harold, 'he is a rapist and a murderer, and the sooner you accept that fact, the better.'

Godwin stared at Harold for a moment before reaching out and clapping his son on the shoulder. 'I understand your frustration, Harold,' he said, 'and I swear I will give the situation much thought.'

'Stay safe, Father,' said Harold. 'I will see you again in a few months.'

He turned to leave the hall, and an hour or so later, after saying his goodbyes to Gytha and the rest of the family, Harold left Bosham to return to East Anglia.

Part Three

Chapter Nineteen

Godwin of Wessex rushed along a corridor of Havering Palace, painfully aware that he was late for the audience King Edward had called only the day before. He pushed past the guards at the door and entered the hall; it was already full of men sitting in a semicircle facing the king and queen.

'Ah,' said Bishop Robert from beside Edward, 'I see you have arrived. How very kind of you to make an effort, Earl Godwin.'

Godwin ignored the sarcasm and took his seat near the king's dais.

'Is that everyone?' asked Edward.

'Bishop Ealdred of Worcester is still to arrive,' said Robert, 'but he has authorised me to speak in his absence. Apparently, he has some very important business and will be here as soon as he can.'

'Then let us begin,' said the king, before looking around the gathered audience. Amongst them were Earls Harold and Godwin representing East Anglia and Wessex, respectively, Ralph of Mantes, who had been gifted Beorn Estrithson's lands after he had been murdered, Earl Siward of Northumbria and the equally powerful Earl Leofric of Mercia. The latter two, in particular, were considered strong supporters of Edward, and their opinions carried great weight at court.

As well as the nobles, the gathering also included the Bishop of London, Robert of Jumièges, and the Bishop of Winchester and Elmham, Stigand of Norwich. Two monks from Canterbury were also at the rear. It was a powerful gathering, and

Godwin knew there were to be important decisions made in that room.

'Gentlemen,' announced the king, 'I am grateful for your attendance at such short notice, so I will not keep you long. A few days ago, we received news that the Most Reverend Archbishop, Eadsige of Canterbury, passed into God's care after many years of ill health. His passing gives me particular grief as it was his hands that placed the crown of England upon my head at my coronation. We give thanks to God for his glorious service to both Church and country.'

'Amen,' said the congregation quietly, crossing themselves in respect.

'The reason I have summoned you here,' said the king, 'is to witness the nomination of his successor. The man who is nominated today will not yet be formally approved, as first we have to lay our dear departed brother to rest. However, it is important to lay the foundations of his archbishopric in an accountable manner in case of objection. It is customary that the monks of the Cathedral Chapter in Canterbury propose a successor, and I am pleased to say that, having already carried out that task, they have sent two representatives to share the outcome.' He looked up at the monks at the end of the room. 'Brother Aelwyn, perhaps you would step forward.'

One of the monks walked into the semicircle of men and, after bowing to the king, produced a sealed parchment from his robe.

'Your grace,' he began, 'my lords and valued friends. After much debate and consideration, the Cathedral Chapter is humbled to bring our recommendation to you. The person named within this document is a truly pious and humble man, yet possesses great spiritual strength and knowledge, attributes that will be essential as he supports the king in his rule of our country in God's name.' He stepped forward and gave the king the document.

Edward ripped it open and stared at the name within for a moment, slightly surprised at the choice.

'The nominee,' Edward said, looking up, 'is Brother Æthelric of Christ's Church Priory.'

A murmur of recognition spread around the room. Many had already anticipated the choice, and nobody had any major challenges. Nods of quiet agreement were shared, and Godwin glanced towards Bishop Stigand, remembering his recommendation to sponsor the monk a few years earlier, advice that now had the potential to reap huge dividends.

'Am I to understand that there are no objections?' asked the king.

'I have one observation,' said Bishop Robert, whose calm exterior belied the fury he was feeling inside. 'Brother Æthelric is indeed a wonderful choice, and I have no doubt that he will serve the office well, but could it be perceived that the appointment of someone who is the cousin of one of our esteemed earls may be a political move, rather than a religious one?'

'Your grace,' said the monk, 'I promise you that no such discussion ever took place in our considerations. Brother Æthelric's name constantly came out as more than worthy in every meeting, and each vote was carried out in private with no outside influence.'

'I'm sure the process was more than honest,' said the bishop, 'I am just voicing my concerns within these four walls so we can be prepared for questions should they arise.' He turned to face Godwin. 'What say you, Earl Godwin? Æthelric is your cousin, is he not?'

'He is,' said Godwin, 'but I have had no dealings with him since he was a child.'

'Yet you sponsor the priory?'

'I sponsor many priories, your grace,' said Godwin. 'I am the Earl of Wessex – it is expected of me.'

'Of course,' said Robert, 'I was just clarifying your involvement for the sake of all present. There is no insinuation of any impropriety.'

'I understand,' said Godwin, 'but as I said, I have had nothing to do with him personally.' He fell silent, fully aware that though

Bishop Robert had publicly stated otherwise, the carefully crafted question had ensured that the seeds of suspicion were now planted in the minds of everyone in the room.

'Thank you, Bishop Robert,' said the king. 'Is there anything else?'

'Not from me, your grace,' replied the bishop.

'Good. In that case, let us disperse and make our considerations. In a few weeks, we will reconvene, but from what I have heard today, I see no reason why the recommendation from the Cathedral Chapter of Canterbury should not be carried out.' He stood up and walked from the room, leaving all the other attendees talking amongst themselves.

Godwin approached Bishop Stigand, talking quietly so as not to be overheard.

'Hello, your grace,' he said. 'We haven't seen you for a while at Bosham.'

'My duties at Winchester keep me busy,' said Stigand. 'How are you and your family?'

'As well as can be expected,' he replied. He glanced around the room. 'I see that your recommendation to sponsor Brother Æthelric was indeed fortuitous.'

'I know not what you mean,' said Stigand. 'I recommend such investments to many people without favour.'

'I understand,' said Godwin, before looking over to see Bishop Robert staring at them with barely concealed disdain. 'He doesn't seem happy.'

'He covets the position of archbishop for himself.'

'There isn't a single man in this room who would support such a move,' said Godwin.

'Perhaps, but let us not forget, the king has the final word in this matter. Æthelric is not Archbishop yet.' As they talked, a servant walked into the hall and approached Bishop Stigand.

'Your grace,' he said, 'the king has asked that you and the Bishop of London join him in his chambers.'

'Of course,' said Stigand, turning back to Godwin. 'Keep your wits about you, Godwin,' he said quietly, 'there are murmurings of unease about you and your family throughout the halls of power.' Without further explanation, he turned away and followed the servant out of the room.

–

The following morning, at his family's London home of Southwark, Godwin was once again summoned to the court of King Edward.

'What do you think he wants?' asked Harold, holding his father's horse as the earl mounted.

'I have no idea,' said Godwin, 'but we'll find out soon enough.'

'What do you think Bishop Stigand meant when he told you to be careful yesterday?'

'Again, I am devoid of answers,' said Godwin, 'though I have noticed Earls Siward and Leofric seem to spend a lot of time at court recently. Perhaps they are the ones spreading discord.'

'I disagree,' said Harold, 'I think the source is the Bishop of London himself. His disdain for our family is known to all.'

'Whichever it is,' said Godwin, 'we will stay alert. Now, I have to go but will stay here tonight before leaving for Bosham in the morning.' He kicked in his heels and walked his horse out of the courtyard.

–

In Havering Palace, the king was already in one of the antechambers, along with Bishops Stigand and Robert. Godwin could see that Stigand was troubled, putting him immediately on edge. He bowed his head towards Edward.

'My king,' he said, 'you sent for me?'

'I did,' said Edward. 'After I left council yesterday, I immediately found out that Bishop Ealdred of Worcester was waiting for me, seeking an urgent audience.'

'I thought he would have been at the confirmation audience,' said Godwin.

'As did I,' said the king, 'but have since found out that he had important news that could not be shared in public. At least, not yet.'

'And this news is?' asked Godwin.

'I think you should hear from him yourself,' said Edward, before nodding towards one of the servants to open a side door. Seconds later, the Bishop of Worcester walked in, acknowledging the king with a low bow.

'Bishop Ealdred,' said the king, 'please tell Earl Godwin where you have been these past few weeks.'

'I have been to Rome,' said the bishop, 'on a pilgrimage to see the Pope.'

Godwin nodded with respect; any journey of such a length was to be commended.

'And did you attend the Holy Father?' asked the king.

'Indeed I did. We discussed many things, but in particular, I sought forgiveness for a young man who has lost his way and seeks redemption in the eyes of the Church.'

'And who is this man?' asked the king, turning to stare at Godwin to judge his reaction.

'The man in question,' said the bishop, 'is Sweyn Godwinson.'

Godwin's heart missed a beat. He had not heard anything from Sweyn in months, so for his name to be brought up in the royal court gave him great cause for concern.

'I am both surprised and grateful,' Godwin said eventually, 'but how did you come about such a decision?'

'I was in Bruges,' said Ealdred, 'and seeking a vessel for my next leg down the west coast of France. My representative came across Sweyn's ship in the harbour and arranged passage. Such a thing is usually expensive, but your son offered it free of charge as he was already going to northern Spain. A most generous gift.'

'Sweyn was aboard?' asked the king.

'He was, and it was during that voyage that he explained the sequence of unfortunate events that led him to his current miserable existence, denied by God, king and country. I was very moved, and in return for his generosity, I promised to raise the situation with the Pope, a conversation that ultimately produced a very satisfactory outcome.'

'What exactly did Sweyn tell you?' asked Stigand.

'I don't think the details are important,' said Bishop Ealdred, 'for does not every man deserve forgiveness in the sight of the Lord?'

'Perhaps,' said Bishop Stigand, 'but to gain representation in front of the Holy Father himself is an amazing outcome. You must have been really impressed by Sweyn.'

'Indeed,' said Ealdred, 'for he is an impressive young man – pious, honest, and most importantly, repentant.'

'Perhaps this is a discussion for another day,' said the king. 'What is important now is the outcome of the audience. What was it?'

'Your grace,' said Ealdred, 'upon hearing Sweyn's wretched tale, the Pope did indeed raise concerns. However, he also said that all men deserved a second chance in the eyes of the Lord and decreed that if Sweyn undertook a pilgrimage to Jerusalem by foot, then he would be absolved of all crimes in the eyes of the Church.'

Godwin swallowed hard. On the one hand, it was good news for his family, but on the other, he had no doubt whatsoever that his son had played down the seriousness of his actions in order to garner favour with the bishop. He looked up at the king, unsurprised to see that Edward was angry.

'Your grace,' Godwin said, 'I do not know what to say. The news is good, is it not?'

'Good for you, perhaps, and certainly good for Sweyn. But I banished your son, remember, only to find out that not only did he return to kill a kinsman but has now sought absolution from the Holy Father himself, a decision that I am bound to honour despite my reservations.'

'Your grace,' said Godwin, 'I knew nothing of his intentions. Perhaps, when he comes back, we can discuss the situation and agree on a mutually beneficial outcome.'

'Oh, there will be no waiting for him to come back,' said the king, 'for he has not yet left. He needs money to pay for his pilgrimage, for apparently, the hardship usually involved in such a journey is not part of his plan.'

'I am at a loss,' said Godwin. 'Do you know how much he wants?'

'Why don't you ask him yourself?' said the king, nodding at the servant again. The door opened, and, to Godwin's shock, his son walked in as if he had not a care in the world.

'Hello, Father,' he said with a grin, 'good to see you again.'

Chapter Twenty

Most of the Godwin family were once again gathered at their London house, ready for the following day's inauguration of Brother Æthelric as Archbishop of Canterbury.

Ever since returning with the Bishop of Worcester, Sweyn had been on his best behaviour, not only because he was keen to reclaim his estates as ordained by the Pope but also because one of the women who had shared his bed years earlier had come forward with a five-year-old son called Hakon, claiming he had been sired by Sweyn. At first, Sweyn had been dubious, but the likeness was overwhelming, and he was soon smitten and more than happy to agree to patronage.

The last few months had been hard, but now the winter was over and the inauguration was upon them, Sweyn also knew it was only a matter of weeks until he was to set out to Jerusalem, a journey that filled him with both dread and excitement.

Harold and his new wife, Edyth Swanneck, had also arrived from East Anglia, having been married *more danico*, the hand-fast tradition favoured by the Danes. As a family, they were comforted after enjoying a peaceful and relatively trouble-free winter.

Those present sat in the hall around a single table. Gytha was quiet, disappointed that others of her family could not attend, but overall the mood was comfortable.

'So, how are you enjoying married life?' Gytha asked, turning to her new daughter-in-law.

'Much as I expected,' said Edyth, sipping on a goblet of wine, 'though Harold is away far more often than I thought.'

'It is a burden of being married to an earl,' sighed Gytha. 'I swear Godwin is at the royal court far more than he is home with me.'

'You are always with me, Gytha Thorkelsdóttir,' said Godwin, 'here in my heart.' He placed his hand over his chest as if to remind her where it was. Everyone laughed at the jest, and even Sweyn looked up from near the fire where he was playing with his son.

'What about you, Gytha,' responded Edyth, 'does life in Bosham sit well with you?'

'Of course,' said Gytha, 'though in summer, when the sun is at its hottest, the smell of the fishing boats is a most unwelcome guest. When it gets too bad, we move to one of the other houses until the weather cools.'

'Do you have many other homes?' asked Edyth.

'A few,' said Gytha, 'as will you as Harold's power and influence increase.' She looked across at Sweyn and Hakon by the fire. 'Are you two going to eat?' she asked.

'Come,' said Sweyn, getting to his feet and picking up his son, 'let us see if we can turn you into a fearless warrior.' He took his place at the table and sat Hakon on his knee, sharing food in a series of joyful games. The boy giggled contentedly, revelling in the attention poured upon him by his father.

'He seems a changed man,' said Harold quietly at his father's side.

'He does,' said Godwin. 'The arrival of the child has softened his heart.'

'Do not be taken in, Father,' said Harold, 'at least not yet. Sweyn has a short attention span, and it will not take much to send him out of control.'

'He will be gone soon enough,' said Godwin. 'Walking to Jerusalem is no mean feat, and by the time he returns, hopefully his spirit will be calmed. Especially with that little one to come home to.'

'I hope you are right, Father,' said Harold, 'I really do, but something tells me he is not a man for changing. When is he going?'

'In a few weeks,' said Godwin. 'I will fund the journey, and he will be accompanied by Owen of Hereford. Apart from that, his only guide and protector will be God himself.'

'Then no wonder he is on his best behaviour,' said Harold, 'for without the Lord's oversight, he is a doomed man, both spiritually and physically. Come, let me fill your tankard, for it is not often this place enjoys such a calmness.'

—

The following morning all the Godwin family made their way to Westminster Abbey, a few leagues away. The ceremony was arranged for mid-morning, and they arrived early, keen not to be late for such an auspicious occasion.

'We have time to kill,' said Godwin, looking around, 'we should seek shelter.'

'My lord,' said one of the many staff on duty in the courtyard, 'the chapel is open, you are welcome to wait in there. I will call you when the doors open to the abbey.'

'Thank you,' said Godwin before leading the family over to one of the few stone buildings on the site.

'The Palace of Westminster is coming on well,' said Sweyn as they walked, looking up at the looming walls of the new building a few hundred paces distant.

'Aye, it is,' said Godwin, 'and despite his many faults, the king is to be congratulated for his ambition. By the time it is finished, it will be worthy of any monarch.' They ducked in through the doors, instantly affected by the peace and quiet inside.

'Sit and be quiet,' said Gytha to the younger members of the family as the adults walked forward to cross themselves at the altar. Once done, they returned to the rear benches, talking quietly amongst themselves.

'I find it strange that a man of your station is denied access to the abbey,' said Gytha to her husband.

'The abbey is still not finished,' said Godwin, 'but I have seen inside. Fret not, the doors will be open soon enough. Besides, it is bound to be warmer in here.'

They waited for just under an hour before the door to the chapel opened, and the same servant who had spoken to them earlier came in.

'My Lord Godwin,' he said, 'your presence has been requested by Bishop Stigand. You are to come immediately.'

Everyone got to their feet, but the servant held up his hands.

'Please,' he said, 'his grace asked for the Earl of Wessex only. The rest of you can wait here.'

'What do you mean?' asked Harold. 'Are we not coming to the ceremony?'

'My lord,' said the servant, 'I am only the bearer of the message. The bishop wants Lord Godwin only.'

'Wait here,' said Godwin, walking to the door. 'I will find out what is going on.'

He followed the servant across the courtyard and through a side door into the newly constructed abbey. Inside, they walked down a corridor and into a side room where Bishop Stigand was pacing the floor, his face contorted with anger.

'Your grace,' said Godwin, 'is something wrong?'

'Shut the door,' said Stigand, turning around, 'lest my curses are witnessed by those who would make merry at my upset.'

Godwin did as he was asked and turned back to face Stigand.

'Your grace,' he said, 'never have I seen you in such a state. What is going on?'

'I'll tell you what is going on,' said Stigand, 'that snake in the grass, Bishop Robert of Jumièges, has snatched the rug from under our feet.'

'What do you mean?' asked Godwin.

'Last night,' said Stigand, 'not only did he manage to convince the king that Brother Æthelric was not suitable for the position of archbishop, but he also succeeded in convincing Edward that there was only one man for the role and that was himself, the Bishop of London.'

'*What?*' gasped Godwin. 'Surely he cannot do that. Tradition dictates that the brothers of Canterbury select the candidate, not the king.'

'That's just it,' said Stigand, 'the process is a tradition only and not enshrined in the laws of the land. It seems that Bishop Robert convinced Edward that he would do a far better job of looking after the Church and the interests of the throne.'

'When did this happen?'

'Late last night. The king issued a proclamation, but I received it only this morning. As of midnight last night, Robert of Jumièges is the new Archbishop of Canterbury.'

'I don't understand,' said Godwin. 'How can this happen by nothing more than a declaration? Surely there must be a consecration?'

'There will be, as soon as Robert comes back from Rome.'

'Why is he going to Rome?'

'To receive his Pallium from the Pope. Once he returns, he will be consecrated by the Church, and all our lives are going to get a whole lot harder.'

'If he returns,' said Godwin.

Stigand stopped walking and stared at the cold look in the earl's eyes.

'Godwin, listen to me,' he said. 'I hate this situation as much as you, but if you are planning to do anything stupid, then wipe such thoughts from your mind. If something happens to Robert while he is away, suspicion will immediately fall upon my head as well as yours. All we can do now is try to make a bad situation as good as it can be.'

'And how do we do that?' asked Godwin.

'I have an idea,' said Stigand, 'one that will go some way to easing the pain, but I cannot instigate it until Robert leaves for Rome.'

'When will that be?'

'In a few days. Take your family home and tell them to act as if the news is welcomed. The last thing we want right now is for anyone to suspect we are less than happy with the situation.'

'And what about this idea of yours?'

'I have to inestigate something,' said Stigand, 'but will come to collect you at Southwark as soon as I am back. Stay there until I return, I will need your support.'

'Of course,' said Godwin.

'Now you should go,' said Stigand, 'but say nothing of this to anyone.'

—

Ten days later, Bishop Stigand and Godwin of Wessex were once more at Havering Palace in the presence of the king. This time Edward was accompanied by Queen Ealdgyth, a specific request made by the bishop when requesting the audience. Both men waited in the corridor until being called in by one of the servants.

'Your graces,' said the bishop, bowing to both, 'thank you for receiving us.'

'On the contrary,' said Ealdgyth with a smile, 'it is always good to see you, isn't that right, Edward?'

'Of course,' said the king, a little less enthusiastically. 'What can I do for you gentlemen? If you have come to voice your opposition to Bishop Robert's appointment, then you are wasting your breath.'

'On the contrary,' said Stigand, glancing across to Godwin at his side, 'we welcome the appointment. Do we not, Earl Godwin?'

'We do indeed,' replied Godwin.

'You surprise me,' said the king, 'for I know there is little love lost between you.'

'Bishop Robert is a holy man,' said Stigand, 'and although the appointment took everyone by surprise, upon reflection, it was an inspired choice, and we give it our full support.'

'And why do you say that?' asked the king, his tone a little lighter.

'As we all know, your grace,' said Stigand, 'before he died, Archbishop Eadsige was a very sick man. His illness laid him up for several years, and despite his best efforts, it has to be said that the abbey suffered from his absence.'

'It had been noted,' said the king.

'Indeed,' said Stigand, 'so the appointment of someone already used to the demands of a bishopric is one that can only produce good results.'

'My thoughts exactly,' said the king, beginning to relax, 'and I appreciate your support. When Robert returns from Rome, I am sure he will also convey his gratitude.'

'I'm sure he will,' said Stigand, 'but that brings me to the reason we are here. While he is in Rome, I feel we are in danger of leaving our people short of spiritual guidance, or at the very least a figurehead to whom the clergy of London can turn for support.'

'What do you mean?' asked the king.

'Well, with Bishop Robert's absence, the positions of both Archbishop of Canterbury and Bishop of London lie empty. This leaves us weak in the eyes of the people, and it could be seen as a void that some may wish to take advantage of.'

Edward nodded as the realisation sank in. 'So are you suggesting that we appoint someone as Bishop of London as soon as we can?'

'I would say it should be done immediately,' said Stigand. 'You have already shown that you are not afraid to act outside of tradition, so why not strike while the iron is still hot?'

'And do you have a suggestion as to who this man would be?' asked the king.

'We do,' said the bishop, 'a man who is pious, loyal and a personal friend of you both.'

'I struggle to call such a man to mind,' said the king, 'who is this candidate?'

'The man whose piety invoked a miracle from St Letard himself, your grace,' said Stigand. 'We strongly recommend that the next Bishop of London is Reverend Father Spearhafoc of Bury St Edmunds.'

Chapter Twenty-one

William the Bastard rode through the gates of his château in Normandy at the head of fifty armed men. His patrol to put down a minor rebellion in a local town had been successful, and the troublemakers were incarcerated until he had the time to decide what to do with them. After he had dismounted and handed over the reins to one of the grooms, he headed inside the building, hungry and tired after the campaign.

'My lord,' said the steward as he entered, 'welcome back.'

'Thank you, Roland,' said William, removing his riding gloves. 'Can you arrange hot water for me to bathe? I stink of the road.'

'Of course,' said Roland, 'but you have a visitor waiting. Shall I tell him to go away?'

'Who is it?'

'Robert of Jumièges, my lord, the Bishop of London.'

'Robert is here?' said William with surprise. 'Did we receive any messages that he was visiting?'

'We did not, my lord,' said Roland. 'Shall I ask him to leave and come back at a more suitable time?'

'Certainly not, the man is always welcome under my roof. Tell him to give me a few minutes, I shall be with him shortly.'

'Of course,' said the servant. Picking up the duke's gloves and cloak, he disappeared into the rear of the chateau.

Fifteen minutes later, William entered the hall and walked over to the bishop, a warm smile upon his face.

'Robert,' he said, 'or should I say, your grace? It is good to see you again.'

'And you,' said Robert. 'It has been a long time.'

'Please, be seated,' said William, 'I have just arranged refreshments to be served. Are you staying in Rouen for a while? Because if so, my house is your house.'

'Alas no,' said Robert. 'Truth be told, I am keen to get back to England as soon as I can, so I need to catch the tide.'

'That is a shame,' said William, 'for there is much to discuss. Nevertheless, let us make the most of the time we have. First of all, what are you doing here?'

'I am returning to England from a visit to Rome,' said Robert. 'I went there to collect my Pallium.'

'Yes, I heard you were the new Archbishop of Canterbury,' said William. 'You have come a long way since last we met.'

'Indeed,' said Robert, 'and I was humbled to be nominated, but that is not why I am here. I need to discuss something of great importance with you.'

'Continue,' said William.

'As you may be aware,' said the bishop, 'over these past few years, I have gained the trust of King Edward and now enjoy the most private of conversations with him, often involving matters of the state.'

'And?' said William, shrugging his shoulders.

'The thing is,' said Robert, 'the queen remains barren, and it looks like Edward will not have an heir anytime soon. This plays on his mind like a gathering storm, so much so that he is now looking outwards to select an heir from anyone who is eligible.'

'And this affects me how?'

'William,' said Robert, 'for the past few months, whenever this conversation has arisen, I have made sure that your name was high amongst those to be considered. Now I am Archbishop, I believe that, with some diplomacy on your part and continued pressure from me, you are best placed to become heir to his throne. In fact, such has been my influence I would go so far as to say that you are the favourite to succeed him.'

William stared at the bishop for a while as the information sank in. Eventually, he got to his feet to walk around the room, his mind racing.

'Is that a problem?' asked Robert, seeing the concern on the duke's face. 'Have I misjudged the situation?'

'On the contrary,' said William from the far side of the room, 'the throne of England has always seemed an attractive prize, but I never gave it any serious consideration. The cost in men would be far too high. But if what you say is true, then it may not come to that.'

'This is what I am saying,' said Robert. 'There is some political manoeuvring to be done on your part, but if this were an opportunity you would welcome, then I think we should start putting some things in place.'

The duke walked back across the room to stand before the bishop.

'I would very much welcome the opportunity,' said William, staring into Robert's eyes. 'In fact, I feel the beginnings of a fire kindle in my gut. Tell me what you want me to do, Robert. What is this path to the English throne?'

–

A few weeks later, Robert of Jumièges emerged from Westminster Abbey surrounded by the clergy and nobles of England. His formal consecration to the position of Archbishop had been a grand affair, and he walked through the streets lined with hundreds of cheering commoners, many there under threat of retribution if their support was less than enthusiastic.

Once the procession was concluded, he returned to the abbey to change his clothes and meet with his bishops behind closed doors, prior to going to Havering Palace to dine with the king and queen.

Inside, the gathered bishops and abbots prayed together before heading through into one of the new halls, now set out with benches on each side for the guests to sit and hear Robert's opening address as archbishop.

As a senior advisor to the king, Stigand sat near the front, while Spearhafoc, the newest bishop to be ordained, sat at the far end of the room nearest the doors. Robert of Jumièges walked in, flanked by the monks and priests of England carrying candles and incense. Each of them took a seat while the archbishop took his place behind the altar.

For the next few minutes, he led the prayers before finally reading from a parchment placed on the table before him. Much of what he had to say was the usual promises and dedications that all such ceremonies consisted of, but just as everyone thought he was coming to a close, he pushed the parchment to one side and looked into the congregation.

'My fellow bishops,' he said, 'brothers of the Church. There is one more thing I have to address, something that is a bit unpleasant but, alas, needs to be done.' He looked around, having commanded the attention of everyone present. 'During my time in Rome,' he continued, 'it seems that there were certain decisions made in my absence, decisions that, though they were well intentioned, are unfortunately impossible to be endorsed by me, or indeed, the Holy Father in Rome. I am, of course, talking about the fact that while I was away, the position of Bishop of London was awarded to Father Spearhafoc of Bury St Edmunds.'

He looked at the new bishop sitting at the rear of the room. 'This award was made in good faith, and Father Spearhafoc is indeed a worthy recipient, but, alas, during my time in Rome, the Pope made it perfectly clear that, with immediate effect, such appointments should be made by me and me alone, and only candidates who have gathered much experience on the journey to their appointment should be considered. Consequently, after much thought and prayer, I have made the difficult decision that Father Spearhafoc has not yet gained the required understanding for such a role, and consequently, after many discussions, the king has agreed that the appointment should be rescinded.'

A murmur of surprise rippled around the room, and all eyes turned to the red-faced Spearhafoc.

'Father Spearhafoc,' continued the archbishop, 'please step forward.'

Spearhafoc rose from the bench and walked down the aisle, his insides in turmoil at the public disgrace. As he neared, Robert stepped from behind the altar to stand before him.

'Do not take this as any sort of slight upon your character,' said Robert, 'for your time will surely come. Your service has been exemplary, and you have the thanks of the king and of the Church.' He leaned forward and kissed the shocked monk on both sides of his face, but before he withdrew his head, he whispered into Spearhafoc's ear.

'*Tell Godwin that, like you, his days at court are numbered.*'

Before Spearhafoc could react, the archbishop stood up straight and made the sign of the cross above the monk's head.

'Thank you, Brother Spearhafoc,' he said, 'you may return to your seat.'

Shocked, Spearhafoc walked back down the aisle, his mind still reeling from the venom in the archbishop's words.

'As Brother Spearhafoc's immediate departure means the Bishopric of London is now vacant,' said Robert, 'I will put my mind to his successor as a matter of urgency. However, today is a day of celebration, and of prayer, so I bid you all depart, and I will let you know my decision as soon as I have made up my mind. Thank you.'

Everyone in the hall stood up as the archbishop disappeared back into the heart of the abbey. Once he had gone, the congregation filed out, with many stopping alongside

Spearhafoc to express their sympathy and sorrow. Finally, there were only two men left, Spearhafoc and Stigand.

'I am so sorry, Father Spearhafoc,' said Stigand. 'If I had suspected for even a moment that he would do something like this, I would never have put your name forward.'

'You were not to know,' said Spearhafoc. 'The fault lies with him and his devotion to the Norman king.'

'Be careful with your words, Father Spearhafoc,' said Stigand. 'Despite his leaning, Edward is English, and these walls have ears. Do not make this awful situation any worse.'

'What should I do now?' asked Spearhafoc. 'Abingdon has a new abbot, and I will not impose upon him the shame that I just endured. It seems that at the whim of one man, I am now no more than a humble monk.'

'I need time to think,' said Stigand. 'Go back to Abingdon and continue your work there. I will make some enquiries and, once my mind is settled, I will come to see you. Stay strong, Father Spearhafoc, this is not over.'

He turned away, leaving Spearhafoc staring at his back. Inside, the monk felt sick, and his head was spinning with implications and shame. But amongst all the emotions, he knew one thing was certain – he was not going to sit back and let Robert or the king get away with it.

'You are right, Bishop Stigand,' he said quietly to himself, 'this thing is nowhere near being over.'

–

Several weeks later, Bishop Stigand arrived at Abingdon and, upon enquiring where to find Spearhafoc, was directed to the workshops where the monk used to spend so much time creating beautiful items for the Church and the king. He headed down the corridor, keen to pass some good news to the monk who had been treated so unfairly by Robert of Jumièges.

He walked through the door and saw several monks sitting at their workbenches, some creating items of jewellery or religious artefacts while others were carefully writing on rolls of vellum and parchment.

'Is Father Spearhafoc here?' he asked.

'Over there, your grace,' said one of the monks. Stigand walked over to find the monk totally focused on gilding a small statue with gold leaf.

'That's beautiful,' Stigand said after a few moments.

Spearhafoc looked up, startled.

'Your grace,' Spearhafoc said, 'forgive me. I was not expecting you.'

'I did not send notice,' said Stigand, 'for I wanted to bring you the news myself.'

'You have had a chance to talk to the king?'

'I have,' said Stigand looking around. 'Is there somewhere we can talk?'

Spearhafoc led the way into the tiny cell where he slept and sat on the side of his bed while the bishop took the solitary chair.

'Well,' said Spearhafoc, 'what did he say?'

'At first, he was surprised,' said Stigand, 'for though you were replaced as abbot here at Abingdon, he was more than happy for me to find you a different post. However, upon hearing the reasoning and supported with considerable cajoling from Queen Ealdgyth, he accepted your request. Your station has now been officially rescinded, and you are no longer an abbot. Instead, you return to the lower orders as a monk.'

Spearhafoc breathed a sigh of relief.

'Thank you, your grace,' he said. 'I was disappointed to lose the bishopric, but in hindsight, it was probably meant to be. I was happiest when I was creating beautiful pieces for the king and queen, and as much as I told myself that I could carry on doing so as a bishop, the truth is it would never have been possible. At least now I can return to what I enjoyed best.'

'I am glad you said that,' said the bishop, 'for there is one important change. Your new title is to be Brother Spearhafoc, official goldsmith to the queen.'

'He has created a dedicated position?' said Spearhafoc, shocked.

'Indeed he has,' said Stigand, 'and that is despite the new archbishop's opposition. It appears you enjoy the queen's favour, and henceforth all such projects will come through you and you alone.'

'I could not have wished for a better outcome,' said Spearhafoc.

'There is more,' said Stigand. 'To start you on this incredible journey and to silence any objections, the king has commissioned a project of such high esteem that anyone who knows of it will immediately realise the importance of your position.'

'And what is this project?' asked Spearhafoc.

'You, my dear friend,' said the bishop, 'are to design, create and bejewel a new crown for the king himself, an adornment that is to be so magnificent everyone will gasp in wonder the moment they lay eyes upon it. Cost is no object, and the only stipulation is that it must be finished by Christmas Day. Do you think yourself capable of such a task?'

Spearhafoc stared at the bishop, half dazed at his good fortune.

'Well?' continued Stigand. 'Shall I tell him yes, or shall I seek someone else to undertake this once-in-a-lifetime task?'

'There is nobody else,' said Spearhafoc with a smile, 'as well you know. Of course I accept the commission, and upon completion, there will be nothing like it in the world.'

'I knew I could rely on you, Brother Spearhafoc,' said the bishop. 'And upon reflection, I suppose this is an even better outcome than the one you had hoped for.'

'Oh, it is, your grace,' said Spearhafoc slowly. 'You have no idea.'

–

Fifty leagues away, at the port of Dover, a covered wagon waited against a wall near the harbour entrance. Inside, Archbishop

Robert sat waiting to meet a very important visitor. A column of men made their way up from the docks, and Robert climbed out to greet the man in front.

'Count Eustace of Boulogne, I presume,' he said, holding out his hand in greeting.

'I am,' said the count, 'and you are?'

'I am Robert of Jumièges, the Archbishop of Canterbury.'

'I am honoured, your grace,' said the count, 'I did not expect to be met by a man of such stature.'

'Not at all,' said Robert. 'The king is looking forward to your visit very much and wanted me to convey his welcome personally. Please, step inside the cart, it is as warm and as comfortable as these things can be.'

'I think I will ride with my men,' said the count, 'that is, if you don't mind.'

'Of course not,' said Robert. 'I will assign you a guide and will see you again at your lodgings.'

'Of course,' said the count, 'I look forward to it.'

Chapter Twenty-two

Dover, July, AD 1051

Several days later, Count Eustace and his men were back near Dover, having enjoyed a pleasant and productive visit with the king at Westminster. With them once again was Archbishop Robert, having insisted on accompanying them back to their ship.

The journey had taken a few days, and they had stayed in wayside taverns and private houses along the way, but the weather had been kind, and, at last, they faced just one more night before the ship sailed with the morning tide.

'This house belongs to Earl Godwin of Wessex,' said Archbishop Robert after they had climbed out of the wagon, 'so I'm sure we will be very comfortable here tonight. Besides, Dover itself is only a few minutes' walk away.'

'The visit has been better than I expected,' said the count, 'but I have to admit that I am looking forward to getting home. We have, shall we say, different standards back in Boulogne.'

'I understand,' said Robert. 'It took me an age to get used to England's customs when I first came here. Even now, I miss the cuisine and traditions of Normandy. Come, let us see what our host has left for us.'

The two men headed for the door of the manor as their retinue started to unload some of the heavy crates from a second wagon. Inside, the steward of the manor led them into the main reception hall.

'It looks comfortable enough in here,' said Eustace, glancing around. 'Is the host at home?'

'He is not,' replied Robert. 'Apparently, he has had to travel elsewhere to sort out some business.'

'Good,' said Eustace, sitting at the table, 'it prevents us from having to repeat the small talk we have had to endure these past few days.' He looked over at a servant standing at the doorway. 'Bring us two more tankards and a fresh jug of wine.'

'Of course, my lord,' said the servant before disappearing out of the door.

'So,' said Robert eventually, looking at Eustace, 'I haven't had a chance to talk to you since we left London. How went your meeting with the king?'

'Very well,' said Eustace, 'In fact, better than expected.'

'Was anything in particular discussed?'

'Nothing of any consequence,' said the count, 'just the usual political agreements to work together more closely. He seems like a good man.'

'It is always a good idea to talk about such alliances,' said Robert. 'The prospect of Normandy and England united as one is an attractive notion.'

The servant returned with the wine, and for the next hour or so, the two men drank and talked until, eventually, Robert yawned and placed his empty tankard on the table.

'The day has been long,' he said, 'so if you will excuse me, I think I will go to my quarters.'

'I am disappointed,' said Eustace. 'My men and I are heading into Dover later. It is said the town has more than its fair share of alehouses. You are welcome to join us.'

'I think not,' said the archbishop, 'the road has worn me out, and I need an early start in the morning.'

'In that case,' said Eustace, 'perhaps I should bid you farewell now.'

Robert got to his feet and shook the count's hand before leaving the hall and heading to his room.

Later that evening, Eustace sat in a tavern in the town of Dover. With him were a dozen of his guards, each drinking heavily in the smoke-filled stable that had been adapted to accommodate the many sailors that plied their trade on the ships using the harbour on a daily basis.

The hall was noisy, and exhausted women tried their best to keep up with the demand for frothing ale whilst avoiding the groping hands of men who had not seen a woman for weeks or more.

'*I've told you a hundred times,*' shouted a woman's voice across the room, '*keep your hands to yourself.*'

Eustace turned around just in time to see the serving girl smash her assailant over the head with a full tankard of ale, much to the amusement of most in the tavern.

The culprit fell off his bench, resulting in even more hilarity for all except one man – a heavily bearded docker sitting at the next table across from the Normans.

'*You whore,*' shouted the victim, climbing back to his feet, 'I'll knock your teeth out.' He lurched towards the serving girl only to be pounced on by his comrades, each laughing aloud at the plight of their shipmate.

'I told you she was a wildcat,' shouted one above the noise, 'sit back down before she does you some harm.'

Another woman thrust an overflowing tankard into the assailant's hands as she passed, and, placated, he emptied half in one draught, though his glares at the first wench suggested he was not finished with her yet.

'This place is full of interest,' laughed Eustace, turning back to his comrades. 'Perhaps we should sail over on a regular basis if only to witness the antics of the locals.'

'I'm glad you find us funny,' said a voice.

Eustace paused, his drink halfway to his mouth. Slowly he placed the tankard back on the table and turned around to face the bearded man.

'I'm sorry,' he said, 'did you say something?'

'Aye, I did,' said the man. 'I said I'm glad you find us so amusing.'

'I meant no offence,' said Eustace, seeing that several more dockers were staring at them. 'I will curb my manner.'

'Make sure you do,' said the man. 'Who are you, stranger?'

'You are talking to—' started one of Eustace's men, but the count held up his hand, cutting him short.

'Nobody of importance,' he said in reply. 'We sailed out of Caen a few days ago and are heading back on tomorrow's tide.'

'You may have sailed out of Caen,' said the man, 'but you are no sailor. Your clothes suggest you are a man of means, a noble even. Which begs the question, why are the likes of you in a place like this?'

'We are having a drink,' said Eustace, 'just like you. Now, if you don't mind, I will rejoin my friends to enjoy the rest of the evening.'

'You see,' said the man, even louder, 'I do mind. You are not from around here, or even this country, yet you see fit to come here with your fancy clothes and fancy way of talking and think it is acceptable to laugh at the way things are done. Now that to me suggests an arrogance that needs to be tempered.'

All the men around the count's table lowered their own tankards, sensing the threat in the man's voice.

'We want no trouble, friend,' said Eustace, his voice lowering. 'We will be gone soon enough, so I suggest, for your sake, you let this go.'

For a few moments, there was silence as the docker stared at the count.

'Nah,' he said. 'I am aggrieved, and we need to settle this.'

He got up from his seat but had taken no more than two paces when one of the count's guards smashed his fist into the side of the docker's face, sending him plummeting to the floor.

Immediately, pandemonium broke loose, and men flew at the visitors from all directions. Eustace and his guards reacted just as violently, but within moments what had started out as a tavern brawl turned sour when one of the Normans produced a blade from his belt and lunged at the nearest docker.

'*Defend yourselves,*' roared Eustace as the situation deteriorated.

Tables and chairs flew through the air, and the whole tavern turned against them, but the Normans were no strangers to conflict, and they fought back viciously, wreaking havoc amongst their attackers.

One of the dockers launched himself off a table onto the count's back, but again one of his guards saw the danger and reached around to slit the attacker's throat. Eustace stared down at the dying man and realised the situation had got way out of hand.

'We have to get out of here,' he shouted.

As one, all the Normans retreated towards the door, using their swords and knives to hold back the mob. The braver amongst the dockers threw themselves into the fray, well used to lives of violence, but against experienced men of war they stood little chance, and several were cut down without mercy.

Within moments Eustace and his men emerged from the tavern, battered but still standing.

'*Is everyone here?*' he shouted.

'All are present,' replied one of his officers. 'You mount up, we'll stay here and hold them back.'

'We leave together or not at all,' replied Eustace. 'Mount up.'

Moments later, Count Eustace of Boulogne and his men galloped away from Dover, leaving a trail of death and destruction behind them.

—

The following morning the count and his men returned to the dock, this time protected by their full force of armed men. Two lines of angry dockers watched as they passed, but they reached their ship without incident, and within the hour, Dover was no more than a sour memory receding into the distance. Count Eustace joined one of his officers standing at the stern of the ship.

'How are the men?' he asked.

'One is badly hurt, but he should survive. What about you, has your wound been adequately dressed?'

'It is but a scratch,' said the count, holding up a bandaged arm. 'I have had worse.'

'Nevertheless,' said the officer, 'the fact is that we were attacked by those men while you were a guest of their king. They cannot be allowed to get away with it.'

'Oh, they won't,' said Eustace. 'I have already sent a message to Edward complaining in the strongest possible terms, and I assure you he will not let this atrocity go unpunished.'

Chapter Twenty-three

Once again, Godwin of Wessex stood before the King of England, and once again, Robert of Jumièges stood at Edward's side, his face barely concealing a look of contempt.

After the Count of Boulogne had left Dover a few weeks earlier, word had reached the king about the violence, and he had immediately sent a message to Godwin, ordering him to mete out punishment for attacking and hurting his visitors. The retribution was to be brutal so as to make an example to the rest of England that such behaviour would not be tolerated.

However, despite a further two letters reminding the earl of his duties, no such punishment had been carried out, and consequently, Edward had demanded Godwin attend him with a full explanation.

'Earl Godwin,' said Bishop Robert, 'is it normal that any man, whether he be noble or pauper, be allowed to defy their monarch?'

'Your grace—' started Godwin, but he was interrupted by the bishop.

'Just answer the question,' said Robert. 'Is it acceptable for any vassal, irrespective of station, to deliberately ignore the direct orders of a king?'

'You know it is not normal,' said Godwin, 'but you also know that to punish a whole town for the crimes of a few is unjust and impractical. It would turn the whole town against the perpetrator and garner hostility for many years to come.'

'So your refusal to scourge Dover is a decision born of self-preservation?' said Robert.

'My decision is one of sensibility and compassion,' said Godwin. 'I am, of course, willing to punish the men responsible, but do not forget, five of our own died that night while the Normans got away with little more than cuts and bruises.'

'I am led to believe that it was the men of Dover who started the fight in the first place,' interjected the king. 'Are you saying that our guests were not entitled to defend themselves?'

'Self-defence does not include the murder of unarmed men,' said Godwin.

'*Curb your tongue*,' shouted the archbishop, 'you will not contradict the king.'

'Your grace,' continued Godwin, his attention solely focused on the king, 'you are a fair man, and I do not believe for one moment that it was your idea to punish so many for the crimes of so few. The man who started the fight was not even one of us – he was harbouring overnight and left at the first opportunity the following morning.'

'So you allowed the main culprit to leave unpunished,' said Robert. 'That is even worse.'

'I did not *allow* him to leave,' said Godwin, 'for as you are well aware, I was elsewhere at the time. The whole town was still in shock, and by the time they had worked out what had happened, he had long gone.'

'That does not excuse the fact that a town under your control allowed a relative of the king to be treated so,' said Robert. 'They need to be punished.'

'Your grace,' said Godwin, turning back to the king, 'five men in the town now lie beneath the soil, their wives and children facing destitution. Is that not punishment enough?'

'No, it is not,' said the king coldly.

Godwin stared in shock. He had been hoping to appeal to the king's sensible side but could now see he was wasting his time. Robert of Jumièges had clouded his mind.

'Then I know not what more I can do,' he said.

'You know exactly what to do,' said Robert. 'Scourge the town and make them publicly responsible for this outrage. I suggest burning every tenth house, imposing a guilt tax to be paid by every man, woman and child directly to the king's treasury, and the immediate execution of all the men involved in that fight.'

Again, Godwin was horrified. He had expected a hefty penalty, but the archbishop was demanding something he could never do.

'I cannot do that,' he said.

'Cannot, or will not?' asked Robert.

Godwin stared at the archbishop. 'Archbishop Robert of Jumièges,' he said coldly, 'heaven knows I am not a perfect man, and I have made many mistakes in my life, but everything I have done has been with a clear conscience. Never have I killed a man purely out of the desire for petty revenge or to make a point. You, however, despite the trappings of your station, now demand that I murder men in cold blood for nothing more than one of your guests possibly being involved in a fight. I would be careful, your grace, for it seems the longer you live, the further away get the gates of heaven.'

'That is enough,' said the king. 'You came here to answer for your crimes, not to insult my archbishop.'

'I have committed no crime,' said Godwin.

'You refused to carry out the orders of your king,' said Robert. 'That is a crime.'

'If it is,' said Godwin, 'then it is one to be judged by the Witan, not by the king's performing jester.'

'*I have heard enough*,' shouted the king, 'and this farce will end right now. Earl Godwin, I will ask you once more – will you or will you not punish the people of Dover for their unprovoked attack on the Count of Boulogne?'

'I will not,' said Godwin.

'Then consider yourself in contempt of the royal court. You will answer to the charges before the council at a time and place of my choosing. Until then, I banish you to stay within the boundaries of your own earldom.'

Godwin paused and stared between the king and the bishop as the seriousness of the situation sank in. He knew there was nothing more he could do and realised the best course of action was to get out of there while he still could.

'Of course, your grace,' he said with a bow. 'May I leave?'

'Yes,' said the king, 'get out of here.'

Godwin bowed again and left the audience chamber.

When he was gone, Robert turned to the king.

'Your grace, you look troubled?'

'Of course I am troubled,' said Edward, 'we have just angered the second most powerful man in England. This is not going to end well.'

'On the contrary,' said the archbishop, 'I believe we have a unique opportunity to put an end to everything that is wrong with this country once and for all.'

'What do you mean?' asked the king.

'What I mean, your grace,' said the archbishop, 'is this could be an opportunity to rid England not just of Godwin but his whole family. What is more, if this is done correctly, it is also the opportunity to resolve the situation regarding your lack of an heir. After all, with the Godwins out of the way, I cannot see any reason why Queen Ealdgyth needs to remain at court as your wife.'

'Let us not get ahead of ourselves, Robert,' said the king, turning to stare at the closed door, 'for there are many hurdles to clear first. But I will tell you this – I, for one, have had about as much as I can take.'

—

Two days later, Godwin paced the floor in the main hall of Bosham Manor. Sat at the great table in the centre of the hall were his wife Gytha and his sons Sweyn, Gyrth, Leofwine and Wulfnorth.

Only two of their sons were absent – Harold, who was in his own manor in East Anglia, and Tostig, who was due back at any moment after being out on a hunt with some local thegns. But despite his family being desperate to know what was going on, Godwin refused to speak until Tostig was back. Finally, the door opened, and Tostig entered before striding across the hall to join his family.

'I received a message to come back immediately,' said Tostig, staring at his father. 'What is going on?'

'We don't know,' said Sweyn from the table, 'we were waiting for you.'

'Sit down,' said Godwin, 'I have worrying news.'

Tostig grabbed a jug of ale from another table and sat across from Sweyn.

'So,' said Sweyn, staring at Godwin, 'what's this all about?'

'As you know,' said Godwin, 'I have recently returned from London, where I was summoned to explain my refusal to scourge Dover. Unfortunately, the meeting did not go as expected, and, despite my explanations, the king, under the influence of the Archbishop of Canterbury, demanded that I carry out his orders forthwith.'

'But that makes no sense,' said Gytha, 'did you explain to him that they were not solely at fault?'

'I did,' said Godwin, 'that and more, but he did not want to hear what I had to say. It was almost as if he knew this was an opportunity to put me under pressure and would not take no for an answer. Eventually, he gave me an ultimatum – carry out the order or face the consequences.'

'What did you do?' asked Gytha quietly.

'I will not chastise innocent people, Gytha,' said Godwin, looking at his wife, 'the punishment he demanded was too great.'

'So what are the consequences?' asked Leofwine.

'I have been declared in contempt of the royal court and will be summoned to plead my case before the year is out. Until then, I am to remain within the boundaries of Wessex.'

'Even so,' said Gytha, 'any man with the sense he was born with would see the unjustness of the situation.'

'Ordinarily, yes,' said Godwin, 'but the problem is all members of the council are loyal to Edward, and the outcome will be what the king desires.'

'That is unfair,' said Gytha. 'Is there any other way to ensure impartiality?'

'Actually, there is,' said Godwin. 'I could appeal for my trial to be placed before the full Witan. That way, my fate is voted on by a gathering of nobles and bishops without fear of favouritism.'

'And if you go to this trial, what are the possible outcomes?'

'If I were to be found guilty, then all punishments are possible, including banishment, imprisonment or even execution.'

'But you are not guilty,' said Leofwine.

'On the contrary,' said Godwin, 'if the charge is disobeying the king, then I am as guilty as any man can be. My defence, albeit honourable, will not be enough to throw out the charge of disobeying the king. Hopefully, it will be enough to mitigate any sentence, but make no mistake – I am guilty of this accusation.'

'What are we going to do?' asked Gytha.

'There is only one thing we can do,' said Godwin, 'and that is to demand I be tried by the Witan. He may or may not agree, so we have to be ready to stand up to him. Our house has many allies across England, and with their support, we can force him to realise that no man, king or not, should be able to order the slaughter of innocent people for nothing more than petty revenge.'

'*You are going to confront the king?*' gasped Gytha.

'I see no other option,' said Godwin. 'The choices are to make a stand now or accept the decision of the royal council. By doing the latter, every member of this family will be at risk, and that is something I will not countenance.'

'At last,' said Sweyn, who had maintained his silence up until then.

'What did you say?' asked Tostig, turning to face his brother.

'I said at last,' repeated Sweyn, placing his goblet on the table. 'It is about time someone confronted the imposter who sits on the throne of England. Did I not request this very thing only a few months ago?'

'You did,' said Godwin, 'but the circumstances were different, as well you know.'

'Either way,' said Sweyn, 'it is about time he was ripped from his gilded throne and sent back whence he came.'

'Hopefully, it won't come to that,' said Godwin, 'but if it does, we have to make arrangements so that, should we lose the fight, we have somewhere safe to flee.'

'We will not lose any fight with Edward,' said Sweyn, 'our allies are too great.'

'Nevertheless, we have to have something in place,' said Godwin, 'and that is why I have summoned you here. We need to discuss our options, should we need to run.'

For a few moments, there was silence as the seriousness of the situation sank in. For as long as they could all remember, their family had been one of the strongest – if not *the* strongest – in England, but now, after a single event out of their control, they were about to discuss running for their lives.

'I have an idea,' said Sweyn, looking up. 'I have a good relationship with King Gruffydd of Gwynedd. I am sure he would be more than happy to help should the situation arise. Perhaps I could speak to him?'

'I thought about that,' said Godwin, 'but his kingdom is too close and easily attacked. Besides, we are still enemies at heart, and I fear that if Edward offered a reward, Gruffydd would not take too much persuading to betray us.'

'Then it needs to be across the sea,' said Leofwine.

'It does,' said Godwin, 'but Normandy is out of the question due to the duke being a close friend of Edward. Boulogne is also off-limits as the count is one of those responsible for these accusations.'

'What about Ireland?' asked Leofwine. 'It is no secret that the King of Leinster is no ally of Edward. Perhaps he could help?'

'It is true that there is no love lost between the two,' said Godwin, 'but let us not forget that King Diarmait's people are Vikings, and there is no guarantee as to how they will react.'

'What about Flanders?' said Leofwine. 'I hear William the Bastard used force against Count Baldwin's daughter for a proposal, and despite Matilda's acceptance, the count still holds a grudge against the duke for the embarrassment he forced upon him.'

'Actually, that is a good idea,' said Gytha, 'we have just had a notification from Count Baldwin approving Tostig's advances to his sister. If we can accelerate this union, we would have a ready-made ally just across the sea. All the details have already been agreed, we just need to decide on a date.'

Everyone turned to face Tostig.

'What say you, Tostig?' asked Godwin. 'Are you happy to marry Judith within the next few weeks?'

'The sooner, the better as far as I am concerned,' said Tostig, 'and I am sure she feels the same.'

'Then that is what we will do,' said Godwin. 'Gytha, send word to Baldwin – tell him that we wish to celebrate the union as soon as we possibly can.'

'Once that is done,' said Sweyn, 'how do you intend to deal with Edward?'

'Leave that with me,' said Godwin. 'In the meantime, we need to contact our allies and warn them that we may have cause to call upon them.'

'I can still call on many men from Hereford,' said Sweyn, 'most of the thegns from my earldom are still loyal.'

'What about your pilgrimage to Jerusalem?'

'If you think I am going to abandon my family in their hour of greatest need, then you are sadly mistaken,' said Sweyn. 'I intend to be at your side, Father, and whether we stand or fall, it will be as a family.'

Chapter Twenty-four

Two young boys sat amid the bracken on the edge of the village, hidden from prying eyes as they shared a piece of bread stolen from the blacksmith's house. The crime had been a risky one, for if they had been caught, they would have spent a day in the stocks at least, if not worse. Still, it seemed the gamble had paid off, for there was no cry of alarm or sign of pursuit, and they enjoyed the fleeting enjoyment of filling their bellies before returning to the fields.

'What's that?' said one, suddenly looking up.

The second boy stopped chewing and listened intently. In the distance, the unmistakable sound of approaching horses filled the air, and not just a few. Carefully, he got to his knees and peered through the bracken at the road below. Coming towards them were four men clad in full chainmail and carrying the flag of Wessex. Each was fully armed and provided an impressive sight, but what came behind them was even more formidable – a never-ending column of soldiers stretching back as far as the eye could see.

'Who is that?' asked the first boy.

'The colours are those of Wessex,' said the second boy. 'What are they doing here?'

'I don't know,' said his friend, 'but we should tell someone.' He got to his feet and turned to run down the footpath towards the village. His friend followed him as fast as he could, leaving the last piece of prized bread behind them.

In the village of Beverton, the constable rallied the few men available that could put up any fight against whoever was approaching. The two rascals were obviously exaggerating, but nevertheless, they had been earnest in their warning, and he had no doubt that something was happening.

'Well,' he said, holding one of the boys by the ear, 'where is this great army? I swear, should this be a jest, you will spend a week sleeping in a cage amongst the headstones.'

'It's true, my lord,' said the boy with a wince, 'I swear it.'

Moments later, the constable let the boy's ear go and stared in shock as the lead elements of Godwin's army appeared over the crest of the hill.

'Oh sweet Jesus,' he said, crossing himself, 'someone go and get the master.'

One of the men ran to the stables and moments later emerged astride a horse to gallop northwards to their lord's manor. The column of men neared until, eventually, it stopped before the constable. The lead rider looked down at the man blocking his path.

'Who are you?' asked the rider.

'I am John Strong,' came the reply, 'Constable of Beverton. Who are you, friend, and why have you come in such numbers?'

'My name is Godwin of Wessex,' said the earl. 'I have a meeting with the king in Gloucester seven days hence and seek a place near water to pitch our camp.'

'There is a river on the far side of the village,' said the constable, 'you can use any of the fields there. But why have you brought an army?'

'Don't you worry yourself about it, my friend,' said Godwin, 'you will hardly know we are here. Just tell the people of the village to keep their distance, and I will do the same with my men, understood?'

'Yes, my lord,' said the constable, before stepping aside as Godwin led over five thousand men-at-arms through the village towards the river.

'Well,' said Sweyn at Godwin's side, 'if Edward doesn't know we are coming yet, he will find out soon enough.'

'Aye, he will,' said Godwin, 'but as we are seven days early for the council, I suspect we will find him unprepared, which is exactly what I had hoped.'

—

A few hours later, in a manor house in Gloucester, Archbishop Robert ran along a corridor, pulling his robes about him. The king's summons had sounded urgent, and he had left a particularly friendly kitchen maid behind in his quarters.

'Do you know what he wants?' he asked as he ran.

'I do not,' replied the servant running alongside him, 'but his mood is sour.'

Robert burst into the king's chambers to see several other men already there, each talking loudly to get their voices heard above the rest.

'*Enough*,' roared the king, bringing the room to silence. 'Everyone be quiet while I think.' He looked up at the red-faced archbishop pushing his way through the throng.

'Your grace,' gasped Robert, 'I came as quickly as I could. What seems to be the problem?'

'The problem,' said the king, staring at the archbishop, 'is that less than two leagues from where I am standing right now, the Earl of Wessex commands an army at least five thousand strong.'

'But that is not what we arranged,' replied the archbishop. 'We said we would meet on the eighth day of the month with both sides equally represented.'

'I know what was agreed,' said the king, 'but it seems that Godwin has set his own agenda. What is more, I have just received word that he is demanding an audience at first light.'

'This is treason,' snarled Robert. 'We should immediately attack and kill every last one of them.'

'With what?' sighed Edward. 'I have fewer than a thousand men under my command. We would be slaughtered in any confrontation.'

'But what about Earls Siward and Leofric? They can both muster at least five thousand men.'

'They can,' said the king, 'and their armies are on their way here, but they are still days away, so I have no other choice but to meet Godwin on his terms or risk an attack on the throne by the County of Wessex.'

'This is unforgivable,' said the archbishop. 'The man needs to be hanged from the nearest tree.'

'I agree,' said the king, 'but at the moment, we are at a disadvantage and need to stall for time.' He turned to one of his courtiers at the far side of the room. 'Tell Earl Godwin's messenger that I will meet with him in the morning, but he is to come alone and unarmed.'

'As you wish, your grace,' said the courtier, bowing from the room.

'He is not going to do that,' said the bishop, 'for he will know that he puts himself at risk.'

'We will see,' said the king, 'for if he does not, that is yet one more example of disobedience to put before the council.'

–

The following morning Godwin and his sons Sweyn, Harold and Tostig rode into Gloucester accompanied by a hundred of Godwin's best huscarls, while outside the town, the rest of the Wessex army spread out across a hill in a show of unmatched force.

When they reached the town centre, the guards were surprised to see the king sitting on a throne outside the doorway of a church at the far end of the square. Alongside him were the

Archbishop of Canterbury and the Bishop of Worcester, while to either side stood five hundred armed guards.

Despite the overwhelming number of potential opponents, Godwin told his men to wait where they were and dismounted. He removed his sword belt and handed it to Sweyn before walking across the square to stand before the king.

'Your grace,' he said with a bow, 'thank you for accepting my petition. As you can see, I have come to you alone and unarmed, as requested.'

Edward looked up at the one hundred heavily armed men just a few paces away and cursed beneath his breath. The earl had met his demands to the letter, if not in spirit.

'I suppose you have,' said the king eventually, 'though your men there seem more ready for war rather than dialogue.'

'The roads are full of brigands these days, your grace, so they made sure I arrived safely.'

'So,' said the king, 'tell me. What is it that you wish to discuss that will not wait until the date we agreed?'

'I saw no point in waiting,' said Godwin, 'for I believe the charges brought against me are nothing more than a distraction guided by someone who is well known to bear a grudge against the House of Godwin. What is more, the person in question spouts the falsehood that I was responsible for killing your brother all those years ago. I feel that if we are to have this conversation, then all accusations on both sides should be tabled, and we can sort this out once and for all.'

'I take it you are talking about the Archbishop of Canterbury?' asked the king.

'I am,' said Godwin. 'Since he arrived from Normandy, he has crawled up the ladder of the Church using his closeness to you as protection against those who see through his ruse. Now he finds himself in a position of unparalleled power, second only to the king.'

'Guard your words, Earl Godwin,' said the king, 'for you are talking about a man who is responsible for the spiritual guidance of our country. He commands great respect along with my unfailing support.'

'He may be the man who carries the title,' said Godwin, 'but let us not forget that the man selected by those who know best, the Chapter monks of Canterbury, was denied his true calling by the lies of the man at your side. I have no doubt that Robert of Jumièges poisoned your mind against Brother Æthelric, your grace, and that, along with all the other falsehoods he propagates, is the reason why he also has a case to answer.'

'That is the most ridiculous thing I have ever heard,' said Robert from the king's side. 'I offer the king spiritual guidance only, not advice on policy or governance.'

'Yet it was you that suggested the extent of punishment to be inflicted upon the people of Dover,' said Godwin. 'Tell me how that is spiritual and not judgemental.'

'That was different,' said Robert with a scowl. 'Your people attacked the king's guests and deserved to be punished. A requirement, I may add, that has yet to be carried out.'

'There will be no scourging of Dover,' said Godwin.

'So once again, in front of all these witnesses, you refuse to carry out the king's command?'

'I do,' said Godwin.

'Tell me,' said Robert, 'what is to stop our men striking you and your men down where you stand? You are outnumbered five to one.'

'Go ahead,' said Godwin. 'But let it also be known that we came here in peace to resolve a situation according to the laws of England. I have been accused of a crime, and as is my right, I demand redress and explanation from my accuser. I break no laws here, archbishop. Perhaps if you had been brought up in this country, you would be aware of that.'

The king held up his hand, cutting short the archbishop's retort.

'Earl Godwin,' Edward said calmly, 'I am fully aware that you have many men surrounding Gloucester as we speak. How can

I take your declaration of peace seriously when you have come here with an army?'

'They are there as insurance only, your grace,' said Godwin.

'So what is it exactly that you want?'

'I want to defend myself before the full Witan of England, not just the royal council. In addition, I want the Archbishop of Canterbury to publicly withdraw his accusation that I was responsible for the death of your brother.'

'*Never*,' hissed Robert, but again the king held up his hand.

'And what makes you think I will accept these demands?'

'I am well within my rights to seek justice,' said Godwin, 'as are all men. As the king, I would expect you to set the example.'

'And if I refuse, will you set your army against me?'

'If I wanted to do that,' said Godwin, 'everyone in this town would already be dead. However, should I be forced into a corner and be denied what is mine by right, then I will have to consider all the options open to me.'

The king stared at Godwin, barely concealing his anger at the veiled threat.

'I think you are bluffing,' said the archbishop. 'There is no way you would attack the throne, not even you are that stupid.'

'There is only one way to find out,' said Godwin. 'Let the king cast his judgement and see what fate awaits us all.'

Edward stared at the earl again. He suspected that, despite the argument, Godwin was still loyal to the throne, but if he were wrong and Godwin did attack, there was no way Gloucester could defend itself from such an army at short notice.

'No,' said the king eventually, 'there is no need for violence between the people of England, and I represent all men, not just those who feel aggrieved. You shall have your audience before the Witan, Godwin of Wessex. Come back to this very spot seven days hence, and we will see what the nobles of England think about this situation.'

'That is all I ask,' said Godwin. 'Thank you, your grace, I shall return one week from today.' With a quick bow, he turned and walked back to his men without being dismissed.

'Your grace,' said Robert, his face contorted with anger, 'why did you cave in so easily? Godwin has many friends on the Witan, and conviction may not be an easy outcome.'

'That is why I have no intention of convening the Witan,' said the king as Godwin and his men rode back out of the gates. 'What we need are more men and plenty of them. Send word to our allies, archbishop – tell them to call their men to arms without delay. I want them mustered on the northern edge of Gloucester within six days. Let us see what Godwin is really made of.'

Chapter Twenty-five

A week later, Godwin once again rode into Gloucester, though this time with just a dozen guards and his two eldest sons, Harold and Sweyn. As they reached the square, they saw the doors to the church were flung wide open and realised the meeting would not take place outside. A priest was patiently awaiting their arrival.

'Earl Godwin,' he said, 'we have been expecting you. The others are waiting inside.'

Godwin looked around, noticing that there were no other horses in the square. 'It looks like we may be the first to arrive.'

'Or it is a trap,' said Sweyn. 'We should go.'

'No,' said Godwin, 'not even Edward would stoop so low as to kill an earl in a church. You stay here, I'll go and see what is happening.'

'Not in a thousand lifetimes,' said Sweyn. 'If you are going in, I am going in.'

'As am I,' said Harold.

All three men dismounted and, after leaving their weapons with the priest, stepped inside the church.

Inside, they could hear the murmur of men talking, and as they approached, they could see the king sitting on a cushioned chair, this time flanked by Archbishop Robert and the friendlier face of Bishop Stigand.

'What is this?' said Godwin, coming to a halt. 'You promised a meeting of the Witan.'

'I said what I had to say to allow me time to gather my thoughts,' said the king. 'Your unannounced arrival with five thousand men-at-arms left me at a great disadvantage, and I felt threatened by one of my own nobles. That is no way to conduct a negotiation.'

'There was no negotiation,' said Godwin, 'I was only demanding what is mine according to the law – the right to be judged by my fellows.'

'And it is my right to decide whether to agree to that demand or not,' retorted the king, 'and in this case, I decline your request.'

Godwin stared at Edward, shocked at the bluntness of the reply.

'I do not understand,' he said. 'We have already discussed the potential consequences of such a denial. Why do you now put the peace of England at stake?'

'Because I will not be dictated to by one of my own vassals,' said Edward. 'I have considered your petition and have decided against it. Instead, you are to be taken into custody and tried in London as a traitor.'

As he spoke, several men appeared out of the shadows, each armed with a drawn sword.

Sweyn drew a hidden knife from beneath his cloak, as did Harold, and they wheeled to face the men.

'Do this,' shouted Sweyn, 'and our men will burn Gloucester to the ground, with you in it.'

'They may well attack us,' said Edward, 'but they will have a fight on their hands. Even as we speak, Earls Leofric and Siward are deploying the men of Mercia and Northumbria around Gloucester, ten thousand men-at-arms more than capable of defeating those you brought from Wessex.'

Godwin stared at the king, realising he had been outplayed.

'Is this what it has come to,' Godwin asked eventually, 'that the King of England resorts to trickery and brigandry in the house of God? I thought you were a just king, Edward, not a plaything for a crooked archbishop. How do you think history will look upon your reign?'

'How will it look when they record that you brought an army to Gloucester to confront your monarch?' retorted Edward. 'That in itself is a hanging offence.'

'I am a minor player on a much wider stage,' said Godwin, 'and it is doubtful my name will even be remembered a hundred years from now. You, on the other hand, are the King of England, and history will judge you by what happens here today. If you arrest me, then my army will attack, irrespective of numbers. Thousands will die on both sides, and even if the men of Wessex are defeated, the history books will say that it was the result of your treachery. That should not be your legacy.'

'So what would you have me do, Godwin?' said the king. 'I cannot and will not cede to your demands. Your actions these past few months are nothing short of treasonous, and if I allow you to get away with it, then you could be the first of many.'

'I have already provided the answer to that question,' said Godwin. 'Let me be judged by the Witan. If I am guilty, then I will hang, and my lands will be forfeited to the Crown. Is that not both just and legal?'

'We know you have many allies within the Witan,' said Archbishop Robert, 'men who have served alongside you in times of war.'

'I also have many enemies,' said Godwin, turning towards the archbishop, 'men who would love to see me dangle at the end of the rope, but you miss the whole point. The Witan consists of the best this country has to offer, men loyal to both sides in this argument. Together they represent our people, and if you think that they can be bought, or will vote against their own conscience, then England is corrupt, and there is no hope for any of us. I, on the other hand, believe they are honest men who will judge me on the facts. But tell me this, Archbishop Robert, why are you so desperate to avoid a fair trial? What is it that you are trying to hide from men of good standing?'

For a moment, everyone fell silent as the accusation sank in, and the king turned to face the furious cleric, but before he could speak, Bishop Stigand took the opportunity to step in and give his opinion.

'Your grace,' he said, 'if I may? There are obviously some very entrenched opinions here on both sides. What Earl Godwin did and continues to do is unacceptable, that much is clear. However, it is also clear that a man of his standing is entitled to be judged by the Witan, and as much as it goes against the grain, I have to say that to deny him that privilege may create further problems with other nobles.'

'I disagree,' said Archbishop Robert. 'I say that if we arrest this man now and execute him for his crimes at the earliest opportunity, it will send a message across England that cannot be ignored – defy your king, and you will reap the consequences.'

'Oh, it will undoubtedly send a message,' said Stigand, 'and if you think that ruling by fear is the path to tread, then go ahead. But the Witan consists of strong men with strong armies at their backs, and if you kill Godwin without a trial, then they are bound to wonder if next time it could be them at the end of your summary judgement.'

'So what do you suggest, Bishop Stigand?' said the king. 'That I cower before one of my own vassals like a beaten dog?'

'I do not, your grace,' said Stigand. 'But nobody has been hurt yet, so I suggest that we all take a step back before something is said that cannot be unsaid. Allow Earl Godwin to leave on the condition that he immediately takes his army back to Wessex and agrees to come to London on the day of the equinox, without men-at-arms. I also suggest that, henceforth, I am used as a go-between to ensure there is no misunderstanding between parties.'

'And what would be the aim of this meeting?' asked the king.

'To allow the earl to present his defence in a rational manner without the need of convening the Witan and to collectively agree on a way forward.'

'Even if that way forward includes punishment?'

'I think the earl knows he has gone too far,' said Stigand, turning to face Godwin, 'and that some sort of punishment is inevitable. Is that not right, Earl Godwin?'

'I have never claimed to be totally innocent in these matters,' said Godwin, 'I just want a fair hearing without being prejudged.'

'So, if I agree to Bishop Stigand's recommendations,' said the king, 'and we hear you at the royal court but without the formality of the royal council, are you saying you will accept my sentence, whatever that may be?'

Godwin paused and turned to look at Stigand, receiving the slightest of nods in reply.

'I will,' said Godwin, turning back to the king.

'No!' shouted Robert. 'He should be dealt with here and now.'

'*Silence!*' shouted Edward. 'I am the king here, and it is I alone who decide what happens next.' He turned back to face Godwin. 'What you have done these past few weeks, no other man would have got away with. By your actions here at Gloucester, you have placed this country on the edge of civil war, a war that would kill the best we have and expose us to invasion from those that covet our lands. For that alone, you deserve to hang, but I also know that if I arrest you now, many men will die. So for that reason, Earl Godwin, I accept Bishop Stigand's recommendations in full. However, there is one condition, one that is not negotiable.'

'And that is?' asked Godwin.

'In order that I can be confident that you will not go away from here and raise an even greater army with which to march upon London, I want hostages. Someone who I know will prevent you from unleashing an unexpected attack on the throne.'

'I will be that hostage,' said Harold stepping forward.

'No,' said the king. 'You are an earl in your own right, and your fate is in your own hands. I want someone who is innocent in all of this, someone whose life means more to Earl Godwin than his own.'

'And who would that be?' asked Godwin.

'I want your youngest son,' said Edward coldly, 'and I want your grandson. Wulfnorth Godwinson and Hakon Sweynson are to be delivered to me within the week, both boys to be held in London until this situation is resolved.'

'You are not having our sons,' said Sweyn, 'forget it.'

'Those are my terms,' said the king, 'and after the way you have acted here, they are nowhere as harsh as they could be. Deliver the boys to me, Earl Godwin, and you will have your hearing. Once the verdicts are in, you have my word they will be released unharmed.'

Godwin stared at the king before turning his attention to Sweyn.

'No,' said Sweyn, seeing the resolution in his father's eyes. 'Do not make me do this. Not my son.'

'It will be for three weeks only,' said Godwin. 'Whatever happens to me after that, he will be released back into your care.'

Sweyn glared at his father but did not reply. Instead, he turned and marched out of the church, slamming the door behind him.

'Well?' said the king. 'Do we have an agreement?'

'We do,' said Godwin with a sigh. 'I will have my son and grandson taken to Havering Palace as soon as we get back. But I swear, if you or anyone else—'

'That is enough,' interrupted Bishop Stigand. 'The king has made his decision, and you have agreed. There is no more to be said.'

Godwin stopped talking and nodded his head in acquiescence. 'In that case,' he said, 'with your leave, your grace, I will withdraw and see you again at the end of the month.'

'You will,' said the king. 'Now be gone before I change my mind.'

Chapter Twenty-six

Godwin and his sons dismounted in the courtyard of their London residence after a hard ride from Bosham. All around them, men saw to their horses and sharpened their weapons, for although they could not accompany the earl into his meeting, they were ready to support him at a moment's notice, as were the several hundred others waiting outside the city.

'Is my wife here?' asked Godwin as he dismounted.

'She is, my lord,' said the steward, 'she is on her way as we speak.'

Moments later, Gytha and Edyth Swanneck, Harold's new wife, appeared from the hall and hurried over to meet them. Both women had arrived several days earlier with Wulfnorth and Hakon, the two young boys being offered as hostages. Both boys had now been transferred to the king's custody in Havering Palace, along with two servants to look after their every need.

'Gytha,' said Godwin, embracing his wife, 'I am sorry we are so late. We had trouble mustering adequate forces. Many of those we had at Gloucester have decided they want no part in confronting the king.'

'What do you mean?' asked Gytha. 'Without men, will we not be at a disadvantage?'

'I know, but there is little I can do. Hopefully, they will not be needed anyway, but I had hoped to have more in case of treachery.'

'Let us pray it doesn't come to that,' said Gytha. 'When do you have to be at the palace?'

'I know not. Apparently, Stigand will let me know when the king is ready. But I should have a few hours, so would like to eat and bathe.'

'I will arrange it,' said Gytha.

'What about the boys?' asked Godwin. 'Are they settled?'

'As far as I know,' said Gytha. 'There were some tears from Hakon, but Wulfnorth stayed brave. I promised them that they would be back amongst us within days.'

'And they will be,' said Godwin. 'Ask the kitchens to arrange hot food for my men; I'll be with you as soon as the horses are stabled.'

'Of course,' said Gytha, walking away as Godwin and his huscarls did what they had to do.

–

An hour later, all the men who had arrived from Bosham sat at the tables around the inside of Southwark Hall, filling themselves up with piping-hot potage and chunks of bread. The mood was tense, and all had their weapons close at hand in case of an unexpected attack.

Godwin and his wife talked quietly to each other, careful not to be overheard, for although the men in the hall were fiercely loyal, everyone knew that careless talk often reached the ears of those who would do them ill. Godwin looked tired, not just from the constant riding and confrontation but from the strain of realising his whole family was now at risk.

'I have heard from Count Baldwin in Flanders,' said Gytha. 'He has assured me that should we need shelter, his ports are open to all who need it.'

'Excellent news,' said Godwin, 'and in truth, that is a load off my mind.'

'What about the ships,' asked Gytha, 'are they ready?'

'Every ship we own has been made ready for sea,' said the earl, 'and are being guarded by two hundred men. If the worst thing happens, we can reach them within two days.'

'There is something else I need to talk to you about,' said Gytha. 'Yesterday, I spent time with Ealdgyth. I did not share our concerns, for she has enough to worry about, but while I was there, I encountered Brother Spearhafoc and told him what was happening.'

'Was that wise?'

'Spearhafoc is loyal to our house,' said Gytha, 'and an opponent of Bishop Robert. If things do not go our way, I fear his life may be at risk, so I thought he should be made aware of the situation.'

'What did he say?'

'He was grateful for the advanced warning,' said Gytha, 'but in addition came up with a suggestion.'

'Which is?'

Before Gytha could answer, the door opened, and one of the guards entered to announce a visitor.

'My lord,' he said, 'the Bishop of Winchester is here and begs an urgent audience.'

'Bring him in,' said Godwin immediately before turning to his wife. 'Hold that thought, we will return to this conversation as soon as we can.' He got up from the table and walked over to the door to welcome the bishop.

'Bishop Stigand,' he said as the cleric entered the hall, 'what news from the palace?'

'Not good,' said Stigand, removing his cloak. 'The archbishop has spent the past few weeks poisoning the king's mind, and Edward's mood has once again turned sour. Bishop Robert has also stated that he heard you threaten the life of the king in Gloucester, which has hardened the northern earls' stance against you. Both have now mobilised their full armies and are camped outside London as we speak. I believe you are in great danger, Godwin, and think you should consider leaving while you still can.'

'Flight is the last resort,' said Godwin. 'Do you believe the king wishes to do us ill?'

'I have not heard that is the case,' said Stigand, 'but he has sent me here with a demand.'

'We should ignore any of his demands until such time as he agrees our own requests,' said Sweyn from near the fire.

'We will hear what he has to say,' said Godwin, turning back to face Stigand. 'Continue.'

'He is still willing to hear your defence in good faith, but your son Sweyn has been declared an outlaw and is to hand himself in for trial before any meeting can go ahead.'

Sweyn stared at Stigand, forcing himself to hold in the rage that was building inside him.

'No,' said Gytha, 'that is not what was agreed.'

'I know,' said Stigand, 'and as I said, the situation changes by the day. Edward now believes he has the upper hand, especially as he has the hostages and a huge army at his back.'

'And he is correct,' said Godwin. 'My army is half the size it was in Gloucester, and most of Harold's thegns have declared for the king. We are disadvantaged.'

As Godwin paced the floor, deep in thought, Bishop Stigand walked over to Gytha and spoke quietly.

'Lady Gytha,' he said, 'did you manage to speak to Brother Spearhafoc?'

'I did,' said Gytha.

'And?'

'The arrangements have been put in place.'

'Have you told your husband?'

'Not yet, but I will as soon as I can.'

'Hold back until we know there is no other option. What we propose is illegal and will add to his woes.'

'So be it,' said Gytha as Godwin approached once again.

'Your grace,' said Godwin, 'the king has backed me into a corner, but I will not be the one to cast the final stone. Tell him that as long as I have his word in writing that he will guarantee my safety and that of my family, then I will still attend the palace for judgement. However, this is on the condition he withdraws the declaration that Sweyn is an outlaw.'

'I fear he will not listen to counter-demands,' said the bishop.

'Nevertheless, convey the message and bring his reply back as soon as you can.'

'As you wish,' said the bishop, picking up his cloak and leaving the manor. When he was gone, Godwin turned to Sweyn.

'I think this is doomed to fail,' he said, 'and we may be forced to flee. If that is the case, we have a fleet of ships waiting in Bosham to take us to Flanders. The king's proclamation puts you at risk irrespective of outcome, so I want you to ride for Bosham immediately.'

'I am needed here,' said Sweyn, 'I need to get my son.'

'*Listen to me for once in your life*,' hissed Godwin. 'You heard what Stigand said, we are outnumbered ten to one, and no matter what transpires here today, you have been made an outlaw. Every man from here to Scotland will soon be seeking the bounty on your head, so the best thing you can do is return to Bosham while you still can. Once there, load my treasury into the ships. Strip the manor of everything of value and spread it amongst the fleet. If this turns sour, we need whatever we can carry.'

'Father,' said Sweyn, 'I cannot leave, my son is in Edward's custody.'

'I understand,' said Godwin, 'but nothing you can do here can change that fact. If I win the argument, they will be released, but if I fail, then all of us are at risk. We do not even know where they are being kept, but you getting killed is not going to help anyone. Do this for the family, Sweyn – do it for Hakon.'

Sweyn stared at his father before nodding his agreement.

'As you wish,' Sweyn said, 'I will take ten men and ride immediately.'

'Good,' said Godwin. 'I also want you to take your mother and Edyth. If we are forced to run, I want them to have as much of a head start as possible. There are fresh horses in the stables.'

'Godwin,' said Gytha, standing up, 'my place is here with you.'

'I know,' said Godwin, 'but I have to know you are safe. If you go with Sweyn now, you can be halfway to Bosham by nightfall. Please do this for me, I need to be focused on Edward, not the safety of my wife.'

'As you wish,' said Gytha before turning to Edyth. 'Come, we should get changed for travel.'

'Take no carts,' said Godwin, 'they are too slow. Today you go by horseback.'

'Understood,' said Gytha, leading Edyth from the hall.

'Now what?' asked Harold once Sweyn and his men had left.

'All we can do now,' said Godwin, 'is wait for the king's reply.'

–

Several hours later, Bishop Stigand returned to Southwark and, abandoning his horse in the courtyard, hurried into the hall. Inside, most of Godwin's men were sleeping on blankets placed around the walls, but as soon as the cleric walked in, they jumped to their feet, keen to hear the result of his petition.

Godwin stood up from the table as he approached and could immediately see the bishop was exhausted.

'Get him watered wine and hot food,' shouted Godwin over his shoulder, 'now.'

Stigand collapsed onto a bench and accepted a half-full tankard of ale.

'What's happened to you,' asked Godwin, 'have you been attacked?'

'No, nothing like that,' said Stigand, 'but I needed to get back here before dark to warn you, and it has been a long time since I sat in a saddle.'

'Did you not use your cart?'

'I did not, for it would have taken too long, and my message will not wait.'

'Warn me of what?' asked Godwin.

'I passed on your message to the king,' said Stigand, 'and he rejected it out of hand. He said that as soon as Sweyn is found, he will be tried and found guilty before being hanged from a gibbet at the gates of London. What is more, he has also outlawed you and your whole family and demanded that you all surrender to his men within three days.'

'That is never going to happen,' said Godwin, 'has the man gone mad?'

'There was one more thing,' said Stigand, 'a declaration that underlines his determination in this matter. He said that he would absolve you and every one of your family of any charges and release both the hostages, on condition you do one simple act.'

'And that is?'

'That you return his brother to him alive and well.'

'But Alfred has been dead for fifteen years. What does he mean?'

'He means,' said Stigand, 'that he now accepts Robert of Jumièges' claim that you are responsible for Alfred's death, and by demanding this impossible task, there is no way he will ever forgive you. The argument is over, Godwin – you are a condemned man. It is time to run.'

–

Within the hour, Godwin, Tostig and Gyrth left Southwark to ride as hard as they could to join the small army gathered to the south of London. Once there, knowing they would have no chance against the king's gathering forces, Godwin disbanded the men and sent them back to their houses and farms across Wessex before following Sweyn and Gytha to Bosham.

Back in London, Harold and Leofwine had stayed behind to escort Stigand back across the city. Once they reached Havering Palace, the exhausted bishop turned to Harold and pulled down his hood.

'Harold,' he said, 'you need to listen to me. I have been a trusted ally of your father for many years, have I not?'

'You have,' said Harold, 'and a truer friend no man has ever had.'

'And have I ever let you down?'

'You have not,' said Harold. 'Where is this going, Reverend Father?'

'I want you to do something,' said Stigand, 'but you need to trust me.'

'What is it?'

'You have to go to Bristol,' replied the bishop, 'and set sail for Ireland. Your father is going to need as many allies as he can get, and his best bet is King Diarmait of Leinster.'

'My father and I have already discussed this,' said Harold. 'Diarmait is a Viking and as such does nothing unless it involves a great deal of money.'

'Worry not about money,' said Stigand, 'certain things have been put in place.'

'What things?'

'I cannot tell you,' said Stigand, 'for if you were to be captured and the information extracted, it will forever ruin the name of your house and bring the wrath of the king down upon my head. In this, you must trust me, Harold – just get to Bristol as quickly as you can and sail to Ireland.'

'But my father is expecting us at Bosham.'

'Do not worry about that, your mother will tell him what is going on the moment he arrives.'

'My mother is involved in this?'

'She is, and we would have told you all sooner, but events played out far more quickly than we had anticipated.'

'Why Bristol?'

'It was the safest port we could arrange, and, as you probably know, Sweyn already has a ship there equipped to take him on his pilgrimage to Jerusalem. The crew are loyal to the family and will not let you down. Just get there as soon as you can, but be careful, for the Bishop of Worcester has also raised an army and is on his way here to support the king. If he catches any of you, your days will be numbered.'

'Are you sure about this?' asked Harold.

'More than anything else in the world,' said Stigand. 'Get to Bristol and sail for Ireland as soon as you can. Do this, and your family's exile may be shorter than you anticipate.'

Harold stared at the bishop before taking his arm in friendship.

'Be careful, Bishop Stigand,' he said, 'and with God's grace, we shall see you soon.'

'Amen,' said the bishop, and as Harold and Leofwine Godwinson turned their horses away, he headed in through the gates of Havering Palace.

—

Two days later, Godwin and his fleet of twenty ships set sail from Bosham to a new life across the sea in Flanders. It had taken more time than they had imagined loading everything they needed, and much had had to be left behind, but he knew more men would follow him as soon as they got organised. For now, all he could do was head into exile.

'Do you think they will be all right?' asked Gytha, staring back towards the harbour.

'Who?' replied Godwin.

'Wulfnorth and Hakon.'

'They will be fine,' said Godwin. 'Edward is many things, but he is no child murderer. Besides, they are worth more to him alive than dead.'

'I agree,' said Gytha, 'and anyway, I'm sure Ealdgyth will make sure they are well treated.'

'She will,' said Godwin. 'Trust me, Gytha, this situation is temporary, and if what you have told me about Harold going to Ireland is true, then they will be back amongst us before this year is out.'

'Oh, it is true,' said Gytha, 'and I would imagine that as long as Harold gets to Bristol safely, he will be surprised at what exactly waits for him aboard Sweyn's ship.'

–

In Bristol, Harold and Leofwine led their horses up the ramp and handed them over to two of the crew.

'Master Harold,' said the captain, 'it is good to see you again. I don't know if you remember me, I served as a mate on one of your ships out of Sandwich.'

'I do,' said Harold offering his arm in friendship, 'your name is Mathew Larkhill if I recall correctly.'

'Aye, it is my lord,' said Larkhill, 'and I am honoured that you remember it.'

'On the contrary,' said Harold, 'your name was mentioned on many occasions, and it was obviously only a matter of time before you got your own captaincy.' He looked around the ship. 'So, have you been told where we are going?'

'Aye, I have,' said Larkhill. 'We are headed to Leinster, though why I have no idea.'

'Are we ready to sail?'

'At your command,' said the captain.

'Good, then let us weigh anchor.'

'As you wish, my lord,' said Larkhill.

'Oh, one more thing,' said Harold, 'I was told that there would be something waiting for me as soon as I came aboard. Something that would explain why we are going to Ireland.'

'I don't know anything about that,' said the captain, 'but there is a man waiting in the stern. I think he may be a monk.'

Harold walked over to the canvas sheet covering the rear quarter of the ship and pulled open the flap. Inside he saw

Spearhafoc sitting on a pile of sacks, a leather bag upon his lap. The monk looked worried and exhausted, but his face lit up when he saw Harold standing in the doorway.

'Harold,' he said, 'thank the Lord. I thought you had been captured, or worse.'

'We had to evade the Bishop of Worcester and his men,' said Harold, 'so took a different road, but I am here now. Why don't you tell me what this is all about? Why are we going to Ireland, and why are you here?'

'Ireland was not my decision,' said Spearhafoc, 'that was decided by your mother. She wants to engage the services of King Diarmait on behalf of your father.'

'That much I know,' said Harold, 'but what I do not understand is how we are going to pay for his men or what your part is in all of this. Is he an ally of yours, family, perhaps?'

'I have never met the man,' said Spearhafoc, 'and have no influence over him. What I do have, however, is the means to pay for an army and a huge one at that.'

'What do you mean?' asked Harold. 'With the greatest of respect, you are but a humble monk and sworn to a life of poverty.'

Spearhafoc stood up and handed over the heavy satchel. Harold untied the leather straps and peered inside, shocked to see it filled with small gold statuettes and precious stones. He looked up, shocked.

'What is this?' he asked. 'I do not understand.'

'It belongs to the king,' said Spearhafoc. 'I was supposed to melt the gold down for a new royal crown and inlay it with the jewels, but in the circumstances, I believe it can all be put to a better use.'

'You stole these?'

'I suppose you could say that,' said Spearhafoc, 'but as I am using them to save England, I hope God will judge me on my motives, not my actions.'

Harold stared into the bag again, astonished at the wealth within.

'This is a gift indeed,' he said eventually, 'but even so, it will not go far when it comes to paying an army.'

'I know,' said Spearhafoc, turning to look at the rest of the sacks, 'but in those bags, there is also a selection of the finest silver ornaments from the king's vaults.'

'I don't know what to say,' said Harold. 'Did you bring all this?'

'I did,' said Spearhafoc. 'All of it was stored in the goldsmith's vaults in Abingdon, but when I heard what had happened, I filled a cart and came here as soon as I could. The valuables are yours, Harold Godwinson. Now let us go and get your father a Viking army.'

Part Four

Chapter Twenty-seven

Westminster Palace, February, AD 1052

King Edward walked into his brand-new audience chamber in Westminster Palace. The building as a whole was a long way from being finished, but enough had been completed to allow him to take up residence whenever he was in London, and as it was walking distance from Westminster Abbey, it was also convenient to keep in touch with his most trusted adviser, Archbishop Robert of Jumièges.

Waiting for him in the chamber were a host of men who had supported him almost four months earlier when he had dealt with the Godwin family. Now, with the burden forever released from around his neck, he had summoned them all to receive recognition for their support. As he entered, the gathering fell quiet, and everyone bowed as he took his seat on the raised dais.

'Gentlemen,' he said, looking around, 'thank you once again for your unflinching support these past few months, especially when my life was threatened by the outlaw Godwin of Wessex. Without your presence, I have no doubt this country could now be at war with itself. Luckily, the traitor and his spawn have long gone, and we are once more free to live our lives according to the laws of our land without fear of contradiction.'

He turned to a servant at his side who gave him a rolled-up parchment.

'I have now had time to consider,' continued Edward, 'and have decided on the following awards. All the men in this room will receive a gift of land, not less than five hides, irrespective of station. However, it is to be noted that the hides come with the usual obligations of taxation and manpower.'

A murmur of approval rippled around the room. It was a generous gift.

'In addition,' continued the king, 'there will be a financial award to everyone present, the value of which will be calculated according to station. Before you leave today, make sure you attend my treasurer, who will inform you of the value of your purse.'

Again the men mumbled their pleasure. It was turning into a profitable day.

'There are, however,' said Edward, 'a few present who went above and beyond what could have been expected, and it is to them I award the greatest gifts.' He looked down at the document and started to read.

'In return for Earl Leofric's support, I grant his son, Aelfgar, the Earlship of East Anglia, lands once governed by Harold Godwinson. The counties of Huntingdonshire and Cambridgeshire shall be awarded directly to Earl Siward for his loyalty. To Odda of Deerhurst, I award a new earlship, made up of part of Earl Godwin's lands and some of those forfeited by Earl Sweyn. To my nephew, Ralph of Mantes, I make permanent his temporary stewardship of the rest of Earl Sweyn's lands and grant him the title Earl of Hereford and the surrounding counties, the boundaries of which will be finalised over the next few weeks.'

He turned to face Robert of Jumièges. 'To the Archbishop of Canterbury, there is no physical gift, for he is blessed with the highest position this country can offer within the Church, but there is no doubt that without his advice and steadfastness, we would not all be here today. So my award to him is twofold: the first is to declare that the thief, Spearhafoc of Bury St Edmunds, is declared an outlaw, and when he is found, he will be tried and found guilty by the royal council before being executed before the gates of Westminster Abbey; the second award is for me to accept his nomination to the post of Bishop of London. To this end, I hereby declare that the monk known as William the Norman fills that position with immediate effect. These are the awards of this royal court.'

The room burst into excited chatter. Everyone was more than happy with their awards, though Earls Siward and Leofric, standing to one side, were quieter than most.

'There is one more thing,' said the king loudly, causing the room to fall quiet. 'I have the unfortunate responsibility to issue one more declaration, one which gives me no pleasure.' He looked around the room, knowing what he was about to say would be unpopular. 'As you know,' he continued, 'I have no heirs, and this is a situation that worries us all. Obviously, the problem lies with the queen, and it is with great sadness that after examinations by the royal physicians and the Archbishop of Canterbury, she has been declared barren and incapable of bearing children.'

This time a gasp of dismay rippled around the room at the devastating news.

'I can assure you,' he continued, 'that we do not hold her responsible for this situation, for it is clear that God did not see fit to give her the gift of motherhood, but nevertheless, England needs an heir. To that end, Queen Ealdgyth has today been transported to the nunnery at Wilton Abbey, there to live the rest of her life in the service of the Lord. All her lands and possessions have been confiscated by the Crown and will be used to further the religious work of the Archbishop of Canterbury. We pray for her wellbeing and for the Lord's forgiveness for her failure to provide me with a son. However, it is England that must come first in these difficult times, so with immediate effect, I have asked the archbishop to start proceedings that will end our marriage. Once done, we will seek a new queen, one that will provide our country with the heirs it so desperately needs. Once again, I thank you for your attendance and your loyalty,' he said. 'This audience is now over.'

Everyone bowed as he disappeared through a door behind the throne, closely followed by the archbishop.

'What did you think of that?' asked Earl Leofric to Earl Siward when they had gone.

'The extra lands and money will be useful,' said Siward, 'but I can't help feeling a little uneasy at how quickly he disposed of Godwin's estates. Just a few weeks ago, there were three of us, all equally important to England. Now, in a blink of an eye, we are down to two, and I worry whether I may be next.'

'My feelings exactly,' said Leofric, 'there is much to consider. Let us keep in touch and have our wits about us.'

'I agree,' said Siward, taking Leofric's wrist in friendship. 'Stay safe.'

Both men left the room along with the others, not realising that their private conversation had been observed carefully by an onlooker, someone who knew their doubts could make a huge difference to the future of England.

–

In Ireland, King Diarmait of Leinster stood near the dock watching woodworkers splitting tree trunks for new ships. For the past four months, he had kept Harold and Leofwine waiting for his decision on whether to aid Godwin's planned return to England. In the meantime, he had made them welcome but was still undecided if he wanted to commit his men to a confrontation with the English king. Now, after finally receiving the information he had been waiting for, he had made a decision and waited for Harold to arrive to give him the news.

At the top of the hill to the rear of the harbour, Harold and Leofwine reined in their horses and stared down at the hive of activity below.

'It looks like he has ordered the construction of more ships,' said Leofwine.

'It does,' said Harold, 'and hopefully that is a good sign. Come, let us see what he has to say.' They urged their horses down the path and entered the docks before dismounting and walking up to Diarmait.

'King Diarmait,' said Harold, 'you sent for us?'

'I did,' said Diarmait. 'I have made my decision.'

Harold glanced nervously over to Leofwine. If the answer was no, then they would have to leave Ireland and seek men elsewhere.

'When you first came here,' Diarmait continued, 'I was taken by the unfairness of your tale and initially keen to support your family's cause. However, I have not lived this long by believing every story that is told at my hearth, so I sent men to find out the truth of the matter.'

'Where did you send them,' asked Leofwine, 'for the tale will surely be different depending upon who you ask?'

'They talked to many people,' said Diarmait, 'on both sides of the argument, but foremost amongst them was your sister at Wilton Abbey.'

'They spoke to Gunhild?'

'They did, for I was already in communication with the abbey about some other matters. Consequently, my representatives took the opportunity to talk to Sister Gunhild and report that she is an impressive young woman.'

'She is,' said Harold, 'but I fail to see what this has to do with whether you will support my father or not.'

'Perhaps nothing, perhaps a lot,' said Diarmait, 'but whatever the outcome, I have decided that I cannot commit my men to an attack on the King of England.'

Harold's heart sank, as did that of Leofwine.

'Your grace—' he started, but Diarmait held up his hand for silence.

'I have not finished,' he said. 'There is more.'

The two brothers stared at Diarmait, wondering where the conversation was going.

'I will not commit my men,' continued the king, 'for they have only just returned from defeating King Eachmargarch in

Dublin. As you may well know, Dublin is now in the hands of my son, Murchard. Now the fighting is over, however, many of the mercenaries involved are looking for fresh engagement. If you are determined to raise an army, then I am happy to help you recruit those men for your campaign.'

Harold looked towards Leofwine. Despite the disappointment of King Diarmait's refusal to join them, they both knew that this alternative was just as good, if not better.

'That is more than we could have expected, your grace,' said Harold, turning back to the king, 'you have our gratitude.'

'Make Gunhild the target of your gratitude,' said the king, 'it is to her you owe thanks.'

Harold nodded with relief. Although he had no idea what part Gunhild had played, at least he could send a message to his father in Flanders to inform him he had managed to raise an army.

'Thank you, your grace,' said Harold. 'You will not regret it.'

'I'm sure I will not,' said the king, looking up to the hill behind them. 'Where is Brother Spearhafoc, is he not joining us?'

'He is not,' said Harold, 'for he is consumed with guilt regarding his theft from Abingdon and has set out to walk around the coast of Ireland as an act of penance.'

'Ireland is a dangerous place,' said Diarmait, 'he will do well to return alive.'

'Nevertheless, he said it was something he had to do,' said Harold. 'We pray that one day our paths will cross again.'

'As will I,' said the king. 'He is a strange yet fascinating character.' He turned back to face the row of partly finished boats along the dock.

'This is a momentous day, Harold Godwinson,' said Diarmait, 'and whatever happens in the next few months, I feel that England will somehow never be the same again.'

In Flanders, Godwin stood on the walled roof of his manor house, staring across the sea in the direction of England. He and his family had settled into an estate near the busy port of Bruges, and with Tostig now married to Judith of Flanders, the two families had become close. Godwin knew that, for the time being at least, they were safe.

Ever since landing in Bruges three months earlier, he had spent almost every minute planning his return. As far as he was concerned, the exile was temporary, and he knew that he still had vast support all across England.

With that in mind, he had sent messengers back across the channel to all those he had been close to during his time as the Earl of Wessex, and slowly but surely, the promises of support were beginning to come in. Overall he was confident that he would eventually be able to sail back to England, but if that confrontation led to armed conflict with Edward, he knew that he would have to win or die trying. There were no other options.

The one thing that concerned him was the position of Earls Leofric and Siward. Both men were extremely powerful, and it was their unwelcome support of Edward in London that had persuaded Godwin to flee to Flanders. But Godwin also knew they were often critical of the king, so their stance had been unexpected. As long as Edward had their support, Godwin knew that any attempt either to overthrow the king or even to get him to withdraw all charges against his family would be unlikely to succeed. It was a problem he had to deal with and, despite his growing forces, one that could ultimately condemn him to permanent exile.

'Father,' said a voice behind him, 'you wanted to see me?'

'Sweyn,' said Godwin, turning to face his son, 'come and stand with me.'

Sweyn walked over and followed his father's gaze out over the sea.

'Over there,' said Godwin, 'through the mist, lies the land of our forefathers. It has seen our ancestors live, toil and die through endless challenges, and no matter how heavy the yoke, how demanding the trials, we came through the other side to win power and influence.'

'That was mainly your doing,' said Sweyn. 'Your alliance with King Cnut all those years ago was a fortuitous decision.'

'Perhaps so,' said Godwin, 'but make no mistake, it was no more than this family deserved. Since then, we have laboured hard to maintain and grow our position while always dealing fairly with our people. Now I find myself banished from the very soil that covers our ancestors' remains through no fault of my own.'

'Some may say we have been too soft in wielding our power.'

'Perhaps so, but every day that passes sees more men commit to our cause, and the time is fast approaching when I must sail back to claim our birthright.'

'And not a moment too soon,' said Sweyn. 'For years, I have preached the injustice of having a king on the throne who sees himself more Norman than English. Now events have proved me right, and I stand ready to lead your armies against Edward.'

Godwin looked over to Sweyn. There was no doubt that he was an impressive man, especially when it came to conflict, but his temperament was questionable at best, and Godwin knew that when it came to diplomacy, he could be a liability.

'Sweyn, you are my firstborn son, and as such, you will always have a prominent place in this family. You are also the only one of my sons so far to have faced any sort of pitched battle, so it should be you who leads us back to England.'

'And I will be proud to do so,' interjected Sweyn. 'Just say when and I will lead our fleet up the Thames to drag Edward from his throne.'

'Sweyn,' said Godwin, 'let me finish. I said that it *should* be you, but alas, I cannot give you that role.'

'What?' said Sweyn. 'If not me, then who? Surely not Harold, he is half the man I am when it comes to the fight, and I will not serve under him.'

'That will not be necessary,' said Godwin, 'for you will not be there.'

'You are not making any sense,' said Sweyn. 'Of course I will be there. Do you think for one moment that I will allow my family to fight without me?'

'You will not be there,' said Godwin, 'because when we finally do go, there will be no place for you. I do not want you at my side.'

'*What are you talking about?*' gasped Sweyn. 'You need me.'

'If there was no other outcome possible than all-out war, then perhaps you would be right,' said Godwin, 'but there is still a chance that all this can be resolved peacefully. However, the king holds you in great contempt, and if you were involved while still exiled, I fear that there would be no chance for negotiations, and England's fields would run red with blood. I can't take you Sweyn, you must stay here.'

Sweyn stared at his father with ill-disguised contempt.

'I knew it,' Sweyn said eventually. 'You have no intention of standing up for this family at all. You are going to bend the knee and become yet another paid servant to Edward's false reign.'

'Think what you like, Sweyn,' said Godwin, 'for you will not believe anything I have to say. The truth of the matter is that I want a strong England with our family at the forefront. However, until the time comes that Edward pardons you for all that you have done, that is never going to happen. I suggest you undertake the pilgrimage that was decreed by the Pope and come back here at length with your head held high. Do that, and I will gladly stand at your side before the king, but until you have absolution, there is no place for you here.'

Sweyn struggled to control his temper, wanting nothing more than to lash out and beat his father to the floor. But he also knew that Godwin had lived a life of conflict, and there was no guarantee he would emerge the victor in such a fight.

'You disgust me,' Sweyn said eventually, 'and you are finally showing your true colours. You are the coward I always knew you to be.'

Godwin stared at his son, swallowing the anger that had built up over so many years.

'I know this is hard to take,' Godwin replied, 'but I am telling you now so you can start your journey back into the corridors of power. Go to Jerusalem, Sweyn, and when you come back, take your place alongside me as head of this family.'

Sweyn paused while staring at his father, still seething at the decision.

'Do you know what?' he said eventually. 'You are right – I should go to Jerusalem. But I tell you this, Father – when I return, it will not be to stand at your side in the House of Godwin, it will be to regain what is rightfully mine and return England's rightful king to the throne – me, the son of Cnut the Great.'

'Sweyn,' said Godwin, 'Cnut was not your father, I am, and you need to accept that fact before this obsession gets you killed. Make this pilgrimage and come home to us a renewed man.'

'You are no father of mine,' said Sweyn. 'Not now, not ever. This is not over, Godwin. I will travel to Jerusalem, but when I return, I swear there will be a reckoning.' With that, he turned away and stormed through the doorway back into the house.

Godwin sighed with frustration. He had known it was going to be difficult, but it had gone worse than expected. Now, though, he had to refocus on the matter at hand and work out a way to return the rest of his family to England.

Chapter Twenty-eight

Hereford, May, AD 1052

King Gruffydd stood hidden amongst the trees, waiting as his men moved silently into position. Since Earl Sweyn had helped him in his struggle against King Rhydderch many years earlier, he had refrained from attacking Hereford, but once the news of Sweyn's fall from grace had reached him in Gwynedd, he saw no reason to hold back any further. Hereford had always been a rich and fertile county, and Gruffydd wanted it for himself.

For months they had harassed any trading caravans travelling through the marches, but they had attempted nothing against the larger towns, knowing that to do so would incur the full wrath of Godwin and the king. But now, with a new earl ruling Wessex, the old alliance was broken, and he had become bolder with his patrols, often crossing the border to plunder the smaller villages and farmsteads. Now, at last, the fortified town at the heart of Hereford lay before him.

'My lord,' said the man at his side, staring at wooden walls surrounding the town. 'I see no signs of weakness in the palisade. Are you sure about this?'

'Have faith, Macsen,' said Gruffydd, 'my spies assure me that there is a weakness in the western wall, and though we may not see it from here, I believe him. This is an opportunity we cannot miss.'

Both men fell silent until the rest of the army reached the forest edge. Eventually, everyone was in place, and as the signal was passed along the line, Gruffydd finally gave the command.

'*Men of Gwynedd,*' he roared, drawing his sword, '*advaaance!*'

On the northeastern coast of England, Godwin of Wessex and one of his huscarls, Osmund of London, lay hidden amongst a pile of seaweed-covered rocks at the water's edge. Behind them, the rowing boat they had used to reach land had been pulled up onto the sand, an arrow's flight away from the fishing boat they had used to get there just an hour or so earlier.

'Are you sure this is the right place?' asked Godwin.

'Aye, I recognise those hills,' said Osmund. 'Besides, we'll know soon enough, and if nobody comes, we'll have to leave soon to catch the tide.'

Both men fell silent again, keeping their heads low, well aware that they were potentially in enemy territory, and all this could be an elaborate trap set by supporters of the king. Nevertheless, the message Godwin had received just days earlier from Bishop Stigand had been intriguing enough to persuade him to cross the channel. All the note had said was that it was important that the earl met with Stigand at a specific location and to tell nobody about the arrangement.

For the next hour or so, both men lay hidden, talking quietly, when suddenly Godwin raised his hand, cutting Osmund short.

'Shh,' he whispered, 'listen.'

A few paces away, an unknown man looked around in frustration, seeking the occupants of the boat.

'Earl Godwin,' he called suddenly, 'if you can hear me, rest assured that I have been sent by Bishop Stigand to take you to him. If you are here, please show yourself.'

'At last,' said Godwin, climbing from his hiding place. 'Who are you, friend, and who do you call master?'

'My name is Fredrick,' said the man, 'but more than that, I will not share. Bishop Stigand is waiting for you half a league from here, but he cannot stay long. Come, we should go.'

The two men followed the stranger up onto the shore and along a path leading inland. Despite them trying to question him about the reason they were there, he kept his silence, saying only that the meeting place was not far. Eventually, they approached a forest and, to one side, could see a tiny woodsman's hut.

'The man you seek,' said Fredrick, coming to a halt, 'is in there.'

'Are you not coming with us?' asked Osmund.

'I am not. I have been paid well, and my work here is done.' He turned away and headed down a different path.

'What do you think?' asked Osmund. 'It could be a trap.'

'If it is,' said Godwin, 'it's an elaborate one. Besides, it is too late now, we are on foot, and that forest could be swarming with mounted men. Come, let us get it done.'

They walked towards the hut, both men drawing their swords. As they neared it, the door opened, and Bishop Stigand stepped out to meet them.

'Earl Godwin,' he said, 'you came. Thank the Lord above.'

'Bishop Stigand,' replied Godwin, sheathing his sword, 'I cannot tell you how relieved I am to see you here. For a while, I thought it might be a trap. The message was short on detail.'

'It had to be,' said Stigand, 'as you will soon find out. Come inside, there is little time.'

Both men ducked into the hut. Inside was a single room with a doorway through to a stable at the rear.

'What is all this about?' asked Godwin. 'Does my daughter fare well?'

'The queen is as well as can be expected,' said Stigand, 'though I assume you know she has been sent to the nunnery at Wilton?'

'So I have been told,' said Godwin, 'though if I am honest with myself, it may be the safest place for her over the next few months.'

Stigand held up his hand to stop Godwin from speaking further, and the earl looked at him in confusion.

'Such details are for another time, perhaps,' said Stigand. 'The reason I asked you to come here in the first place is that there is someone I want you to meet.'

'You are not alone?' asked Osmund, his hand creeping to the hilt of his sword.

'I am not,' said Stigand, 'but I guarantee you are perfectly safe.' He turned to the door leading into the stable. 'You can come out now, they are alone.'

Godwin and Osmund watched as the door opened and a man stepped through to greet them.

'Hello, Earl Godwin,' he said, 'it is good to see you again.'

Godwin stared in shock as he recognised the man standing before him.

'Earl Siward,' Godwin said eventually, holding out his arm.

–

Back in Hereford, King Gruffydd's army had overwhelmed the town's defences and now rampaged through the streets, killing anyone who was deemed a threat and stealing whatever goods they could carry. At the centre of the town, a timber castle sat upon a raised mound surrounded by a deep ditch filled with timber spikes.

Up on the palisades, the armed men of Hereford looked down in frustration. The suddenness of the attack had caught them unprepared, and though they had managed to put up some initial resistance, the Welsh numbers were overwhelming, and they had quickly retreated to the castle. Now, with the town and its people completely under his control, Gruffydd turned his attention to the fortification.

For over an hour, his archers had fired volley after volley at the walls, but without any sort of siege engines to hand, Gruffydd knew that unless part of the palisade caught alight from the many fire-arrows, there was little chance he could breach them, at least not until the rest of his men turned up with rams and ladders.

'*Hold*,' he roared, 'and withdraw.'

Gradually his men withdrew to just out of range of the archers within the palisades.

'Macsen,' he said as the noise of battle eased off, 'come with me.' He stepped out from behind the wall where he had been taking cover and started walking up the path towards the castle gates, his hands in the air.

'Hold your arrows,' he shouted as he walked, 'I only wish to talk.'

'Stay back,' roared a voice, 'or we will cut you down where you stand.'

'Just listen to me,' replied Gruffydd, 'there is no need for anyone else to die here today. I just want to talk to your leader.'

'I am here,' shouted another voice. 'What do you want, Welshman?'

Gruffydd stopped in his tracks and stared at the man looking over the palisade.

'What is your name?'

'Who wants to know?'

Gruffydd hesitated, knowing that if he was to reveal his identity, he was making himself a target.

'Do not reveal yourself,' hissed Macsen at his side.

'I need him to trust me,' said Gruffydd. 'Warn me if you see any man draw his bow. My name,' he shouted, turning back to the palisade, 'is Gruffydd ap Llewelyn, and I am here to speak to Ralph of Mantes.'

The men on the battlements looked at each other with confusion. If the man below was indeed the Welsh king, they could easily kill him before he had the chance to run.

'If you are Gruffydd,' shouted the man, 'why do you put yourself at risk? We could cut you down where you stand.'

'You could,' replied Gruffydd, 'but I wanted to earn your trust to prove that what I have to say is true.'

'And what is that?'

'Let me speak to Ralph of Mantes. He is the Earl of Hereford, is he not?'

'He is, but he is not here. My name is Alan of Hereford, and I am in command in his absence. You can speak to me.'

'Where is your master?'

'Aboard a ship leading the king's fleet in the channel. There are reports that Godwin's ships have sailed from Bruges and Edward sent Ralph to sink them.'

'If that is true,' said Gruffydd, 'I suspect your master may come off second best. I hear they call him Ralph the Timid. Is that not true?'

'What do you want, Welshman?' asked Alan of Hereford. 'For you talk better than you fight.'

Gruffydd paused for a moment before responding.

'For your sake,' Gruffydd said eventually, 'I will ignore the insult, but you need to listen to me carefully. Hereford is already ours. My men have taken the town with few casualties, and by tonight we will double in number as well as having siege ladders and rams. Tomorrow morning at first light, we will tear down these palisades and kill every living person inside without quarter. That is not a threat, it is an oath, and if you are truly a man of war, you will see that there can only be one outcome. However, I already have what I came for, and nothing you can do can take it from me. So, I am here to offer you a chance to live. Surrender to me at dawn tomorrow, and you have my word that I will let you and all your men ride out of Hereford carrying your weapons. Refuse, and I will have no choice but to show the people of Hereford what sort of deaths await them should they try to rise against me. And I promise you it will not be pretty.'

The men on the palisade looked down at the hundreds of warriors surrounding the castle. There was no doubt that the defenders could hold them out for a while, perhaps even days, but with no way of sending for help, it was only a matter of time before the walls fell, and when that happened, there was only one possible outcome.

'How do I know you are telling the truth?' asked Alan of Hereford. 'You could slay us all as soon as we open the gates.'

'We could,' said Gruffydd, 'but I am a king, and my men have heard me give my word. If I were to break it, they would know I could never again be trusted.'

'I need time,' said the defender, 'there is much to consider.'

'Do not think too long, Alan of Hereford,' said Gruffydd. 'You have until dawn and not a moment longer.' Without waiting for an answer, he turned away, leaving his back exposed to the archers on the wall.

—

On the coast of East Anglia, Bishop Stigand, Earl Godwin and Earl Siward sat on three stools around the remains of a fire in the centre of the room. Osmund stayed at the door, keeping watch in case anyone came.

'I'm sorry I can't offer you any hospitality,' said Siward, 'but as you can see, the venue is not the best.'

'Meat and wine I can get in abundance once I leave,' said Godwin. 'I am far more interested in why I am here.'

'You are here at my behest,' said Stigand. 'At some of the audiences we have shared with the king recently, I suspected that Earl Siward was not comfortable with the way things were going. Eventually, I risked approaching him and found my suspicions were correct, so I asked if he would be willing to meet you.'

'To what end?' asked Godwin, turning to face Siward. 'You have already declared for Edward, surely you are not going to change sides now?'

'You are correct,' said Siward, 'for my loyalty is to the throne of England, irrespective of occupier.'

'So I ask again, why am I here?'

'I may be loyal to the Crown,' said Siward, 'but I am not blind, and even I can see who the true power behind the throne is.'

'Robert of Jumièges?'

Siward nodded.

'He has always been a concern,' said Siward, 'but lately, he has taken it upon himself to decide strategies in matters of both state and defence.'

'Does the king know of this?'

'Oh, he knows,' said Siward, 'but it seems as if the bishop has some sort of control over him, and he often just waves away our concerns without consideration. Lately, Earl Leofric and I have found ourselves more and more sidelined.'

'Not as much as I,' mused Godwin.

'Indeed,' said Siward, 'and what happened to you is an even greater worry. If he can simply dismiss the second most powerful man in England, then who is next?'

'Ah, so this is an exercise in self-preservation?'

'In part, yes,' said Siward, 'but it is more about the security of England itself. The way Edward is going, he will soon sideline every man in power except those of French birth, and if that happens, civil war is inevitable.'

'So what do you suggest?' asked Godwin. 'You have already said you will not turn on Edward.'

'And I stand by my oath,' said Siward, 'but what I can do is question his decisions and be slow to the table if it comes to conflict.'

'What do you mean?'

'What I am saying,' said Siward, 'is that if you stand up to the king and demand to be reinstated, there will not be many dissenting voices.'

'Talk does not make a king bend,' said Godwin, 'especially with you and Leofric at his back.'

'We will be there,' said Siward, 'but our armies will not. Unlike at Gloucester, you would only face the king's forces, and if it should come to a fight, although I am sworn to the Crown, our men would still be days away. With that disadvantage, I feel Edward will be more prone to listen.'

Godwin stared at Siward for a few moments as the proposal sank in.

'And what if it comes to blows?' he asked eventually.

'As I said, we will have to support the king, but it could take days for my men to arrive; who knows what you could achieve in that time. But one thing is certain – should you defeat the king's forces, there will be no point in more Englishmen dying, so we would not take arms against you.'

Again, Godwin fell silent. What he was being offered was basically an open road to London with whatever army he could raise. Once there, he had three days to convince the king to change his path before his men would be attacked by the forces of Siward and Leofric.

'You paint an interesting picture, Earl Siward,' Godwin said eventually, 'and there is much to think about. Allow me to give it some thought.'

'Of course,' said Siward, standing up. 'Send a message to Bishop Stigand when you have decided. But the situation grows worse by the day, and if you don't act soon, I fear England will soon be overrun by Frenchmen without a sword being drawn.'

'I will let you know within the month,' said Godwin. 'Now, we should go.'

'Travel safely, Earl Godwin,' said Siward, 'and may God bless England.'

Chapter Twenty-nine

Dungeness, England, 24 June, AD 1052

Godwin and Osmund walked down the gangplank and headed towards a group of three men waiting nervously at the harbour wall. Behind them, another dozen men disembarked, each battle-hardened and fully armed.

'Earl Godwin,' said one of the men, stepping forward, 'welcome to Dungeness.'

'Lord Beresford,' said Godwin, holding out his arm in friendship, 'thank you for doing this. Is everything ready?'

'Aye,' said Beresford. 'This is my son, Gareth; he will be your guide.'

'Greetings, my lord,' said the young man, nodding to the earl.

'And to you,' said Godwin. 'Did you manage to get the horses I requested?'

'I did, my lord, they are waiting in the stable outside the dock gates. We are ready to go as soon as you say the word.'

'Good,' replied Godwin. 'We should waste no time, for we need to get to as many towns and villages as we can. As soon as word gets out that I am here, I have no doubt that Edward will send his men after me.' He turned back to Beresford. 'Do you have any more news?'

'Aye,' said Beresford, 'the mood is turning sour against the king and his pet archbishop. Everyone I talk to yearns for your return, and support spreads like wildfire. I reckon that if you do return, you will have the whole of southern and eastern

England at your back. When are you coming back, my lord? When can we expect to see your fleet on the horizon?'

'Soon enough,' said Godwin. 'And the support of the people is welcomed, but I still need to recruit experienced men-at-arms to my banner.'

'I reckon I can call on about two hundred,' said Beresford, 'but few are willing to sign a commitment lest your campaign fails to materialise and the document is found.'

'I understand,' said Godwin. 'Just assure them that I will return and, signature or not, I will need their support.'

'I will, my lord,' said Beresford. 'Now, you should be going.'

Godwin nodded and followed the guide out of the harbour along with his men. A few minutes later, they galloped out of Dungeness and headed inland to begin recruiting the men they would need for the day they confronted the king.

-

In Dublin, Harold, Leofwine and King Diarmait of Leinster walked along a line of ships in the harbour. The fleet was ready to sail and was fully equipped to service the needs of over five hundred mercenaries, each of whom was currently enjoying the alehouses of the city.

'This is more than I could have expected, your grace,' said Harold. 'Five hundred fighting men will make a huge difference should it come to a confrontation.'

'I hope it doesn't come to that,' said Diarmait, 'but if it does, you can rely on these men to be your vanguard. Pretty they are not, but as fighting men go, you will find none better. Just keep them supplied with ale, meat and women, in that order.'

'I will try my best,' laughed Harold. 'Are you not coming with us?'

'I am not,' said Diarmait. 'With these men, my commitment to you is over. What happens from here onwards is your business only.'

'I understand,' said Harold. 'You have my eternal gratitude, King Diarmait. If there is anything I can ever do to repay you, please let me know.'

'There is one small thing,' said the king. 'I want you to take something to Wilton Abbey and make sure your sister receives it personally.'

'You have a gift for Gunhild?'

'You could call it that,' said Diarmait. 'Your sister is studying the life of St Brigid of Ireland and last year reached out to me for any information I might have. We started corresponding, and I found her thoughts to be very enlightening. She seems to be a very spiritual person, so I would like to give her something that deserves to be in the hands of someone far more likely to look after it than I.'

'What is it?' asked Harold.

Diarmait turned and called out to one of the following servants, who ran over carrying an ornate box. Diarmait opened the lid to reveal a small piece of fading red fabric.

'This,' he said, 'is what is left of the Mantle of St Brigid. It has been kept in a local chapel for centuries, but I want your sister to have it. I'm sure she will see it gets a more suitable home.'

'Who was St Brigid?' asked Harold. 'And what is so special about her mantle?'

'As a young woman, she used it to perform a miracle to win lands from a king to build a monastery,' said Diarmait. 'The details escape me, but I'm sure your sister can tell you more. Take it – Gunhild will make a far better custodian than I.'

Harold took the box and handed it to Leofwine at his side.

'My work here is now done,' continued Diarmait, 'and I intend to leave tonight. When do you sail?'

'Tomorrow at noon,' said Harold. 'It will probably take the morning to round up those still suffering from too much ale.'

'Aye, it will,' laughed Diarmait, 'but trust me, it is a price worth paying. Travel well, Earl Harold, and give my regards to your father.'

'I will,' said Harold taking the king's wrist. 'Live long, King Diarmait, and may God watch over you.'

—

In London, King Edward sat in his council room with his advisors. Chief amongst them, as usual, was the Archbishop of Canterbury, Robert of Jumièges. The mood was troubled, for not one man amongst them had good news to report.

'What do you mean you cannot find him?' snapped the king to Earl Ralph of Mantes. 'You and Earl Odda have spent weeks in command of my fleet. Why have you not brought Godwin's head to me on a spike?'

'Your grace,' replied the earl, 'we have scoured the coastline from north to south, but no sooner do we arrive at a confirmed sighting than we are told he has gone. Either he has the will of the people on his side, and they sow untruths to keep us on the wrong path, or God himself enables his escape with storms and fair winds.'

'God is not with Godwin of Wessex,' interrupted Robert of Jumièges. 'He is, and always has been, on the side of the King of England. You would do well to remember that, Earl Ralph.'

'Of course,' said Ralph, 'but it has to be acknowledged that somehow he remains at least two steps ahead of us at all times. The weather has also not aided our task, for we spend more time in harbour than we do at sea.'

'Yet this is the same weather that Godwin encounters,' said Robert of Jumièges. 'Perhaps it is you that is not up to the task.'

'Your grace,' said Bishop Stigand from across the room, 'in fairness, all of Godwin's men are experienced sailors, as is Godwin himself. Earl Ralph, despite his undoubted commitment, is new to the sea, and it is perhaps ill-advised to judge him too harshly in this matter.'

'Bishop Stigand,' said the king, 'when I allocate tasks in my name, especially ones that involve the defence of England, I expect them to be carried out as instructed. This is neither the time nor place for excuses.'

'Forgive me, your grace,' said Stigand, 'I was just trying to find alternatives to achieve the same aims.'

'And these alternatives are?'

'I think we should remove Earls Odda and Ralph from command of the fleet and replace them with men born to the sea. I hasten to add that this is not a judgement on the abilities of either man but would better allocate your resources where needed. When this is done, the fleet would be more effective, and Earl Ralph can focus on wresting Hereford from the hands of the Welsh. For several weeks now, King Gruffydd has used Hereford as a base from which to launch attacks further into England, and if we are not careful, Leominster itself could fall, and that would be a disaster.'

'I have to admit I am concerned about the Welsh,' said Edward. 'Perhaps I should consider leading an army there myself and finish this man once and for all.'

'In time, yes,' said Archbishop Robert, 'but for now, I would suggest your attention remains focused on Godwin. We have heard that he is recruiting men up and down the coast of England, and if that is true, then it can only mean he intends to return. When he does, we must be ready for him.'

'I agree,' said the king, 'and I also agree that Earls Ralph and Odda are out of their depth.' He turned to the two men in question. 'Where is the fleet now?'

'In Sandwich, your grace,' said Ralph.

'Bring it to London,' said Edward, 'and moor it on the Thames alongside Westminster. In the meantime, I will seek more experienced commanders to relieve you of your positions. Once done, I expect you to reclaim Hereford in my name. Is that clear?'

'Yes, your grace,' said Ralph.

'Good. In that case, this audience is over. You may leave.'

Just over two weeks later, Godwin was back in his temporary home in Bruges, enjoying a rare meal with his wife Gytha and Harold's wife, Edyth Swanneck. His continued recruitment drive along the southern coast of England had been hampered by bad weather, but he had been encouraged by the number of men who had sworn support. In addition, his son Harold had sent news that he had managed to raise an army in Ireland to support his cause and would come to Bruges as soon as he could, but first needed to take care of some business in Porlock on the way.

'When are you sailing back out?' asked Gytha, setting her wine down on the table.

'Not for a few months yet,' said Godwin. 'First, I need to see the mettle of the men Harold has recruited. We have managed to avoid the king's fleet so far, but our luck cannot hold forever.'

'Did you not say that Earls Ralph and Odda were inept?'

'As seamen, perhaps, but they still command land armies made up of the best England can offer. If we were to be caught and forced to beach, there is no knowing which way the battle would fall. No, I need more men and more ships.'

'Have you heard anything about Wulfnorth and Hakon?'

'I have not,' said Godwin, reaching for the platter of chicken in the centre of the table, 'but that is a good thing. As long as I am alive and pose a threat, they both have value to Edward.'

'And if you die?' asked Gytha.

Godwin sighed and picked up his tankard. 'Then I suppose he has no more need for them, so they will be released.'

'Or killed,' said Gytha, voicing the worry that played on everyone's mind.

Godwin paused with the tankard halfway to his mouth.

'Wipe that thought from your mind,' he said. 'As I said before, Edward is a lot of things, but he is no child murderer.'

'He may not be, but I wouldn't put it past Robert of Jumièges.'

'But he is a man of God,' interjected Edyth, 'surely he could never do such a thing.'

Godwin and Gytha did not answer, both knowing that some men of the cloth had committed far worse crimes in the name of God.

'Look,' said Godwin eventually, 'it should not come to that. You saw what happened in Gloucester. Edward had a chance to kill my men and me but decided not to. A civil war is no good to anyone, and certainly not to England.'

'Then why are you raising an army?' asked Edyth. 'Can you not just petition him again and ask to be heard?'

'I could, and indeed will,' said Godwin. 'But alas, without an army at my back, and as long as Robert of Jumièges has the king's ear, I am just opening myself up to be condemned without a hearing. At least this way, he will see that I am serious and will, at the very least, agree to my case being heard by the Witan.'

Before Edyth could answer, the door opened, and two men entered, each wearing sodden cloaks from the downpour outside. Both removed their hoods, and Godwin could see that the first man was Osmund, his favoured huscarl, but the second was a stranger to him.

'My lord,' said Osmund, walking towards Godwin, 'I have news.'

'Can it not wait?' asked Godwin. 'It is not often I get to break bread with my wife.'

'It will not,' said Osmund, turning to beckon the stranger. 'Karl,' he said, 'come forward.'

The second man joined Osmund and bowed his head to all three sitting at the table.

'My lord,' he said, 'my ladies.'

'This man is a deckhand out of Sandwich,' continued Osmund. 'He arrived in Bruges yesterday aboard a trading ship but fled after beating one of his shipmates half to death over an insult. He was to receive twenty lashes but made his escape before anyone could lay a hand upon him.'

'Then why is he here?' asked Godwin. 'At sea, the captain's word is law, and he should be whipped. In fact, the number should now be doubled for desertion.'

'Aye,' said Osmund, 'I agree, but in an effort to save his own skin, he begged an audience with you. He said he had important news and would share it in return for a pardon.'

'I do not trade in such things,' said Godwin. 'Take him away and give him back to the captain.'

'I tried to,' said Osmund, 'so he told me what he had to say. You need to hear this.'

Godwin looked back at the prisoner.

'Well,' he said, 'say what you want to say. But I warn you now it has to be something special for you to save your skin.'

'It is, my lord,' said the sailor, 'your man here is telling the truth. I am indeed a deckhand out of Sandwich, but I do not normally serve on trading ships. I was only on this one because that was the only work I could get. Until a few days ago, I served on one of the ships seeking you up and down the coast of England under the command of Earl Ralph and have been for many weeks.'

'And?' said Godwin, his interest piqued.

'As I said, my lord, there was plenty of work for men such as me, but a few days ago, we were dismissed along with many of the men-at-arms still aboard. The ships were left with skeleton crews only.'

'Why would they do that?' asked Godwin.

'The talk was, my lord, that Earls Ralph and Odda were to be replaced, and until that happened, it was pointless retaining so many sailors while the ships lay idle in the harbour.'

'So the fleet lies unprotected in Sandwich?'

'No, my lord, those still aboard were tasked with sailing them up the Thames to Westminster. They left a few days ago.'

'*What?*' gasped Godwin, getting to his feet.

'It is true, my lord, I swear it. I needed work and managed to get aboard a trading ship, but I fell out with a Frenchman and broke his teeth. I am sorry about what I did, my lord, I truly am, but he deserved it, as God is my witness.'

Godwin held up his hand to demand silence.

'If this is true,' he said, turning to Osmund, 'there is no way the ships can go back to sea. At least not until the king appoints a new fleet commander.'

'But he just said that the earls were going to be replaced,' said Osmund.

'It is not as easy as that,' said Godwin. 'Such men are hard to find, especially any that are loyal to the king.'

'What are you going to do?'

Godwin did not answer but turned back to face the sailor.

'If what you say is true,' he said, 'I will pardon your crime in full and give you a purse of silver. In the meantime, you shall have two silver pennies for your message and a position on one of my ships.'

'Thank you, my lord,' said the sailor, 'they said you are a just man.'

'Just, I may be,' said Godwin, 'but I am no fool, and if your tale is a lie, I will hang you myself. Now be gone and keep your mouth shut about this night.'

'I will, my lord,' said the sailor before turning away to leave.

'Well,' said Osmund when the man had gone, 'what do you want to do?'

'First, we must find out if he tells the truth,' said Godwin, 'and if he does, we need to get word to Harold. This is an opportunity we cannot afford to let slip through our fingers.'

'I thought you said you did not yet have enough men to confront the king,' said Gytha.

'Perhaps not in open battle,' said Godwin, 'but he doesn't know that, and without a fleet, the heart of London is at risk.' He turned back to Osmund. 'Prepare our ships, my friend – tomorrow we sail for England.'

Chapter Thirty

Harold Godwinson stood in the bow of the lead ship, peering through the gloom to the banks of the River Severn. To the west were the distant hills of Wales, but he was more interested in the eastern bank and, in particular, the town of Porlock in his brother's former earldom of Somerset.

When Sweyn had first been exiled by the king, many of his towns and villages had pledged their continued allegiance to the Godwin family, but one town, Porlock, had made it clear that they were glad to be rid of anything to do with the Godwins and had even supplied ships to pursue the fleeing family when they had escaped to Bruges the previous year. Now, with an army of mercenaries under his command, Harold wanted retribution. The sails had been lowered, and the oarsmen pulled quietly, taking the ships closer in to shore.

'Steady,' said the captain behind him, 'there is a good landing spot just ahead. We are less than a league away from Porlock and can reach there undetected.'

Callum One-eye, leader of the mercenaries, was an Irishman of Norse descent. His name reflected an injury he had received in one of the many fights he had been in throughout his life, but despite the disfigurement, his prowess in battle was undisputed, and the men both feared and respected him in equal measure.

'So be it,' said Harold, turning to look at his crew. Many sat at the oars, pulling steadily, but many more sat on the benches between, each fully armed and waiting impatiently to disembark.

'We are almost there,' said Harold. 'When we land, we will wait for the rest of the men before heading upriver. If we meet anyone on the way, make sure they are silenced as quickly as you can. Once we are in sight of the town, we will re-form and make our assault. Is that clear?'

'Aye,' came the murmured reply from most of the men as Harold turned back to face the approaching shoreline. His revenge on Porlock could have been delayed, but he knew his mercenary army were impatient for blood and plunder, and this was a perfect opportunity to keep them interested.

The boat shuddered to a halt as the hull ground against the rocky riverbed, and one of the men immediately jumped overboard, landing in waist-deep water with a coil of rope over his shoulders. He waded to the shore before wrapping the rope around one of the many boulders. To either side, the other ships did the same, and within moments hundreds of men waded through the water to the shore.

Once they were all on land and the ships were secured, Harold led his army upstream, and a few hours later, looked down from a bracken-covered hill above Porlock. The sun was just rising behind them, and a low mist still lay amongst the houses of the town. A few people had appeared in the streets, most heading to their place of work, but overall the town was quiet, a situation that was about to change drastically.

'Get ready,' Harold said from his position in the undergrowth. 'This town pledged loyalty to Odda and provided ships to pursue my family. The thegns deserve all that is coming to them, but we hurt no women or children, is that clear?'

'Aye,' said One-eye at his side, turning to pass the word down the line. 'Food and plunder are ours, as are the lives of those men in charge, but women and children are to be untouched.'

'The time has come,' continued Harold, as the mercenaries got up from their hiding places. 'Let us get this done.' Without another word, he started walking down the hill, and as almost five hundred men joined him, broke into a run.

In one of the streets of Porlock, a young priest walked towards the church carrying a flask of wine for the day's services. As he walked, something caught his eye, and he looked up to see hundreds of men swarming down the hill.

'*Oh, sweet Jesus,*' he gasped and, dropping the wine, ran to the church just a few paces away. Racing inside, he made a beeline for the bell rope, and within seconds the bells of Porlock rang out across the town.

'*Alarm,*' the priest shouted at the top of his voice, '*we are being attacked.*'

Over and over again, he pulled on the rope, and throughout Porlock, men jumped from their beds to seek their clothing and weapons; but it was too little too late. By the time any of them emerged onto the streets, the Irish mercenaries were amongst them, now in full voice as they roared their terrifying battle cries.

The attack was overwhelming, and many of the ill-prepared defenders were killed even before they had chance to don their clothes, cut down by men bursting through their doors with nothing but violence and plunder on their minds. Screams echoed through the town as the men struggled to form any sort of coherent defence, but in the outlying villages and farms, the sound of the church bells had also roused men from their rest, and they had more time to react.

Harold led the attack through the town and headed towards the main hall. To one side, a half-dressed man burst from one of the doorways and threw himself sobbing at Harold's feet.

'Mercy, my lord,' he begged, 'spare our lives in the name of God.'

'Where are your thegns?' demanded Harold, grabbing the man's hair and forcing his head back. 'Tell us where they are, and we will let you all live.'

'Some are in the hall,' gasped the man, 'but most live outside the town. Please, have mercy, my lord.'

Harold threw the peasant to one side and called out to the mercenaries working their way through the houses. 'Leave what you are doing,' he roared, 'and head for the hall. A purse of silver for every man who brings me the head of a thegn.'

Reinvigorated, the Irish mercenaries forged forwards, searching for anyone who held any office of responsibility. As they passed, Leofwine looked up the slopes to a hill overlooking the village to the east. At the top, he could see a column of smoke snaking high into the morning sky.

'Harold,' he shouted, 'look.'

Harold cursed. Someone had lit a warning beacon, and men for leagues around would soon know they were there.

'I'll take some men up there and tear it down,' said Leofwine.

'Leave it,' said Harold, 'the damage has already been done. Besides, if that beacon is meant to rally the thegns of Somerset, then let them come.'

'Shall I recall the men?'

'Not yet. Let them finish what we came to do, but in the morning, I want them ready to move. We are not finished here, brother. The greater task is still before us.'

–

On the Isle of Wight, Godwin's men were just as industrious and swept across the island, collecting stores and valuables. With no men-at-arms to oppose them, there was far less bloodshed. Nevertheless, some died in a foolish attempt to defend their properties against the banished earl.

Within days the island had completely capitulated, and people queued up to pay the earl a tithe, only interested in staying alive. Godwin held court in one of the captured halls along with Osmund of London and his ships' captains.

'Have we lost any men?' asked Godwin.

'Five that I know of,' said Osmund, 'but those responsible for the slaying have suffered the same fate. A dozen more are wounded, of which three will not see another dawn.'

'Make sure their families receive a purse,' said Harold. 'Are there any places that still stand against us?'

'No, my lord, the island is ours.'

'How are we doing for supplies?' asked Godwin.

'Meat we have aplenty,' said Osmund, 'both on the hoof and salted. We are loading two of the ships as we speak. We also have many barrels of grain and dried fish as well as enough ale for the thirstiest of armies.'

'Good,' said Godwin. 'Do not kill any of the living animals yet; we will slaughter them only when we are about to sail.'

'And when will that be, my lord?' asked one of the captains.

'I know not,' said Godwin, 'for we await my sons from Ireland, but as soon as they arrive, we will turn our attention to London.'

–

Back in Porlock, it had been two days since the initial attack, and Harold's men now occupied every house in the village, enjoying the spoils of their victory. Up on the hill, several lookouts stared inland, watching for any sign of retaliation, but so far, there was no indication that the warning beacon had had any effect.

Harold was growing impatient, for though he had succeeded in his aim of punishing Porlock, the main people to suffer had been those who held little in the way of power. He had hoped to capture the thegns who had betrayed the house of Godwin but had only managed to find a handful of less important men, their heads now adorning the gates of the village.

Harold left the hall at the centre of the village and walked towards the stables, meaning to take one last look inland for any movement, but was only halfway there when a horn echoed from the hill above. He turned immediately and stared upwards. The signal could only mean one thing – they were about to come under attack.

'*To arms*,' he roared, 'and muster at the top of the hill.'

Men ran from everywhere, and within moments swarmed up the slopes to where the lookouts waited. Harold followed them and, at the top, stared across the valley to see a large body of men marching towards them. At least half were mounted, and even from this distance, he could see the foot soldiers carried axes and spears.

'It looks like they've summoned the fyrd,' said Leofwine at Harold's side. 'There are at least two thousand men there.'

'Aye,' said Harold, 'a decent number.'

'They have horses,' said Leofwine, 'and all our men are afoot. What do you want to do?'

Harold looked down at the lower ground between him and the approaching men.

'I don't think they will use their horses,' said One-eye from behind them, 'the ground is uneven, and they would lose too many in the charge.'

Harold agreed and made a decision.

'Pass the word to form up, brother,' he said, 'and lead us down into the valley.'

—

Within the hour, Harold and his army of mercenaries stood in formation a few hundred paces away from a shallow stream that cut through the wide valley.

To the fore were those with the strongest shields, ready to present a wall against any attack. In the second and third ranks, the men bore axes and swords, and to the rear, another hundred or so stood ready to launch their spears into the advancing enemy.

'Remember,' shouted One-eye, pacing back and forth before his men, 'when I give the order, let fly your spears but keep one about you to support your comrades in the wall. Any man not giving his all will have me to deal with.'

Across the valley, the English forces paused at a narrow but deep stream.

'Why have you stopped?' shouted one of the thegns on horseback. 'Get across and form up on the other side.' The soldiers waded across while those on horseback dismounted and followed them, their better weapons and chainmail singling them out as men of power and influence.

Harold stared at them, knowing that they were the men he had come to find. His heart beat faster, and though he and his men were outnumbered, he had every confidence that they would emerge the victors should it come to battle.

The approaching army came closer, eventually forming up just a hundred paces distant. Once they had formed their own shield wall, one of the commanders stepped through and walked towards the Irish lines.

'Who speaks for you?' the commander called, coming to a halt.

Harold pushed his way through his own lines and walked forward to face his opposite number.

'I do,' he said, 'Harold Godwinson. Who are you, stranger?'

'I am Henri of Normandy,' came the reply, 'lord of this county. You, Harold Godwinson, are not wanted here.'

'Ah, yet another Frenchman ruling where he is not wanted,' said Harold, 'why am I not surprised? This is England, Henri of Normandy, not France. Why don't you go back to your own country?'

'That is an interesting viewpoint,' said the Frenchman, looking over Harold's shoulder, 'for if I am not mistaken, your men are Irish. If I am an interloper, then what are they?'

'Paid men to rid England of people such as you,' said Harold, 'and when the task is done, they will leave us to rule our own lands as we have done for hundreds of years.'

'Alas, those days have long gone,' said the Frenchman, 'and it is only a matter of time before you bend the knee to people like me and accept us as your true masters.'

'That will never happen,' said Harold.

'No? Then look around you, Harold – these men at my back once thought the same. Now they fight for the rightful king while you lead nothing more than an army of pirates.'

'I see nothing but thirty traitors leading men who do not know better,' said Harold. 'It is a shame that they will also die today, but that is something out of my hands.'

Both men stared at each other for a few moments, trying to judge the strength of their opponent's mettle and character.

'What do you want, Harold?' asked Henri eventually. 'Why have you come here?'

'To inflict retribution upon those who turned their backs on my family,' said Harold.

'You talk of the House of Godwin,' said Henri, 'yet you were all declared outlaws. These people did no wrong.'

'Neither did my father,' said Harold. 'Many people were undecided, but only Porlock actively recruited men and ships to pursue us. The town has paid the price, but there are still debts unpaid.'

'So, many innocent people are dead because of you?'

'Not as many as you would think,' answered Harold, 'for it is men like you that we have come to kill, and here you are, all lined up like lambs to the slaughter.'

'We outnumber you two to one,' said Henri. 'I suggest you leave while you still can.'

'We are going nowhere,' growled Harold, staring at the Frenchman. 'Not unless you hand over every thegn responsible for supplying the men who crewed those ships. Do that, and you may just leave this place alive.'

'You are truly mad, Harold Godwinson,' said Henri. 'There will be no handing over of anyone, and before this day is out, I will be riding to London with your head tied to my saddle.'

'In that case, Henri of Normandy,' said Harold, 'you know what you have to do.'

Both men turned away and returned to their lines.

'Well,' said Leofwine, handing Harold his helmet, 'what did he say?'

'Nothing of any interest,' said Harold, pulling his helmet onto his head. 'Now look to your sword, brother – we are about to teach a lesson to those who would betray our house.'

Chapter Thirty-one

Both armies stared across the narrow strip of ground between them. The Englishmen far outnumbered the Irish, but most were ordinary village folk summoned to the fyrd by their lords. Armed with basic weaponry and farm implements, they were unused to warfare and stared at their opponents with fear and trepidation.

The Irish, on the other hand, were paid mercenaries and made their living from fighting. Experience told them that there was little to fear, and their confidence was high.

'Harold,' said One-eye, 'you are in charge, but I suggest you leave this battle to me. I know these men well and know how to win this fight.'

Harold looked at his massed ranks before turning back to the mercenary. 'What is your plan?'

'Those before us are nothing more than children compared to my men,' said One-eye, 'it is almost a shame to kill them, for they know not what they are facing. They will think their greater number will overwhelm us, but my men are strong and disciplined. We will let them wear themselves out attacking our shield wall before retaliating, and when we do, it will be without mercy. You and your brother should stay here and let us do what we came to do.'

'I am happy for you to take command, One-eye,' said Harold, 'but Leofwine and I will not stand back while others fight in our name. Tell us where you want us, and if that is in the front line, then so it shall be.'

One-eye nodded his approval. 'In that case,' he said, 'each of you can command a flank until we advance. At that point, you can join my men.'

'So be it,' said Harold, walking away to the right flank as One-eye took his place in the front line.

Across the open ground, the thegns of Somerset roused their men to action, striding amongst them whilst screaming about the heathen threat. Heroes from battles long gone were invoked, and gradually the noise increased as many struck their shields with their weapons in time with their beating hearts. With blood boiling and knowing their fate lay in the hands of God himself, they stepped forward as one, heading towards the Irish ranks just a hundred paces away.

'*We will hold the line,*' roared One-eye amongst his men, 'and will not break until I give the order to do so or I fall beneath their blades. Do you hear me?'

'*Aye,*' roared the men, and all the shields tightened against each other as the men braced for impact.

Onwards came the Englishmen, and as they reached halfway, Henri of Normandy roared out a command from behind the rear line of men.

'Men of Somerset, we are here to protect our homes and families from these intruders. It is time to show courage and to drive these heathens from our lands in the name of God and of the king. *Chaaarge!*'

With an almighty roar, almost a thousand men raced across the intervening ground and crashed into the Irish shield wall. The initial impact drove the defenders a few paces backwards, but the experienced mercenaries straightened their legs and leaned into their shields. A few buckled under the impact but no sooner did one fall than another immediately stepped forward to take his place.

With furious rage, the Englishmen smashed their weapons down onto the shields, desperate to get through to the men behind, but with each shield overlapping the next, there was no way through.

Over and over again, the attackers broke off to catch their breath before being ordered back into the fray by Henri and the thegns. On the flanks, the spearmen led by Harold and Leofwine held their own, stretching into an outward curve like a bull's horns and stopping anyone from seeking a path to outflank the defenders.

Many of the English fell from the spears launched from behind the shield wall, while others were struck down by sword thrusts from between the shields. Men also fell in the Irish lines, most cut down with a sword blade after being smashed to the ground by a giant axe, but overall the casualties were heavier on the attacking side.

Gradually the ferocity of the attack eased off, and though they still came, the effect on the shield wall became less and less. One-eye saw his chance and gave the command everyone had been waiting for.

'*Men of Ireland,*' he roared, '*advaaance.*'

As one, the whole shield wall marched forward ten paces before re-forming. The whole thing took less than a few seconds and had taken the attackers by surprise.

Henri stared in shock and caught his breath as the Irish lines repeated the move, marching another ten paces forward before stopping to reset. Over and over again, they did the same, striking their weapons against their shields in time with their steps.

Unprepared for such an unexpected manoeuvre, the Englishmen gave ground, running backwards towards the stream.

'*Where are you going?*' roared Henri. '*Attack them.*'

Some of the men lurched forward, but over half hesitated, watching their comrades being cut down and trampled underfoot. Suddenly one turned and, dropping his pitchfork, ran back towards the stream.

'*Stop him,*' roared Henri, '*cut him down.*'

One of his men gave chase, but the damage was done, and more men followed the first. Within moments the attacking lines broke, and men turned to run in their hundreds.

'*Nooo*,' roared Henri, realising they had lost the initiative, 're-form!'

In the Irish lines, One-eye saw them break and knew the time had come. '*Men of Dublin*,' he roared, 'they are ours for the taking. *Break lines*.'

Immediately all the mercenaries broke formation and charged forward. This was the moment they had been waiting for and the sort of fighting they did best – in open ground, unrestricted by discipline or formations.

With an almighty roar, they fell upon the rear of the retreating lines, cutting them down without mercy. Some men fought back desperately, but the combination of fear and panic saw them fall to Irish steel.

Those at the front of the fleeing fyrd reached the stream and plunged in, desperate to get away from the slaughter, but as some stumbled on the rocky bottom, those behind crashed into them, causing even more confusion and panic. More and more men fell or turned to find a better way across, but the hesitation proved costly, and the Irish fell amongst them with unbridled ferocity.

Men fell on both sides, but despite the numerical disadvantage, the experienced mercenaries were far more ruthless and slaughtered their opponents where they stood. Within minutes the battle was over, and although some of the English managed to escape to the far side of the stream, most had been killed or were now cowering in terrified submission, surrounded by One-eye and his men.

'Throw down your weapons,' he shouted, 'and get to your knees.'

The prisoners did as they were ordered, each sure they were about to die.

'One-eye,' said Harold walking over, his chainmail covered with blood, 'well fought, your tactics were admirable.'

'Some escaped,' said One-eye, glancing over his shoulder towards the riders disappearing into the distance, 'but the haul is good.' He looked back at the prisoners. 'They will bring a good price in Ireland.'

'We have no time to take prisoners,' said Harold, 'our work has only just started, and we need to join my father.'

One-eye looked at Harold with disgust. 'Do you not realise the value of these men?' he asked. 'They are strong and will make good slaves.'

'Not this time,' said Harold. 'Besides, you already have the plunder from Porlock.'

One-eye shook his head in disbelief, but he was well paid and knew the decision had to stand. 'Oh well,' he said, drawing his sword again. 'How do you want them to die, swiftly or screaming in pain?'

'There is no need for them to die,' said Harold, 'most are just farmers doing the will of their lords. Let them loose to go back to their families.'

Again, One-eye shook his head in disgust. 'Peasants or not,' he said eventually, 'set them free, and you could meet them again on the battlefield in the days to come. Do you want to risk that?'

'As I said,' replied Harold, 'they are the innocents in all this. Let them go in return for a pledge never to bear arms against my family.'

'And if they refuse?'

Harold looked at the group of desperate prisoners, each hanging on his every word. 'If they refuse,' he said, loud enough to ensure he was heard, 'you can do with them as you will.'

He turned away and walked across the battlefield to join his blood-soaked brother.

'Leofwine,' he said, 'how do you fare?'

'Unharmed,' said Leofwine, sheathing his sword. 'The day went well.'

'Aye, it did,' said Harold. 'We lost quite a few men but nothing in comparison to Henri.'

'Where is he?' asked Leofwine. 'Did he fall?'

'He escaped,' said Harold. 'As soon as he saw his men break, he fled like a frightened child.'

'Still,' said Leofwine, 'it looks like we killed many of his thegns.'

'We did,' said Harold, 'and that gives me great comfort. Come, let us get back to the river and wash this blood away.'

Both men headed back over the hill and down to Porlock. A few hours later, One-eye joined them in the hall, clad in a shiny chainmail hauberk.

'One-eye,' said Harold, 'your armour is different.'

'I found it on a dead thegn,' said One-eye. 'He has no more use for it.'

'Talking of thegns,' said Harold, 'did you count how many fell?'

'Aye, I personally saw over thirty, but when I saw this hauberk, I gave up counting.'

'What of the prisoners, have they been released?'

'They have,' said One-eye. 'My men were not happy to let them go unpunished, so gave each of them a beating before releasing them.'

'I told you they were innocents,' said Harold, 'there was no need to do that.'

'Yet only moments earlier they were trying to kill us,' said One-eye. 'It is what it is, Earl Harold. You should let it go.'

'Leave it, brother,' said Leofwine, 'at least they are alive.' He turned back to the mercenary. 'Our work here is now done,' he said. 'As soon as we have buried the dead, we head back to the ships.'

'And then?'

'First to the Isle of Wight, and from there, who knows.'

'Good,' said One-eye, 'for my men now have a taste for blood. The English dead will stay where they fell; let their own families dig their graves. As for our own dead, we will build them a funeral pyre, and tonight, as we watch them burn, we will celebrate the victory in the way they would have wanted, with ale and with women.'

Leofwine started to say something, but Harold cut him short.

'So be it,' Harold said. 'I will send a cask of ale to pay homage to those that paid the most, and in the morning, we shall see you at the ships.'

'Aye, you will,' said One-eye, turning to leave the hall.

The brothers watched him go before Leofwine turned to Harold.

'Why did you not say something?' he asked. 'Burning men is not a Christian thing to do, alive or dead.'

'It is their way,' said Harold, 'and not for us to judge. Besides, it is no less Christian than piercing a man with a blade. Come, we have things to prepare.'

Chapter Thirty-two

Godwin once more stood in the prow of his ship, though this time one of fifty sailing from the Isle of Wight. For the past few weeks, he had recruited men and boats from all along the English coast and at last knew he had a force at least equal to that commanded by the king, not just at sea but also on land, where an army of thousands headed towards London.

The morning was still young, and the sight of so many ships sailing up the Thames caused a stir amongst those watching from the two shores. Many recognised the earl's banners and word spread quickly on the northern bank, with some loyal to the king racing through the muddy streets to sound the alarm.

Godwin knew this would happen but had planned carefully. The tide was low, which meant they could not sail further upriver than London Bridge, but similarly, the king's fleet could not sail to meet them until the tide changed, a situation that meant that he could get his ships deep into the heart of London without being challenged.

His estates at Southwark were all south of the river, while those solely controlled by the king started on the northern bank, and allegiances differed wildly. Most in the north favoured the king, while in the south, the people tended towards Godwin, especially as their lives had become significantly harder since his exile. In addition, Godwin had sent hundreds of men into the city weeks earlier, spreading disquiet against the king and gathering support for his forthcoming campaign. Now, at long last, he sailed his ship into the docks at Southwark, knowing full well that whatever happened over the next few days, the situation would soon be at an end, one way or another.

Several hours later, he walked back into his manor, finding it empty and the doors unlocked. Since he had been exiled, it had been in the hands of a minor lord loyal to Archbishop Robert, but as soon as word had arrived that Godwin was headed that way with an army, the occupants had fled.

As he inspected the building for damage, his men spread out along the timber fortifications, creating a defensive position in case of attack. More and more men arrived throughout the day, and by nightfall, the hall was crammed with those loyal to Godwin waiting for instructions as to the next step.

In the centre of the hall, a huge cauldron of bubbling potage hung above the fire, available to any man in the manor, and throughout the evening, servants kept topping it up with shredded meat and cooked vegetables to ensure nobody went hungry.

Godwin sat at a long table at the end of the hall, deep in conversation with his advisors and chief huscarls. Their journey up the Thames had been more successful than they could have hoped, with not a single blade drawn in anger. Now their fleet was safely anchored along the shores of Southwark and guarded by thousands of well-armed men. Encouraged by their progress, they now had to decide what to do next.

'I say we just sail straight to Westminster,' said Osmund, 'and get it done while we still can.'

'Are you saying we attack the king directly?' asked Leofwine.

'Why not?' replied Osmund. 'We know we are stronger than him and that the northern earls are still not in London. We will never have a better chance to drag him from the throne.'

'And replace him with who, exactly?' asked Leofwine.

'That is a question for the Witan,' said Osmund, 'not I. All I am saying is that we cannot afford to wait. In a few days, Edward will have rallied all those loyal to him and, should it come to a fight, we are unlikely to emerge the victors.'

'Hopefully, it will not come to that,' said Godwin, 'I have already sent Tostig to the king requesting an audience. If Edward has any sense at all, he will realise this is the better way forward.'

'It is not the king that worries me,' said Harold, 'but that Norman bishop. As long as he has Edward's ear, he is unlikely to listen to reason.'

'Perhaps so, but we have to be seen to try. If we were to attack without attempting dialogue, then it would be seen as just a power grab from the house of Godwin and would turn the Witan against us. All I have ever asked for is a fair hearing, and that request still stands. If, however, we hear nothing from him by tomorrow night at the latest, then Osmund will get his wish, and we will sail across the river to march on Westminster.'

'Well, we will find out soon enough,' said Harold, standing up. 'I'm going to get some sleep. Wake me if you hear anything.'

-

Just over a league away, in Havering Palace, King Edward sat on his throne in his audience chamber. Before him were his military commanders and at his side his advisor the Archbishop of Canterbury. One of the men had briefed those gathered with the current situation, and now they all awaited the king's guidance.

'How many men do you think he has?' asked Edward, looking at the officer.

'It is hard to say, your grace,' replied the officer, 'but he has in excess of fifty ships, and there are reports that many more men are rallying to his banner south of the river.'

'And how many do we have to hand, should they attack?'

'Two thousand at most. I have already sent word summoning all the fyrds, but it will still not be enough. We need the armies of Earls Siward and Leofric if we are to have parity.'

'And our ships?'

'All moored in Westminster,' said the officer. 'They have skeleton crews, but their men-at-arms were sent home until you recruited new commanders of the fleet. We are disadvantaged.'

'What about an attack overnight?' asked one of the other men. 'We could set fire to their fleet before they sail north of London Bridge.'

'And how do we do that?' asked the first man. 'The bridge has been heavily fortified on the far end by Godwin's men with nobody allowed to pass. Similarly, we do not have enough smaller boats to ferry our men across, and even if we did, Godwin has his own boats out on the river acting as lookouts.'

'The man has thought of everything,' said the king quietly.

'Your grace,' said the archbishop, 'all is not lost. If we can just delay him long enough, the northern armies will arrive in a matter of days. Once they are here, Godwin will have no choice but to stand down.'

'And if he doesn't?'

'Then you must smite him with everything you have in the name of God. Yes, men will die, but if you do not rid England of this traitor once and for all, I fear he will not rest until he sits upon the throne himself.'

Many in the room gasped at the accusation. Few were happy with the way events were unfolding, but nobody thought for one moment that Godwin coveted the throne.

Before the king could answer, the far door opened, and one of his staff approached to talk quietly to the steward before returning to his post.

'Well?' asked the king, staring at the steward. 'What is so important that he needs to interrupt my audience?'

'Your grace,' said the steward, 'you have a visitor. Tostig Godwinson is waiting outside and begs an audience.'

Everyone in the room gasped at the audacity, and the king stared in disbelief.

'Turn him away,' shouted the archbishop, 'or better still, run him through. The man is the spawn of the devil himself.'

'No,' shouted a voice, 'that would be murder.'

The room erupted into argument until the king himself stood up.

'*Silence,*' he roared, '*you are acting no better than barbarians.*'

The hall fell quiet, and Edward looked around him with anger, finally settling on Robert of Jumièges.

'Archbishop Robert,' he said, 'yet again I find myself reminding you that it is I who am king and as such it is I who will make decisions as to the fate of those who have come to parley. This court never has and never will take the life of any message-bearer, no matter who he represents.'

'My apologies, your grace,' said Robert, 'I spoke impulsively but only with your wellbeing in mind.'

'Do not presume to judge my thoughts or deeds,' said Edward. 'Advice is one thing; decisions are something completely different.' He turned back to the steward, 'Tell Tostig to come forward,' he said, 'we will hear what he has to say.'

A few minutes later, Tostig and one of his huscarls entered the chamber and walked between the gathered men to stand before the king. Both bowed deeply, acknowledging the king's rule.

'Your grace,' said Tostig, 'thank you for receiving us. I know these are trying times, but I bring a message of hope and peace from my father.'

'You may bring a message of hope and peace,' said the king, 'yet you also bring an army the likes of which London has seldom seen. How do the two balance?'

'These are dangerous days,' said Tostig, 'and there are many who plot against both my father and the Crown. It seems that strength alone commands safety now, instead of trust and respect as in days gone by.'

'And who are these outside forces that threaten the crown?' asked Edward.

Tostig glanced towards the archbishop but stopped short of accusation and turned back to the king.

'You only have to look across the channel, your grace,' said Tostig. 'This island is of great value to every king or noble with any hint of ambition, and those that have often broken bread with you would not hesitate to attack should they get a chance. You know it, my father knows it, and every man in this hall knows it. All they need is an opportunity, and they will fall upon us like vultures.'

'Yet it is *your* father who comes with an army at his back,' said Edward. 'Is that not exactly the sort of opportunity they look out for – Englishman fighting Englishman?'

'We did not come here to fight,' said Tostig, 'but to strengthen England against such threats.'

'And how exactly do you intend to do that?' asked Edward.

'By reuniting the three great earldoms in your name,' said Tostig. 'Today England stands divided and fragmented, all because of a misunderstanding and outside interference. My father's continued exile means you have only two earls strong enough to provide you with an army, while the rest of the country bickers as to whom they call lord.'

'Your father refused a direct command,' said the king. 'He needs to be punished.'

'My father questioned something he saw as an injustice,' said Tostig, 'nothing more. Perhaps he was wrong, but as one of your most loyal and trustworthy earls, surely the punishment meted out to him already far outweighs the seriousness of his alleged crime? I suspect that there may be other forces at work here, forces that take great comfort in seeing your power base fractured and turned against each other.'

A mumble of agreement rippled around the room. Tostig was voicing fears that many of them already held, and hearing them voiced in the presence of the king only reinforced their doubts.

'Your grace,' interjected Archbishop Robert, 'if I may comment?'

'Go ahead,' said the king.

'Your grace, Tostig is a clever young man and provides an eloquent case in the name of his father, yet the fact remains that not only did Godwin disobey a direct royal command, but he also raised an army to confront you, not once but twice. Surely that alone is enough to prove the extent of the man's loyalty?'

'I don't know,' said the king with a sigh, 'the arguments laid out in this manner do suggest that perhaps all this could have been avoided. I need time to think.'

The archbishop walked up and whispered into the king's ear. 'Earls Siward and Leofric are only days away, your grace. Delay making any decisions until our army matches that of Godwin, then you can deal with him as you will.'

Edward continued to stare down at Tostig. What the archbishop said made sense, but he could not help believing that there was a solution to all this where all sides emerged with integrity.

'Tostig Godwinson,' he said eventually. 'You proclaim your family's loyalty, yet your brothers Harold and Leofwine recently led a Viking army against the innocent citizens of Porlock. How do you justify this?'

'They killed nobody who had not raised their swords against us in the first place,' replied Tostig. 'The Frenchmen to whom you gifted Sweyn's lands raised an army as soon as our fate became known and, rather than let us leave in peace, actively gave chase with the aim of killing our family. It was those whom my brothers sought, giving them an opportunity to fight real men, not women and children.'

'Yet Englishmen died at the end of your blades,' said Edward.

'They faced those who the thegns raised to fight their battles for them,' said Tostig, 'this is the way of war. But once the battle was won, they released all of their prisoners back to their families, taking neither bounty nor slaves.'

'There is much to consider,' said the king, 'but in the meantime, go from this place and tell your father this – the presence of an army lined up against me is an affront to the throne of England. However, in the interests of peace, I am willing to meet and discuss his grievances on one condition – that he withdraws his men and crosses the river with no more than his family and his huscarls for protection. Do this, and I give my word as king that there will be no trickery employed to detain or injure any of his party.'

'My lord,' said the archbishop, 'you should not—'

'Be quiet, Robert,' interrupted the king, 'I have made my decision and will stick with it.' He turned back to face Tostig. 'Well?'

'I will convey the message, your grace,' said Tostig.

'There is one more thing,' said the king, 'you will take Bishop Stigand with you to act as an intermediary. I am aware he looks favourably on the house of Godwin, but nevertheless, he is an honest man, and I am sure he will do everything in his power to forge a peaceful outcome. Now leave us to our musings and send back your father's answer no later than tomorrow night.'

'As you wish, your grace,' said Tostig with a bow before turning away to leave the court.

Chapter Thirty-three

The following day Godwin met with his sons and advisers early, painfully aware that if he needed to launch his fleet, it would need to be within the following two hours to take advantage of the tide.

'Gentlemen,' he said once everyone was gathered, 'you will have heard by now about my son's meeting with the king. You will also know that he demanded we withdraw all our men from London except for those standing in this room. If we cede to his demands, we have his word that there will be no treachery and all will be safe. I would be grateful for your thoughts on this matter.'

'My thoughts,' said Osmund, stepping forward, 'are that I do not trust the king, or those that stand alongside him. This is a ruse to gain time until the northern armies arrive, and when they do, we will be disadvantaged. I say we sail now and attack him while we still can.'

'Aye,' shouted several voices in the hall.

'And don't forget what happened in Gloucester,' added Leofwine, 'we gave him time to consider, but when we returned, he had amassed his armies against us. Is this not the same situation?'

'I agree,' said Godwin, 'but the last thing we want is to go to war with the king, so let us explore other options before we draw our swords.' He turned to face Bishop Stigand standing to one side. 'Bishop Stigand, you were there last night and know the king better than all of us. Do you think this is a trap?'

'Ordinarily, I would urge caution,' said the bishop, 'especially as Robert of Jumièges still holds so much influence. However, last night I sensed something had changed in the king's manner, something that could be favourable to your cause.'

'Can you explain further?' asked Godwin.

'Well, for a start,' replied Stigand, 'he was quick to silence Robert of Jumièges on more than one occasion. That is a first, at least in public, and demonstrates that he grows tired of the archbishop's constant advice. I suspect that he is now far more open to a mutually agreeable outcome than he was in Gloucester.'

'And yet he wants me to withdraw all my men and place myself at his mercy.'

'He does, and I have to admit that makes me uneasy. The archbishop is a clever and persistent man. He will not just stand back and allow the king to make decisions without doing everything in his power to influence him. Who knows what might have changed since last night.'

'And your counsel?'

'I think you should not put yourself at risk by removing your army. However, it is still worth pursuing a path of mutually agreed peace. If you can find a way to do that, not a single drop of blood needs to be spilt.'

Godwin looked around the circle of men, knowing that each and every one of them would fight and, if necessary, die in his name. That was the life they had been born into or had chosen to pursue in support of the House of Godwin. But he knew that to confront the king in any military capacity risked invoking the wrath of the Witan itself, and that was something he dared not do.

'Father,' said Harold, stepping forward, 'if I may?'

Godwin nodded towards his son.

'From the day we landed in Flanders over a year ago,' said Harold, 'we have been planning how and when we would return. That was never in doubt, and we have spent a fortune in time and money recruiting loyal men to our cause. At last, we are in a position to match anything the king can send against us, but for a limited time only. If we even consider standing down now, after everything we have done, then it has all been for nought. Yes, there are risks, and we always knew that, but here we are, with everything at hand that we wanted.'

He paused and looked around the room. 'None of us wants a war with Edward, but if that is what it takes, then that is what we must do.' He turned back to face Godwin. 'You have an opportunity to right this wrong, Father, and to finally remove the influence of Robert of Jumièges. For make no mistake, while that man stays at court England will never be safe. I say take this chance and do what we came to do.'

He stepped back into the circle of men, his ears ringing with the cheers of his comrades. Eventually, the noise died away and all eyes turned to stare at Godwin.

'My son has spoken well,' he said, 'and has reminded me of my responsibilities, not just to my family and my comrades but to England itself. This is not a time for faint hearts, so in a few moments, we will leave this place and head for the river. Once there, we will use the tide and sail the fleet past London Bridge to moor on the opposite bank to Westminster. At the same time, we will summon our men from the outskirts of London, as well as any citizens who support our cause. By doing this, it will show the king that although we do not want to fight, we will if we have to. However, I will also stress to Edward that all we want is justice, peace and an end to the influence of those who will not rest until England is ruled by the lords of Normandy.'

Again the hall erupted into cheers, and Godwin glanced across towards Stigand, receiving the slightest of nods in return.

'The time for talking is done,' he shouted, turning back to the men. 'The time for action is upon us. To the ships, my friends, and may God go with us.'

A few hours later, Archbishop Robert of Jumièges and one of his loyal monks forced their way through a gathering crowd on the riverbank. On the far side, over a dozen of Godwin's ships were already moored to the dock, with hundreds of men disembarking to form up on the shore. Downstream the scene was no less worrying, the river seemingly full of ships being rowed past London Bridge to moor opposite the still unfinished Palace of Westminster.

Robert was furious, knowing that such a display of force could mean only one thing – that Godwin was willing to fight, a situation that could go very badly for the archbishop.

'The man is a traitor to the king and to England,' he spat, watching as more and more ships came into view.

'What are we to do?' asked the monk at his side.

'I need to speak to the king,' said Robert, 'and advise him of this treachery. But we must also prepare in case this goes against us.'

'What do you mean?'

'If the northern armies arrive in time,' said the archbishop, 'then Godwin will have no other choice but to surrender. However, just in case they are delayed, we need to put some things in place to ensure our own safety.'

'What things?'

'Let us get back to the abbey,' said the archbishop, 'there are some preparations I want you to make.'

–

Across the river, men disembarked from the ships and assembled along the riverbank. More men joined them from the city, and as the army grew, so did their confidence, their voices ringing out across the water, taunting the forces of the king on the other side.

Godwin and his sons stayed aboard one of the larger ships, staring over towards the towering buildings of the recently finished abbey and the half-built Palace of Westminster. Those loyal to the king also gathered along the riverbank, and soon the two armies exchanged insults and threats safe in the knowledge that there was a large body of water between them.

'Has Stigand gone?' asked Godwin.

'He has,' said Harold, 'he crossed London Bridge just before we set sail. He should be at the king's palace by now.'

'It will be interesting to see Edward's reply,' said Godwin. 'Is there any news about the northern armies?'

'Not yet, but there is a rumour that Earl Siward has been seen in London, so they must be near.'

'We have no time to waste,' said Harold, 'or we will lose all advantage. Make sure our men do not stray too far. Time is running out, and if we do not have an agreement by this time tomorrow, we will have to act.'

–

On the northern side of the Thames, Edward paced his hall, frustrated at the whole situation. Some of his advisors were already there, as were Bishop Stigand and Archbishop Robert of Jumièges.

'The man haunts my every waking moment,' gasped the agitated king. 'I exile him, he returns; I demand he disbands his army, he assembles it even closer. What is it with him? Is he stupid?'

'I would say confident, your grace,' said Stigand. 'He knows he is in a powerful position and is not willing to weaken it without some guarantee of safety.'

'But I have already given him my word, what more does he want?'

'With respect, your grace, he only remembers what happened in Gloucester and is cautious he is not treated the same way.'

'The man is a traitor and a coward,' said Robert of Jumièges. 'We should not pander to his will. I say let them come and meet him on the streets with what men we have to hand.'

'He outnumbers us many times over,' said the king, 'as you well know. If it comes to a fight, we will never win.'

'We do not have to win,' said Robert, 'all we have to do is delay him long enough for the northern armies to arrive. My spies tell me they are only a day or so away.'

'What say you, Bishop Stigand?' asked the king.

'Your grace,' said Stigand, 'unlike the archbishop, I do not have spies to call on. I find such things to be unnecessary in the service of the Lord. I do, however, have the trust of the House of Godwin, and if I assure him he will come to no harm, I am certain he will attend.'

'Then why have you not told him this already?' asked the king.

'Because I am not comfortable that this is the case,' said Stigand. 'I too have witnessed words being broken and promises being withdrawn.'

'*Are you calling the king a liar?*' gasped the archbishop. 'I will have you excommunicated for this.'

'Who said I was talking about the king?' asked Stigand, staring implicitly at the archbishop. After a few moments, he turned back to face the king. 'Your grace, I can assure you he has no desire to wage war upon you or the realm. All Godwin wants is the opportunity to speak in safety, not only about the exile of his family but about the deep concerns across England over the growing influence of Normandy.'

'What do you mean?' asked the king. 'I have little contact with any of the Norman lords. How could they possibly influence my decisions?'

'With the greatest respect, your grace,' said Stigand, 'it is well known that the Most Reverend Father, Robert of Jumièges, is a passionate Norman empathiser, and whether there is ill will intended or not, there is a perception that perhaps he may have too much influence on your daily decisions.'

'*That is preposterous*,' shouted the archbishop, 'never have I heard so much nonsense.'

'Nevertheless, the rumours abound,' said Stigand, 'and it is of those things that the earl wishes to speak.'

'He is no longer an earl,' said Robert, 'as well you know. He is nothing more than an outlaw and should be hanged as such.'

'My apologies,' said Stigand, 'old habits die hard.'

The king sighed and dropped into his seat.

'I am willing to meet him, Bishop Stigand, and I am happy to guarantee his safety, but what can I say or do to prove my pledge?'

'There is one thing, your grace,' said Stigand, 'and that is to swear upon the Holy Bible in the presence of witnesses. If you do that, then I will be happy to assure Godwin that he is safe.'

'You ask too much,' snarled Robert. 'The word of a king is enough, and no man may demand more.'

'I am only trying to help,' said Stigand. 'With so much at stake, perhaps it is a small gesture to make, especially if the vow is true.'

'Someone bring me a bible,' said Edward from his chair.

'Your grace,' said Robert, 'do not demean yourself by bowing to Godwin's whim. Who is the king here, you or him?'

'You heard what I said,' repeated Edward, 'I want a bible brought here right now. I tire of all this and would bring it to an end.' He looked up at Stigand. 'You will have your vow, Bishop Stigand, but this is his last chance. Either he comes here by the next tide, or he and his men will be at war with England itself, no matter the cost. Is that clear?'

'It is, your grace,' said Stigand. 'Let us hope that God himself guides both your paths.'

Chapter Thirty-four

Godwin and Harold walked through the corridors of Havering Palace towards the king's audience chamber. With them were Bishop Stigand and Osmund of London, along with an escort of twenty of King Edward's best men.

Once Stigand had reported that Edward had sworn upon a bible that there would be no attempt on his life, Godwin had accepted the invitation and had wasted no time in making the crossing in one of his ships.

But now, as the moment approached, he was having doubts as to the wisdom of his decision and knew that whatever happened in the next few hours, his fate would be decided one way or another. Finally, they arrived at the main doors and, as two servants pulled them open, he could see the hall was lined with many lords and thegns known to be loyal to Edward. Undaunted, he walked through them to the front of the hall and bowed deeply before the king as the door slammed shut behind him.

'Godwin of Wessex,' said Edward with a deep sigh. 'It has been a long road, but at last, you have your wish to stand before me amid a group of your peers. Perhaps now we can get to the bottom of this matter.'

Godwin looked around him. Among those present were many important men, but there were no earls, so it could hardly be called a gathering of peers. Nevertheless, he decided to ignore the situation and take advantage of actually being able to voice his concerns.

'Your grace,' he said, finally turning to face the king, 'you have my gratitude for agreeing to this audience, and whilst it is a difficult situation for all of us, I can assure you that my thoughts here are only for the future of England itself.'

'We will see,' said the king. 'Let us get down to business. First of all, I hear that you wish to press your family's right to reinstatement due to the fact that you were treated unjustly after the confrontation in Dover. Is that correct?'

'No, your grace,' said Godwin, 'it is not.'

Everyone around him, including Stigand and Harold, turned to stare in shock as a murmur of surprise rippled around the room. It was the last thing anyone had expected him to say.

'I do not understand,' said the king eventually, 'surely that is why you are here?'

'Originally, it was my only focus,' said Godwin, 'and there was never a moment when I was not planning on doing exactly that. But these past few months have opened my eyes to something far more important and far more sinister.'

'And this is?'

'Your grace, for months now, I have been sailing the coastline of England recruiting men. I admit my reasons were personal, and I thought it would be difficult to recruit such men. However, it soon became clear that I was wrong. Everywhere we went, from coastal villages to inland towns, men flocked to my banner, each happy to pledge allegiance. From lords to peasants, the mood was sour, and I recruited far more than I imagined, men who now wait impatiently across the river to see the outcome of this meeting.'

'You say the mood was sour,' said Edward, 'to whom?'

'To the throne, your grace,' said Godwin, again to gasps from the gathered men. 'They see your kingship as weak and fear their lives are at risk from men across the sea.'

'Treachery,' shouted a voice. 'Cut him down.'

Before anyone could move, the king held up his hand.

'Listen to me,' Edward shouted, 'I gave this man my word before God that as long as he is here, his safety is not in doubt.

Any man drawing a blade to Godwin or any of his entourage will be taken outside and executed without trial. Is that clear?'

A few men murmured a response, but Edward was not happy.

'I said, *is that clear*?' he shouted.

'*Aye*,' they replied in unison, and Edward turned back to face Godwin.

'My apologies,' he said, 'that will not happen again. Now, Godwin of Wessex, explain exactly why there is so much ill-feeling towards me.'

'Your grace,' said Godwin, 'it is not against you directly but against the power of the throne.'

'Which by implication means me,' replied Edward.

'To some extent, perhaps, but even if you were to stand down, which I am not suggesting, there is a feeling that it would be too little too late, and eventually there would be a reckoning.'

'But why? Am I not a just king?'

'That is for God to judge, your grace, not I, but our people are not blind, especially those who trade with the French and the Normans. Not a day goes by when those who work in the docks and on the ships do not hear tales of strong lords across the sea, each coveting the throne of England. Ordinarily, they would pay no heed to such boastfulness, but lately, it has become apparent that we offer succour and favour to those we once called enemy.'

'I know not what you are talking about,' said the king. 'I do no such thing.'

'You may not,' said Godwin, 'but look around you. How many of your court are English born? Most are Norman, French or Flemish, from lords to pot washers. The palace is being invaded, your grace, one person at a time.'

'I have no direct input into who is engaged,' said Edward. 'The matter is dealt with by those who run my household.'

'I understand that,' said Godwin, 'but you only need one man in a position of power to start the process, and those decisions trickle downwards and outwards. Soon men of all stations are replaced, and before you know it, your court is full of people with allegiances elsewhere.'

'What are you saying,' said the king, 'that there is a traitor at court?'

'The term traitor depends on who the person vows allegiance to in the first place,' said Godwin. 'If his alliance lies with Normandy, then he is loyal, just not to you.'

'And you know of such a man?'

'Aye, your grace,' said Godwin, 'and I am happy to accuse him in front of all these good men.' He turned around and pointed straight at the archbishop. 'That man, your grace, has plotted against England since the day he first landed on the shores of England. Remove him and those in his service, and I swear I can turn Wessex back into the loyal earldom it once was. Fail to do so, and I cannot be held responsible for what comes next.'

The mood in the hall changed yet again, with murmurings of agreement and dissent from both sides. Archbishop Robert's face was red with rage, and it was all he could do to contain his outburst, yet he had one more significant development to deploy in his case against Godwin.

Edward held up his hand for silence before turning to face the archbishop.

'Reverend Father Robert,' the king said, 'this man has laid a great accusation at your feet. My instinct is to immediately dismiss it out of hand, but I promised him a fair hearing. If this is one of his main complaints, I am duty-bound to ask you to respond.'

'Your grace,' said the archbishop eventually, 'it will be no surprise that I refute all such charges, and to be honest, I find it absurd that I stand here answering the accusations of an outlaw. He and his family have caused nothing but trouble since your coronation and indeed before that date. Can I remind you and everyone here that it was Godwin who arranged the death of your brother when he was next in line to the throne? It was he that raised an army and sent it to Gloucester to try and force you into an agreement. It is his son, Sweyn Godwinson, who kidnapped and raped an abbess before murdering his cousin in cold blood just to get his lands. Even his daughter, Ealdgyth, has failed you by not producing an heir. The whole family is like an anchor around your neck, yet somehow it is I who stands accused of treachery.'

Robert turned to face Godwin and Harold. 'It is obvious what is happening here – you are using the strength of your army across the river to force yourself back into the king's favour. Well, it will not happen, outlaw, for we have seen through your ruse and are now able to face force with force.' He nodded to one of the servants at the end of the room, who immediately turned to open the doors.

Everyone turned to see who entered, and gasps of astonishment rippled around the room as both Earls Siward and Leofric walked in, their garb still dusty from the hard ride south. Both men walked up to bow before the king as the archbishop watched on, a satisfied smile playing about his mouth.

'Earl Siward,' said Edward, 'Earl Leofric, you have arrived. We did not expect you until tomorrow at the earliest.'

'We rode through the night, your grace,' said Siward, 'at the behest of the archbishop. He sent a message yesterday saying our presence is urgently required and that your life may be in danger.'

Edward turned to face the archbishop.

'Do you think my life is in danger from just two men in front of all my court?'

'Perhaps not here,' said Robert, 'but his army stands ready to fight just across the river. With the northern armies now camped on our doorstep, Godwin's dominance has been negated, and we can treat him as the outlaw that he is.'

'If something happens to my father,' said Harold, 'all England will know that the king went back on his word, and our men will tear down these very walls.'

'And there it is,' said the archbishop, 'the threat that we all know has been simmering just beneath the surface.' He turned to face the room. 'You all heard Harold Godwinson threaten the king, every man here is a witness.'

'It was a threat of retribution,' said Bishop Stigand from the side, 'only issued as a counter to any broken vow issued to God himself. We all know the king would not break that vow, so it is not even worth listening to.'

'We also all know on which side of the argument you stand, Bishop Stigand,' said the archbishop. 'Your name should be Godwinson, so strong is your allegiance.'

'I have served four kings, including King Edward,' said Stigand, 'and stay neutral in all affairs.'

Robert of Jumièges turned away in disgust, deciding that when the situation had been dealt with, he would write to Rome and have Stigand stripped of all his offices. 'The bishop clouds the issue,' he said, 'but nevertheless, the truth lies before us. Godwin and his family are still outlawed and have once again raised an army against you. He came here thinking he could strong-arm the throne into reinstating him to his old earldom, and indeed that might have been successful, but now, with the arrival of the northern armies, that threat no longer exists. I urge you, your grace, if you are not going to punish him here and now, at least make it clear that his race is run and he will face your wrath.'

The room fell silent as all eyes turned to Godwin.

'Your grace,' said Godwin, 'may I address Earls Siward and Leofric?'

'You may,' said the king.

Godwin turned to face the two newcomers.

'My lord Siward,' said Godwin, acknowledging that, at least for the time being, Siward outranked him. 'Is it true that you have your army with you?'

'It is,' said Siward, 'almost five thousand men-at-arms and a thousand lancers.'

'And you, Lord Leofric?'

'About the same,' said Leofric.

'That makes around ten thousand,' said Godwin, 'and with those that the king already commands in London, a total in excess of twelve thousand of England's best men. In return, I have around five thousand. I think it is safe to say that should it come to a fight, I would lose. Do you agree?'

'I do,' said Siward.

'But that will not happen, will it?' asked Godwin.

'It will not.'

'Can you tell the court why?'

'Because we have not come to fight you,' said Siward, turning slowly to face the king, 'we came to join you.'

A gasp of astonishment echoed around the room, and Edward got to his feet in anger.

'*What,*' he gasped, '*you come here to oppose your king?* That is just as treacherous as the charges laid before Godwin.'

'We have not come here to oppose you, your grace, but we will not wage war on a fellow countryman whose only concern is to protect England from those who would do us ill. Earl Godwin is a good man, and in my view, has been poorly treated. However, whether you reinstate him or not is not of my concern. I have only come here to see we do not end up with a situation where brother kills brother.'

'So if I attack Godwin's army, you will not fight with us?'

'We will not, but if your life is at risk, we will protect you.'

'This is absurd,' gasped the archbishop, 'you are the king's men and have a duty to fight on his side.'

'And we will, if necessary,' said Siward, 'but only to protect his life. Otherwise, my men and those of Earl Leofric are neutral in this matter.'

The king sat down, totally bemused. It was a stalemate, and he knew not what to do. Beside him, Robert of Jumièges was still seething, and he knew his argument was rapidly losing strength. Finally, he took a deep breath and turned to face Edward.

'Your grace,' he said, 'never in my life have I witnessed such a situation. Within this very hall, you have an outlaw who has threatened you on more than one occasion and two more earls who refuse to carry out their sacred duty. Yet still, you hesitate to do what has to be done. However, there is one more piece of evidence I need to present, a witness so powerful that you will demand that Godwin is hanged from the city gates immediately.'

'And who is this witness?' asked the king.

'Alas, I know not his name, but he appeared before me only last night with a testimony against Godwin so grievous it will turn your blood cold.'

'Where is he?' asked the king. 'Send for him immediately.'

'He is not far from here,' said the archbishop, 'but he is so scared of retribution that if he sees anyone but me approach, he will disappear like a frightened bird. If we can adjourn this audience temporarily, I will bring him here to testify.'

'What charge does this man make against me?' asked Godwin.

'You will find out soon enough,' said the archbishop. 'Until then, I recommend that you are kept under guard lest you choose to flee.'

'My conscience is clear, Robert of Jumièges,' said Godwin, 'there will be no flight from me. Bring your witness so we can prove both he and you are the liars we know you to be.'

The archbishop ignored the insult and turned to the king.

'Your grace, do I have your permission to leave?'

'You do,' said the king. 'Be back here by nightfall with your witness. If you are not, I will have no other option but to dismiss all accusations against Godwin of Wessex.'

'Thank you, your grace,' said the archbishop, turning away to leave the hall by a side door.

'The rest of you can return to your business,' said the king. 'Only the nobles need return at dusk to witness my judgement.'

He turned to face Godwin and Harold. 'You are under no obligation to stay,' he said, 'but I would appreciate it if you would, if only to demonstrate the continued trust demonstrated here today.'

'We will happily stay,' said Godwin. 'This situation needs to be resolved once and for all.'

'Good. Bishop Stigand will ensure you are well looked after.' He got to his feet, and as the rest of the court left the hall, he followed the archbishop out through the side door.

'What did you make of that?' asked Harold as Bishop Stigand walked over to join them.

'I know not,' said Godwin. 'For the life of me, I cannot think of anything I have done that would demand the retribution the archbishop demands.'

'Perhaps he is lying,' said Harold.

'Oh, he is definitely up to something,' said Stigand, 'I just cannot fathom what it may be.'

'Well, we'll find out soon enough,' said Godwin. 'In the meantime, could we get something to eat?'

'Follow me,' said Stigand, and the three men followed the rest of the audience from the hall.

Chapter Thirty-five

Several hours later, Godwin, Harold and Stigand walked back into the hall. This time there were just a few dozen men present, but amongst them were Earls Leofric and Siward. The night was drawing in, and the hall had been illuminated by hundreds of candles, casting dancing shadows upon the walls.

The mood was muted, yet there was an anxious feeling in the air. Everyone present had been more than aware of what had happened over the preceding few years and knew that it all had to come to an end, for the sake of England and of unity.

The side door opened, and everyone bowed as the king entered and took his place on the throne. He looked around, seeking the archbishop, but he was nowhere to be seen.

'Has anyone seen Archbishop Robert?' the king asked. 'He should be here by now.'

Nobody responded, so the king turned to his steward standing at the door.

'Send someone for him,' he said, 'and remind him that I gave him until dusk to return. I will grant him a little more time, but if he is not here, he knows the consequences.'

'Aye, your grace,' said the steward, and as he left the room, Edward turned to face Godwin and his son.

'Godwin of Wessex,' he said, 'thank you for returning. I feel that at last we have at least reached a mutual level of trust, and that can only be a good thing.'

'As do I,' said Godwin.

'Your grace,' said Bishop Stigand, stepping forward, 'while we wait for the archbishop, I have a request to make on behalf of the Godwin family.'

'Continue,' said the king.

'Your grace, as you are aware, last year when tempers were at their hottest and the trust we now enjoy was at its weakest, you may recall that Godwin of Wessex and his son, Sweyn Godwinson, each allowed one of their own sons to be taken as hostages to provide assurance that they would continue to talk in good faith. As you can imagine, this situation has created enormous worry for the Godwin family, especially during the darkest days when there seemed there was no way back. However, as you can see, Godwin himself now stands before you, unarmed and without any of his bodyguards. He has put himself completely in your hands and, as such, exhibits a trust over and above what could reasonably be expected.'

'What do you want, Bishop Stigand?' said the king, cutting him short.

'Your grace, whatever happens in these next few hours, whether Godwin is found guilty or whether he is absolved of all accusations, this situation will soon come to an end. Surely there is no longer any need to involve the children, so I would respectfully ask that they are returned to their families immediately.'

'Would not that relinquish any leverage I have?'

'What better leverage could you have than the man himself standing unarmed before you amongst those you call loyal? If you could grant this one favour, it will not only exhibit trust in the process of our laws but also demonstrate to the people of England what a just and compassionate king you truly are. In amongst all this bad feeling, your grace, irrespective of fault, it is only the children that are truly innocent.'

Edward stared at Stigand, realising he had constructed a well-worded trap. To deny the request in front of so many witnesses would send out a negative message across the country.

'As you wish,' he said before turning to one of his courtiers. 'Simon Williamson, take someone with you and bring the children to court.'

'Yes, your grace,' said the man, leaving the hall.

'So,' said the king, turning back to face Godwin, 'here we are. It seems you have finally got your way, Godwin of Wessex. Your children are to be released, and in a few moments, you are to be judged by your peers for crimes against the king. How do you feel?'

'I asked for the Witan, your grace,' said Godwin, 'but I'm happy to accept those present as my jury. I believe my actions have been misrepresented by the archbishop, and when the truth is told, these good men will see that there was no crime against you or England, only a reluctance to submit to the judgement of a Norman bishop. If that is proven, then they will have no other choice than to acquit me of all charges.'

'And if they do not?'

'Then I will submit to your will without question.'

'Tell me,' said the king, 'what is the best outcome you could possibly hope to achieve?'

'That I am acquitted of all charges and all my family's lands and titles restored in full.'

'And if you are acquitted but I refuse to reinstate those privileges?'

'You are my king, your grace, and I am subject to your whim. All I ask is that you open your eyes to the real danger that the archbishop represents.'

'We will see soon enough,' said the king, looking over to the side door, impatient for the archbishop to arrive. Over the next few minutes, the mood in the room changed from pensiveness to worry at the archbishop's continued absence.

Finally, the king decided to carry on without him, but as he was about to begin, the steward burst into the hall, a look of concern etched deep onto his face.

'Ah,' said the king, 'here they are, at last.'

'Your grace,' said the steward, 'alas, I am alone. The arch-bishop is not with me.'

'Why not? Did he give a reason?'

'He did not, your grace, for he was not there, and his servants said they had not seen him since this morning.'

'Perhaps he is still seeking his witness?'

'I do not think so, your grace, for I checked with the stables, and one of the grooms told me that just after noon, the arch-bishop selected the best horse he could find and headed out of the abbey at a great pace. He also told me that last night a cart full of the archbishop's belongings left for Dover.'

The king's face fell as the realisation sank in. 'He said nothing of this to me; why would he do that?'

'I suspect he was preparing the way for flight should the need arise,' interrupted Godwin, 'and now he knows he can no longer build a case he has taken the opportunity to escape while he still has a chance.'

'He could still be seeking that witness,' said the king. 'Perhaps we should afford him some time.'

'Then why send a cart with all his belongings to Dover?' asked Harold. 'I think he feared such an outcome and prepared his escape.'

'He must have a ship waiting,' said Godwin, 'and intends to get away with the next tide. He could already be at sea by now.'

'Not necessarily,' said Harold, 'but even if he is, we have some of the fastest ships in England at our command. We could set sail immediately and try to catch him.'

'We cannot,' said Godwin, 'all our ships are north of London Bridge, and with the tide already out, we will not be able to sail until early tomorrow morning. He has thought this through well, your grace.'

The king sat back on his throne and stared at Godwin. If all this was true, then he would have no other choice but to reinstate the Godwin family, yet still he hesitated, wondering if it were not all just a mistake and the archbishop would soon return with his witness in tow.

Every noble in the hall was talking loudly, most siding with Godwin, but fell silent when the guard sent to retrieve the hostages burst back into the hall, hurling a woman to the floor before the king.

'Simon Williamson,' said the king looking up, 'why have you not brought the Godwin children?'

'I could not, your grace, for they had already gone.'

'What do you mean, gone? They were in a locked room and were under the protection of the court ladies.'

'They were, your grace, and this is the woman in question. I found her locked in the empty room.'

'What happened?' shouted the king to the woman as anger spread through the room. 'Why did you not care for them as instructed?'

'Your grace,' she replied through her tears, 'I opened the door for moments only, I swear I did. There were two monks, and they said they had been sent by the archbishop to talk to the children.'

'And you believed them?'

'I did, your grace, they were known faces in the company of the archbishop. But when I opened the door, they burst in and knocked me to the ground. The first two tied me up while another two grabbed the children.'

The room burst into noise as every man voiced their anger. Edward held up his hand, trying to get some order.

'Do you know where they went?' the king shouted.

'Your grace,' replied Simon over the noise, 'on my way back here, I was told that last night two guards were murdered at the eastern gates. Witnesses say that there were at least two horsemen.'

'Which way were they headed?'

'Eastwards, your grace, towards Dover.'

As the hall once more burst into noise, Godwin and Harold turned away and strode towards the back of the room.

'*Godwin of Wessex,*' roared the king, getting to his feet, 'how dare you turn your back on me? I have not dismissed you.'

Godwin stopped and turned back to face the king.

'After all that has happened here today, your grace,' he said, 'I believe there are no more charges to answer. My fate is in the hands of God and these men, so you do what you have to do. I am going to find my son and grandson.'

Chapter Thirty-six

Outside the stables, Osmund of London and one of his fellow huscarls sat at an upturned barrel, playing a game of dice in the light of a smoky oil lamp. They had been there all day along with another dozen men, awaiting the return of Godwin and his son, but despite the boredom, they remained alert, knowing that they were potentially in enemy territory.

'I know not if you are lucky or a clever cheat,' said Osmund as his comrade took another silver penny from him.

'I am hurt you think such things,' joked the huscarl. 'I am as honest as the day is long. Some say I should be in the Church, such is my honesty.'

'And since when is that evidence of honesty?' laughed Osmund. 'Some of the most crooked men I know ply their trade around the churches of England.'

'That would not be me,' said the man. 'I would be the most pious and honest priest ever to walk the roads of England, unless they wanted to play dice, of course.'

Both men laughed but looked up urgently when they heard Godwin calling Osmund's name.

'My lords,' shouted Osmund, seeing Godwin and Harold running from the palace, 'are you in danger?'

'No,' shouted Godwin, 'but we need to get the horses, *quickly.*'

'You heard him,' shouted Osmund, turning to his men. 'Get moving.' He turned back and waited as Godwin and Harold came to a halt. 'What's happened,' he asked, 'have you been absolved?'

'Never mind that,' said Godwin, 'Robert of Jumièges has abducted Wulfnorth and Hakon and is headed for Dover. We have to get to them before they take ship.'

'When did this happen?'

'The children were taken last night, but the archbishop left earlier today. Apparently, he was astride one of the king's best horses.'

'It will be difficult to catch him,' said Osmund, 'especially with such a head start. I suspect he will not be stopping for much rest.'

'Neither will we,' said Godwin. 'The chances are slim, but we have to try. If they have kept the children in the cart, then we have a chance.'

Osmund nodded and turned to see his men leading their horses out of the stables. 'Drop all your packs,' he said, 'and lighten their loads as much as you can. We need to ride these horses as we have never done so before, to the death if needs be.'

Harold and Godwin walked over to retrieve their own mounts, and as soon as everyone was ready, headed out of the gates east across London.

–

Wulfnorth sat on two sacks of hay in the back of a covered cart. Next to him, Hakon lay curled into a ball, frightened and tired after many hours travelling in the wagon. Across from them were the two monks who had dragged them from their temporary home in the Palace of Westminster, one of whom held a single candle, giving just enough light for the monks to see by.

Wulfnorth stared at his captors. He had no idea what was happening but knew he had to do something soon, or their lives were in serious danger.

'Where are you taking us?' he asked eventually.

'Away from here,' sneered the monk. 'Somewhere where your unearned station will carry no weight. I think they may even make you work hard for your bread, something your father and brothers never had to do. I would pay a silver penny to see your fingers bleed from pulling rocks from the ground.'

'And who knows,' said the second monk, 'if you do not work hard enough, you may be beaten.'

'Or killed,' added his comrade.

Wulfnorth glanced down at his sleeping nephew, not wanting the young boy to be frightened more than he already was.

'If you release us,' he said, looking up, 'I will tell my father that it was you that saved our lives. He will make you a rich man.'

'I am rich enough,' said the monk, 'and can't think of anything worse than doing the House of Godwin a favour. No, you are coming with us, my friend, but let me make something clear.' He looked down at the sleeping boy before returning his gaze to Wulfnorth. 'I have no doubt that you think you can escape. You may even succeed, but let me tell you this – whatever happens, there is no way that little one will get away from us, so if you even try, we will skin him alive. Do you understand?'

'Yes,' said Wulfnorth, his heart sinking.

'Good. Shut your mouth, for we have a distance to go.'

–

Harold and Godwin rode through the night, stopping only to exchange their horses in a village halfway between London and Dover. As soon as they had made the exchange, they set out again, shoving handfuls of bread and cheese into their mouths as they went. The road was long and hard, but still they pushed on, stopping only to water the horses, knowing that there was the slightest of possibilities that they could at least catch the cart, if not the archbishop.

Finally, night approached again, and though they still had several leagues to go, they pushed their exhausted horses even harder, desperate to reach Dover before it got too dark. They raced up a hill, and Godwin reined in his horse to peer down into the valley below. He lifted the water-skin from his saddle and drank deeply before throwing it over to Harold.

'My lord,' shouted Osmund, 'look there.'

All eyes turned to where the huscarl was pointing, and their hearts soared to see a cart and two riders in the distance travelling along the road towards Dover.

'That must be them,' said Harold, 'thank the Lord.' He threw the water-skin to one side and, with a kick of his heels, sent his horse galloping down the hill towards the fleeing cart. The men followed close behind, and within minutes bore down on the wagon, their swords already drawn for retribution.

The two riders heard the approach and turned to stare in fear. Realising they had no chance, they immediately threw their swords to one side and held up their hands as the cart master jumped down and started running towards the nearby treeline.

Despite the surrender, Harold was in no mood to talk, and he increased the pace before riding past the first man and smashing him in the jaw with his mailed fist, sending him flying to the floor. Osmund did the same to the second rider before jumping from his horse and marching over to place his boot on his victim's face, pressing it hard into the dirt.

'I am going to ask you once and once only,' snarled Osmund, 'where is the archbishop?'

'I know not, my lord,' the man groaned, 'only that he was going to join us before boarding a ship to Normandy.'

'You are lying,' said Osmund, pressing harder. 'Tell the truth, or I will kill you right here.'

'I swear, my lord, we were to transport his personal belongings only and wait at the dockside for him to arrive.'

'And what about the children?'

'Lord, I know nothing about any children, we are carrying baggage only. I swear it; take a look inside.'

Osmund turned to stare at the wagon where Godwin was cutting the ties on the canvas covering. Harold joined his father, and they ripped the fabric wide open before Harold climbed inside. A few seconds later, he re-emerged, a look of worry on his face.

'They are not here,' he said, 'they must have been taken off somewhere after leaving London.' He strode across and placed his blade on the fallen rider's throat. 'Where are they?' he snarled. 'Tell me, or you die here.'

'I know not what you are talking about, my lord,' cried the man, 'there have been no children aboard the wagon since we left London. All I know is that we were paid a handsome purse to escort this cart to Dover as fast as we could. It has remained sealed all this way, and whatever is inside remains exactly as it was.'

'What's in the boxes?'

'The archbishop's personal possessions, my lord – that's what he told us.'

'Empty it,' shouted Harold. Some of the men ran over to drag the boxes and sacks out of the wagon. Every one was bound tightly, and the men cut the ropes before emptying their contents onto the floor.

'My lord,' shouted one, 'you should see this.'

Godwin and Harold walked over and stared at the scattered contents in shock. It was no more than piles of cut firewood.

'We have been duped,' said Godwin, his heart sinking. 'The archbishop has tricked us.'

—

Just over sixty leagues away in Bristol Harbour, Wulfnorth and Hakon were dragged from the cart, their hands bound before being led onto a dock. Despite the darkness, they could see an unassuming ship being loaded with dozens of boxes.

'Try anything,' said one of the monks, 'and I'll throw the little one in the sea. Got it?'

Wulfnorth nodded in silence and walked towards the gangplank.

'Get up there,' said the monk, following the two boys onto the ship.

As he stepped aboard, one of the crew grabbed Wulfnorth and threw him across the deck to land heavily against the mast. Wulfnorth was temporarily stunned, but as he came to his senses, he realised there was a tall man looking down at him.

'I know you,' he said, looking up. 'When my father finds you, he will rip out your heart.'

'He has to find me first,' said Robert of Jumièges. 'In a few days, I will be safe amongst my allies in Normandy. Say goodbye to England, Wulfnorth Godwinson, for I highly doubt you will ever see her again.'

Chapter Thirty-seven

Godwin and Harold stood alongside each other in the bow of their ship after spending the previous few weeks sailing up and down the coast of England, seeking any information they could about the whereabouts of the children or the archbishop. Although they knew the exercise was unlikely to provide any answers, it was important to spread the word as far and as wide as possible, just in case the archbishop was still hidden somewhere, waiting for the opportunity to escape.

Inland, Godwin's other sons and huscarls spread out across all the counties, also seeking information, but to no avail. There was no trace of the archbishop anywhere.

During their absence, Edward had granted Godwin's family temporary occupation of Bosham manor until the crisis was sorted out, but the whole time they knew the final decision regarding his guilt still had not been made. Now, having received word that Edward had made his judgement, Godwin was returning to Bosham before heading back to London to receive it.

The ship docked, and after paying the harbour master, the two men walked up the hill towards Bosham manor, followed by the dozen huscarls that had served them loyally over the past few weeks.

'We will find them, Father,' said Harold as they walked. 'I swear I will make it my mission in life to do so, and when I do, the screams of Robert of Jumièges will sound louder than the strongest bell.'

'The fate of the archbishop is secondary in importance,' said Godwin, 'I am more concerned about the boys. I fear they are in France by now, and the chances of finding them recede by the day.'

'If they are, then so be it,' said Harold, 'but when the truth comes out, as it will, I suspect few men will want to associate themselves with a man of God who deems kidnap and murder to be acceptable practices.'

'He is a clever man,' said Godwin, 'who knows what he is capable of and what allies he can influence?'

'This is not over, Father,' said Harold as they walked through the gates to the manor. 'In fact, it has hardly begun.'

As they entered the courtyard, Harold's wife, Edyth Swanneck, saw them arrive and gasped in relief before running across and throwing herself into his arms.

'Harold,' she gasped, 'I thought you would never return. Thank God you are safe.'

Harold returned the embrace before she pulled away and turned to Godwin.

'My lord,' she said, 'it is good to see you again. Do you have any news?'

'Alas, we do not,' said Godwin, 'but we have eyes everywhere. We will find them soon enough, I am sure of it. Is my wife here?'

As if in answer to his question Gytha appeared in the doorway before hurrying over to embrace her husband.

'Anything?' she asked, pulling herself away with tears of hope in her eyes.

Godwin shook his head.

'Nothing,' he said. 'Is there any news from Leofwine or Tostig?'

'They have both returned,' said Gytha, 'but nobody has seen the archbishop or the boys. It is as if they have just disappeared into thin air.'

'Someone, somewhere, must know something,' replied Godwin, 'and I swear I will find out where they are.'

'Come inside,' said Gytha, 'the fire is lit, and there is hot potage in the pot. You too,' she added, turning to the huscarls, 'there is enough for all.' She took her husband's hand and led the way into the smoky hall.

All the men sat at the main table, mentally and physically exhausted. They were looking forward to hot food and a good night's sleep.

'I'll tell the kitchens you are here,' said Edyth, kissing Harold on the cheek before disappearing through a door.

Harold and Godwin removed their wool-lined cloaks and walked over to stand near the fire as Gytha brought them each a mug of ale.

'I am glad you are back,' she said, handing over the mugs. 'I have not slept since you left, such is my worry.'

'I have only returned to face the king,' said Godwin, 'and once done, depending on his decision, I intend to sail to Flanders to see if Count Baldwin has heard anything.'

'There is no need to go to London,' said Gytha, 'I have received word that Bishop Stigand is on his way here with the king's judgement.'

'Stigand has the decision?' said Godwin. 'Why would Edward do that?'

'I know not,' said Gytha, 'but he will be here by tomorrow.'

'That is something, I suppose,' said Godwin with a sigh. 'I know that at the very least I am to retain my freedom.'

'Unless Stigand leads an army in the king's name,' said Harold. 'Do not anticipate anything until we hear the judgement for ourselves.'

Across the room, a door opened, and Edyth walked back in, followed by a dozen servants carrying bowls of hot potage and platters of roast pork.

'Come,' said Gytha, 'enough talk, we need to get you all fed and rested. You look exhausted.'

The following morning Gytha Thorkelsdóttir stood in the courtyard, watching as Bishop Stigand's wagon pulled to a halt before the manor stables. With him were four horsemen, armed bodyguards against the brigands of the road, but there was no sign of any army, and deep inside, Gytha felt an overwhelming sense of relief.

One of the servants ran over with a small set of steps and pulled the rear flaps open to allow the bishop out. Gytha walked over and helped Stigand down, catching him as he stumbled from the step.

'Careful, your grace,' she said, 'we would not want to be responsible for your demise. We have more than enough going on in our lives as it is.'

'Lady Gytha,' said Stigand, straightening up, 'it is good to see you again.'

'And you, your grace,' replied Gytha. 'Are you well?'

'My bones ache from the journey, but the pain is a price I pay for my position.' He looked around the courtyard. 'Is your husband here?'

'All the family are here,' said Gytha. 'We thought we should hear the news together – what affects one affects all.'

'In that case,' said Stigand, 'let us waste no more time. Where are they?'

'Waiting in the hall,' said Gytha. 'Come, they will be pleased to see you.'

They both walked across the courtyard and entered the hall. Inside, the mood was sombre, and the Godwin family were joined by their loyal huscarls as well as all the manor staff.

'Godwin of Wessex,' said the bishop, removing his cloak, 'this is quite the reception. I thought we would be meeting alone.'

'Welcome back to Bosham, Bishop Stigand,' said Godwin. 'And yes, the room is full, but as far as we are concerned, everyone present is part of our family, and as such, is affected by the king's judgement. We have no secrets, so feel free to speak freely.'

'As you wish,' said the bishop, 'but first, may I have a drink?'

'My apologies,' said Gytha, 'you have only just arrived, and we are demanding answers before offering you hospitality. That is unacceptable.'

'Not at all,' said Stigand, 'this is important news and has to be shared immediately.'

He accepted a mug of ale and, after quenching his thirst, placed the mug back on the table.

'So,' he said, looking up, 'the judgement.'

'Wait,' said Godwin, 'I see no parchment? Was there no need to commit such important things to a document?'

'Not at all,' said the bishop, 'it is all up here.' He tapped his head. 'But fret not, Godwin of Wessex, for, despite my advancing age, even I am able to recall the king's message.'

'Which is?'

Bishop Stigand took a deep breath before looking around the room.

'King Edward,' he announced, 'has thrown out all charges against Godwin of Wessex. With immediate effect, all lands and chattels that belonged to the earl prior to his exile will be returned in full, as will his titles and allowances, as well as those of his family and dependents. His decree is that all accusations are proved false and are to be removed from the record completely.'

The room erupted into cheering, and Stigand waited for the noise to lessen before holding up his hand for silence.

'Wait,' he said, 'there is more. As of today, the Archbishop of Canterbury, Robert of Jumièges, has been stripped of all titles and privileges awarded by the king and is declared an outlaw. There is a price upon his head and any man bringing him to justice will be well rewarded.'

Again the room cheered, but Godwin and Gytha remained stony-faced, waiting for the one piece of information that would make the news complete. Bishop Stigand returned their gaze, knowing what they were waiting for. Eventually, the noise lessened, and again he held up his hand for silence.

'Alas,' he said, 'we have no news about Hakon and Wulfnorth, but there is one more piece of information that may lessen your pain and shed light in the darkness.' He looked around the room before returning his gaze to Godwin and Gytha.

'My lord,' he said, 'my lady. I am humbled to announce that the king's wife has returned from the abbey where she was incarcerated and has had all her titles and privileges restored with immediate effect. Not only is she safe and well, but your daughter, Ealdgyth of Wessex, is once more the Queen of England. May God bless her and guide her path.'

Epilogue

As most of the Godwin family celebrated their return to normality, hundreds of leagues away, Sweyn Godwinson and Owen of Hereford sat at a campfire alongside a forest path near the town of Lycia in Turkey. Their journey to Jerusalem had been completed, and now they were returning to England, with Sweyn still fully focused on raising an army to challenge the king.

For the past few months, Owen had lived alongside Sweyn, listening to his plans and grudges on a daily basis. The longer time went on, the more convinced he was that not only was his master deluded, but he was turning into a dangerous man, convinced that he was going to be the next King of England.

Sweyn's temper was also getting shorter and more violent by the day, and many travellers they met on the road suffered at his hand, with most losing their lives for nothing more than refusing to hand over their valuables. In addition, many women also suffered at Sweyn's demands, finding themselves forced upon after rebuffing his attentions.

'The thing is,' said Sweyn, staring into the fire, 'when I am king, you will be Earl of all England as a reward for your loyalty. You will have riches beyond compare, and any woman alive will be yours to do with as you will.'

'I find no pleasure in taking women against their will, my lord,' said Owen. 'And anyway, will not your father have something to say about such ambition?'

'Forget about him,' said Sweyn, 'for he will join Edward on the gibbet, as will my brothers. England will be mine, Owen, and mine alone, and with you and your armies at my side, we will be unbeatable.'

Owen sighed inwardly. The constant delusion was wearing him out, and now they were headed back to England, he grew worried about the consequences. Sweyn had lost his mind, and he knew he had to do something about it.

Before he could respond, two figures appeared out of the gloom and stopped just short of the fire, staring at the pot of food hanging above the flames. Owen got to his feet and walked over. One was an old woman, and the other was a young girl, no more than eight years of age.

'Greetings, fellow travellers,' Owen said, 'what can we do for you?'

The old woman responded quietly, but her language was unknown to Owen, and he shrugged his shoulders in response.

'I'm sorry, old woman,' he said, 'I do not understand.'

The young girl at her side pointed at the pot.

'*Gida?*' she said, looking at Owen with pleading eyes. '*Gida?*'

Owen glanced at the pot and, realising what they were after, beckoned them closer to the fire.

'Who are they,' asked Sweyn, looking up, 'and what do they want?'

'I think they are just hungry,' said Owen. 'We have plenty in the pot, so I thought we could share.'

'Can they pay?'

Owen stared at Sweyn. Experience had taught him that his master was a hard man, but he never ceased to be amazed at how cold he had become.

'My lord,' he said, 'look at them. They are destitute, and we have plenty. Just let them eat, and I will send them on their way.'

'No,' said Sweyn. 'If they want to eat, they must pay the price.'

'I'm sure they have no money,' said Owen, 'so they can have my share.'

'They will have nothing,' snapped Sweyn, 'until they pay the price.'

'What price?' gasped Owen. 'The woman has nothing of value.'

'On the contrary,' said Sweyn, 'she has her.' He pointed at the young girl.

Owen stared in shock. Over the years, he had seen Sweyn kill men in cold blood and rape women indiscriminately. But never had he seen him force himself on a child.

'My lord,' he said, 'you know not what you are saying. The girl is still a child and has not yet come into her womanhood. Take the old woman if you must, but do not touch the girl, I beg of you.'

'Why not?' asked Sweyn. 'This country is full of such people, and they are not human in the eyes of God. I, on the other hand, am the future King of England, and as such, can do whatever I want to whoever I want.' He got to his feet and stared at the girl with lust in his eyes. 'Get rid of the woman,' he said, unfastening his belt, 'and leave me with the girl.'

Owen turned to stare at the unsuspecting travellers, his conscience torn by what was about to happen.

'*Gida*,' said the girl again, holding her hands together in prayer. '*Gida?*'

Owen's heart ached, and something inside him changed. For too long, he had stood aside and allowed Sweyn to kill and rape as he saw fit, but after their time in Jerusalem, he knew he could stand it no more. He turned back to face Sweyn, a cold look of determination on his face.

'No, my lord,' he said, 'I will not stand aside. If you do this, it will be an affront to God himself.'

Sweyn stared at Owen, his anger evident upon his face.

'Are you defying me, Owen of Hereford?' he asked eventually.

'I am, my lord,' said Owen, 'only in so much that I will not allow you to rape a child.'

'I told you,' growled Sweyn, 'I will do as I like, when I like, to whoever I like. Now stand aside or suffer the consequences.'

'I will not, my lord,' said Owen, looking at the dagger in Sweyn's hand, 'and if our journey together ends here, then so be it.'

Sweyn stared again, but suddenly his manner changed, and a smile spread upon his face.

'Ha,' he said with a laugh, 'I was only jesting. Of course, they can have your food, mine as well. Let them come, Owen – they are welcome.'

Owen was surprised at the sudden change of character, and as Sweyn walked away, he turned back to face the travellers.

'Come,' he said, 'you are welcome to share what we have.'

But before anyone could move, the old woman let out a scream as Sweyn threw himself at Owen's back, knife in hand.

The split-second warning was enough, and Owen spun to one side while drawing his own knife. As Sweyn stumbled past, he instinctively thrust his own blade forward, plunging it deep into his master's stomach, stopping him dead in his tracks.

Both men stared at each other in shock before looking down at the blood now oozing past the blade.

For a moment, Owen was horrified, but as the realisation finally sank in, he knew that it had only been a matter of time before something like this was going to happen. Slowly he withdrew the knife, and as he cast it to one side, Sweyn Godwinson collapsed into his arms.

'*Owen,*' gasped Sweyn, '*what have you done?*'

'Forgive me, my lord,' whispered Owen, 'but the path you described could never come to pass. It is better that it ends here.'

'*I need a physician,*' gasped Sweyn, '*there is so much more I have yet to do.*'

Owen felt Sweyn's body growing weaker and lowered him gently to the ground.

'*Am I dying?*' asked Sweyn.

'You are, my lord,' Owen replied, 'but I swear I will pray for your soul.'

'*I am not afraid,*' said Sweyn, his voice barely audible, '*for am I not of royal blood?*'

'Of course you are,' said Owen, seeing his master of many years slip away, 'and your name will live for ever more.'

'*Aye,*' said Sweyn, '*that it will. Tell my family...*'

'Tell them what?' asked Owen as Sweyn fell silent. But it was too late. After a life conflicted between loyalty and brutality, Sweyn Godwinson finally died in the arms of the man who had been the most loyal of them all.

–

The following day, Owen buried his master in a shallow grave before marking a nearby tree so someone could find it at a later date. He knew he had to get back to England to tell Godwin the truth, for though Sweyn's actions over the years had caused great concern, he had been well loved and deserved a final resting place more befitting a man of his station.

Owen also knew that when it was revealed that it was he who had wielded the blade, he would probably be executed; but that was in the hands of God, and he would accept his fate graciously, whatever it might be.

With a heavy heart, he picked up his pack to begin the long journey home. There was no doubt that Sweyn's death would have a devastating effect on the family, but even in his darkest dreams, Owen could never have anticipated just how devastating it would be.

Author's notes

In the telling of this tale, I have tried to maintain historical accuracy as much as possible, but as is usual in such novels, there has had to be some artistic licence to allow the story to flow. Any inaccuracies are mine alone, and I hope they did not distract from the story too much.

William the Bastard

There are many versions of William's origins, including the following. In approximately AD 1027, a Norman duke called Robert the Magnificent peered down from the ramparts in one of his many castles across Normandy. In the courtyard below, several women were trampling leather in the stone dyeing trenches.

One of the women, Herleva, the daughter of a tanner, caught the duke's eye, and he arranged for her to be brought to him a few days later. Herleva went on to become the duke's concubine, and the following year gave birth to a child called William.

In normal circumstances, the chances of the child having any sort of privileged life was unlikely, but with no other heirs, it soon became apparent that the bastard child would inherit the title when the duke died. This attracted the attention of many men, both honourable and otherwise, and when William inherited his father's title at the tender age of eight, members of the Norman aristocracy battled each other with a view to furthering their own ambitions.

Many of the boy's guardians died during these turbulent years, and it is claimed that his protectors often had to hide him away in the cottages of peasants when his life was in danger, a claim that he often repeated later in life. On one occasion, when William was approximately ten years old, one of his guardians, a man called Osbern, was killed in the boy's bedchamber by an assassin. Why the murderer did not proceed to kill the young duke is not known, but if he had, the history of Britain would have looked so much different.

Regarding his betrothal to Matilda, there are several versions of events, but most include the story that after Matilda refused his proposal on the grounds that he was not worthy of her, William rode to Bruges and pulled her to the ground by her braids while she was heading for church. Other versions say it happened at her home, and again some element of physical violence was involved, but before her father could intervene, she proclaimed that he was the one she was going to marry.

Godwin of Wessex

Earl Godwin made his name fighting for King Cnut and rapidly rose through the ranks to become one of the most powerful earls in England. When Cnut died in 1035, the throne of England was reportedly claimed by Alfred Ætheling, but some sources say that Godwin tricked him and had him blinded before he could claim the throne. Alfred later died from his injuries.

When the subsequent king, Harold Harefoot, died in AD 1040, Godwin supported Edward's claim to the throne. Edward subsequently came to England after twenty-five years of exile.

Godwin held great power in the court, even getting his wayward son a pardon, but when he refused to punish the town of Dover in 1051, the king took the opportunity to banish him and all his family from England. However, the following year Godwin returned with a great army, and all his lands were restored.

Gytha Thorkelsdóttir

Gytha Thorkelsdóttir was the daughter of a Danish prince and linked to King Cnut through marriage. She eventually married Godwin of Wessex, and they went on to have at least nine children together.

Her daughter, also called Gytha, was renamed Ealdgyth when she married Edward, while her other daughter, Gunhild, devoted her life to worship and became a nun in Wilton Abbey.

Harold Godwinson

Harold was the second son of Godwin and was already the Earl of East Anglia when our story starts in 1045. He seems to have been a character blessed with a level head, and over the years, gradually gained the trust of King Edward.

Harold married a woman called Edyth Swannesha, a name sometimes referred to as Edyth Swanneck. In our tale, we refer to her as being the daughter of a nobleman called Gerald of Wessex. However, her true parentage is unknown, and they were almost certainly married 'more danico,' the Danish hand-fast marriage custom. She gave birth to at least five children and seems to be the same person referred to in the Domesday Book as one of the richest landowners in England at the time of the Norman Conquest.

Harold's siblings

Depending on what source of reference is used, Harold Godwinson is reputed to have had nine or more siblings. In this book, I have deliberately focused on just those who have a direct bearing on the story – his brothers Tostig, Gyrth, Sweyn, Leofwine and Wulfnorth, and his sisters Ealdgyth and Gunhild. Birth dates are vague at best but are approximately relevant to their actions within our tale.

Sweyn was certainly the black sheep of the family. Not only did he seek alliances with the Welsh kings, but he has also been accused of abducting the Abbess of Leominster and keeping her prisoner for almost a year. Whilst some records say she went of her own free will, there is nothing known for certain either way. Eventually, Sweyn was forced to return the abbess, and he was exiled from England, seeking refuge in Flanders and Denmark.

His lands were shared out between his cousin Beorn and Harold, but he soon returned to seek a pardon and the restoration of his estates. Both men refused, and Sweyn lured Beorn away before murdering him in cold blood and hiding his body alongside the river Dart. Harold Godwinson had Beorn's body reburied adjacent to his uncle King Cnut in the Old Minster, Winchester. Sweyn again fled but returned to England with the Bishop of Worcester in AD 1050.

When the Godwins were banished from England, Sweyn embarked on a pilgrimage to Jerusalem, presumably as a penance for his sins, but even though he apparently reached there unharmed, he died on the return journey. Some say he died of illness, some say he was murdered, but whatever the truth, he was certainly a colourful character.

Spearhafoc

The monk in this tale is based on a real character – Spearhafoc was indeed a talented goldsmith based in the abbey of Bury St Edmunds. He went on to become a favourite of Godwin and was made Abbot of Abingdon in or around 1048. In 1051 King Edward promoted him to Bishop of London, but the newly ordained Archbishop of Canterbury, Robert of Jumièges, refused to consecrate him.

After the fall of Godwin in 1051, Spearhafoc fled, taking with him the gold and gems intended for King Edward's crown as well as other treasures accumulated from the Church's stores. There are no records of his fate from that point on.

Robert of Jumièges

Robert of Jumièges was the Abbot of Jumièges from approximately 1037. He became friendly with Edward during his early exile in France and subsequently followed him to England when Edward became king in 1042.

He was made Bishop of London by the king in 1044 and Archbishop of Canterbury in 1051. He was considered hostile to the Godwin family, even accusing them of plotting to kill the king, an accusation that instigated the crisis in 1051.

When Godwin finally returned to England in 1052, Robert fled to Normandy and told William the Bastard that Edward had nominated him as heir to the throne of England, a message that contributed greatly to the eventual invasion in 1066. There are also some reports that he took Wulfnorth and Hakon Sweynson with him, handing them both over to the duke.

Stigand, Archbishop of Canterbury

At the time our story starts, Stigand was Bishop of Elmham for the second time, having been deposed but then reinstated by King Edward. Stigand appears to have held favour with Godwin of Essex, and when Robert of Jumièges was outlawed and exiled in 1052, Stigand was appointed Archbishop of Canterbury by King Edward.

By then, Stigand was already Bishop of Winchester, but though he accepted the new position, he refused to give up his existing bishopric. This angered the Church, and his new appointment was never recognised by the Pope. During his life, he served six successive kings, including William the Conqueror. His life was controversial, and he was not afraid to ignore the demands of the Pope.

When Godwin and his family fled to Flanders in 1051, Harold and Leofwine headed to Bristol and used a ship intended to take Sweyn on his pilgrimage, to reach King Diarmait of Leinster in Ireland.

King Diarmait helped Harold raise an army of mercenaries, and they eventually sailed from Dublin to support Godwin's fleet. It is assumed that it is around this time that Diarmait gifted Gunhild the Mantle of St Brigid, a holy relic that she eventually gave to the Cathedral of St Donaas in Flanders.

During the months between the Godwins being exiled and their ultimate return, Godwin harried the coast of England – in particular, the Isle of Wight – with his ships. To combat this, the king tasked Ralph the Timid and Odda of Deerhurst with catching Godwin with his own fleet out of Sandwich, but when they had no luck, they were withdrawn, and the fleet disbanded. It is also during this period that Godwin was known to land ashore up and down the coast of England, recruiting allies for his eventual return.

Finally, when he took his chance to confront the king, Godwin sailed up the Thames and moored his fleet opposite the king's ships. At first, the northern earls were not present at the negotiations, but when they did arrive, they made it clear that their men did not want to fight fellow Englishmen. With both sides concerned that such a war would leave England open to invasion, they finally agreed terms, and Godwin, along with all his family, was completely reinstated.

All Godwin's titles and lands were restored, and Robert of Jumièges was declared an outlaw for causing the animosity and plotting against the Crown. He and his supporters murdered some men at the gates of London before fleeing to France, taking the two young hostages with him.

The Mantle of St Brigid[1]

One of the more commonly told stories is of Brigid asking the King of Leinster for land. She told the king that the place where she stood was the perfect spot for a convent. It was beside a forest where the members could collect firewood and berries, there was a lake nearby that would provide water, and the land was fertile. The king laughed at her and refused to give her any land. Brigid prayed and asked God to soften the king's heart. Then she smiled at the king and said, 'Will you give me as much land as my cloak will cover?' The king thought that she was joking and agreed.

She told four of her sisters to take up the cloak, but instead of laying it flat on the turf, each sister, with face turned to a different point of the compass, began to run swiftly, the cloth growing in all directions. The cloak began to cover many acres of land.

'Oh, Brigid!' said the frightened king, 'What are you about?'

'I am, or rather my cloak is about covering your whole province to punish you for your stinginess to the poor.'

'Call your maidens back. I will give you a decent plot of ground.'

The saint was persuaded, and if the king held his purse-strings tight in the future, she had only to allude to her cloak to bring him to reason.

Soon afterwards, the king became a Christian, began to help the poor, and commissioned the building of the convent. Legend has it; the convent was known for making jam from the local blueberries, which were sought for all over Ireland. A new tradition is to eat jam on 1 February in honour of this miracle.

---

[1] The note on The Mantle of St Brigid is quoted unabridged from Wikipedia, please see copyright page for further information.

More from the author

The Blood of Kings
A Land Divided
A Wounded Realm
Rebellion's Forge
Warrior Princess
The Blade Bearer

The Brotherhood
Templar Steel
Templar Stone
Templar Blood
Templar Fury

Novels
Savage Eden
The Last Citadel
Vampire

Other-Worlds
The Legacy Protocol
The Seventh God
The Last Citadel
Warrior Princess